LAST SHOT

ALSO BY GREGG HURWITZ

Gregg Hurwitz

LAST SHOT

wm

WILLIAM MORROW
An Imprint of HarperCollins*Publishers*

HarperCollins books may be purchased for educational, business, or sales promotional use. For information please write: Special Markets Department, HarperCollins Publishers, 10 East 53rd Street, New York, NY 10022.

FIRST EDITION

Designed by Paula Russell Szafranski

Library of Congress Cataloging-in-Publication Data

Hurwitz, Gregg Andrew.
   Last shot / Gregg Hurwitz.— 1st ed.
     p. cm.
   ISBN-13: 978-0-06-073146-5
   ISBN-10: 0-06-073146-X
    1. Rackley, Tim (Fictitious character)—Fiction. 2. Prisoners—Fiction.
3. Escapes—Fiction. 4. Psychological fiction. I. Title.

PS3558.U695L37 2006
813'.54—dc22   2006041938

---

06 07 08 09 10 WBC/RRD 10 9 8 7 6 5 4 3 2 1

For Marjorie Hurwitz,
my mother

LAST SHOT

Chapter 1

The mood inside was nice and mellow until Spook taped razor blades to his hands and slashed up two Aryan Brothers and half a correctional officer. So that meant Terminal Island was on edge and the population unshaved—disposable razors being accountable items the screws hadn't kept accountable. Every morning this week, Walker had to stand in line with the other boarders for his shot with a piece-of-shit Norelco, the CO dipping the cutting head in Barbicide between shearings.

The inside heated up in August. Air like fever. Men slept worse, got antsy. Got violent. Some, like Spook, got creative. Walker steered clear, as always, of the ensuing bullshit. He kept out of the yard—too much trouble brewing—to sit on the stacked footlockers in his house upstairs and take in the sights.

Two wind-battered palm trees, row of Dumpsters, anchor resting atop a concrete pillar at the coast guard facility across the way—all strained through two layers of chain link and some nifty coils of razor wire. The view wasn't much. But it was all he had. He loved the two palms—Sally and Jean Ann. Loved how their crowns could hold the evening light, bathed in gold a good half hour after the grounds were puddled in shadow. If he mashed his face to the concrete wall, he could make out the edge of a third tree, but he didn't know that one well enough to name her.

Walker pulled back from the iron bars and regarded his house. He knew this view well, too. All six by eight of it. Bunk beds, metal, one solid piece. Stainless steel toilet and sink. Technically, the walls were supposed to be bare, but by the window Walker had used chewing gum to put up a picture of Tess, mostly because he didn't know what else to do with it. Aside from the photo and a few cigarette burns on his footlocker, he hadn't made much of an imprint on the place in two and a half years.

His cellie, a soft-spoken rapist renamed Imaad, had been more active in his nesting. An Arabic phrase, rendered in gold calligraphy, glittered from a black velvet banner. Below it a postcard of a mosque was stuck to the wall with paste, since he claimed that chewing gum contained—Allah forbid—gelatin. A prayer rug, woven from lovingly twisted cords of toilet paper, stood rolled up in a corner. Atop the frayed end, safely above belly level, rested a worn Koran, the leather binding long gone to pieces. Imaad, who was well behaved and aggressively introverted, tolerated Walker as Walker tolerated him. Yesterday Imaad had drunk ammonia with his Cup o' Noodles, his puking buying him a lay-in at the infirmary so he wouldn't have to mix with the general pop. A good move for a model prisoner, given the smoke on the horizon.

After Spook's Schick escapade, the Gorillas and the Aryans were due to let more blood. And the cholos weren't about to get left out either. The Norteño cell lieutenant's punk had gone renegade and gotten picked up by a jocker from Surrenos, stoking the embers of a dormant vendetta. An unnatural silence had permeated the block the past few nights. Convicts were stockpiling food. Despite the heat, gang members only ventured out in canvas jackets, padding their undershirts with magazines and newspapers as insurance against stickings. It was like gas had been leaking through the grounds all week and everyone was holding their breath, waiting for somebody to strike a match.

Walker's right arm sported a dark comma above the biceps—yin of yin-yang fame. Tommy LaRue from D-Block was the ink slinger, but the tattoo had gone unfinished after his kit was confiscated in the wake of the May riot. Walker had smuggled the needles out of Unicor, where the prisoners toiled for a buck twenty an hour stitching and packing and making useful things like paper targets so cops could practice shooting them. He'd shoved the needles beneath the surface of his heel callus and delivered them to LaRue, who tied them with a shoelace to the point of a pencil. The ink was easy—burn a Bic pen filler heroin style in a spoon, then mix the soot with toothpaste and soap. The lace soaks up the ink, the needles open the skin, and—had no shakedown occurred—Walker would've gotten his yang. But since Kelly O'Connell felt inspired to throw a flaming mattress off the third tier, Walker had to walk around for three months like an asshole with a big tadpole on his arm. To be fair, Kelly's riot had also provided free entertainment. First the bedding and burning trash raining down onto the range floor, showering sparks. Then the boarders got to sit on the bare mesh of their beds and watch the mini-frontloaders at work, scooping up the charred mounds below. That one had made the papers, and they'd paid for it. Petty reprisals for a month. No basketballs. No magazines. No dessert.

Walker glanced at Tess on the wall and felt his thoughts sharpen, pricking him with imagined scenarios. The only treatment, he'd learned, was to tune out. Weights, headphones, or the four-star view.

He was just reconvening with Sally and Jean Ann when Boss sent for him. Walker didn't like being sent for, and if it was anyone else, he would have ignored the summons, but Boss hadn't sent for him in months, and when Boss sent for you, you went.

Sweet Boy repeated the request, leaning against the doorway with a bent wrist propped against a smooth cheek, and Walker said, "I heard you."

"Boss says now."

"Boss can wait."

Sweet Boy's eyelashes flared, as if Walker had wiped his nose on the pope's robe, and he made a snitty little noise at the back of his throat and withdrew.

Walker rose and stretched. The powdered eggs from breakfast had left a foul taste in his mouth, so he brushed his teeth, tapped the rubber Department of Corrections toothbrush on the lip of the sink, and dropped it into a cup from the chow hall. A titanium cross escaped his shirt when he leaned to spit. His first month in, LaRue had gotten the thin black cord—more like a shoestring—for Walker to hang the pendant on. LaRue could get anything, from Albanian hash to the e-mail

3

address for Catherine Zeta-Jones's publicist so you could write and get a signed head shot. LaRue was the closest thing to a friend Walker had in here. Or, for that matter, anywhere. He served everyone and no one, and Walker liked him for his democratic refusal to cultivate alliances.

Walker stepped out onto the catwalk, glancing over the waist-height rail to the concrete plain of the range floor forty feet below. He could hear the clink of weights and shouts from the boccie court out on the North Yard. The echoes bounced off the high ceiling, came back distorted.

LaRue was scurrying toward him, head down, elbow pressed to his side to hold firm whatever contraband he was muling under his shirt. They clasped hands, bumped opposite shoulders.

"Let's see the tat." LaRue shook his head at Walker's forlorn yin. "We'll get it finished up as soon as this shit blows over."

"You got word for me?"

"Expect to have it by lunch." He produced a cigarette from thin air, handed it to Walker, and scurried off to finish his rounds.

Walker stuck the cig in his mouth and continued down the catwalk. Boss Hahn, a shotcaller for the Aryan Brotherhood, occupied the best cell on J-Unit's third tier, right next to the TV room. Kelly's arm greeted Walker at the cell door, but Boss tipped his chin in a faint nod, the limb withdrew, and Walker stepped inside.

A red sheet over the window cut the light to a soft glow. Sweet Boy reclined on the bed reading a romance paperback. Boss's cellie, Marcus, was taking a dump, one foot out and clear of his pants in case a brawl broke out; if nothing else, prison kept you ready for dirty fighting. The smell mixed with that of the ramen noodles on the hot plate. After a while you barely notice stuff like that. An AB strongman, Marcus was missing two front teeth, so he could smile clench-jawed and still stick his tongue out at you.

His weight bowing the footlocker he straddled, Boss leaned over a paper chessboard. The pieces were carved from soap, half of them blackened with shoe polish. A bottle cap stood in for a missing pawn. Boss tapped a knight's head. Blunt fingers, wide at the nails. His arm was so loaded with muscle that the bulges met one another in tangential circles—delt, biceps, forearm. Like Walker, Boss wore the standard

fare: khaki pants, tan button-up. His influence showed in his Nikes—
Walker wore issued canvas slip-ons—and in the red-and-white cartons
stacked up the wall opposite the bed. Boss was rich in cigarettes, and
in prison cigarettes bought you anything from a punk to a shiv in your
enemy's kidney. Inked on Boss's neck was the Aryans' symbol: shamrock and triple sixes. He was old-school AB, before they wised up and
started hiding the brands.

Kelly returned to his seat across the board from Boss. Boss continued to study the situation, a mildly pained expression on his face. He
jerked his wide head in Sweet Boy's direction. "Why didn't you come
when she told you to?"

Walker shrugged. Shifted the unlit cigarette from one corner of his
mouth to the other.

"*Answer* him." Kelly sprang up in Walker's face. "You gonna make a
move, GI Joe? No? Then fuckin' answer the man."

Four men. Sure, they could take him, but it wouldn't be worth the
injuries. Walker repeated his mantra. Sixteen months. Two weeks. Four
days.

Boss made a noise of assent, though nothing had been said. "Walk
don't talk much, ya see. He keep to hisself. Ain't that right, Walk?" He
picked up the knight, tapped it to his lips thoughtfully, set it back down.
"Things are coming to a head. Jiggers are watching all my regulars.
You're a fighter. All that army time. I need you to blade up Spook when
he comes off lockdown."

"What do I get?"

"Protection."

"I'm being serious."

Boss snorted, waved a hand at the wall of Marlboros. "You can live
like a king. Hell, you never know when someone wants in for better living."

Walker took in Marcus wiping himself. "Thanks anyway."

"You'll be part of the new order."

"I don't even like the old order."

"Right. Serve your time like a good Christian and get back to the
world. Like it's always been."

"Like it's always been."

"Okay," Boss said. "Okay, okay, okay." He raised his head slowly, gave Walker the famous blue stare. "I keep order 'round here. Don't you go forgetting that." With sudden violence he added, "And keep the *fuck* outta my way."

Sweet Boy lowered the book to his chest. It took a moment for Marcus and Kelly to untense. Walker waited to see if he was dismissed, but Boss had returned his attention to the makeshift chessboard. He occupied himself with his fingers, fussing with the miters of the Ivory bishops.

Boss finally grimaced and settled his weight back. "Never was any good at this game." A resigned sigh. "How many moves he gonna beat me in, Walk?"

Walker's eyes flicked to the board. "Three."

He stepped back and walked out.

Plastic picnic tables bolted to the concrete. Crumbly meat loaf, watery corn, a stiff cube of cake on a white saucer. Despite the food, Walker had gained fifteen pounds on the inside, mostly lats and chest. A joint body, they called it, built by barbells and bench presses and having nothing better to do. The added weight—and a few early, effective displays of his hand-to-hand prowess—had earned him the right to eat alone. Nonaligned. Even LaRue left him be during meals, preferring to zip around and work chow-hall deals.

That's why Walker was pissed when Moses Catrell ambled up to his table at dinner and took a seat. On Moses's ebony forearm, the Black Guerrilla Family dragon coiled around a prison tower, a correctional officer in its clutch.

"Spook was just retaliating," Moses said, picking up the strain of an argument Walker didn't know he was having. "Boss had him ganged in the learning lab, two big fuckers. Eight stitches."

Walker had sixteen months, two weeks, and four days to go, and the last thing he needed to be concerned with was the state of Spook Roberts's asshole. He choked down a mouthful of meat loaf, took a pull of apple juice.

"If Boss gonna escalate this motherfucker," Moses said, "people gonna die up in here."

"I got no beef with Boss. I keep outta his business, he keeps outta mine."

"You the only one could do something 'bout the shit comin' down the pipeline."

"Not my concern."

"Shit, fool." Moses blew air through pursed lips, seemingly unimpressed by Walker's grasp of altruism.

Walker knew his type—little-boy temper backed up by a hood's body. Still trying to wrangle fair from life. Never learned that the world doesn't care about just and right, not when it comes to fuckups and down-and-outs like them.

"You take Boss the peace pipe," Moses said, "he'll listen to you."

Walker let corn juice drain through his plastic fork. "That so?"

"Hell, yeah. I heard about how you fight."

"Stories."

"Then why's even the AB stay off your back?"

"Don't involve me."

"That all you got to say?"

Walker considered for a moment. "Get off my table."

Moses's mouth twitched to one side in an elaborate display of indignation. He sucked his teeth at Walker and withdrew. Walker downed the rest of his juice, chased some more corn around the plate. When he looked up, he saw LaRue coming toward him—not quite a run, more a walk with a charge in it.

Walker said, "Well?"

LaRue bent over, breathing hard from making double time, his whisper humid against Walker's cheek. "Left."

Walker did his best to take in the news calmly, his fist tightening around the fork until his fingers went numb like the rest of him.

LaRue gave him a concerned glance, tapped him on the back solemnly, and darted away.

Walker bailed out the toilet to make it a conduit for eavesdropping down the unit. He sat, head tilted over the empty metal commode, listening to a rape under way down in Boss's house. The sounds of five or six large men moving quietly around a cramped space. Guttural cries stifled by a cloth gag, loud enough to reach Walker and maybe even the CO below, who sat at a sad little desk before the unit's sole exit, a rolling steel-reinforced door. The kid getting initiated was Orange County, a surfer type with shaggy hair. He was tan and skinny and didn't stand a chance. It was fifteen minutes past count time, so it wouldn't be over for him till it was over for everybody. Terminal Island was medium security, no supermax, so no central lever locked the cells. The old-fashioned key-in-door setup meant lockdowns were few and night movement easy.

Good for the wolves, bad for the sheep.

Finally the muffled struggle ceased. Boss would make his trip to the shower room at the end of the tier. He was a creature of habit, Boss, and a stickler for hygiene.

Walker moved to sit Indian style by his open cell door, looking out at the black drop beyond the railing. The silence, when it asserted itself, was awesome. A concrete warehouse, shocked at its own purpose. From time to time, the COs put on moccasins and crept into the pipe chases between cells to spy on the boarders. Of course, everyone heard them, shuffling behind the walls like giant mice.

He could still smell the aftermath of the day. The musk of a hundred close-quarters men with poor ventilation. Lingering odors off illicit hot plates—rice, beans, noodles stirred in tuna cans. He closed his eyes, waiting for the creak of the catwalk. A stress that said 280 pounds, a familiar cadence of steps. He'd spent enough time alone in the dark to read the whine of the mesh underfoot, the identities behind the breath patterns. He hadn't acquainted himself with the specific noises of men this intimately since his days with Recon.

First the vibration came through the floor, then the faint groan of metal on a half-second repeat. Another few steps and the raspy inhale joined in.

The harmonics of Boss Hahn on the move.

Walker rose, staying just inside the dark of his cell. He counted the steps, gauged the approach, and pivoted onto the catwalk, face-to-face with Boss. A ragged white towel wrapped the big man's waist and thighs. Exertion pulled Boss's lips back, revealing oddly square teeth. His cheeks and chest shone with sweat. The startled expression gave way to an arrogant smile.

Walker clenched the hard plastic against his palm. His hand was down at his side, and then it swung up and tapped Boss high on the neck. A black spray fanned two feet in the air, and Boss grunted and waved his dense arms as if trying to keep his balance. Walker put one hand on the bullish slick chest and one under the chin and flipped Boss over the rail. He fell into darkness, the white afterthought of the towel fluttering down in his wake.

An instant of silence.

Then he hit the floor. The CO flipped the lights, and there Boss lay, gasping and shuddering, limbs bent in the wrong places. Blood pumped lazily from beneath his ear, widening the pool that had already encircled his torso. One arm managed a single paddling rotation against the concrete, painting a sloppy arc, then stilled.

The CO stared down at the pink body, its mouth caught in a perfect O. He stepped slowly back to the single steel door that could make J-Unit airtight, his hand grabbing for the radio at his belt and catching it on the second try. A moment of breath-held anticipation as a hundred sets of eyes peered out from fifty cells. A giant roar came all at once, as if from a single throat, and then the convicts charged from their cells.

Chapter 2

Decked out in Spider-Man shoes, an empty belted scabbard, Evel Knievel helmet, and wearing a goatee of chocolate ice cream, Tyler rose from a crouch that dangled his pale butt to the carpet and sneezed a Spidey-web of snot into his spread fingers. He studied the result, impressed.

"Bless you," his mother said.

An encore.

"Bless you."

Yet again.

"Enough already." Dray grabbed a flailing arm and tugged Tyler around Bear's legs toward a waiting Kleenex. Ty dropped his milk, kicking it across the floor, its airtight roll reinforcing Tim's perpetual regard for the inventor of the sippy cup. In an act of nearly unprecedented stupidity, Tim and Dray had recarpeted the house—in white—shortly after Tyler's second birthday. They still hadn't figured out just to let the rug get appropriately stained, their neurosis about spills an indication of how basic their lives had become.

Over by the fireplace, Tim finished duct-taping carpet scraps onto the corners of the raised hearth. Tyler had scraped a shin on one yesterday, and tonight the offending stone was paying the price. Bear reclined on the couch, a dessert plate on each knee.

Bear fingered his own plate and licked the frosting, then regarded Tim's untouched square longingly. Tim had doubted the wisdom of entrusting his piece of birthday cake, which amounted to the shaky *th* in *Happy 38th*, to his partner's custody. Though enormous, Bear had little flab. He was more like a shaped block. It was a lot of mass to support, and his stalwart reliability ended when food entered the picture.

Since Tyler's screeching arrival, Tim and Dray had enjoyed staying home more. Slowing down and speeding up to a domestic pace. Eating dinner when it was still light out. Going to bed before Letterman. They'd had good practice for the seven years of Ginny's life, and with Tyler's birth they'd returned to the once-familiar lifestyle with renewed appreciation.

Bear had filled in increasingly over the past year as Tim and Dray had started to spend some evenings out alone. Early on, Dray's mother had trooped over religiously, bringing with her onion-intensive casseroles and a vast collection of unwarranted fears—"You'd better childsafe that toilet lid." "There's no juice in this juice!" "Do you know the *crap* in the air on this side of the freeway?" Dray, realizing that her mother was augmenting Tim's own overprotectiveness, finally informally banned her from the house. They met once a week at a park or a mall, which was about fifty times a year more than they did before Tyler. Tim's father, an inveterate and accomplished con man, had sent a postcard on Tyler's first birthday saying he wanted to meet his grandson, but Tim had not replied. The card represented the sole correspondence between them since their latest falling-out three years before.

Dray released Ty, who tottered around Boston, Bear's Rhodesian Ridgeback, and regarded the pajamas he'd kicked off—yet again—moments before. "Kaiyer hot," he declared.

"So you've indicated," Bear said. "Several times."

Dray, looking as if she had grave doubts about having extended her maternity leave from the Sheriff's Department, regarded Tim's work and shot a blond wisp out of her face with an expertly directed exhale. "Missed a corner or an edge somewhere." Her index finger roamed, sweeping across the carpeted backyard step, the rugs muffling the kitchen linoleum, the foam taped over the corners of the coffee table. "Huh. Guess not." Her smile tugged left—her smart-ass grin—and her hair fell across her light green eyes. Thirteen years of marriage, and still the impossibly pale shade of her irises could catch Tim off guard.

She glanced over at the couch, and her eyebrows, two of her most expressive features, tilted sternly. "I said that's *enough* cake."

Bear, Tyler, and Boston all reacted to her tone with hurt expressions.

Tim rose from the hearth and dusted his hands. "Not you, Bear."

"Oh." Bear glanced down and saw Tyler's hand, sneaked around his midsection and embedded in frosting. "You little rat. Get outta here."

Tyler squealed and ran away, avoiding a tap on the naked rear end from Bear's size sixteen boot. It was good to see Bear smiling again. He'd had to put his other dog down three months ago and had been smothering his grief with Two-Dozen Tuesdays at Krispy Kreme all week long.

As Dray had suggested on more than one occasion, Bear needed a woman.

Tyler stalked around the back of the sofa, licking his blue-smeared hand, coming back for another pass at Bear's plate.

"Don't even think about it." Tim claimed his cake, smashed by the hand imprint. To Bear he said, "Nice work."

Bear shrugged. "Off duty."

Tim checked his watch—9:05 P.M.—and set down his plate. "Come on, bub." He swung Tyler up onto a hip. "Say good night."

Ty blew kisses, which involved knocking a sticky hand against his chin and then flinging it outward.

"Night, Typhoon," Bear said.

"Night, Bautin." More awkward gesticulation at the dog, who lifted his eyes solemnly in acknowledgment. Tim headed toward the back.

Bear's cell phone revved up into a flat rendition of Zeppelin's "Kashmir." He stood, hefting his jeans, tugging the Nextel from his belt. From his reaction, the text message was something more pressing than a confidential informant trying to sell a tip.

Predictably, Tim's phone vibrated next, startling Tyler. Tim handed him to Dray, tilted the screen, scowled.

Bear said, "Happy birthday."

Tim started back again. He returned to the living room a moment later, holstering his Smith & Wesson. He leaned over, kissed his son on the forehead. Bear pocketed an oatmeal cookie.

Dray raised an eyebrow. Tim nodded in affirmation, kissed her as well, and followed Bear out.

Chapter 3

Bear accelerated down the Harbor Freeway, his overused Ram protesting with a whine of engine and shocks. For a prison break, as with a missing-persons, the first twenty-four hours are key. Since 1979, when the Justice Department shifted responsibility for fugitives from the FBI to the Marshals Service, federal prison escapees had fallen into the Service's domain. Tim and Bear had swung by the district office downtown to grab whatever files Guerrera had been able to pull together. Consigned to light duty in the squad room after a questionable use of force during a raid last spring, Guerrera had accompanied them down the hall on their way out, right up to the awkward moment when the elevator doors banged shut in his envious face.

Bear, proud godfather, kept a photo rubber-banded to the cracked sun visor—himself holding Tyler upside down by the ankles before Legoland's pint-size Empire State Building. He laid on the horn, then passed a soccer mom in a Hummer with a NO WAR FOR OIL bumper sticker, the Dodge, hardly fuel-thrifty itself, shuddering its disapproval.

Tim thumbed through a sheaf of printouts, stopping at Walker Jameson's presentencing report and squinting at the fax-squashed letters at the periphery. *U.S. Marine Corps. Enlisted. MOS: Infantry Rifleman.* If the brief, unofficial write-up of his nine years in the Corps was accurate, Jameson had seen action in Jordan, Kosovo, Somalia, Sudan, and Iraq. After 9/11 he'd requested to retrain on an Anti-Terrorist Task Force and attended Scout/Sniper School at Quantico, making corporal as a sniper with First Force Recon. A photocopy of a grainy picture showed a lean, powerful man, fist tensed around a combat knife. His camo-smeared face was turned to the shadows, a near-perfect seam of dark claiming the left side. His rifle was slung, stock to his right shoulder, barrel at his opposite knee.

Having spent eleven years as a platoon sergeant with the Army Rangers, Tim was only too aware of the experience Jameson had amassed in his diverse deployments. Tim studied his fugitive's face. A Spec Ops warrior trained at taxpayer expense to think as Tim once thought, to stalk as he stalked, to shoot as he shot. Tim set the photo on the dash. His eyes pulled to the bottom line of the PSR. *Dishonorable discharge. Reduced to E-1. Six months in Leavenworth.* No further explanation.

"Remind me to tell Guerrera to get ahold of Jameson's SRB."

"His who?" Bear asked.

"Service Record Book. His file." He and Bear had worked together for so long he sometimes forgot that their shared lexicon didn't extend to military jargon.

Jameson's personal section was surprisingly spare. Thirty-one years old. Married once, long separated, though the divorce wasn't on paper yet. No kids. One sister, five years older. During his marriage he'd lived in Littlerock. The rural community of about ten thousand was located fifty miles northeast of L.A., smack in the middle of pretty much nothing. After his last deployment and vacation in Leavenworth, he hadn't returned. From what Tim knew of Littlerock, it was easy to see why.

The Dodge veered onto one of the Long Beach exits and flew across the channel on a green suspension bridge. Bear finally eased off the gas as they arced down onto Terminal Island. Home of the prison that had accommodated inmates ranging from Al Capone to Charlie Manson, the island was also an integral part of the Port of Los Angeles. Semis lined the roads end to end like building fronts. Shadowy container ships crawled in and out of berths, some large enough to give the illusion that it was the land that was casting off, washing the Ram with it. The white, ribbed tube of a pipeline twisted overhead through the island like a monorail.

Jameson had been handed a five-year sentence for stockpiling explosives. He'd gotten rolled up in a federal sting attempting to acquire two crates of frag grenades. Good-behavior credits had won him a one-year reduction.

"Five years seems a bit steep for a first-time weapons beef," Tim said. "Did Guerrera give any background?" When Marshal Tannino, roused from sleep, had pulled Tim aside at the office to remind him in a rare facile lapse of the importance of a quick takedown, Tim had missed Guerrera's full rundown.

Bear raised his voice to be heard over the loose dashboard and the garbage truck rattling by. "Jameson refused to cooperate—wouldn't name names, wear a wire, nothing—so they played up the aggravating factors and stuck it to him. Cost him years, probably."

The watchtower loomed into view. The dark plain of the harbor, glittering to the east beyond an ornamental strip of well-tended grass, underlined the tower's beaconlike appearance. The prison rose above a cyclone fence, its concrete blocks pallid yellow. Coils of razor wire formed a dense and forbidding underbrush. Rust-red bars obscured dim windows and the thousand-man confraternity of the Terminal Island Federal Correctional Institute. To the west stood a cluster of coast guard administrative buildings. They looked ready to crowd the prison right off the land, its eastern wall hanging over the water. Officers jogged along the building's walls, hauling semiautomatics, their shouts faint in wind off the ocean. The tower spotlight glared off the fake quartz rocks in the narrow run between expanses of chain link, making Tim squint. The escape had to have been as spectacular as billed. Again Tim found himself musing on Jameson's considerable training.

Bear flashed his creds at the guard in the station, who spit tobacco into a paper coffee cup and said, "Warden's expecting you. Guns stay in your vehicle."

They pulled through the gate, parked, and slid their guns into the glove box. Tim removed the handcuff key from his key chain and taped it under his watch.

He frowned at the file in his lap, and Bear plucked up the top page and studied it, as if to pin down the cause of Tim's taking offense. Tim chewed his cheek and conned the choppy harbor. The air smelled strongly of tar. The distant, sonorous call of a tanker vibrated the window.

Tim said, "Why's a guy who's racking up good-behavior credits serve most of his sentence, *then* break out?"

"Convicts move in mysterious ways." Bear jiggled the key to free it from the ignition. "But we work that out, we're in the game."

Across the parking lot, the warden stepped from the building and raised a hand in greeting. Tim waved back, and he and Bear unsnapped their seat belts.

Tim threw open his door, then paused. "Gimme his identifiers again. Jameson."

Bear held up the sheet to the faint light. "Six feet. Hundred ninety pounds. White."

"Great. He looks like everyone. He looks like no one."

Bear glanced at the photo on the dash. "He looks like you."

Chapter 4

The guard at the console gave them a cordial nod on their way into the secure room, where they found five men arrayed around desks and tables of inmate manufacture. The conversation stopped abruptly.

The warden, an exacting former Indian Affairs commissioner with a trimmed mustache and a limp, paused at the door. "John Sasso's our operations lieutenant, and this is Daniel McGraw, our intel specialist. They're here to assist you. Now, if you'll excuse me, I've got a media shitstorm to forge into."

He withdrew, and the silence resumed. Neither Sasso nor McGraw—who remained standing in a clear display of annoyance at having been summoned from more pressing matters—offered a word of greeting, and the three COs who hadn't been introduced continued wearily at their sandwiches and files. The vibe, while uncomfortable, wasn't unexpected. Deputy U.S. marshals were outsiders, and they generally got called into prison business only when correctional officers or intel specialists—who were supposed to keep their fingers on the pulse of prison underlife—failed at their jobs.

Tim offered a hand. "Tim Rackley. My partner, George Jowalski."

Whereas Sasso was dressed to code—gray slacks, white collared shirt, maroon tie with a blue blazer—McGraw had gone SWAT casual, his short sleeves cuffed over his biceps and his camo pants stuffed into the tops of unlaced boots. Sasso's belt was laden with gear: radio, two key-ring clips, a baton slotted through a metal circle. From his blazer pocket protruded an inmate rule book and a blue pad Tim guessed contained union guidelines.

"I'll walk you over to Jameson's cell," Sasso said. "You'll have to see it to believe it."

"Actually, we'd like to watch the tape of the assault first," Tim said. "Would you mind taking a look at it with us?"

"Seen it about fifty times, thanks," McGraw said.

"We were hoping to get your perspective."

"Pretty cut and dried. Guy got shanked in the neck."

Bear rose to his tiptoes and made a shape with his mouth as if to whistle—gonna be a long night.

Tim said, "Maybe we could ask you a few questions before we head over."

McGraw snapped a cell phone from his belt, tapped a button to quiet it. "If we can make this quick. Full plate, as you can imagine."

"We'll do our best," Tim said. "You catch any whispers from the snitches this week?"

"None at all."

"I saw Jameson kept perfect behavior."

A glimmer of a smirk. "Until now."

"How was he today?"

"How are any of them any day?" Sasso said.

"Anything different?" Tim asked.

McGraw again: "Another day, same shit."

"We don't keep track of every mood shift in every prisoner," Sasso added.

Bear cleared his throat. "All that sensitivity training gone to waste."

Tim forged ahead. "Can we get his medical files?"

"Nothing in 'em," McGraw said. "He's a healthy guy."

"I'd like to look at them anyway."

"Maybe we should get a sample of his toilet water, too."

"You volunteering?"

McGraw's radio squawked, and he muttered into it, "I told you—be there in a sec," then glanced up at Tim and Bear. "Look, I'm sure all this background shit helps when you're running down a serial rapist in the world, but it's different in here. Not like the street. We've got cages and captives. It's the jungle, and it's got different rules."

"It would seem he's no longer in here," Bear noted evenly.

Tim tried another tack. "I've spent some time inside."

"Unless you're full-time, you don't understand."

"Twenty-four/seven."

McGraw looked perplexed, so Bear clarified. "He means as an inmate."

This shut McGraw up. He studied Tim. Then his eyes glinted with recognition and he sat down. Spun by the media, Tim's vigilante rampage after Ginny's murder was remembered by some—particularly in law enforcement—as Charles Bronson–style legend.

"Listen," Tim said, "we're not here to bust your balls. Our job is to find your inmate and deliver him back to you, and to do that, we're pretty much dependent on *your* expertise."

McGraw matched Tim's stare, then thumbed down the volume on his radio.

Tim said, "Any tracks or sightings outside the facility?"

"Would we all be standing here?"

"Any security irregularities?"

"A family of raccoons wreaked havoc a few weeks back with two of eight motion sensors along the beach, so we turned 'em off. Just those two. You can't do anything from that point anyways except swim straight out—if Jameson tried a hook-around, the tower would have him in seconds."

"Any chance of a water escape?"

"Unlikely, but possible. We have coast guard out in the harbor."

"What was the murder weapon?"

"We still aren't sure. You know there was a building mood in here, right? The slashing last week? I briefed your guy—Guerrera?—over the phone." McGraw waited for Tim's nod. "After the incident, we tossed the cells. Took everything—razors, pens, even spoons. So I've got no clue what Jameson used for the stabbing, and you can't make it out on the tape."

"Did Jameson seem caught up in the tension this week?" Bear asked. When McGraw didn't answer right away, he added, "On edge?"

McGraw's first hesitation. "Not that I noticed, no."

Bear said, "Tell us about the victim."

"Boss Hahn. Shotcaller for the AB, good for three murders. Armed heist that went south. He was serving his second—life on the installment plan."

"Jameson have a beef with him?"

"No more than anyone else. Boss ran the show."

Sasso added, "But you never know when someone steps on someone else. What sets them off. They're good guys, most of them. The only difference between them and human beings is the length of their fuse." He held up his pinkie.

"Why do you think Jameson would risk an escape with a year and change on his sentence?" Tim said. "He was serving perfect time? Why now?"

"Why does anyone break out?" Sasso said. "To be free. People flip out sometimes, can't do the time anymore."

McGraw shook his head, and for the first time Tim sensed an element of rivalry between the two of them. "He *had* to escape. You don't kill Boss and stay alive in here."

"Square one," Bear said. "What's Jameson have against Boss?"

"Nothing," Tim and McGraw said at the same time.

"Who'd Jameson run with?" Bear asked.

"No one, really," Sasso said.

"Was he religious?"

"He wore a cross, but he never went to chapel," McGraw said. "I monitor attendance personally."

No chaplain to question—another dead end.

Bear pressed on. "Tight with his cellie? Imaad Durand?"

McGraw hoisted his eyebrows and riffled through the nearest mound of paperwork. "Bill, toss me Jameson's jacket." One of the mute COs threw Walker's central file across the table, and McGraw thumbed through it. Exasperated, Bear blew out a breath—they were looking for the kind of information that wouldn't be recorded in a prisoner's C-file. Still reading, McGraw said, "Not particularly."

"He have any females come to see him?"

"You mean like conjugal visits?" Sasso asked.

McGraw grinned. "We don't have a Felon Reproduction Program in the federal system."

"Right. I meant regular visits," Tim said.

McGraw shuffled back through the files. "Not a one."

Bear whistled, jotting in his notepad.

Tim asked, "He have any jobs?"

McGraw's eyes scanned down the page. "Food service, Unicor, maintenance detail, trash orderly, laundry detail. The usual shit."

"How was his money situation?"

McGraw flipped the page. "He had about seventy bucks on the books. Put twenty on his canteen account this morning."

"What was the balance before?"

"Eleven bucks. Would've lasted him another week or so."

"Why bother adding to it if he was planning to escape that night?"

As it became apparent that no one was going to produce an answer, the door opened and a young CO leaned in. "Look what we just picked out of the shitheap." He let a plastic Baggie unroll dramatically; it gave a satisfying snap. Nestled in the bottom was a blue toothbrush.

"Lemme see that, Newlin." McGraw laid the bag on the table, and the men leaned over it. The hard rubber end of the toothbrush had been whittled to a point. A good two inches of red stain. Strips of cloth wrapped the handle, secured with paste. A shoelace served as a pommel. The bristles were dark with ash.

"Where'd he get the paste?" Sasso asked. "Unicor?"

"Imaad kept a little jar of it for his posters. He won't use gum, cuz he's Muslim and they can't chew gum for some reason. So he made his own paste out of soap and wax he traded for with Zeller." Newlin offered Tim and Bear a slightly embarrassed look and smoothed his sandy mustache, which he no doubt wore to try to add years to his boyish face. "I've worked J-Unit six months now."

Sasso offered a dry smile. "Long enough to remember your jacket, I'd imagine."

"Right. Sorry." In place of a union guidebook, Newlin had a pack of cigs stored in his breast pocket. On his belt, in addition to the normal accessories, was a latex-glove packet. Informed, relaxed, and prepared. He'd even referred to Walker's cellie by first name. Bear and Tim shared a quick, impressed glance.

"Listen," Tim said to Sasso and McGraw, "we've already taken up enough of your time. If . . . ?"

"Cary Newlin." The youthful CO offered his hand to Bear first, then Tim.

". . . wouldn't mind showing us the tape and walking us over, we can get out of your hair."

"Me?" Newlin shrugged his accord. McGraw bowed his head, extending his hands as if in benediction. Sasso steered them out, depositing them in the control center across the hall.

Manned by another team of zombie COs who barely noted Tim and Bear's entrance, a bank of closed-circuit TVs monitored the various prison buildings. The screen labeled "J" showed mini-frontloaders clearing away mounds of smoldering trash. Officers patrolled the perimeter of the mess while workers loaded more burned refuse into rolling bins. A few roaming COs wielding fire extinguishers continued to blast real or imagined embers, mist settling in a sci-fi layer about their knees. The barn-style steel door had been shoved back to accommodate the equipment, while an officer with an M4 guarded the ten-foot gap and checked the creds of the workers and COs passing through.

Newlin grabbed one of the three tapes atop the corner TV/VCR that Sasso had indicated and began fast-forwarding it. An unlit stretch of empty catwalk, blurred in bands by the tape's movement. It was a tight shot; the security camera must have been mounted on the tier just above.

"The brass chaffing you in there?" he murmured to Tim.

"How ever did you guess?"

"From the way you jumped on my bandwagon." He offered Tim and Bear a wink with a tip of his head. "Fellow chaffee."

Bear pointed at the activity on the live-feed J-Unit screen. "What are they still looking for in there?"

"Well, no inmate has technically *left* J-Unit," Newlin said. "The only door was secured seconds after Boss's body hit concrete. We figure maybe Walker's still lodged in a duct somewhere. Though at this stage it's wishful thinking. We've been through every inch of the unit twice. He literally vanished. Like, thin air, you know?"

"How'd you settle the riot so quickly?"

"This wasn't a riot, just a tantrum. We're only medium security. Once the last chair and TV get thrown, the inmates lose their juice. Plus, we had a full CO response and DCT—Disturbance Control Team. Power in numbers. We got the boys back in their houses without too much hassle."

"You notice anything different about Walker's behavior today?"

Newlin swapped out the tape for another one and resumed fast-forwarding. "Uh-huh."

The response caught both Tim and Bear by surprise. "Yes?" Tim said.

"Sure. His mood shifted at night. He was quiet—well, I guess Walker's always quiet. He seemed fine heading off for chow hall. But he came back from dinner, I dunno . . . *off.* Sat out TV time."

"Hadn't done that before?" Tim asked.

"Not that I remember."

Tim's gaze drifted across the bank of closed-circuit monitors, finding the "DH" screen. Rows of picnic tables, barely visible in the darkness. "Can we pull footage from dinner?"

"Hear that, Earl?"

One of the COs, without turning from the screens before him, offered Newlin a lethargic thumbs-up.

Newlin hit "play." The time stamp in the bottom right corner of the screen counted up from 20:14:32. Boss Hahn appeared, glimmering with sweat, his chest and stomach muscles pronounced above the towel. He moved with his weight on his heels, his arms bowed to accommodate their girth. A flash of shadow entered the screen, and Walker stood before him, facing away from the camera. A split-second pause, then the rise of the arm, the tap to the neck, the shove over the railing, and Walker vanished in the direction from which he'd come. An instant later the camera vibrated slightly on its mount—Boss Hahn's body hitting the floor.

The entire assault took place in about three seconds.

Rapidly, the catwalk filled with screaming inmates, churning and shoving. In short order they were heaving blankets and microwaves off the tier. The muted action and gloomy lighting gave the scene a sinister, old-fashioned feel.

"His cell's that way?" Tim pointed in the direction from which Jameson had entered and exited the screen.

Newlin nodded. "Just out of view. So he could've returned to his cell or kept going on the catwalk and shot down the south stairs. The thing is, the stairs are exposed, and the housing unit officer would've seen him."

"Unless Jameson waited for the riot and *then* split."

"Right. By that time the officer would've been out of the unit with the door locked."

"Anything on the other tapes?"

"They're limited view, as you can see. We've got one on the middle of each tier, like this, and then the general cam"—he pointed to the J-Unit screen—"which only really picks up the range floor and the center of the first tier. We've got a team going over everything, and they've yet to pick anything up."

"Let's roll the stabbing again," Tim said. "Tell me what you see."

Boss flew up over the railing, landed on his feet. The blood sucked back into his neck. He waddled backward, then headed forward to get murdered again.

"It's an expert strike," Newlin offered.

"Sure is." Tim's voice contained an element of admiration. "He struck right between the skull and the back shelf of the jaw, where it's good and tender. From the look of the blood pressure, he punctured the external carotid, straight up from the heart. Makes for a quicker bleed-out—about seven seconds. Jameson's right-handed, so it's a natural strike."

Newlin's eyes shifted from the screen to Tim's face, a reappraisal of sorts in the works. "How do you know he's right-handed?"

"Photo from his days in the Corps shows his rifle slung right to left." Tim tapped the screen. "Can we take another look at it?"

They watched the segment through a few more times. The spurt from Boss's punctured neck, when viewed frame by frame, was spectacular. They were just getting ready to leave when Newlin came out of his chair with excitement. "Hang on. Right there. Check it out." As Walker moved to shove Boss, his shirt pulled up on the left side, revealing the hems of several undershirts for a split second. "I *thought* he looked bulky. He layered up." Of Bear's puzzled glance, Newlin added, "Wearing a bunch of shirts. It's a defense against getting stuck. And it lets you pull a quick appearance change after you shiv someone."

"Why would he need to switch outfits?" Bear said. "He knows he's on tape."

"Plus, it's *his* ambush," Tim said. "I doubt he was worried about getting stuck."

"Maybe he put the shirts on earlier," Bear offered.

"Pretty damn hot in here to hang out in quadruple layers," Newlin said.

Bear bobbed his head in agreement. "Weird."

Newlin rose and headed for the door. "Not half as weird as his cell."

Chapter 5

Unlike Sasso, who pivoted corners on the ball of his foot to preclude a break in stride, Newlin slouched along, swinging the keys around an index finger. In the breezeway, cameras rotated to follow the three men's progress. They reached J-Unit and were promptly halted at the door.

"Creds and badges." The officer glanced quickly at Tim's and Bear's IDs, his hand never leaving the stock of his M4. "You're the marshals, huh? You figure this one out, you're better men than me." He handed Tim an electronic clipboard of the type carried by UPS drivers.

Tim perused the category labels—*Name, Position, Time In, Time Out*—before punching in his information. "You've kept this crime-scene log since the stabbing, right?"

"No one has crossed this threshold without signing here and walking past the barrel of my gun."

"Can we get a look at the records you've kept?"

The officer said sharply, "I know all these guys. Each name. And I look *everyone* in the face. No way our boy threw on a uniform and slid past me. No way."

"All the more reason, then, to give us a hand."

The officer tugged the clipboard out of Tim's grasp, entered a code, and returned it. The on-screen list had the names of everyone who had entered or left J-Unit after the Disturbance Control Team had secured

26

the building and extinguished the small fires. McGraw was first, at 8:43 P.M. Then a host of COs. Maintenance men. Sanitation workers. The warden. More sanitation workers. Most names had been entered going in *and* out.

Anticipating Tim's next question, the officer said, "Yes, the eleven outstanding are all still inside, and I know every one of them."

Tim handed over the clipboard with a nod and pressed forward with Bear and Newlin. Stagnant air filled his lungs, thick with the bitter scent of burned debris. An ambitious tech had done his best to lay down a chalk outline on the range floor, but it had been blurred by swept ash. Elsewhere dark puddles remained. From the cells, inmates cheered the mini-frontloader's progress as its bucket tray scooped up detritus like the distended mouth of a bass. Tim stared up the dreary rise of metal and concrete, wondering if Walker could in fact be hiding inside the walls.

Their footsteps shuddered the metal staircase as they climbed. Newlin led the way along the third-tier catwalk, Bear fanning the front of his shirt against the humidity. The facility was on full lockdown, the cell doors secured. As they drew near, palm-size mirrors, held by dark arms, retracted back through the bars. A huge Samoan kid offered Tim the finger from his perch on the toilet, where he sat with one leg free, his loose pants puddled around a laceless sneaker. A few of the cells remained neat, their mattresses and spartan furnishings intact, but most were torn apart. Posters had been ripped from the walls, leaving behind taped corners of azure water or tanned flesh.

The inmates peppered Newlin with questions: "CO, you guys all buy your ties at the same place?" "CO, who're them Newjacks with you?" "CO, this clogged toilet's *killin'* me."

The correctional officers milling by Jameson's open door stepped aside, one sweeping his arms melodramatically toward the cell as if indicating a just-unveiled statue.

Perfectly centered on the floor stood the bottom halves of two plastic Coke bottles—makeshift cups that had been filled, one with green liquid, the other with yellow.

Newlin followed Bear's gaze and nodded, lips pinched. "Mouthwash and urine."

Bear peered around the cell, summing up Tim's thoughts: "What the *fuck*?"

Two of the grid window's safety-glass panes had been broken. No jagged edges, just fist-size circles and a scattering of glass pebbles on the sill. A roll of green dental floss had been tied to a bar and dropped through one of the holes. Tim glanced through the glass, eyes tracing the thread's path down to the quartz rocks forty feet below. A breeze picked up the floss, floating it over the razor wire. A bedsheet rope, complete with a cartoon-prisoner knot and secured in similar fashion to a bar, dangled through the second break, the end swaying no more than ten feet below the bottom of the window ledge. Any drop from the rope, even if Walker could have shrunk himself to Mighty Mouse proportions and squeezed through the bars and the tiny gap in the glass, would have resulted in a death plummet to the razor wire.

Tim lingered on the view—two vast fences, coast guard headquarters, Dumpsters piled with charred refuse, a couple royal palms.

He gestured for a pair of latex gloves, then picked through the trash can. Three balls of tissue unfurled to reveal snot. The other contents were equally enlightening: a few empty Styrofoam cups and lids, two plastic Coke-bottle caps, a shorter string of dental floss, a wad of red gum. He set the can back down and eased to all fours to look under the bed. It took him a moment to identify the delicate blue shavings: rubber gratings from where Walker had whittled the toothbrush against the edge of the metal leg.

Tim stood, mused for a moment, then rapped his knuckles on the steel platform of the top bunk. "He threw his mattress over the rail?"

"That's right."

"He usually participate in stuff like that?"

Newlin took a moment, reflecting on the question. "We don't have Attica break out that often, but no. Walker's not a joiner. He didn't take part in the May riot."

"He left his cellie's mattress." Tim crossed the space and crouched, studying the frayed prayer rug of two-ply tissue. "This would've made for good burning, too." He glanced up at the black velvet banner and the postcard of the Sultan Ahmet, its six minarets pushing into a rich blue sky. "And that."

"So he didn't trash Imaad's stuff," Newlin said. "What's your point?"

"Seems like a pretty selective temper tantrum."

Bear beckoned Tim over to a color newsprint photo adhered to the wall by the sink. It was a studio shot of a woman in her thirties, awkwardly posed, fist to chin. Sears, perhaps. Amused, private eyes, angled to the side as if the photographer couldn't hold her attention. Maybe she was self-conscious, but it looked more as if she would've rather been someplace else. A too-slender nose prevented her from being beautiful, but it also added a sharpness to her otherwise even features, conveying an impression of intelligence, of resolve. The lavender retro-eighties Swatch dangling loose from her right wrist matched a pattern repeat in her shirt. Noting that Dray had a similar, Target-bought button-up, Tim pegged the woman's outfit as stylish but basically cheap. The dated haircut—short and excessively windswept—and the woman's makeup suggested the photo was from the late nineties.

"That his girl?" Bear asked.

"Sister," Newlin said. "She killed herself a few months back."

Bear jotted this down. "He take it hard?" Tim asked.

"You wouldn't know with Walker. When the wheels are turning, when they're stuck, you know?"

"Were they close?"

"I don't know, really."

"Given the visitor log," Bear said, "not that close."

Tim knelt before the footlockers. The top lid creaked back to reveal several kufis, shirts, and toiletries thrown together with a collection of postcards of pilgrimage-class mosques. By contrast, the bottom footlocker was meticulously ordered. Toothpaste, neatly rolled. Shirts and pants folded with military crispness. Some yellowed papers peeked out from beneath a row of socks. Tim withdrew them, finding an obituary and a handwritten letter. The obit's torn top border aligned with the bottom edge of the photo stuck to the wall.

Tim scanned the brief newspaper write-up. *Theresa Sue Jameson (38), born April 1, 1966. Theresa, a Littlerock native, worked as office manager for Westin Dentistry in Canyon Country. Her friends remember her irrepressible spirit. She leaves behind a son, Samuel (7). Services will be held at St. Jude's Church June 12 at 6pm.*

The footer read *June 11, Littlerock Weekly.*

As good a way as any to reduce someone's life into one and a half column inches. Tim remembered how his father always worded those he placed, rarely, for old associates to come in under the six-line minimum.

Bear, reading over Tim's shoulder, remarked, "Regular hotbed of journalistic panache, the *Littlerock Weekly.*"

It also was a publication of insufficiently wide circulation, Tim figured, to be taken by the Terminal Island library. He tilted the worn rectangle of newspaper and picked up faint indentations in the corner. Maybe a return address from the envelope it had been mailed in, written after the clipping had been enclosed. Bear opened his notepad, and Tim slipped the piece of paper in; they'd have it looked at later.

Bear glanced at it a moment longer before shutting the pad. "Least we know he didn't break out to attend her funeral like that jackass we bagged at his granny's wake in Chino Hills."

The letter proved to be from Theresa, though it was dated a couple years prior, a few months after Walker's term at TI began. Feminine handwriting crossed the page at a slight downward tilt. The cheap, lavender-tinted stationery, torn from a pad, hadn't held the ink well; some of the letters' upstrokes were smudged.

> Walk,
> So I started going to a free counseling center out here. The shrink's younger than I am, so we'll see how that goes. I've been doing a lot of work on myself in therapy for Sammy's sake—shit, there I go again. For <u>both</u> our sakes, for Chrissake (I suck at this). And I figured out all these ways I can't hold my boundaries to protect maybe what's best for me and for Sammy. I don't think I'm strong enough to say no to you, Walk, for much of anything, so the best thing I can do right now is to take some time off. Please, please, please don't be upset with me. I know you just got in there and I know you've got no one, but please remember this is me. I love you and I think of you still and always as my baby boy. We went through some times, me and you, didn't we? I know we haven't been in touch much since you went to Iraq. I always

thought it's a shame you never got to know the little guy.
He's tough as nails, but he's got heart. He reminds me of you
when you were younger, before I lost you to the Marines. I
bought you this cross, in place of me, I guess. I bought it in
titanium, so even you can't break it (kidding).

Love you always,
Tess

Tim offered the note to Newlin, who read it before handing it off to Bear. After perusing it, Bear slid it also into his notepad. "Why would he leave this behind? I mean, obviously, it's highly personal. He could have at least flushed it."

"Points to a rushed escape," Tim said. "Just because it was smartly planned doesn't mean he didn't swing into action quickly when he got set off."

"So Walker finds out something awful about Señor Hahn at dinner, gouges him that night, knows he's in deep shit unless he flies the coop?" Bear's tone made clear he wanted more to tie down the theory. Like Tim, Bear had started thinking of the man they were pursuing by his given name. A good sign—they were starting to build a relationship with him.

They stood in silence in the cramped space. It smelled of metal, virile and unforgiving. A familiar smell. Tim tasted it back by his molars, as if he were chewing a piece of foil. He crouched before the Coke-bottle cups, taking in the cell with a long, slow sweep of his eyes.

One of the COs at the door said, "So what you got, Sherlock? What's mouthwash and piss got to do with the breakout?"

"Nothing," Tim said.

Newlin now: "Nothing?"

"They don't mean anything. They *can't.* They're a diversion. He wants to draw our attention away."

"Away from what?"

Tim studied the twinning holes in the window. "From what he doesn't want us to see."

Newlin sounded slightly exasperated. "What does he not want us to see?"

"I haven't figured that out yet."

Chapter 6

Tim, Bear, and Newlin sat on frail rolling chairs in the control center, shoulder to shoulder before the TV, watching Walker Jameson work his way through a slab of meat loaf. On the way back, they'd stopped by the infirmary to speak to Jameson's cellie and gotten little from him save a sullen indifference that Tim had found credible. From the tape they'd confirmed that Walker appeared to be wearing no other layers under his tan button-up at dinner. Now a hulking black prisoner whom Newlin identified as a BGF leader cruised up to Walker's table. They spoke briefly, and then, judging by the man's expression, he left displeased.

Walker ate hunched over his tray, shoulders rounded, a man used to guarding resources. Another inmate hustled over to him and whispered urgently in his ear. Walker's body stiffened. The inmate patted his back almost regretfully and headed off. He was a wiry man who walked with a forward lean. Head down but eyes flashing—very alert.

Walker sat for a long, stunned time, then rose slowly and strode to the exit.

"Who's the whisperer?" Tim asked.

"Tommy LaRue. He's the go-to guy for the prisoners. We turn him upside down now and then just to see what'll fall out. Porn, dime bags, unlisted numbers of guys' ex-girlfriends. You'd be amazed. I found him with a wedge of wrapped Brie once, I shit you not. He's well respected. A nice, gentle guy."

"What's he in for?" Bear asked.

"Double homicide."

They inched the recording forward, frame by frame. LaRue had cupped his hand by Walker's ear, so there'd be no lip-reading magic. He'd had time to deliver a few words, tops.

"Let's see where he's coming from. LaRue." Tim indicated the side door through which LaRue had entered.

A painstaking twenty minutes passed as the other COs, with reluctance, helped Newlin sort through archived security tape to find the appropriate segments. Slowly, Tim and Bear pieced together LaRue's backward journey. The hall camera caught him flashing by. A breezeway lens captured a stretch of his hurried stroll from the yard. A wide-angle mounted on the roof of C-Unit showed him moving, a dot among dots, to the B-Unit door. And, finally, the last bit of footage traced him to his origin: the phone mounted on the range wall.

During the call, lasting less than ten seconds, LaRue faced away, blocking the numbers as he dialed. He'd strolled into the building casually but left with an intensity of purpose.

Something he'd heard had lit a fire under him.

Tim and Bear had to wait to get clearance to enter the Special Housing Unit, where LaRue would be spending the next few nights in solitary. During the post-escape cell checks, a CO had found a vial of heroin secreted in his pillow.

Frank Zarotta, the North Yard officer, had the bearing and temperament of a bulldog, a resemblance strengthened in no small measure by his persistent gnawing on a greasy Slim Jim. He studied Tim with wide, dark eyes, as if he were privy to a dirty secret.

Zarotta's radio crackled, and he pressed it to an ear, and then there was a buzz and the door clicked open. He beckoned Tim and Bear with a sturdy finger. They headed into the trap, an eight-by-twelve-foot chamber. Through a big window to their right, encased in a metal cage, two SHU officers looked up from their game of cards and returned Zarotta's flick of the head. One of them reached under his desk, and the inner door popped open.

Zarotta led Tim and Bear to the left, down a concrete corridor lined on either side with cell doors. "Now, remember," he said, "no strikes to the head. Maybe he gets a tooth through the lip, some blood on the brain—it's trouble. Aim low for the shin, or catch the floating rib." He paused and leaned back, a broad comic gesture with both arms spread. "Hey, what am I telling *you*? You guys know what you're doing." His eyes lingered on Tim. "Ain't that right, Troubleshooter?" He enjoyed a good laugh. "I'm just messin'. Shoulda seen you guys' faces."

He unlocked the steel door and led them in. The concrete cell had the usual stainless steel furnishings, the bed bolted to the concrete. A tiny window on the rear wall, no more than six inches by two feet, peered out on the darkness like a bunker gun slit. The metal reflected the harsh blue overhead light. Despite the scaled-down space, LaRue looked small, sitting with his back to the far wall, knees drawn up. He had a fingernail between two molars, digging at something.

"Deputy marshals are here," Zarotta said. "It's sharing time."

"Shit, I ain't no cheese eater. Get these jokers outta here."

"No can do, pal. And watch your mouth or you're gonna catch a case."

"I want to talk to some rank."

"Sure thing. I'll get Condi Rice on MSN Messenger." Zarotta closed the door and chuckled his way back down the hall.

"Real cutup," Bear said.

"Oh, I get it," LaRue said. "Here's where we establish camaraderie."

"Nah," Tim said, "let's skip it. Are you a friend of Walker's?"

LaRue was really working the tooth now, his elbow rising level with his head. "Ain't no one a friend of Walker's. But yeah"—and now a flash of pride—"I'm the only one he'll talk to in here."

The warden had not put out word of Walker's escape to the population, but inmates were second only to socialites at acquiring and disseminating sensational information. Tim decided to float the obvious to gauge LaRue's willingness to talk.

"He escaped."

LaRue's eyes stayed uncharacteristically steady. "Did he, now." He gave up on his fingernail, tugged a strand of yarn from his sock, and flossed out a green fleck. "Walk was short, sixteen-some months to the door. Why would he bust a move like that?"

"We were hoping you could enlighten us."

With a flourish of his hand, LaRue made a cigarette appear, and then his fingers fussed in the hair behind his ear and produced a match. Centering his thumbs on the phosphorus head, he carefully tore it and the tinder in half. He flicked one of the half matches against his tooth and lit up, pleasure closing his eyes on the inhale.

"What do you know about his sister?"

"Walk has a sister?"

"How about his wife?"

"His *wife*? Shit, that's been years. I'd bet a spoonful of chiva she's put on a sport coat by now."

"Sport coat?" Bear asked.

LaRue smiled sourly. "A man your lady slides on to keep her warm while you're doing hard time."

Tim asked, "Did Walker have a problem with Boss?"

"Walker didn't have a problem with no one. Not even with the screws."

"So why'd he kill Boss?"

"Beats hell outta me."

"I think you know."

Same flat stare. "Do you, now?"

Tim walked over and sank to his haunches so he was eye level with LaRue. "You made a phone call just before dinner. Then you busted ass getting to the dining hall so you could whisper in Walker's ear. You're gonna tell us what you found out."

For the first time, LaRue looked uneasy, but his composure snapped back, smoothing his face like a mask. "I don't much seem to recall that particular phone call."

"LaRue. I want an answer."

LaRue shrugged and showed off a set of clean white teeth. "What you gonna do? Put me in jail?"

"He's exactly right," Tim said, charging back down the breezeway. "We've got no leverage with *him*. He's a lifer already. We need the guy he *called*."

Bear shuffle-stepped to keep up. "And how are we gonna get to him?"

Tim moved down the brief hall and through the door into the control center, where Newlin was making decisive gains on a cruller.

"Do you monitor inmate phone calls?" Tim asked.

Newlin looked up from the recording—LaRue's whispered pronouncement again—and wiped a smudge of grease from his chin. "Course."

"Record them?"

"Only if we're keeping an eye. We wouldn't have recorded LaRue, probably. We're not that concerned about the seamy underworld of Brie."

"Can we get the number he called?"

"Yeah, the prisoners have to use a PIN number before dialing. They can only call approved numbers, which we database at Investigative Services. It's just a matter of digging around the records. I'll call over."

"And see if you can rustle up any information on who LaRue used to run with." Tim tapped Bear on the shoulder. "Let's get Guerrera on that, too. He's probably boring a hole in the phone with the patented Little Havana stare."

Newlin dialed and said as it was ringing, "Oh, and they sent over an update of the crime-scene log." He handed a printout to Tim.

Tim perused the already familiar names. COs and sanitation workers.

His pulse quickened as he sensed—finally—some of the data pulling together. A pattern shifting shape, still eluding him.

Newlin finished his call, and he and Bear reviewed the chow-hall tape yet again. LaRue's bend at the waist. Cupped hand rising to Walker's ear. Fist tightening around fork.

"What the hell could he have told him?" Newlin's curiosity had lapsed into frustration. "Some pickup waiting out in the harbor? A green light for Boss's killing?" He snickered at himself. "His Manchurian Candidate activation code word?"

Tim sank into a chair, glancing at the J-Unit monitor. The wreckage had been largely disposed of, the trash orderlies brought in to mop up the remaining sludge. Walker *seized his opportunity* in the mayhem?

Tim closed his eyes, considering the cell. Two severed Coke bottles. Piss and mouthwash. Walker's padding himself with shirt over shirt.

One mattress untouched, one missing. Two windowpanes punched through. Nothing beyond the bars but razor wire, palm trees, and Dumpsters. The trash can—Kleenex and bottle caps. But what *hadn't* the trash can contained?

Tim flipped to the log's next page. More COs. The frontloader operator. John Sasso. The same maintenance man from before. McGraw again. Sanitation worker.

Tim stood up abruptly. The chair tilted over with his momentum, clattering on the cheap laminate flooring. He met Bear's and Newlin's startled gazes.

"I know how he did it."

Chapter 7

The crow lurched from one foot to the other on its spongy nighttime perch, its black marble eye shifting in its socket in sudden, awakened alarm. The ground beneath it swelled, and the crow screeched, spooking the roost, which took flight in a grand exodus of flaps and squawks. The dark upsurge lifted out of the San Pedro Municipal Landfill and wheeled south, undulating in the night murk, a few beaks still sounding their agitation.

The charred mattress bulged again, and then an arm slid from the incision, scattering tufts of ash-streaked batting. A plastic cone protruded from the striped ticking like a snorkel, the Coke label rubbed off from friction. The blackened hand groped the uneven terrain, gauging it eyelessly, grotesquely. A head fought its way out next, red-raw cheeks showing in patches through the soot.

Walker pulled himself free and collapsed backward, taking in deep breaths between spasms of coughing. He used the still-moist inside of his shirt collar to clean the grime from his swollen lids and opened his eyes. The moonless sky above seemed impossibly vast.

Aside from a heat-induced ruddiness and a few healthy scrapes along his arms, he was in surprisingly good shape. The mattress stuffing, repositioned to conceal his form and soaked with water from the cell sink, had staved off the fire. He'd dropped the mattress over the railing, then run down to slither through the slit as the ignited trash began raining down. Once inside, he'd had to turn his head to breathe, his lips sealed over the mouth of the upward-facing Coke bottle—his channel to oxygen. When the smoke had been most stifling, in the moments before he'd felt the rescuing scoop of the frontloader, he'd plugged the makeshift snorkel with a finger and sucked what little air he could through a wet rag. The five shirts had insulated his torso from the heat. Though most of the fires, he knew from the last riot, were small and isolated and quickly burned themselves out, he'd had a scare at one point when the heat had pulsed relentlessly through the soaked padding, making him writhe before it backed off.

He sat up and surveyed his surroundings. Lucky as hell—he'd gotten dumped near the top of a heap within the dug-down pit, though he was still a good ten feet below ground level. He laid the blackened remains of a table on end and used them to gain traction against the dirt wall, the crumbling border giving way as he clawed, then squirmed his way over the brink.

A dense film of seagull shit coated the ground. Above the smell of rotted fish and soot, a distant whiff of ocean.

Walker peeled off his top two shirts and threw them aside. He went with the fourth shirt since the third still bore traces of ash and the bottom one was drenched with sweat. His pants were filthy, but they'd do. They were baggy and low-slung—inmates couldn't be trusted with belts—but prison couture had spread to the outside, so he'd blend right in with the other lowlifes. Retrieving the plastic bag from his waistband, he slid out the last dripping cloth and used it to wipe off his face, his hands, his forearms.

By the time he cracked his back and began to jog toward the stream of headlights far off to the west, he looked by most accounts like an average citizen.

Chapter 8

Bear crouched with his prodigious ass floating above his heels and let his flashlight beam pick over the trash below. At his side Tim watched. It couldn't have been much clearer. The mattress, split like a pita. One Coke-bottle segment pushing clear of the top fabric, the second one smothered in the trash below. Finger furrows up the wall of the pit. And then, a few strides from the lip, a puddle of ruined clothes.

A B-movie monster hatching.

Bear spoke with a sharp, wounded intensity. "So he sawed off a Coke bottle, then peed into it just to draw our attention away from the missing bottle *tops*?"

Tim said, "That's right."

They'd raced over from the prison. The garbage-truck driver, a rotund bearded man, had forged over hills and around sunken plots to show them where he'd made the dumps. Now, a scant forty minutes later, flashlights were visible across the landfill, bouncing like fireflies. Dogs stood slack on their leads, and deputies hollered their frustration over the wind. If there was any amalgam better at killing a scent trail than garbage and ash, Tim didn't know what it was. Bleach and civet, maybe.

San Pedro PD units were prowling the surrounding streets, but the landfill was close to a number of thoroughfares and the 110, and they weren't working on a time frame that made Tim optimistic. A tech had identified the blood type as O from a streak on the mattress, giving them a match. She was running a DNA to be sure, but Tim already was.

Bear said wryly, "Got us looking the wrong way."

"That's right."

"A stall."

"Uh-huh."

"Bought himself time."

"That he did."

"The dental floss? The bedsheet?"

"Set design."

"Clever fucker." Bear rose and planted his hands on his hips. "So now he's out. Maybe he moves to Cambria, opens an antiques store."

Tim recalled Walker's face in the dining hall once the shock had faded and he'd stood and made his way to the exit. Steel and focus. Whatever Walker was out for, he had risked being incinerated, compacted, or buried alive to get it done.

"Doubt it," Tim said.

"Me, too." Bear heaved a world-weary sigh. "Bakery, maybe."

Bulldozers peered over the edges of the wide pits. In the distance a queue of landing lights dotted the darkness, a lineup for John Wayne Airport. Rats tugging at the bent pizza box that Tim was standing on retreated a few feet when he shooed them with his boot. He preferred his rodents demure. And his fugitives less inventive.

Every household and business in San Pedro generated trash, and it wound up here. Tim thought about the garbage pipeline stretching back from this foul hub to all those places and then to all the places beyond those. A million spots for a smart fugitive to hole up and plan his next move.

A smart fugitive with extensive combat training.

More than anyone that Tim had squared off against since joining the Service six years ago, Walker Jameson could take him head-on, test his limits. He hoped it wouldn't come to that but already knew better.

As Tim followed Bear back to the truck, glass and eggshells crunching underfoot, the Nextel vibrated at his hip. He flipped it open and pressed it to his ear.

Newlin said, "I got you a phone number."

Chapter 9

Fifth and Wall. The nucleus of a few blocks that stoically held out for squalor, resisting tooth and nail the gentrification of downtown Los Angeles. Two homeless guys were fighting by an overturned shopping cart, bears spinning in rags. They were well padded and badly coordinated, their blows decelerated to a slow-motion tempo by alcohol or exhaustion. They stumbled off as Tim and Bear drew near, their fleeing shadows stretching several stories up. One storefront remained lit, leading Tim to ponder the age-old question: Who buys a mini-motorcycle at eleven-thirty at night?

Shouts from various open windows called for someone to shut up, demands so self-defeatingly persistent that Tim couldn't discern their target. When the yelling quieted, the source confrontation became audible—a stern domestic lecture emanating from a parked Cadillac.

Happily for Tim and Bear, Guerrera had sublimated his pent-up frustration from being deskbound into working the databanks. He'd not only produced an address for them from the phone number LaRue had dialed, but he'd also ferreted out the apartment records. A gas bill had been paid three months ago by a check on First Union Bank, account of Freddy Campbell, the same Freddy Campbell who'd celled with Tommy LaRue in Victorville for a few years before LaRue's transfer to TI. The apartment leaseholder was thrice-divorced Bernadette Monroe, whom Guerrera pegged for Freddy's girlfriend, given that they'd traveled together last

March to Rio. Freddy had no driver's license, no registered vehicle, and no major credit cards in his name.

Tim and Bear made their way up sticky stairs to number 214, rang the bell, and stood to the side of the door, hands on their guns.

"*Better* be your sorry-ass ass," they heard, and then the door pulled open to reveal an imposing woman, bathrobe barely containing a mass of flesh and frilly nightshirt. "The *hell* are you?"

Bear and Tim peered past her into the one-room apartment.

Bear said, "U.S. Marshals, ma'am. Mind if we come in?"

"Hell, you can drag the National *Guard* through here, all I care. Maybe they can find the fool calls hisself the *man* of this crib."

Bear brushed past her, moving to safe the apartment. She exaggerated, stumbling back from the intrusion, her eyes flaring. "Oh, no you didn't just! Oh, no you *di*'int!"

"I'm terribly sorry," Bear said over a shoulder, "but I did."

He disappeared into the bathroom, and Tim heard him rake back the shower curtain. Tim checked the closet—empty—and peered under the bed. Boxes littered the water-warped floor, cardboard lids torn back to reveal every order of merchandise—pedicure kits, baby lotion, bootleg purses, dolls, bags of balloons with Chinese ideograms, coffee mugs with corporate logos. Cosmetics overflowed a vanity beneath the window. Papers, mail, and half-burned candles covered an embattled wooden table.

Bear emerged, running a forearm across his brow. "We're looking for Freddy Campbell. Do you know if—"

"Don't you be talkin' to me after you *shoved* me outta the door."

Bear tried to voice an apology but found himself talking to the hand.

"Ma'am," Tim interrupted, "does Freddy Campbell live here?"

Bernadette whirled, suddenly calm and regal, head withdrawn. A delivery worthy of a screen diva: "Not anymore."

"Are you expec—"

"*Hayell* no. And that fool better not think he can limp his nappy ass home with an empty wallet *again.* Stankin' of cheap liquor and knockoff perfume. Uh-*uh.* I said he *beh*'a not."

Tim held up Walker's booking photo. "Do you know this man? Walker Jameson?"

From her face it was clear she didn't. "He your brother or something?"

Tim shook his head, sliding the photo into his back pocket. "Did Freddy ever mention a guy named Boss Hahn?"

"Quit playin'. Ain't no fool named *Boss* nowhere 'cept on the *TV*."

"Do you know where we might find Freddy?"

But already she was hustling them toward the door, literally leaning into Bear with the heels of both hands. "You come all *storm*-troopin' through here, and me in my drawers."

The phone rang, and she gave up momentarily, holding up one finger while she hunted for the cordless. "I ain't done with y'all."

As Bernadette rooted through the bedding for the source of the trill, Tim surreptitiously flipped over the top pieces of mail on the table, scanning a few bills and junk-mailers.

Bernadette slammed a fist to her cocked hip and shouted into the phone, "Do I *sound* like I wanna refinance?"

As the phone sailed back toward the bed and Bernadette began a dramatic pivot to face them, Tim tossed the mail to the table and dropped his hands to his sides. The paperwork mound slid over a few inches, revealing a torn paycheck stub bearing the golden arches.

July 27. $375. Freddy Campbell.

Bernadette came at them, leading with a long maroon nail. "Get to steppin'. Or come back with some paper."

Tim's eyes found the address beneath Ronald McDonald's grinning face an instant before Bernadette propelled him out through the door.

Chapter 10

The rusting horizontal slats groaned their displeasure as the metal door slid up, Walker's long shadow darkening a swath of the broad, garagelike interior. A generous space for a self-storage. He'd set up shop here at Parson Bros Stor-Yor-Self under a false name, paying the full term in cash so he could give all his tools and trinkets a home before reporting to serve his five years. The subdivided cinder-block depot sat on a throw of worthless real estate in the southern reaches of Antelope Valley. After what he'd come through, the barbed wire had been a breeze. No nighttime guard, no security cameras, nothing to distract the Parson boys from their apparent policy of considered inattentiveness.

Around the edges of Walker's unit, crates and cartons rose in the dimness. And among them, in smaller cases or folded in oilcloth, hid some of his favorite collectibles, items he'd picked up over the years at shows or smuggled back hidden in pallets sealed by diplomatic immunity. An antique musket. Flintlock dueling pistols. A stainless ten-gauge double-barreled shotgun pistol with teak handles he'd salvaged from the conning tower of a sunken U-boat. Electrical cords snaked underfoot, terminating in power strips. In the middle a patch of concrete floor remained bare, flanked by high benches.

His workshop.

He unzipped the outer pocket of a black duffel and tugged out a camo Mag-Lite. Just where he'd left it. He slid in two new C cells, gave the head a twist, and a beam hit the far wall. He jerked the combination lock from its dangle and yanked the door shut.

Walker had requisitioned a Toyota—an older model favorable to hot-wiring—thoughtfully left at a gas station a jog from the San Pedro dump. A steady sixty up the 405, and he left the Camry in long-term parking near LAX. He'd picked up a newish red Accord, one of thousands in the city, from a metered spot on the street. A back window had been left down far enough for him to unlock the door, and then he'd popped the trunk and removed the tire-change kit. The ignition keyhole snapped off under pressure from the jackhandle, and then he'd jammed the flathead into the gap and twisted. Once the engine turned over, he'd made sure the pry bar had fooled the ignition system sufficiently to give him full range of the wheel, and then he'd made the drive north to the auto deal-ers around where Oxnard Boulevard meets Van Nuys. While the linger-ing salesman busied himself hawking minivans to an exasperated mother in the glow of the sole surviving overhead, Walker had removed two dealer tags from the outermost car on the lot. After dropping the old li-cense plates down a storm drain and affixing the pleasingly blank new ones, he'd made the drive north to the 5 and hit the 14.

Aided now by the flashlight in the dark cave of his storage, he picked his way over a few cardboard boxes filled with military books and sat on the cowhide swivel stool before the U of the workbenches. He lit a hurricane lamp and the gas ministove beside it. The newfound light made visible the oilcloth bundle centered on the front bench. He slipped his hand into the stiff fabric, feeling the perfect fit of his weapon even before it emerged into view.

A Ruger Redhawk. Stainless steel. Double action. A classic six-shot, more compact and holster-friendly than its newer competitor, the Su-per Redhawk. A large-thread four-inch barrel increased the wall thick-ness where it entered the frame. Beefed-up support around the cylinder kept the specs tight even after heavy use. Not a gun lover's gun. A gun for someone who respects guns.

Even inside the drawer, his safety glasses had collected a film of dust, which he blew off before seating them on his face. He removed his necklace and let his pendant cross slide down the black cord and fall into a ceramic crucible, which he set on the gas stove. He adjusted the flame down to pure blue. Though the titanium didn't need to be alloyed, he added lead for mass and tin for castability and waited the requisite twenty minutes as the metal liquefied, becoming ready to flux. Tallow, beeswax, lubricant—he found the tiny jars with recovered instinct. He worked quickly, meticulously, and with the hands of a seasoned card dealer. The bullets that fell from the parted mold blocks were perfect sextuplets.

He repeated the process twice, then lined up the bullets on the workbench. He shot rarely and with precision and imagined that a Redhawk wheel charged with titanium bullets would serve his purpose, but it never hurt having a few spare speedloaders on hand. He filed the bullet edges and lubricated the grooves to prevent barrel leading, all the while picturing the ragged slugs of his melted cross shredding through the soft fiber of a heart.

Or several.

Prepping the cases took about a half hour and required the same exactness. He tumbled, resized, trimmed, and chamfered them. A hand's natural oil could deactivate the tiny primers, so he used tweezers and a swing-mount magnifying glass for the insertions. Next came charging the cases—his favorite part of the process. Dispensing measured allotments of powder from the hopper. The folding balance scale. The tiny aluminum funnel.

And last, cycling the press handle, firm against his palm as the rising ram seated a bullet into the perfect fit of the case mouth. It was a great deal of craft and a bit of art as well. Calming and fulfilling. All focus, devoid of thought and emotion.

He stood in the center of the clear space and stripped. When the door rolled back up, the cold bit at him. A handleless spigot by the building's corner, when cranked with his pliers, gave a steady gush. Squatting, he shoveled icy water up to his face, through his hair, under his arms. He returned to his storage space and changed into the least conspicuous clothes he found. An army-green T-shirt, tan cargo pants, white socks, black jungle boots.

He loaded his six dedicated bullets into his long-waiting Redhawk, relocked his unit, and headed into the night.

Chapter II

Even at 12:21 A.M., cars lurched past the drive-through window. The manager, affable Ken Wade, had proved helpful to the point of oppression. He'd seated Tim and Bear at his prize corner booth, all the while peppering them nervously with details of his store's operation. To Tim's irritation, Bear encouraged the fast-food trivia, urging Ken to expound on everything from the introduction of the rib sandwich—"*Mc*Rib, actually, and it was 1981"—to the proportion of treats to ice cream in a well-crafted McFlurry. Ken even offered them their choice from the menu, a proposal that paralyzed Bear with indecision between professionalism and carnal desire.

Ken had jumped ship after a three-year stint as a quality evaluator for KFC, a position of numerous considerations, Tim and Bear quickly learned, all of which led back to the acronym CHAMPS.

"Cleanliness, hospitality, accuracy, maintenance, product, and . . ." Ken's face reddened. "Product and . . ." His hands neatened the front napkin in the tabletop dispenser. "Maintenance, product, and . . ."

"Safety?" Bear offered.

"No." Ken dabbed at his neck with a handkerchief. "It's not *safety.*"

"Sanitation?"

"No. That's certainly an industry value, but not one that's part of CHAMPS."

Tim again braved the magnetic field between Ken's pride and Bear's fascination, finally managing to steer the topic back to Freddy Campbell.

"He didn't show for work again yesterday or today," Ken said. "And we're busy Sunday evenings, as you can see." He wrinkled his nose prudishly. "We get the late-night crowd spillover."

"Maybe *serenity*?" Bear volunteered.

Tim shot an elbow into Bear's McRibs, not wanting to break his own line of inquiry. "You've had problems with his employment?"

"McDonald's Corporation is extremely active in supporting the community," Ken said, as if reading from a brochure. "We do our best to help parolees reenter society, but we need some help and accountability as well, you know?"

"Sure," Tim said, nodding him along.

"I've certainly broached the topic with Freddy on numerous occasions. Customers mistake him for a homeless guy. I mean, you have to give back, but I also got a business to run, you know?"

Tim knew.

"He did this two weeks ago, too. A no-show Saturday *and* Sunday. Cutting out at four forty-five Friday afternoon, leaving the rest of his team to cover those last fifteen minutes. He claimed to have gotten sick with the flu, but that's the shortest flu I ever heard of. I'm thinking he had the hung*over* flu, if you catch my drift."

Tim did indeed.

"Plus," Ken continued, with mounting outrage, "not even a phone call so I could cover the shift. I told him one more time and—"

"Two weeks ago," Tim interrupted. "He didn't come to work the weekend after the Friday he got paid. July twenty-seventh."

"Right, that's right."

"You pay biweekly."

"Correct. So when he doesn't call . . ." It took a moment for the quarter to drop, and then Ken's eyes widened, and he fussed with his polyester tie indignantly. "*This* is the weekend after a Friday payday also. A pattern. You think he goes on a *binge* of some sort? After getting paid?"

"I'm thinking precisely that." Tim slid his card across the table to Ken, who regarded it as if assessing the corporate logo. "Next time he comes in, please give us a call. *Before* you fire him and send him on his way."

They stood at the curb in the unseasonably crisp night air, staring out at the strip of Century Boulevard and its host of vivid signage advertising burrito shacks, banks, tattoo parlors, pubs, auto detailers, gentlemen's clubs, window tinters, and all order of strip-mall industry. Cars and LAX shuttles clogged the streets even at this hour—travelers who'd stumbled off red-eyes or bleary partiers chasing the last-call schedule all the way to the seedy after-hours joints by the airport. Bear munched a Big Mac, which he'd paid for himself; he'd shot Tim the evil eye as he'd slid the bills across the molded counter with his index finger.

"All right," Tim said. "It's payday Friday. You get your check. No autodeposit. You don't have a car. You're a binge drinker. Your home life is not altogether pleasant. Where do you go?"

Bear guided the last double-decker wedge of beef and patty into his mouth and pointed at the bus stop a few storefronts up before something made his jaw halt midchew. He made some sort of sound around the mouthful of Big Mac.

"What?"

Bear's Adam's apple jerked once, and then he said, "Four forty-five. Friday. That's when Freddy left."

"Right. What are you . . . ?"

Bear gestured at the sign, barely in view above the bus-stop shelter: FIRST UNION. Freddy's bank. "He goes to cash his paycheck before the bank closes. He wants cash in hand right away to go to . . ." His finger drew an arc down the block, past an Irish pub, to a woman's neon silhouette blinking, beckoning: THE BACK NINE. 24 HRS. "The one reliable place a man who looks homeless can go to drink around the clock and get covered with the 'stank' of knockoff perfume."

It was at such moments that Tim remembered why he was lucky to have Bear, with his bachelor proclivities, as a partner. They were almost out of the parking lot when a shout turned them around. Ken scrambled toward them, trailing the strings of his McDonald's apron.

"Speed!" he cried triumphantly. "The *s* stands for *speed*."

"Right," Tim said, and gave a sincere thumbs-up.

Bear shook the manager's hand weightily. "Thank you, Mr. Wade." He looked down at his palm, surprised; he'd come away with Ken Wade's business card.

Ken was still breathing hard from his run, but he flashed Bear a smile. "Nice to meet you, Deputy Jowalski. And just so you know, there are a lot of opportunities in the hospitality sector should you ever be interested."

"Why, I think it's a fine idea," Tim said. "Fry Guy George Jowalski."

"You done yet?"

"You'd fill out the Grimace costume rather well."

"Still going, huh?"

"Plus, you could put your prior job skills to use . . ."

Pausing with both huge hands on the padded door of The Back Nine, Bear swung his tired eyes in Tim's direction, awaiting the punch line. "Get it over with."

". . . taking down the Hamburglar."

Bear released a weary sigh and pushed into the strip club. The doorman rose from his barstool aggressively, but Tim fended him off with his badge. Brass, mirrors, and ice cubes bounced images off one another, endless reflected corridors in which to get lost. A scattering of the usual clientele around the usual four-tops. Three college guys were having more fun than seemed plausible—elbows on the catwalk, hoarse laughter, backward baseball caps. A comb-over-gone Al Pacino gangster behind oversize sunglasses ran a doughy hand up the thigh of a between-sets dancer delivering cocktails. A young lady announced as Pinch wrapped snakelike legs around the brass pole, her magenta hair skimming the creased singles littering the stage. A hall, lit purple by cloth-and-bead sconces out of a Gypsy catalog, led to the bathrooms and the optimistically titled private lounges.

Tim and Bear took a walk around the horseshoe of the runway. Despite Pinch's best efforts, their entrance put a chill on the festivities—they weren't the usual cops paid off so the booze could flow during restricted hours and the flesh could undulate closer than the state-mandated six inches. Ignoring the nervous eyes of the manager and bartender, they peeked into the private rooms, some ornamented with couches, others with tall aquarium windows blocked by metal shades. The men's room featured a urinal encased in a frame of crumbling dry-wall, and a doorless stall.

"Well," Bear said as they headed out, "it was worth a try."

Tim set a hand on the ladies' room door and pushed it quietly open. A better-kept space, probably used by the dancers. Even a can of air freshener by the sink. Two stalls, one with the door closed. Tim crouched, tilting his head parallel to the floor for a better vantage.

Someone sitting, one foot free, a pair of jeans loose around the other ankle. Jailhouse habits die hard.

Tim rose, eased the door closed, and nodded at Bear. They waited in the narrow hall, arms crossed, Bear flattening himself politely against the wall as the house dancers passed in fragranced hazes. The toilet flushing sounded like a rocket taking off, and then the door creaked open, revealing a man in a ragged sweater, stretched sleeves hanging down past his hands. He wore Walkman headphones around his neck, unplugged, a fashion statement. Dreadlocks fell like incense sticks across his shoulders. A clouded eye floated left.

"Freddy Campbell?"

"Shit." With the word, a waft of pure gin. "What'd I do now?"

Bear put an arm around Freddy's waist, hand moving in a subtle frisk as he steered him into the nearest private lounge. He held him steady, easing him into the middle of five movie-theater seats lined up before a window. An impossibly tall East Asian girl in platform heels and nothing else pressed both hands to the glass, leaning over. A dollar-bill feeder stuck out of the wall like the neck of a hungry goose.

Freddy bit his lip, studying the girl and bouncing his head as if to a beat, though the room was oddly silent. "Now, *that's* what I'm talkin' 'bout."

Bear, momentarily distracted by the breasts swaying mere feet from his head, took a moment to find his focus. "Do you know Walker Jameson?" He nodded for Tim to produce the photo, which Freddy studied intently. "Or Boss Hahn?"

"Okay. Okay." Freddy seemed to be trying to sort his way through a drunken muddle of thoughts. "Who are y'all?"

Bear shifted his weight against the glass, showing off the Marshals star on his belt.

Freddy bobbed his head a bit more, as if considering his options. "Don't know that cat," he finally said, tapping a dirty fingernail against the picture, "but I know *of* Boss Hahn. Big mofo in the AB, ain't that right?"

"He was recently demoted." Bear settled heavily into the seat beside Freddy. "We had a little chat with Tommy LaRue yesterday evening. I guess you did, too. Right around, say, five-thirty P.M. We want to know what you told him."

"I ain't gonna bitch up for y'all. Not on Tommy. We're road dawgs, man. Thick and thin."

"We're not interested in LaRue," Tim said. "Not at all. We're after someone else, and we'll be as happy to ignore LaRue as we'll be to ignore you."

The metal screen slammed down, leaving them alone in the darkness. Bear fumbled in his pocket, fed a crumpled bill into the machine, and then there was light. And breasts.

He shrugged at Tim. "Ambience."

"And say I don't want to talk to y'all?" Freddy asked amiably.

"Then we'd probably have to poke and pry around all that merch in your pad. Irregularities in your First Union account. How you afforded to fly yourself and Bernadette to Brazil. Who you saw there, what you brought back."

Freddy's eyes registered surprise at some of the proper nouns. "We don't want that," he agreed. The woman stopped dancing in her glass box and folded her arms, annoyed at the sudden lack of attention. Freddy fussed with the edge of his sweater sadly. "You talked to Bernadette, huh?"

"Tough lady," Bear said.

Freddy shook his head. "Word."

"What'd you tell Tommy LaRue?" Tim said. "Answer the question and we were never here. And we won't make trouble for LaRue. Or you."

Freddy squinted at Tim in the faint light. "Hey, you that dog killed them people?"

"Lotta dogs kill a lotta people in this city."

"A'ight. I'll bump gums. You cross me, I go *public* on your ass." Freddy winked good-naturedly. "Now, I don't know what it means. I'm just a relay man. Tommy can only call certain phone numbers from the inside, and I'm one of them. I'm his clearinghouse, right? Yesterday I get word to go to a pay phone at a certain time, someone would call. So I go. And they call. Just a grumble. Three words. Tommy calls me at our usual time today. I tell him. *He* hangs up. That's all I know. I just relayed the message."

"Which was?" Bear asked impatiently.

" 'The left side.' "

As if on cue, the metal screen slammed down, bathing them in darkness. At the same time, Tim and Bear repeated, " 'The left side'?"

"The hell does *that* mean?" Bear said.

"'F I supposed to know, they'd be no point in tellin' me in code, right?" Freddy held up his hands. "Like I said. I don't know too much so I don't know too much."

"I'm beginning to feel the same goddamned way."

After the next few questions went equally nowhere, Tim and Bear left the strip club in silence. Finally Bear said, "Maybe the left side was a meet point for after the break. The left side of a road. Or a river. Something."

"I think it's more than that. Walker had an emotional reaction to it. It put him in motion. It's the *answer* to something."

"So maybe it was a signal for the break. The bedsheet? Wasn't that on the left side?"

"I keep thinking it's gotta have something to do with Boss Hahn."

"Walker stabbed Hahn on the left side. Though I doubt that directive would've puckered him in the dining hall. Let's take a spin through the files again, have Guerrera do a keyword search on the Aryans, the prison, the Black Guerrilla Family, whatever we got." Bear pulled himself behind the wheel, slamming the door a little too hard. The dash clock showed 2:03 A.M., and it was ten minutes slow.

A long night, and they'd wound up with three words. Three words that could mean a lot of things but were cause enough for Walker Jameson to kill Boss Hahn and break out of prison.

And were likely cause enough for him to do more than that.

Chapter 12

The run-down community within earshot of freeway traffic showed off couches, carports, and rusted truck bodies languishing on dirt lawns. The street was 3:38 A.M. quiet. Walker pulled over his Accord, shut the door soundlessly, and prowled.

Shadows, shrubs, tree trunks—even the pit bulls didn't pick him up. A light through a particular kitchen window caught his interest. He crept close, on his toes, peering. An open refrigerator door cast a golden glow across the sleep-puffy face of a slim brunette in her mid-thirties. Attractive features starting to wear down from work and worry. A pert mouth showing the pull of gravity at the edges. Shoulder-length hair cut in no particular style and parted in the middle. Her body, visible beneath a too-long L.A. Clippers T-shirt, still looked fit. Firm in the chest, pinched at the waist when the fabric shifted. Wide, flat feet, nails covered with chipped pink paint.

She returned the water pitcher to the refrigerator shelf and shuffled back down the hall with her glass. His steps muffled by the barren flower beds, he mirrored her movement outside, picking her up in her room through a seam in the blinds. Converted den, fold-out couch. She eased back beneath the sheets, took a final sip, and set the glass on her bedstand. He followed the movement of her torso in the faint blue glow of the night-light. After a few minutes, her breathing grew deep and steady.

Walker withdrew silently, circled to the back of the house, and found a sliding glass door with a broken latch. He moved down the dark hall as if floating—not a creak beneath his boots. The doorknob turned soundlessly. Five well-placed steps and he was bedside. He inched the top sheet back, exposing a bare shoulder, and took in the swirl of brown hair on the pillow.

He stood over her sleeping form, the cool metal of the Redhawk pressed to the small of his suddenly sweating back.

Chapter 13

Boston bounded past Tim over the porch, leapt through the truck's open passenger door, and Bear pulled out from the curb with a wave. Tim entered the house quietly. Dray was out cold on their bed, paperback butterflied on her chest.

She stirred, grinding a hand into her eye. "Your son requests your presence."

Tim checked his watch. "He's not down?"

"Is he ever? He doesn't fall asleep for good until he sees you. We know this."

Tim crossed the hall and saw Tyler's head poke up over the padded guardrail of his bed. Snowball, the aptly named hamster, snoozed on his exercise wheel. Habitually lazy, Snowball had never evolved into the playmate they'd hoped for; he'd just evolved into a larger hamster.

"Fuff pillow."

"It's fuffed. You want me to fluff it again?"

A solemn nod. Tim tapped the pillow on either side then kissed the outsize head. "Sleep tight."

"Elmo funny."

"I love you."

"I want a dog."

Then Tyler was asleep.

Tim sat on the glider rocker and watched him. Most parents he knew remarked that their children looked like angels when they slept. Not Tyler. His chin inexplicably weakened and his lips pressed out like a duck's bill. He wound himself in the sheets, contorted like a head case fighting a straitjacket. Sweat matted his fine blond hair. His head felt to be two hundred degrees—it had taken Tim and Dray months to figure out that he wasn't running a nightly fever, that he just slept hot.

From the time Tyler was a baby, Dray had dealt with him directly and easily—"Sorry, pal, the breastaurant's closed." Tim had been largely responsible for Ginny during her first three weeks of life when post-C-section complications had kept Dray bedbound; from the gates, his relationship with his daughter had felt more natural than his with Tyler. Ginny's murder at the hands of convicted child molester Roger Kindell, Tim worried, had taken away a part of him that he'd yet to recover or re-place. But he was also ever more certain that during his and Dray's two-year childless gap, he'd revised Ginny's brief upbringing into something idyllic. He'd forgotten how thin a kid could wear a parent's patience. How irritating it was fighting tiny socks onto uncooperative feet. The exhaust-ingness of a child, this living machine designed to eat and cry and poop and resist and *require,* all from within an impenetrable shell of self-absorption.

The first time they'd taken Tyler to the park, Tim had hovered over him, righting him when he stumbled, steering him clear of metal and asphalt. Finally Dray had called him over. "The world doesn't work that way." She gestured at the playground equipment. "It has sharp edges and hard surfaces. He's gonna learn that. The longer he takes, the worse it hurts." Even as she was talking, Tim had scooped Tyler midair from a fall off a slide. Dray's grim silence on the walk home had an air of conde-scension to it.

Tim had been freed up by Ginny's removal from their lives to take insane—inane—risks. No human had been wholly reliant on him, in his charge. It was a kind of liberty that he'd put to use. And exploited. In the squalling calm of the past two years, he'd wondered whether he was still the deputy he'd been in the void between Ginny and Tyler; there was no doubt, his softening back into affection and concern had dulled his edge. It was just a question of how much.

Tim rose and padded down the hall. He picked up the copies of the

TI security tapes from the counter and popped one into the VCR. As it rewound, a commercial was kind enough to inform him of one more pediatric disorder with which he wasn't familiar.

"An estimated one in every two thousand individuals is affected worldwide by alpha-1 antitrypsin deficiency," a movie-trailer voice alerted over a slow-pan shot of a particularly pathetic little boy with a stained shirt, frown dimples, and too-big glasses.

Pointing the remote, Tim set the tape in motion. He viewed Boss's stabbing a few more times, looking for intricacies he might have missed, then switched tapes and watched LaRue's scamper across the dining hall. Matching words with image, he played the whispering scene again and again, speaking the words as LaRue did. "The left side." "The *left* side."

Getting up from the couch, he sat on the carpet before the TV and frame-by-framed Walker's reaction after LaRue delivered the news. Walker's head settled slightly on his neck—a split-second recoil. Tim froze it on-screen. The instant revealed a look on Walker's face Tim hadn't caught previously. A hidden expression, but one Tim recognized immediately. Grief.

Walker's mouth shifted, as if it were still working on the corn, though he'd swallowed seven frames back. Sorrow shifted to rage—an emotional logic with which Tim was intimate. Finally Walker rose and strode off camera, purpose quickening his step.

Dray's voice from behind caught Tim off guard. "How's the Need Monkey?"

Tim kept his eyes on the screen. "Down."

"The Tyrant keeps me up half the night, and now that he's soundly snoozing, *I'm* wide awake."

"I'll come give you Sleep Hold in ten minutes. Put you out like a stale cigarette."

"I love it when you talk dirty about sleep. Only problem is, a ten-minute estimate when you're working, based on previous findings, *really* means"—a pause, during which she pretended to crunch numbers—"an hour and fifty-three minutes. And we have to be awake by then."

"Twenty minutes tops."

"Do I hear thirty?"

Tim reversed a few frames, capturing the recoil again. Emotion loosened Walker's features, giving them an almost vulnerable cast. He wore the expression awkwardly; it had barely managed to slip to the surface.

Dray slid down behind Tim on the carpet, her sturdy legs on either side of him. She wrapped her arms around his shoulders and chest and gave him a squeeze, then rested her chin on his shoulder and watched Walker's exit from the chow hall.

"I miss it sometimes," she said. "The job. Almost as much as I don't miss it."

"It's always there. You're still your captain's favorite."

"I'd rather partake vicariously. Better hours." She waited through a moment of silence, then turned, lips brushing his cheek. "That was your cue, dummy."

He found himself re-sorting the information as he told it to her, ordering his thoughts. She listened quietly and attentively, her muscular body still enfolding him. In the intense yet comfortable silence that followed his account, he could sense her working over the facts.

"The Palmdale Station covers Littlerock, right?" Tim asked. "You still in touch with Jason Elliott up there?"

"Now and then. You're thinking as a maybe-former sheriff's deputy, I could get a fuller picture of the sister's suicide investigation?"

"More than we'll get out of the crime-scene report and a CYA phone conference."

He switched the tapes—back to the toothbrush through the carotid artery.

Dray watched, rapt, and made a noise at the back of her throat as if she'd just seen Barry Bonds send one into the Bay. "Impressive. No hesitation."

"Former military."

"You know how *those* boys are." She plucked the remote from Tim's hand and rewound the tape. "Look at that. Not even adrenaline. No anger, no tremor in the hand, nothing."

"He seems to be a dispassionate guy."

She paused the video, inadvertently capturing Boss's grotesquely twisted face as he sailed over the rail. "If you buy the veneer. But in the dining hall footage, your boy's working through some material. Here he's not. He doesn't even slow down to take in Boss's reaction to getting stabbed. Doesn't seem personal to me, as far as murders go."

"That's the problem. No one—not the guards, LaRue, *or* Freddy— came up with a motive for why Walker would whack Boss."

"Maybe there isn't one."

"There must be. If we can find it, we'll at least be on the right trail."

"Like if you could find out what the mint mouthwash was for?"

Tim shifted, regarding her across his shoulder.

She clicked "play," sending Boss to plummet into darkness. "Helluva spectacle, this murder. Blood spraying. Free fall. This wasn't no quick- and-quiet on the catwalk. Remember, Walker's a strategist. He used de- coys in his cell. To sidetrack you."

"So you think he killed Boss to create a diversion?"

"I think you're looking at this backward. There's no need to pitch the guy three floors just to hear the thud. Boss's murder wasn't the reason Walker decided to escape." Dray pointed at the inmates mobbing the screen. "It created the spectacle that *allowed* him to escape."

Tim felt the range of possibilities crank wider, a sensation that was both exhilarating and alarming. "Okay. But we're still stuck with this one: What's a guy that close to the end of his sentence escape for?"

Dray rose, tugging Tim to his feet and leading him back to the bed- room. "Something that couldn't wait a year and a half."

Chapter 14

Walker sat on the sagging couch watching the dust filter through the slant of early-morning light that fell through the back slider. He stayed leaned over, elbows on his knees, his fingers laced to form a pouch. On the scratched glass coffee table before him lay a dish of stale potpourri, a cluster of keys linked to a blue rabbit's foot, and, enigmatically, a used electric label maker with a red gift bow on it. A few ambitious commuters whined by on the freeway, the distant sound carried into the family room almost as a vibration. A clock ticked. Somewhere up the street, a dog barked. He'd forgotten what the world sounded like.

"Get out of my house or I'll fucking shoot you!"

Calmly, he turned his head, getting a partial view of the woman behind him. She stood in the mouth of the hall, clutching a gun with trembling hands before her L.A. Clippers nightshirt.

"Safety's on," he said.

"Walker?" And again, angrily. *"Walker!"* Kaitlin squared her shoulders when he stood, as if to meet force with force. She'd slid on a pair of jeans, and the black box of a beeper showed at her hip. For a few moments, she was at a loss. He watched determination forming on her face, an act of will, and when she spoke again, her voice was steady. "You're bigger. New and improved." Her lips tensed. "You stopped drinking."

He nodded.

"Why?"

"Lack of supply."

She pointed at one of the crooked cabinets hanging beside the TV. "There it is. Go get it."

"Other things on my mind right now."

She ran a curious gaze across him, like a decade had passed, though it had been only three years. Prison must have altered him more than he thought. His sleeve was wrinkled back from his biceps, and he sensed her eyes catch on the fucking paisley tattoo and then, mercifully, move on.

"You're out early." It was not quite a question; she was still sorting through the possibilities.

He nodded again, slowly.

"Oh, *Jesus*," she said. "Wonderful. Another rehabilitation success story." She shook her head and let a hand clap to her thigh, looking away like she didn't know where to start. The freeway noise had increased to a drone. "Well, while you were otherwise detained, I inherited a *mess* here."

A quietly hurt voice from the hall behind her: "I never asked you."

Walker was on his feet, hand at his lower back.

Kaitlin turned, the anger smoothing out of her face. "Honey, I didn't mean—"

A boy, about seven years old, peeked around Kaitlin's hip to see who she was talking to. He took note of her lowered gun with fear and natural excitement.

Walker let go of the Redhawk handle protruding from his rear waistband and brought his hand back to his side. "The hell is this?"

"Your nephew."

"Oh. I thought he was . . ." He couldn't bring himself to say *yours*. He didn't want to admit his thoughts had gone to a new boyfriend, to possible stepchildren.

"He is now."

The boy eased out from behind Kaitlin's back, scared but defiant, a terrier holding ground against a rottweiler. Anorexic arms poked from the sleeve holes of a Dragon Ball Z shirt. Camo pants bagged around his legs. A pair of clumsy glasses magnified the yellow tint that had overcast the whites of his eyes.

Walker tried for a name. "Sam."

"My uncle is in the marines, you know. He killed terrorists."

Kaitlin leaned to whisper to the kid, her fine brown hair falling to block her face. Sam swallowed once, hard, like he was tamping something down. His stare fixed on Walker; he took a step back, then another, then he ran back down the hall. A door slammed.

Kaitlin shoved her hair up on either side of her head and gave a sigh that said that this exchange was just a tiny glimpse of a grander downhill slide.

"Why do *you* have him?"

"We couldn't work out building a bunk bed in Terminal Island."

"Every cell comes equipped."

"If only we'd known." She shouldered against the wall, keeping the space of the room between them. "You knew she had a son. It never occurred to you what would happen to him, did it?"

"Someone would take care of it."

"Right. Me. I'm taking care of 'it.' "

At thirty-six, Kaitlin was five years older than Walker, just two younger than Tess. During their marriage the relationship between his wife and his sister had been tepid. Two tough women with strong feelings for and about the same man and not enough geography or age separating them. It was hard to make his recollections fit with the current arrangement here under Tess's roof.

"That's why you're living here," he said.

"Consistency for Sammy. And more space. I just had a crappy one-room across Pearblossom. You might remember it."

Walker tipped his head to indicate the hall. "What's wrong with him?"

"His liver's shutting down. He needs a transplant. Yeah, it's nonstop fun here. We're in the biggest donor region, you see, which means the longest waiting list. And he's an O, the worst type. Someone dies with an O liver, it can go to an O, A, B, *or* an AB—pretty much anyone. But he can only take an O. So guess how many people that puts ahead of us on the list?"

"Tess knew about this?"

Kaitlin laughed, but her eyes stayed cold. "You are amazing. Of course she knew. What do you think she'd been dealing with these past two years?"

He took a step back and sat on the arm of the sofa.

"There was a shorter list for a while in Region One—Maine and all that—but she didn't have the money to relocate and establish residency," Kaitlin said. "By the time she scraped together three grand for the flights and an apartment there, the wait list had grown enough to make it pointless."

"She couldn't figure out enough money to move?"

"Oh, right, like with all the cash you were sending from prison to help her out? I think we both know that gravy train wasn't running on schedule." She studied him, clearly spoiling for a reaction, but he was too tired to take the bait. "She had some money from the divorce, but I don't know where it went. You know Tess—not the world's best financial planner. Till this."

"Meaning?"

"I dunno, Walk, maybe finding out your kid's gonna die unless you get your shit together is a pretty good motivator. She worked two jobs, went back to school nights, got an accounting certificate. I started watching Sammy sometimes to help her out. An overtime here, maybe even a movie there. This was two years back, just after you went down for your repeat performance."

"She never told me."

"Were you interested?" She studied his blank face with enmity. "You didn't even *recognize* him, for Christ's sake."

"I been gone for three years."

"How about before that?"

"I was fighting a war. A few of them."

"How about before *that*?"

"You tell me. You were there. Tess was living with that asshole out in Simi Valley. I didn't see *you* blazing any trails to their door."

Kaitlin's bearing stayed combative—*sad* and combative—but for once she wasn't ready with a quick response. He took her sudden silence to mean that she knew she was overloading her charges. When she spoke again, her voice was softer. "We had a shot with this biotech company. Gene therapy or something. They even used Sammy in one of their commercials."

"The new refrigerator."

"What? Oh—that's right. The commercial bought them that and took a bite out of Sammy's medical bills. Tess's paycheck barely kept them afloat. We're hardly in the money now, but at least we can eat. And if we time our checks right, we can keep the bills from going to collection."

"Memories of my childhood."

"Memories of our present tense." She rubbed her eyes. "Goddamned health companies bleed you dry. When Tess got Sammy on the trial list for this gene thing, it was like they'd hit the lottery. It was gonna be free, too. He should be in line still to get the treatment—it comes available in a week or two. But the study was oversubscribed, and they dropped him. Just like that." Her hand bobbed, and he heard the snap. "It might cost him his . . ." She made a sound like a hiccup, and Walker realized it was the start of a sob that had caught her off guard. She pressed her hand to her mouth, and he gave her the silence until her cheeks stopped quivering. "I guess Tess couldn't take it."

"Tess could take a lot."

Kaitlin shoved a wrist across her eyes. "I'm not sure *I* can." It was unclear whether she wanted comfort and unclearer yet if he remembered how to lend any.

They waited out an awkward silence, and then she laughed like she'd remembered something amusing, thumbed her pager, and approximated a Pollyanna voice: "Back to the liver. We wait. And pray."

"I never got much mileage outta prayer."

"It's about all we have left. I just don't want him to get scared. Anything else, I think I can take. But not scared. All the doctors. Needles. I get him a present for after each visit."

Walker glanced at the gift on the coffee table. Used but repackaged. The bow was creased from where it had been removed from another gift and restuck. "You got the kid a *label gun*?"

"It's what he wanted. I don't know. It was eight bucks on eBay."

"Was Tess in some kind of trouble?"

"I see the conversation I was having no longer interests you."

"New guy, something like that?"

"I don't know. We weren't real close."

"Why are you raising her kid, then?"

"You mean your nephew?" She waited, displeased with his silence, then said, "Because I have weak boundaries and a compulsion to take care of people so I can bitch a lot."

"Was she in touch with her ex?"

"You tell me. She was your sister."

"She stopped talking to me. After I went in the second time."

He saw in Kaitlin's face that Tess hadn't confided that to her, and he also saw that Kaitlin had a good handle on what that would've meant to him. The empathetic lines over her eyebrows lasted only a moment before merging in an angry dip. "Smart girl."

"I'd say so."

"Her ex is in Lompoc, where he's been the past four years. Small-time embezzling or something. I don't think they've been in touch since Sam was a baby."

"Is my mom dead?"

"What? No, she's at the Valley Glen Retirement Home."

"How 'bout my dad? Where's he?"

"He's the one oughta be dead."

"Ah. A boundary."

Her mouth tensed at the edges, but instead of smiling she said, "You got a place?"

"No."

"Money?"

"No."

"Anything?" She met his uncomfortable gaze, then strode into the kitchen and returned, prying the lid off a coffee tin. She teased out a wad of singles, but he held up his hand. "Come on," she said brusquely. "It's the emergency fund. I think this qualifies."

"Keep it for you and the kid."

"We've survived without your looking out for us this far, thanks. Besides, I get paid in a few hours. What's your plan?" She kept the cash extended toward his unmoving hand until the scene felt childish. "Take it, god*damn it*! It's forty bucks. Get a meal and a shower."

Reluctantly, he reached up and took the money.

She studied him with her hard, gray eyes. "What's your deal, Walk? What are you doing here?"

"Unfinished business."

"Whose?"

"Tess's."

"Tess finished her own business."

He looked down, worked the inside of his lip between his teeth.

She seemed to grasp what he wasn't saying. "So you're what? Honoring her memory by breaking out of prison and rolling some heads?"

"Something like that."

"Whose?"

He didn't answer.

"Why don't you honor your sister in a way that would mean something to *her*?"

A spark of indignation charged his voice. "You don't know Tess. You weren't there. You weren't there in the B—"

"The Buick. Right. The winter you guys lived in a car by Griffith Park. Get over it. She did. She pulled it together. And for what? To give you opportunities?"

"I took them. That worked out well. Fighting Dick Cheney's war for him."

"So you didn't get a fair shake. Guess what? You're not entitled to one. People like us don't get a fair fucking shake. Not you, not Tess, not me, sure as shit not Sammy. And there's nothing you can do about it."

"Oh," Walker said, "there's something."

"As I figured, it's not about Tess aft—" The telephone rang, and Kaitlin broke off her pronouncement and her stare, hurried into the kitchen, and leaned over the caller ID screen. "Damn it. It's Sammy's insurance. They call at ungodly hours so they can leave messages. I need to grab this."

Walker pointed down the dark hall to the closed door opposite the converted den where Kaitlin slept. "That where she died?"

Kaitlin nodded. "Don't go anywhere." Ring. "I haven't decided if I'm gonna shoot you yet." She picked up, her nervously polite tone following him into the hall. He passed a door through which emanated the exaggerated sounds of video-game bloodshed, and paused outside Tess's room. Squares of bare wood marked either side of the jamb where the crime-scene tape had pulled up the paint. He turned the handle and paused, collecting himself.

The smells hit him first and strongest. The curtains remained drawn, and day after day of sunlight had baked the air of the closed room to a choking staleness. Bleach. Cleanser. And barely lingering beneath the chemicals, an express lane back to his childhood, the comforting scent of Jean Naté. There it was on the bureau, the yellow bottle with its curious cursive scrawl. He popped the cap and inhaled. The scent covering the sun-faded smell of the Buick's maroon crushed velour bench seat that had served as his bed for two months when he was eight. Sleeping cuddled into Tess for warmth. Her veil at her all-wrong wedding dinner in the back room of the Olive Garden as he'd leaned to kiss her cheek, struggling and failing to come up with something meaningful to say. What *was* there to say? After what Tess had risked for him? With their mother furloughed to another dry-out of questionable sincerity and their estranged father in the clink, Tess, at fifteen, had packed the trunk of the Buick with saltines, peanut butter, off-brand canned soup, six-packs of Tab, clothes, and a flashlight and taken Walker on the lam to keep them clear of the social workers. And she'd succeeded, right up until fifty-seven nights later, when they'd passed their mother's house on their weekly drive-by and seen—with relief so great Tess had sobbed for the first and only time he knew of—the light back on in the kitchen. What *could* he have said to his sister, years later, over bad table red and a warbly nuptial rendition of "That's Amore"? Thank you?

A spiral-bound weekly planner, sized to fit in a woman's wallet, sat beneath the cologne like a coaster. A picture of Tess in a paper Benihana frame was wedged in the mirror nailed above the bureau. He slid the photo and the datebook into his pocket. Covering the rest of the Formica walnut veneer and stuffed into the neighboring bookshelves were stacks of files containing Xeroxed articles from medical journals, printed reports, and pamphlets on what he assumed was Sam's condition. A few videos with professionally printed VECTOR stickers on the spines caught his attention. The same name and logo appeared on various brochures and reports. He figured Vector Biogenics for the gene-therapy outfit

Kaitlin had mentioned. One of the Vector tapes was labeled in kid's handwriting: *My News Segmint.* A laminated visitor's pass to the "Vector Campus" dangled from a lanyard Tess had hung on her closet door-knob.

Bracing himself, Walker turned to face the bed, which he'd half seen upon entering. At the foot a bleached blob stood out from the rust carpet, the loop threads poking up like maggots. The missing comforter had probably been disposed of, leaving a yellow top sheet folded back neatly over a worn blanket. The crime-scene cleaners had scrubbed the wall above the headboard, leaving an uneven patch of discoloration.

Kaitlin's voice carried down the hall: "I *know*, sir, but I thought the ER copays *also* applied against the urgent-care deductible."

Walker trudged over and sat where his sister must have in her final moment, his back to the headboard, his feet centered in the white spot of carpet. He tried to reconstruct her position; her head must've been turned. He curled a bit, shoulders rising, stomach jerking—the convulsions of crying, though his eyes stayed dry. His palms sweated. Then he clenched his jaw and straightened back up.

The door shushed across the carpet a few more inches. Sam's terrified gaze moved about the room—he couldn't help himself—and then the wireless joystick fell from his hand and he retreated silently from the doorway.

Walker found him just outside the room, back to the wall, breathing hard.

"She visited Nona," Sam said once he'd caught his breath. "I heard you asking."

"Her mother? Your grandmother?"

"Yup."

"How often?"

"Once a week. I went, too, usually."

Walker continued toward the family room. Kaitlin's voice reached an exasperated pitch as she paced the tiny kitchen. She didn't notice Walker flash past the doorway. He got halfway to the glass slider, stopped, and returned. Sam had closed Tess's door and was standing before it, fingers still clenching the knob.

"Can you keep your mouth shut?"

"Course I can."

"Good. You'll get me killed if you don't. I'm not fucking around. You don't know me. You never saw me. Got it?"

Sam's lips trembled, and then he stormed into his room and shut the door, hard. Kaitlin glared at Walker this time as he passed. He stepped through the rear slider, hooked around the side of the house, and, after scanning the street from the cover of the neighbor's misshapen juniper, made his way to his Accord. He drove a few blocks before he pulled over. The air smelled of tar and fried breakfast meat—something sugary, packaged sausage. He opened Tess's calendar to the date of her death. Blank. The last entry, on June 1 in the 7:00 P.M. slot, read *Vector Party, The Ivy—Bev Hills.* Exactly one week before her death.

Walker scanned back over the preceding months. Vector was listed in March and April, often several times in a given week. Staring at the company name rendered again and again in Tess's neat hand, he felt his curiosity sharpen.

Chapter 15

Dolan cracked his knuckles for the third time that morning, psyching himself up for the confrontation he'd been rehearsing in his head since he woke up. A glance around the lab and his anxiety gave way momentarily to pride at all his work had given rise to.

He'd stumbled into the field, awed by the progress made by those scientist-pioneers who'd come before him. They'd made a brilliant leap. An imaginative leap. Brilliant and imaginative the way that Darwin's mechanism for evolution had been—simple and sound. Once you got it, it was all but obvious. All the pieces had been there; it was just a matter of assembling them to form the right picture. And unlike natural selection, viral vectors could be tested over weeks, not eons.

Gene therapy arose to correct genetic disorders that were deemed incurable. The bench work, while complex, was straightforward. Take a virus, designed through natural selection to penetrate human tissue, and excise the DNA sequences that make it virulent. Once it's been defanged and declawed, what remains is a biological vehicle with plenty of cargo room—a microscopic Trojan horse. Insert a therapeutic gene and the formerly threatening virus acts as benign transport. Once the viral vector is introduced into a subject, it finds its way to the target DNA sequence on the appropriate chromosome and the transgene insinuates itself, replacing the faulty gene.

Dolan had always been taken not just with the medical ramifications of viral vectors but with the elegance of the mechanics. And over the past few years, under the auspices of his own Vector Biogenics, he'd made not one but two breakthrough contributions to the field. They had come in relation to alpha-1 antitrypsin deficiency, an obvious disorder to tackle, since all its complications arise from a single set of faulty genes. Other grails were out there, sure, cystic fibrosis, maybe even familial hypercholesterolemia after that, but for now his (and Vector's) hopes hung on perfecting a viral vector that could deliver a gene to correct AAT deficiency. A dire disorder, usually diagnosed in childhood. Instead of producing a protein that helps coat and protect the lungs, the liver of an afflicted patient generates an abnormal enzyme that accumulates *inside* the liver and eventually shuts it down.

Dolan had chosen lentivirus and smallpox for his development models because they were nice roomy viruses, Mack trucks to the Mini Cooper of the more experimentally plumbed adenovirus. His first landmark vector—and still his pet project—had been born in relatively short order.

Lentidra.

The lentivirus vector (the latest model was code-named L12-AAT) had been his favorite from the gates because it seemed consistently to provide permanent integration of the transgene into the genome—one shot and the subject was cured. Optimistic from all theoretical indications, he'd handed over his creation to the study director who would conduct animal trials. But Lentidra's preclinical studies were abruptly suspended, after initial reports had come back riddled with problems. After this first, failed model, Dolan had to set his sights lower, temporarily relinquishing the dream of long-term gene expression and, at the board's urging, turning his focus to his redheaded stepchild, the smallpox vector (now known as X5-AAT and by its more marketable title, Xedral).

Rather than integrating into the host's genome, Xedral allowed only for short-term gene expression; the DNA floated in the nuclei of the target cells, got expressed briefly, then faded. The treatment was effective—86 percent effective from trial indications—but not a cure, and it required a booster shot once a month for maintenance. Otherwise the subject would slide back into his failing condition. In animal studies,

Xedral was looking to be safer than Lentidra and more effective. These trials showed a stability of transgene expression sufficient to bring Vector to the verge of FDA Phase I human studies. A number of volunteers, mostly children, would begin trials within the month.

Dolan still mourned the loss of Lentidra. The idea of *cure* was tantalizing. Next to prevention, it was the best thing a medical scientist could deliver.

In fact, the notion of long-term transgene expression was what had sparked Dolan's interest in the field. When, while coasting through UCLA as a biochemistry major, he'd first learned of the huge advances scientists were making using viruses to shuttle genes, he'd been possessed intellectually. Casting aside a (lukewarm) aspiration for medical school, he'd dived into research, fretting over mitochondrial-derived activators for a promising but uninspired senior thesis. He'd stayed in the department for a Ph.D., blissfully engaged in his research. He loved playing detective, tugging at analytical knots, plank-walking out to areas of specialization where he alone could generate answers to the questions he was posing. And, better yet, he was gifted at it, his dissertation work knocking the experimental frontier forward a longitude or two.

Dolan's thoughts returned to the concern at hand, and he leaned forward, resting his elbows on his workstation. For all its sloppiness, his bench was organized precisely to his liking. It was the one place he felt at home. *His* machine-sharpened Faber-Castell number-twos, *his* DNA samples, *his* microfuge tubes.

When he strayed beyond his bench, however, the particulars of ownership became a bit hazier. Beacon-Kagan, the pharmaceutical behemoth that was Vector's parent company, brought its influence to bear in imaginative and indirect fashion. Ostensibly, Vector had its own management, but it was a wholly owned subsidiary with plenty of Beacon-Kagan executives on loan and more cross-board memberships than would have been orthodox a few presidential administrations ago. In return for these unnegotiated concessions, Dolan, as the principal investigator and senior scientist, enjoyed a relative freedom from budgets and business concerns. He mostly kept to his domain, what others called research but he always called science, constructing his viral vectors in his sheltered corner of the lab.

LAST SHOT

Having assumed the lease at the board's insistence from a failing digital-TV company, Vector occupied the ground floor of the twenty-six-story Beacon-Kagan building in Westwood, located just below UCLA on Wilshire. In his private moments, which were many at work and few at home, Dolan likened Beacon-Kagan to a twenty-five-story ogre perched on his shoulders. But what a rich infrastructure for Vector to flourish in. And flourish it had—thanks to Xedral—to the brink of a closely watched IPO. Watched from the Street and from above.

Dolan pivoted now in his barstool-height architect's chair, working up the nerve to confront the board's pet study director (in title at least, Dolan's employee) about the aborted Lentidra trials. Casting nervous glances across the lab through the two glass walls into the test-subject suite, he waited for Huang's head of shiny black hair to appear. It was early—6:00 A.M. early. Any Beacon-Kagan employees (and that meant any Vector employees) who didn't want to wither in the corporate culture started their days before their days.

Huang finally swept into view, wearing his knapsack, an accessory—like the Trek twenty-one-speed he "commuted" on—that Dolan had always thought an affectation of youthfulness. Dumping the knapsack onto his desk, Huang tugged his lab coat from his chair back and slipped into it, completing his transformation into authority figure. Sipping a Starbucks, he pulled himself to his monitor.

Dolan stood, trying to override unease with indignation. Why shouldn't he confront Huang? After all, wasn't it Dolan's company? Vector Biogenics wouldn't exist were it not for him. As the father of the process and the senior scientist, wasn't he entitled to a few simple information requests?

He started for the door, muttering to himself, drawing curious gazes from the junior researchers. His resentment flared, putting an uncharacteristic conviction into his step. He gowned up and passed into the baking heat of the production room, a massive incubator where thousands of bottles rotated slowly on racks lining the walls. Made of polypropylene, a plastic on which cells readily grow, the roller bottles were filled with a red medium liquid. This growth fluid created a wet environment for the genetically altered smallpox to reproduce. In the batch currently spinning all around Dolan like living wallpaper, a mere three days into production, the virus had already swollen the cells and begun to bud out of them. A few more days and the production team could pour out the infected liquid and filter it. Once the Xedral was purified, it could be formulated, dispensed into vials, and freeze-dried, just like a standard vaccine. After that, just add purified water and inject.

Dolan stepped into the airlock, then out into the test suite, the monkeys grunting and banging their cages in greeting. With relative ease, Dolan had designed a viral vector to "knock out" the AAT gene, so that Huang could create an animal test group that simulated humans with alpha-1 antitrypsin deficiency (destroying—especially when it came to genetics—was always easier than repairing). Rabbits, mice, pigs, and woodchucks had all come and gone before Huang hit upon cynomolgus macaque monkeys, whose clinical presentation of the deficiency was sufficiently comparable to that of humans to make them useful in determining the effectiveness of Lentidra and Xedral. Simple intravascular injections, like flu shots, were administered, and thirty-six hours later the test monkeys no longer had functioning AAT genes. Their livers started to shut down; they lost weight; their sclera yellowed. Dolan had created the problem to fix it. And fix it he had.

How permanently his viral vectors could keep that fix in place was another question. The recovery of the monkeys had been staggering to witness. An added advantage in using higher animals was that the trials could continue longer; it wasn't until the eighth month of L12-AAT's second trial that Huang had caught the complications that had made the board pull Lentidra from development.

Dolan arrived at Huang's side, but the study director continued tapping at the keyboard, the monitor's glow reflected back in his glasses. "Just a sec, D."

Waiting, Dolan offered a salute to Grizabella, and she bared her teeth kindly and returned the gesture. One of 128 composing the final longitudinal Xedral study, Grizabella was the gentlest and (on those rare occasions when Dolan ventured into the test-subject suite) his favorite. Huang had started with 130 macaques but lost two to simian hemorrhagic fever, which was common enough in monkeys imported from the Philippines and, thankfully, harmless to humans.

Huang sent an e-mail with a flourish of his hand and spun on his chair to face Dolan. He flashed a boyish grin. *"Herr Direktor."*

"Chris, I took a spin through the preclinical reports you got me from the last Lentidra trial. I'm still having trouble reconciling the figures with the results. I'd like to take a look at the raw data."

"Again? We've gone around on this a few times now."

"And every time I found inconsistencies in what you submitted to me. I'd like *all* the raw data so I can rerun them myself. Top to bottom."

Huang blew out his cheeks. "Well, we're focused on Xedral now, right? We've got a functional model, and we're readying to hit market."

"Xedral's more or less autopiloting to Phase Is next week." Dolan set his fists on his hips, Superman style. "My work there is done."

"So don't we need you to move on? Lentidra didn't pan out."

"Exactly. But, you see, everything *I* oversaw on Lentidra did bear results—"

"In a petri dish."

"Which is why I want every piece of data since my vector crawled out of my petri dish and into your monkeys."

Huang laughed. "Fair enough. It's a ton, though. I'll need some time to pull it together."

"What's the challenge? Attach it to an e-mail and click 'send.' "

Huang jigged the chair back and forth so it gave off little squeaks. "Look, the board's been clear where we need to be putting our focus. Don't you think—"

"The board doesn't want to burn resources chasing a failed model for the sake of the senior scientist's ego. I get it."

A tension-releasing laugh. "You said it, not me."

"But you've got to remember, this company's based on vision, not just corporate expediency. The upside to Lentidra—*permanent* transgene integration—is huge. It's worth devoting a small percentage of our resources to backtracking and troubleshooting. I hate to sound like a commercial, but if I get a handle on the problem, I think I could engineer an alternate Lentidra design that would offer us the best of both worlds—the stability and safeness of Xedral with long-term genetic expression. If we nail it, who knows what the other applications will be?"

"Okay. I'm with you. I'll help. But we're *all* working late. And early." A gesture at the computer-screen clock. "We've still got limited time, and time—as our CEO is so good to remind me in our now daily meetings— is our most valuable capital. Based on what I'm getting from upstairs, obsolete vectors are *not* where our aim is right now. Our aim is the IPO. As soon as we get through the next few weeks, I'll dig out all the old data. Then we'll start breaking it down together in our copious spare time." Huang offered a hand and a smile. "Deal?"

Dolan did a quick translation: In his zeal to serve the board, Huang had put all his focus into Xedral, leaving the other data in sloppy condition. Though Dolan couldn't relate to Huang's lack of curiosity, he'd found it all too common in corporate researchers.

Dolan returned the handshake but not the grin. When he turned, Grizabella extended her hand through the bars and slapped him a solemn five. He passed through the automated glass sliding doors into the hall, Dean Kagan's pious oil portrait beaming down at him.

Chapter 16

Maintaining a disciplined stillness at the head of a pre-
posterously long conference table, Dean Kagan held his executives'
pained attention a moment longer. The tip of his tongue poked into view,
wetting his lips. "Permit me to list the excuses so we can skip the whining
phase this morning. Consumers are pissed off about climbing prices. The
AARP is on the warpath and has allies on the Hill. Canada's undercutting
our supply and pricing. The pipeline's not what it was. Twenty-eight
states and counting have passed legislation to regulate drug pricing. *I
know.* Your job is not to reiterate the obvious but to come up with creative solutions. I'd like each and every one of you to hear me on this
point." A creaky shift forward and then a firm finger jabbed across the
grain of the mahogany. "I'll be pushing up daisies before I permit this
company to backslide on its P&E multiple. I want blood from a stone.
And I want it staining our next quarterly sales estimate. Booked sales
will be up before the shareholders' confab in November. I am not having
another week's golf at Wailea rained on by those Wharton clones from
the pension funds."

Twenty faces stared back at him, male and female, black and white,
doughy and chiseled, but attentive to a one. Dean scrutinized them,
amused by himself, the market challenges, the tension in the room. His
hair, silvered but as yet unthinned by age, was short and expertly
styled. A forty-five-hundred-dollar suit disguised his softening athlete's

build, enhancing his shoulders, firming his posture, creating a more tapered waist. Dean Kagan had never been forthcoming about his age, but an average of the conflicting public-record accounts put him at seventy-three.

The air smelled of linseed oil and leather, still new-car strong though twenty-seven years of weekly 6:30 A.M. "stratcom" meetings had passed through the war room since it was constructed. The impressive plane of wood on which rested elbows, reports, and various mugs of designer coffee was Bolivian mahogany, acquired for a pretty penny before the import laws clamped down. The brass fittings of the cabinets were polished to a boot-camp gleam, and the window that stretched the length of the north wall, providing a twenty-six-story view of Westwood and the smog-shrouded Santa Monicas beyond, was spotless.

The solid-core oak door had been calibrated to bulletproof, as had been the door leading into the anteroom, one of many details put into effect by the same overpriced Beverly Hills firm that had sent contractors to secure the oil fields of Kirkuk. Stem-cell research that Beacon-Kagan sponsored on three continents had led to increased threats, but there'd be no shoot-em-ups here, nor at the Kagan estate, where the windows were tactical glass and Dean's security adviser—who lived full-time in a guesthouse—was always within handgun range. The master suite even had a walk-in closet that converted to a safe room in case of burglary or attack. Dean had cut a swath through the world of international commerce over the past half century, and he wasn't going down because some mouth-breathing crusader with a hair-trigger twitch couldn't shake a fit of empathy over the treatment of his primate brethren.

Beacon-Kagan had sprung up fast and hard in the late seventies, stealing talent from the universities and competing corporations and developing a slate of solid but unexceptional meds that kept the company reasonably profitable from the start. As it grew more innovative and reactive, it began to reap higher dividends. Beacon-Kagan had added its name to the roll of the Pharmaceutical Research and Manufacturers of America, at last muscling up to the table with Merck, Bristol-Myers Squibb, Pfizer, and its other better-regarded, higher-market-cap competitors. Over the past several decades, Dean had driven the company—and its stock—north with relentless focus and vigor, Beacon having long fallen out of the picture, slumped into his potatoes au gratin at a corporate luncheon in his fifty-ninth year with a blown aorta. Today Beacon-Kagan was poised not only to compete but to trailblaze.

Dean punched an intercom button built into the desk. The door creaked open, and a nervous assistant stood in the gap, her hands clenched before a tasteful charcoal skirt.

"My coffee," Dean said.

The assistant relayed the message to someone out of sight, and a demitasse, gold rimmed, appeared almost instantly through the gap. She delivered it to Dean and backed away, ready to respond if he chose to make eye contact.

The leather chair cocked under his weight. "Now," he said, with the relish of a football coach assigning a particularly grueling hitting drill, "let's trot out the workhorses."

The senior VP of Sales and Marketing ruffled her notepad, then pulled off a stylish pair of glasses and set them on the table. Jane Bernard was a tenacious, steely woman with handsome features and a shell of coiffed gray hair. "Why don't we begin with Midachol?"

Dean tipped his head in a nod.

They'd added their own statin to the cluster behind the counters and, with aggressive promotion, managed to squeak out an 11 percent market share to the tune of a billion and a half a year. To approve a new drug, the FDA demanded only that it be shown superior to a placebo, not to other drugs. In Beacon-Kagan-conducted trials, Midachol had beat a sugar pill at lowering cholesterol nine times out of ten.

The young man across from her looked up from his BlackBerry and shot Jane a wink. In an approximation of an arranged marriage, he was engaged to her daughter, currently back east finishing a clinical social work degree at Smith. Chase Kagan returned to his e-mail, holding the wireless device in both hands like a GameBoy. His navy jacket hung over the back of his chair, freeing him to display the rich colors of his madras shirt. A knee, clad in artfully rumpled linen, was propped against the table's lip. His eyes were small and pale, set in pouches of loose skin accented by lashes so light they disappeared unless the sun hit them. He carried an air of uninterest—not apathy but boredom, as if he knew all the answers before the questions had been asked. A precocious but well-earned affectation for a twenty-eight-year-old a few promotions out of B-school.

Jane offered her future son-in-law a terse smile, folded her arms, and said, "We've stayed horizontal for June and July—"

Dean said, "Lobby the panel, get them to change the parameters of high blood pressure. We already got one-forty over ninety moved to one-twenty over eighty, see if they'll give us another adjustment. It'll open up the market for everyone. Two of the panel members are our consultants—I'm sure the other fine M.D.'s are living subsidized lifestyles on someone else's dime. Sandeep, put out a pigeon to our brothers-in-arms. We can play well with others at this stage, fight it out over market share later. What else?"

"We need a more aggressive ad campaign," Jane said. "We have to go up against the competition directly."

"Who's stopping you?" Dean said. "Here's what we do: Pick off the top dog. We run a quick trial comparing Midachol to Lipitor—twenty mgs of ours against ten mgs of theirs. We don't have to disclose dosage—"

"Better yet"—all heads swiveled to Diane Little, head of Legal—"nor do the guidelines specify how we need to *administer*. So for the Lipitor sample group, we can give the drugs other than as recommended—say, topically instead of orally."

Dean's head panned the table. "What else? I want to hear those gears clanking, hamsters running on their wheels. Earn those stock options."

Jenner, Research, cleared his throat. "If we're moving toward comparative branding, how about an obscure safety test? We'll stress that Midachol usage *doesn't* cause testicular cancer. Since the other companies haven't tested for it, it buys us a 'proven safer than' tag in the commercial."

"We do, however, have some FDA complaints about the incomplete list of side effects on the current commercials. *That* we might need to address," Little said. "We capped them at five seconds for a thirty-second spot, but we need at least ten."

"No," Dean said. "I'm not paying two-fifty K per prime-time hit to air voice-over about burning urination and flatulence. Refer viewers to a Web site."

"We'll hear about it from the FDA, Mr. Kagan."

"I've been hearing from the FDA for twenty years. What do we care about fines? We negotiate the levels of the fines every lobbying season. Now—do you know how many people the FDA employs to review industry ads for accuracy and balance, Ms. Little? Thirty. *Thirty* people for thirty-four *thousand* ads annually. They're slow. By the time they send us a warning letter, the campaign's run its course and the ads are off the air."

"And if we're nailed?"

"Our bottom line can handle a few nickels out and a page-twenty-seven mention in the *Journal* better than explosive diarrhea as declaimed by Mr. Moviephone. Next."

"We think you at least want to consider—"

"*Next.* How are we looking in the ambulatory-suicide department?"

"Strong," said Patrick White, VP of Product Management. "We gained two on Prozac, nearly as much on Zoloft. But we're losing the patent on Pastol next year, so we need some strategies for extending—"

"Make it a weekly drug instead of a daily. Or change a molecule, have P&A pick a new name and color, and ram it through. There's an idea—make it a suppository. Whatever. Pick us up a fresh twenty years on the patent. We'll market it as improved, phase our users over to the new product, and discontinue the old model."

"We'll also have to smear the old model before the generics get their hands on it," Chase offered, his eyes still on the LED screen of his Black-Berry. "A few well-timed press releases about this side effect or that."

"There you go. I thought I was gonna have to send all you people to the remedial group." Dean burned with pride, his mind feasting on the possibilities. "Thanks, Chase. Everybody: Ours is a *highly creative* business. Don't come here needing to be reminded of that."

"If we start the process now," White jumped in, "we'll be in good position for the big holiday push. Advertise hard on Christmas depression—"

"Make generalized depression a bit more generalized," Jane interjected playfully.

"—push the docs to prescribe away the blues. We do a mass sample mailing in November to get patients habituated, then we send the doctors free Christmas trees."

"You jackass." A good-natured smile graced Dean's lips. "These are doctors. Send dreidels." He didn't wait for the scattered laughter to die down. "I want a clean entry to prescribers. The repackaged Pastol has to be the New Best Thing for depression, and our data's gotta support that."

Dean Kagan was in his element now. As the best and brightest argued over placebo bumps and cherry-picking test subjects, he leaned imperceptibly back and quit listening. The meeting had done what he loved—taken on a life of its own.

"How's Boneral?" he half heard someone ask. A fresh wave of laughter, though the quip had long worn thin.

"Well," Jane began, "our head-to-head campaign didn't fare well. You'll remember we had banners at NASCAR—'Viterol: What Viagra Wants to Be When It Grows Up,' 'Viagra on Steroids'—that stuff, but it didn't take. We need a face for the product."

Jenner again: "How about A-Rod?"

"Too expensive, overrated, and can't hit postseason," Dean said. "I want an extreme athlete. How about that rock-climber kid who sawed off his own arm a few years back? I doubt he's wading through offers. Plus, I want to buy soft mentions—pardon the pun. How much would it cost to get Sean Connery to shill Viterol in a Matt Lauer interview? Get me numbers."

The director of Sales pitched in: "We can't get around the fact that Pfizer's outpricing us."

Now Bernie, Accounting: "We can't price down any further. Our profit margin's too tight."

"Then inflate the wholesale and sell it to doctors for cheaper," Chase said. "Let them keep the spread."

"Temporary fixes," Dean said, with a flick of his hand.

The dismissal brought a few moments of reflection.

"To boost earnings in a way that's significant," White ventured, "we need to widen out its applications, push doctors to prescribe off-label."

They went in various directions at once. Dean tuned out. Taking potshots at Viagra. Christ, what pikers.

Eighteen pens were scribbling on eighteen pads in sixty-five hundred dollars' worth of Coach and Gucci notebooks.

Little again: "Come on, we've got Viterol covered from every angle, from the shape of the pill to the coating—"

"Can we patent taste?"

"Bad taste, sure. Would Beverly Hills exist otherwise?"

Dean cut in on the yuk yuk yuk. "Remember, all of you"—he cast a hawkish gaze around the table—"examiners in the FDA receive bonuses based on how many applications they handle, and a patent app is easier to approve than deny. It just comes back the next year anyway, adds to the pile."

Jane watched Chase mouth the final clause as Dean spoke it.

Dean went on. "What's next?"

Chase said, "Vector."

A deep inhalation brought Dean upright in his chair. For the first time, his expression brightened.

Biogenics was the future of the big drug companies, and Dean had sensed it in his brittle bones. As the progenitor of a $40 billion pharmaceutical company, he was no fool; he'd long anticipated the need for fresh technologies to replenish the drying pipeline of conventional meds. The major PhRMA companies had spent the past twenty years chasing one another with me-too drugs, creating ever paler imitations of meds already in profitable existence. Me-too drugs targeted common, lifelong conditions—arthritis, depression, high blood pressure. Antibiotics were seldom blockbusters because infections don't last long enough for repeat sales. People with rare diseases formed a limited market, and thus their conditions were of little economic interest. Meds geared toward lethal diseases were a losing bet because the consumer didn't stick around long enough to rack up substantial expenses. So Big Pharma had focused on picking off the low-hanging fruit, letting their development wells run dry. Except Beacon-Kagan, which had implemented an aggressive biogenics strategy early on. Beating the competition into the field, Dean had supported Vector to a tune of $80 million, an amount expressly chosen to shatter the start-up biotech funding record. He'd since poured in tens of millions more.

The others' focus remained on the head of the table, so Dean made a show of deferring to his son, whom he'd installed as Vector's CEO at the outset.

Chase nodded his thanks, glad to assume brief command. "Do you want the good news or the good news?" Polite chuckles. "Since with Xedral there's no need to moderate dosage levels or study metabolism effects, and because kids are dying from AAT deficiency every day, the FDA approved our request for a combined Phase I and II. Three months long, randomized, double blind, placebo controlled, starting next week as planned. Once the Xedral injection is shown to take, and if the kids don't combust"—a current of polite laughter generally reserved for Dean—"we roll out wide before the new year."

"Any trouble securing subjects?" Jenner asked.

"We've been beating off a virtual stampede."

Various impressed nods and noises from the others. Scarcity of human subjects usually caused the biggest delay in getting a new drug to market.

"Families are desperate," Chase continued. "They have kids languishing on the liver waiting list. No need to pay bounties to doctors for enrollees—these parents just want our help."

Bernie said, "Let's have those numbers again."

"There look to be about a hundred thousand people in the U.S. with AAT deficiency and an equivalent number in Europe. Calculating in other moneyed populations—Australia, Japan, what-have-you—brings us to at least three hundred thousand. But. Most estimates show that less than ten percent of people with AAT deficiency have been diagnosed, even though it can be determined by a simple blood test. So we can push for more screening as a public health measure, which will allow doctors to identify the disorder early, save lives, and raise our consumer population. To that end we're rolling out a preceptorship program for pediatricians, hepatologists, pulmonologists, and geneticists. We'll get young, attractive drug reps—"

"New blood," Dean said. "Redheads seem smarter. Troll the campuses."

"—to shadow doctors, educate them about Xedral, even get in the room with patients. For their troubles the sponsoring docs will receive three hundred dollars a day. Going off the most conservative numbers—the three hundred thousand *diagnosed* patients—an annual treatment cost of twenty thousand dollars grosses us over six billion dollars our first year."

Bernie again: "Isn't that treatment cost too ambitious?"

"Yes. It is." Chase drew out the silence an extra few seconds, a trick, Dean noted with satisfaction, he'd appropriated from his old man. "Of course, for people with resources it isn't. Is your child's life worth twenty thousand dollars a year? Absolutely. But for middle- and lower-class patients, we have a few hurdles. However, Vector has invested a sizable sum of money in an AAT deficiency public health rationing study, the results of which will post the week after the IPO. Our argument is simple: This is a lifesaving treatment, and poor patients shouldn't be deprived of it because of cost. Frankly put, it's unethical, akin to class genocide. We'll capitalize on the momentum from the study with continued aggressive lobbying in Washington. We have word from inside that if we bring the heat, Medicaid will widen eligibility and reimburse for half cost."

A literal gasp went up from around the table.

"We've been upping our sponsorship of AAT deficiency patient-advocacy groups over the past year to ensure they have a voice, which we'll continue to make use of. In a few months, we'll do a big fat airlift to a few poor countries. That'll make 'em teary even in the red states, gets us a hundred million bucks in publicity for a million in cost. In the meantime, we'll keep booking local network and nationals and continue to spin marketing off the advertising to pick up extra mileage. Our polling showed that the KCOM news segment last month made a favorable market impression."

"The story about the kid?" Jenner asked. "That was great. Really moving."

"And we found our new mascot." Chase held up a design layout of the corporate brochure. The boy's picture on the cover had been replaced by a doe-eyed girl, strawberry blond pigtails, lopsided smile, smear of chocolate artfully positioned on her chin. "Cute as hell, and they don't break the bank."

Dean punched the button on the table, the door clicked, and the assistant again slid into view. "Summon Dolan from the Ivory Tower."

"I'm here already, sir." The door creaked open another fifteen degrees, and Dolan stepped into the boardroom, a spray of Coomassie blue staining his lab coat from pocket to hem.

"Glad you dressed for the occasion." A few laughs, and then Dean added, with manufactured pride, "The absentminded professor."

"Sorry I'm late."

"You're not late. You were joining us at seven-thirty. It's seven-ten. But have a seat. We're always eager to talk Vector."

All the plush leather chairs around the table were occupied. Dolan tugged over the stool from the telephone nook. Jenner and Bernie made a show of shifting their chairs to make space, but there was nowhere for them to go.

Dolan folded his hands over a knee and stared down the spit-shined length of mahogany.

"I have good news," Dean said. "The business and legal counterparts have reached an equitable and mutually beneficial arrangement. Beacon-Kagan will pay Vector a licensing fee—a *significant* licensing fee—to become the exclusive worldwide manufacturer for Xedral. Your first eight-figure deal. Nine by this time next year. How does it feel?"

"Great." Dolan mustered a smile. "What are the terms?"

Chase slipped his BlackBerry into a pocket and tapped the circle of his fingertips on the three-inch-thick document before him. "Sucker boilerplate."

"Vector obviously doesn't have the infrastructure to manufacture big numbers," Dean added, "and big numbers we'll be doing. This is a fine deal, and you're to be congratulated."

"We can't put it out until after the IPO of course," Chase said, "which brings us to our big news. We got approval for the S-1. Vector goes public a week from Wednesday."

A round of congratulations. Dean was smiling now, a genuine grin. "Vector will be upping laboratory tours for patients and key investors as a ramp-up to Friday's pre-IPO presentation." His eyes found Dolan. "Be cordial. And dress. But remember, you're in the quiet period until the stock's been trading twenty-five days. No leaks, no asides, no press releases." Chase rolled his eyes at Jane—like Dolan's plugged in tight at CNBC. "For the next month, accessible but low-profile is the rule. We'll celebrate tonight at the house." His head cocked, his grin fading. "You're not jumping up and down?"

The other eighteen sets of eyes shifted to Dolan. "I think we have a window to bring Lentidra through another stage, see if we can attain permanent transgene integration."

"Chase says the numbers—"

"He's not a scientist, sir," Dolan said.

Chase's posture firmed, bringing him out of his slump. Jane coughed into a curl of manicured fingers. The other execs got busy examining papers and PalmPilots.

Dean glowered at Dolan. "There is more than one kind of numbers."

The fair skin of Chase's face had colored. "While you're busy stamping out disease, we're building an infrastructure around you and other researchers so we can effectively deliver your theragenes to patients in need."

"They're actually called transgenes," Dolan said.

"Not anymore. Show some appreciation for the work the *rest* of us do. Without us you're a guy with an idea and a university stipend."

Dean watched Dolan squirming in his chair. Dolan's birthright and duty as the elder Kagan offspring should have been to inherit one day the helm of the vast family-run corporation, but he'd eschewed business for science. As a sacrifice of sorts, on the eve of acquiring his doctorate and a humble NIH STTR grant, Dolan had offered up his gene-therapy research to his father in the form of an amateurish business pitch. After a consult with the director of UCLA's Office for Technology and Trademark Licensing, a gray old friend, Dean had taken over Vector Biogenics as he took over most matters, funding it in return for owning it lock, (especially) stock, and barrel.

Dean had raised two sons, one in his mold, the other who still required molding. But it was the latter who'd come up with the winning lottery ticket.

Dolan lifted his hands, palms out. "I guess I'm just disappointed in myself. For Lentidra's failure. For Vector's."

Winifred said, "You've done top-notch work, Dolan, on a remarkable timeline."

"We have an eager market and dying kids," Chase added. "Plus. We're on a clock with the IPO. That is gonna give you and Vector the longevity to pursue twenty-five times what your present resources would."

"Let's get to new business." Dean's festive mood had dissipated. He waved a pale, smooth hand at his younger son. "Chase, please?"

This was also Dolan's exit cue.

Offering a curt nod, Dolan withdrew. Dean waited impatiently for the door to close behind him.

It was early, and there was much work to be done.

Chapter 17

Tyler's sturdy legs flexed as he tried to reverse his head out of the railing of the plastic slide. His face turned red, his ears poking forward like a monkey's. Tim heard the deep breath but couldn't get there quick enough to avert the wail. He guided Ty's head through the gap and held him, standing on the dew-wet grass and checking his son's soft skin for scratches.

"Come on, bub. Let's go draw."

He stepped back into the living room and set Tyler on the plastic sheet laid down between Magic Marker and carpet. Distracted by scribble potential, Ty finally stopped crying, trading tears for a fist grip on Blinding Yellow. He attacked a length of butcher paper with vigor.

"Kaiyer draw Daddy."

Evidently Tim was an anatomical freak, stick legs and bread-loaf feet topped by a head like a nineteen-inch Trinitron. He tried to help Tyler clutch the marker effectively but had trouble translating finger placement to his son's left-handed grip.

Muffin stuck in her mouth, Dray came around from the kitchen, bringing Tim a smoothie and a piece of peanut butter toast. She halved her muffin, offered Tyler a chunk he inverted on the mat beside him, and turned a quizzical gaze to Tim's manipulation of their son's tiny splayed fingers.

Tim said, "Can't we just force him to be right-handed?"

"Bind his left arm behind his back and call him a devil child? I've read that's bad for self-esteem these days." She took a bite of Tim's toast before handing it to him. "You got him his OJ?"

"Right over there." Tim checked his watch—a little past 7:00 A.M. Eager to start digging into Walker's background, he'd do better at the office than at home on just a few hours' sleep. His colleagues could be distracting as hell, but they didn't cry and spill things. Well, Bear spilled things, but at least he didn't cry.

Dray said, "I got Elliott. He said he'd be happy to. He's working a P.M., so I'll meet him at Palmdale Station, walk through the files with him to get the skinny on the sister's suicide, and bring copies by your office tonight." Before Tim could thank her, her attention shifted to the Typhoon. "Did he get up the steps and down the slide by himself?"

"I worry about that slide. It gets his head stuck."

"*He* gets his head stuck. And he'll learn how to get it *un*stuck. That's what playground equipment is for."

Tim followed Dray's sharp stare to Tyler, who was standing with his knees pressed together, cupping his crotch.

Tim hoisted him up by his armpits, swept him down the hall, and deposited him on the kiddy toilet. In solidarity Tim followed suit once Tyler was done, without the aid of the red plastic booster.

As Tim flushed, Ty applauded clumsily. "Good job, Daddy."

"Thanks, pal. I been at this awhile, so it actually no longer constitutes a big accomplishment."

As Tyler toddled back to his markers, Tim heard him sneeze a couple times. Holstering his .357 as he came back into the living room, Tim asked, "You're gonna take him to the doctor today, right? Check out his cold?"

Dray toed the carpeted hearth. "You don't want to keep doing this to him."

At her tone he straightened. "Doing what?"

"The plastic railing and a doctor's trip after three sneezes. You'll make him a sick kid. You're teaching him that's how to live in the world."

Capitalizing on the distraction, Tyler had his shirt off and Ernie and Bert negotiating a fine domestic matter at too-loud volume.

"What's your biggest fear?" Tim asked.

"Having the hiccups indefinitely?"

"Dray."

"Going to jail for a crime I didn't commit? Speculums?" Eyebrows raised, she studied his irritated expression. "Okay, I give up."

"Mine is having something happen to him that we could have prevented."

"Okay." Dray took a few steps forward, arms folded so her firm biceps showed against her cutoff academy T-shirt. "I don't have a 'biggest' fear. I gave them up with best friends. But here's one of my *bigger* ones: raising a timid, shy boy who's terrified of adventure and risk and regards the world as a dangerous place. And right up there with that is the fear of being a parent who'd do that to him."

"The world *is* a dangerous place."

"Right. But that's not just a fact of life, it's one of the facts that gives life meaning and excitement. Even a kid can learn enough anxiety to lose sight of that."

Tim looked at Tyler, nakedly scribbling with a stunt helmet on. "I don't see that in him."

Dray's gaze shifted, then caught. Tyler was studying his feet intently, holding the uncapped yellow marker like a wand. "Ty, what are you doing?"

In response he leapt up and spun in circles.

"Okay," Tim said, "I'll work on it."

"Do more than that. Work on your head, sure. But *act* differently in the meantime. Now, finish your toast and go catch Walker Ja—" Dray stiffened.

A trail of tiny yellow footprints across the white carpet betrayed Tyler's escape route. The markers were kicked in all directions, food spilled across the sheet. Dray studied the scene, her jaw tensed. She drew a deep breath, closing her eyes and exhaling slowly as if to decelerate her temper. Finally she took a few steps over and studied the sticky TV. Orange juice had been splashed right into Elmo's hapless face.

"Field analysis would indicate the absence of a sippy cup," she said, "an open container being the only reasonable explanation for the spatter on the television screen."

Tim worked on keeping a straight face. "Sorry 'bout that."

"Crumb distribution suggests that the UNSUB ate his muffin imitating the Cookie Monster, not realizing that *he* actually *has* an esophagus, while said puppet does not." She assessed the stained fibers seriously. "The footprints, which are thankfully rendered in *fluorescent yellow*"—a brief pause as she pretended to regain her composure—"show the UNSUB headed west down the hall. . . ."

Blinding Yellow proved surprisingly robust as they followed the splotches.

"Preliminary evidence points to UNSUB coloring his feet bottoms with Magic Marker. *Permanent* Magic Marker." Dray shoved their bedroom door the rest of the way open, revealing the Typhoon jumping on their mattress, giggling at the sight of them, a puddle of jaundiced comforter at his feet.

Tim waited for Tyler to draw a breath between screeches. "What was that you were saying about timid?"

Chapter 18

Within the hour, when their stretches get stuck in traffic, I'm gonna have calls from the mayor and from Sutter's Fort or wherever the hell the governor lives. To ask what they can do to help. To inquire politely what *we* need. We need this guy nailed. Nothing shakes consumer confidence like a prison break." Sitting sideways on Tim's flimsy desk, hands laced across his knee in his trademark pose of paternal authority, Marshal Tannino flashed an ironic grin at Tim, Bear, and Guerrera. "Go restore order."

One of the few of the ninety-four U.S. marshals who'd risen through the ranks, Tannino preferred sweating over case files to the more prestigious—and dull—responsibilities of his appointment. He was supposed to be attending a fund-raising breakfast in Long Beach, but he liked to spend Monday mornings reviewing cases with his deputies in the squad room. The Service's central district warrant teams occupied the Roybal Building's Garden Level, so named because a bank of windows overlooked a spotty lawn and a few tired trees drooping under exhaust from Temple Street traffic. The desks were laden with laptops and red-markered maps. Crime-scene flyers, faxes, and booking photos flew back and forth over the waist-high partitions as the deputies waged an endless war of attrition against a horde of escape, parole, and drug cases.

The City of Angels also happens to be the nation's fugitive capital. Sleaze, after all, is just glamour that falls short of the mark. For every

Hollywood release, there were five skin flicks staining their way into existence on a Van Nuys bedsheet; for each set of celebrity handprints pressed into pavement on the Boulevard, there was a crimson spatter across glass-strewn asphalt.

Alongside LAPD's Parker Center, the federal courthouse, City Hall, and a variety of seventies-style landscape sculptures of questionable appeal, Roybal sits on Fletcher Bowron Square, which honors a brief but valiant stab at wresting city government from rackets and vice taken by L.A.'s forty-second mayor. Bowron's campaign met with far less success than did his subsequent effort to root out, dispossess, and intern Japanese-Americans, but his later apology stands as the sole capitulation by a major political leader in the postwar years. Tim, perhaps unnervingly early in his own career, identified closely with a man whose good intentions were overshadowed by recklessness and regret.

This morning Tannino looked uncharacteristically casual, salt-and-pepper stubble darkening his handsome Italian face. Rumors of retirement had been floating through the federal corridors, and he'd been complaining more often, confiding to Tim last week that his age—a youthful fifty-seven—already had him pissing in Morse code. But Tim couldn't see Tannino relinquishing his hold on his beloved Arrest Response Team, the Service's SWAT-like strike force composed of various warrant-squad deputies. Tannino oversaw tactical operations more closely than his predecessors, though Supervisory Deputy Brian Miller headed up ART in title. Thomas, the one colleague who continued to give Tim friction over past transgressions, had risen to team leader, spending so much time at the side of the supervisory deputy that the others had dubbed him "Miller Lite." Thomas and his partner, Freed, an independently wealthy deputy with a knack for unraveling shady finances, had proved themselves invaluable resources. Though Tim was technically a rank-and-file Escape Team deputy and ART member, his Spec Ops training bought him point-man status when they were pursuing a fugitive with Walker's expertise.

"You need to reconsider a task force," Tim said. "One way or another, Walker's heading for an escalation."

"An escalation?" Tannino said. "Like he'll break out of a *bigger* jail?"

"He's got an agenda. He didn't break out to go lie on a beach."

"Okay. What's the agenda?"

"I don't know yet," Tim admitted after a pause.

" 'I don't know yet' doesn't quite buy us a task force. Not with our caseload. I have faith in your premonitions, Rackley, but I also have faith that you and Bear can plot some trajectories of Jameson's mission before we go rolling out deputies with MP5s to chase each other around in the streets"—a dissatisfied glance at Guerrera—"and let's hope Che here can keep from kneeing any registered voters in the face this go-around if he's chained to his desk." Tannino squeezed Tim on the shoulder and rose to head back to the tranquillity of his well-appointed office at the rear of the courthouse. "Do what you do. And maybe even keep it off TV."

Tannino strode under the row of sanctimonious cabinet-member color portraits. They'd just gotten around to scraping Ashcroft off the wall, but Cheney remained, his smirk pulling to one side as if jerked by a string. Taking advantage of Tannino's having vacated, Guerrera planted himself on Tim's desk, hooking a chair with an extended boot and rolling it over for a footrest. His pop-singer Cuban features narrowed as he studied the photograph of Walker that topped the Service Record Book, freshly faxed. Guerrera, who'd always been openly in awe of Tim's tactical capabilities, flipped the page and whistled. "Think our boy Rambo's got it on you, Rack?"

"Yep." Tim took the file. "More practice. More recently."

The SRB revealed that Walker had been attached to First Platoon, Bravo Company, Fifth Marines, First Marine Expeditionary Force out of Pendleton. Walker had gone over to Iraq early in 2003 with the first troops to serve a half-year deployment. But the paperwork showed otherwise. *Extended six months. Extended three months. Extended three months. Extended three months.*

Page eleven showed a handful of discipline infractions, some conduct-unbecomings, and a few minor insubordinations, but the specifics of the incident that got Walker court-martialed were excised. Rather than clearing up the mystery of the Leavenworth sentence, the SRB was vague, affording the incident just three words: *assault and disrespect.*

Bear matched Tim page for page on his copy of the report to keep their thinking synced. "Why'd they demote a guy if they were just gonna kick him out anyways?"

"Your stay in Leavenworth is more unpleasant the lower your rank."

Bear let out an admiring chuckle. "Nasty fuckers, aren't you?"

"Did you locate any of the guys he served with?" Tim asked.

Guerrera said, "Most are still deployed or heading back."

"How about the injured?"

"They've been warehousing them in Germany."

"Of course." Tim clicked his teeth a few times, thinking. "Call Pendleton, see if you can get one of Walker's officers on the line."

Just short of San Diego, Gomer Pyle's old base was an easy drive for an interview if anything panned out. The air conditioner blew processed air into Tim's face. Across the partition, Thomas and Freed were arguing with Denley and Maybeck about a parolee who skipped a court date to go on a honeymoon.

Tim asked, "Do you think Walker's ex-wife is worth a visit?"

Maybeck picked up the question from two desks over. "Ex-wives are *always* worth a visit."

"Separated three years, though. Never visited him in jail."

Maybeck shrugged. "The more she hates him, the more you want to talk to her." He had faint freckles and a snub nose. He was ART's top breacher, though Denley joked that he'd look more at home in a varsity sweater than a ballistic vest.

Freed asked, "We got a girlfriend, maybe?"

"Working on it," Guerrera said.

"The family information is sketchy in Walker's presentencing report *and* in his SRB," Tim said. "See if you can fill it in for us. At this point don't rule anything out. Keep the lines out for family members, platoon-mates, associates, everything. The sister mentioned a shrink in her letter to Walker—see what you can dig up there, too. I know shrinks are uphill battles, but maybe we can get an insurance diagnosis."

Guerrera scribbled notes on his expanding to-do list.

"Who's looking into the Aryan Brotherhood?" Bear asked. "Enemy of my enemy and all that."

AB had tentacles everywhere. And a retaliation killing of Walker would be essential PR. Zimmer raised his arm without looking up from his monitor.

Thomas called out, "I think you should send Guerrera to talk to them. Alone."

Guerrera offered Thomas his slender middle digit and a few choice descriptions of his mother in rapid Spanish.

" 'The left side'?" At his desk Denley flicked a finger against Tim's case briefing. Even before he'd lost some hearing in an explosion a few years back, his hoarse Brooklyn-accented voice had been audible from a room away. "That's all you got? How do you know LaRue passed along to Walker the same message he got on the phone?"

"We don't."

" 'The left side'?" Denley said again. "What the hell?"

Bear cut in, riding his own stream of reasoning. "We get anything back from San Pedro PD?"

"Sorry, *socio*," Guerrera said. "Not a damn thing."

San Pedro had kept five units on alert through the night, combing the landfill and canvassing the surrounding area. Tim pictured the thousands of hiding places among the refuse, the networks of nearby streets, the blanket of distant rooftops. Walker's meticulous orchestration during the escape showed him to be a planner capable of thinking several moves in advance. Tim put himself in Walker's place, tumbling from a garbage truck into a hole filling with trash. What next?

He abruptly sat upright in his chair. "Stolen car. We should run down any stolen-car reports from last night. Within a five-mile radius of the landfill."

Guerrera cracked a smile, his response cut off by the stern voice coming from the forgotten speakerphone: "Yes, this is Second Lieutenant Lefferts."

Tim picked up the handset, and the deputies working the case popped on their headsets and kept working. Tim introduced himself and lobbed a few basic questions to test the ground. Lefferts relied on formality and briskness of tone to convey his authority. Tim had him pegged within moments, having endured similar officers on deployments of his own.

"Walker Jameson," Lefferts said. "I remember him. He was under my command for the better part of a year in Iraq." With exaggerated irony he added, "Jameson stood out."

"Had all the answers?" Tim prompted him.

"Nope, not that type. He just . . . *quietly knew better.* And he did as he pleased, always toeing the line of acceptability."

"Was he popular?"

"Walker Jameson was the kind of loose cannon who passes for a leader among the undisciplined and the foolish."

Thomas leaned heavily on the partition with both elbows, directing a pointed look at Tim, his handsome, muscular face tensing around a blond mustache too thick for the twenty-first century.

When Tim related news of Walker's escape, Lefferts seemed almost pleased. "I can't say I'm surprised. Sometimes we train the wrong ones. Then what the hell do you do with them?"

Thomas renewed his silent interrogation of Tim, his eyebrows wondering, *Well?*

Tim asked, "Does the phrase 'the left side' mean anything to you in relation to Jameson?"

"Not that springs to mind," Lefferts said.

"We think he's after something now. So whatever we can find out about grudges he holds or unsettled scores would be helpful. Would you mind filling me in a bit on his court-martial?"

Lefferts tightened up even further. "If the Marine Corps didn't see fit to include that in the SRB, Deputy, it would be because it's sensitive information. If you're a former Ranger as you claim, you should very well know that."

"I can get sensitive information, Lieutenant. What I want is your perspective."

"Walker Jameson is off my roll," Lefferts said with calm satisfaction. "He's your problem now."

Chapter 19

There was no lock on the door, which made Walker nervous, but if he sat with his chair pressed to the wall, he could watch the front parking lot through the sash window, which he'd struggled to push up and open. The room, sized like a generous walk-in closet, was bare-bones—bed, nightstand, visitor's chair—but clean and private. The occasional waft of lemon disinfectant rose from the linoleum tiles to relieve the scent of decay. A stiff top sheet crossed Bev Jameson crisply at the chest, her bare arms lying at her sides like they'd been placed there by someone else. An oxygen tube ran from a cluster of bedside equipment to rim her upper lip. Her copper hair rested in loose coils on a rouge-stained pillow. A few pencil sketches by a child hung on the walls, dragons and Vikings and muscular robots, some of the depictions surprisingly proficient. At the bottom of each, rendered proudly in a wobbly hand, was the artist's name. *Sam J.*

Bev licked her cracked lips, her unblinking eyes remaining on her son. "Tess had problems, all right. I couldn't count them on four hands. Money. Sammy. She burned all her time with the medical stuff—Lord knows, it's a pain in the ass. Dealing with insurance, doctors, referrals. She was excited about some new technology, gonna switch up Sammy's genes or something, but it didn't pan out. The things she did for that boy."

"Any new friends?"

"Not that I knew of."

"Boyfriend?"

Bev coughed for a good while, not bothering to raise a fist. When she finally finished, her smoky eyes grew smaller and darkened with remembered anger. "Jesus, you're just like your father." She squinted, not wanting to miss a second of Walker's reaction. "Out of the loop for how long? Then here you are, poking around, demanding answers."

"Pierce asked questions? Why would he give a shit?"

"Why would *you*?" Bev's laugh turned into a wheeze. "Of course you hate your father. You're stamped outta the same press." She raised a trembling tissue to her face and blotted her lips. "Once we split, he never wanted to acknowledge Tess. Or you. Or me, for that matter. But someone lays a hand on her, all of a sudden she's *his* flesh again." She shook her head, her neck tensing with surprisingly firm tendons. "His old ways." She kneaded the ragged tissue in a liver-spotted fist. "Now you come clamoring in over Tess's body like some Greek play. But when she was scraping bottom? No, sir." She spoke observationally, as if cruelty were far from her mind. "She was twice the person you'll ever be."

"Ain't that the truth."

Gurney wheels wobbled by out in the hall, accompanied by faint moaning.

"Early to see you, by my calendar." Her wise, wet eyes appraised him. "What next?"

"I don't know."

"Sure you do," she said, her voice coming smooth and steady now. "You'll get ahold of your father, and you'll do what you came for."

They regarded each other, mindful of the rumbling of ancient resentments, neither eager to spark the barely contained animosity. Walker supposed this is what vulnerability felt like—a reluctance to pick certain fights. Bev broke the silence with a coughing fit that racked her shoulders from the pillows and did not seem inclined to end. She spit into a bedpan, neatly dual-purpose, and settled back, a band of sweat sparkling through the foundation smoothing her forehead.

"There's some unspoken rule about all this, but I'll break it. I don't want to die. I know I'm supposed to be stoic and noble and all that crap, but I'm not. I'm scared. I don't want to die. I don't know what's waiting for me." She looked around her tiny quarters and let loose a cynical cackle. "I suppose it's gotta be better than this."

Walker again felt the sharpness of her stare, its hidden edge of accusation. The rough, cracked skin of his hands rasped when he rubbed his palms together. "I'm sorry I didn't work out." He paused to clear his throat softly. His voice was reflective, without self-pity. "I know I wasn't what you wanted."

A flicker of emotion altered her face, though what it was he couldn't say. She started to reply, but then the door clicked open and Walker darted across the room, hands resting on the windowsill. But it was just a young nurse smiling from the doorway.

"I didn't know you had a son, Beverly." She blushed. "I mean, it's just that your daughter visits so much more."

"Visited," Walker said.

More blood darkened her cheeks. "Right. I'm sorry. I, uh . . ."

"I'd like more apple juice," Bev said.

Grateful for the excuse, the nurse nodded and backed out, easing the door shut soundlessly, as if to convey remorse about her intrusion.

Walker stood beside the window, but Bev kept her head turned away. "They'll come looking for me," he said. "I'd appreciate it if you'd—"

"I don't think you've got ground to ask any favors here, Walker."

He dipped his chin once. "Don't worry," he said to the back of her head. "You won't see me again." He stepped through the window, setting one foot on dirt, then paused, straddling the sill. "I always thought I was gonna get to know you better."

A polite rap on the door, and then the nurse entered, bearing a glass of apple juice. "Where'd your son go? What's wrong, honey?"

Still as a corpse, Bev held her gaze on the blank wall.

The nurse set the glass on the nightstand. "Here's a Kleenex."

Bev waited for her to leave before pressing the tissue to her moist cheeks.

Chapter 20

Multiple-voice yelling rose above the blaring TV inside. Tim gave the doorbell a double ring and flattened himself to the wall beside the knob. Bear waited back from the porch, thumb break unsnapped on his holster.

Half-moon indentations pressed into the soft wood of the upper doorjamb, baton or flashlight impressions from domestic-disturbance calls, a warning for future responders. Repeat customer. Tim banged the door with a fist, not eager for a door-kick entry after he'd broadcast his presence. The Aryan Brotherhood was a "blood-in, blood-out" gang, and whatever they might learn here wasn't worth being somebody's initiation kill.

More shouting. Tim looked at Bear and shrugged. Probable cause? Probably not.

He tried the knob, and it gave up a full turn. A sign from the Locksmith in the Sky.

Past the raised step of the entryway, in the living room, a hefty woman in a stretched off-white undershirt sat angrily against the arm of a couch. A white male wearing muscle pants paced before her, the tattooed bulges of his muscular torso glimmering with sweat. An inked shamrock, complete with three sixes, stood out on the pale dip between his shoulder blades. A small stalactite of blood stained the woman's shirt, hanging from the collar. Matted hair clung to her face, pasted around the nasty gash beside her eye. Pinned down by various remote controls, a newspaper lay sectioned on a cable-spool table. On a TV split with undulating gray stripes, Rachel and Chandler bemoaned some intricacy of Monica's anal retentiveness. In the corner a Doberman lay curled up, inexplicably asleep.

"Howdy, folks!" Bear yelled against the din of the TV.

Yves Dagrain turned, perfectly calm, the rectangles of his six-pack shifting like the scales of a snake.

The woman continued chattering. "Course I didn't fucking call, baby. What do you think I am? I'd never call." And then, to Tim: "Get *out* of here." She heaved her purse in their vicinity. A ganglion of key chains hit the carpet at their feet, along with a sprinkling of change and a travel bottle of Dermablend, the preferred makeup of battered women. Given the amount of purse debris littering the carpet, a direct hit would've knocked Tim's head off.

Bear said wearily, "You had to go and do that."

Yves chuckled as Bear frisked her and tightened flex-cuffs around her chubby wrists. Then Bear fought with the remotes, clicking past a vacuum-seal storage bag infomercial and a parrot on ice skates before finding a mute button. The abrupt silence was blissful.

"Okay," Tim said. "Let's start this over. We're deputy U.S. marshals. We have a few questions for you."

Bear deposited the woman on a La-Z-Boy. Yves remained standing.

Tim walked over to the adjacent kitchen and dug through the freezer. He tossed a bag of frozen corn at the woman, which she pressed to her eye.

"Thanks," Yves said. "Now, what the fuck do you want?"

"I want to ask you about Walker Jameson."

"Can't say I've had the pleasure."

Tim reached over, pulled the *L.A. Times* front section from the cable-spool table, and held the photo of Terminal Island's watchtower in front of Yves's face. "Really?"

"I don't know nothin' 'bout that," Yves announced proudly. "I don't read."

Tim's eyes flicked to the silenced TV. Melissa Yueh, KCOM's tireless anchor, was gabbing from location at the San Pedro landfill, a photo of Walker Jameson occupying the upper right quadrant of the screen. "Blind, too?"

"My eyes work good enough to see an illegal search of my private property."

"Okay. You want to play this game? Battery on your woman here. You're the AB's top dog for Southern California, you've got responsibilities now. Do you really want another stint in the pen?"

"That shit only works on smart people."

"Reason?"

"Intimidation."

"Pretend you're smart, then."

Yves took a deep breath and held it. His exhale smelled of marijuana. He aimed a finger at Walker's picture on the TV. "I ain't makin' no specific threats, and I ain't sayin' I'll do nuthin', but that boy's a dead man. Period."

"Thank you," Bear said.

"For what?"

"For punctuating your sentences. I have a hard time keeping up otherwise."

Tim rose and pulled the woman to her feet.

"Don't you fuckin' talk to Jenna. You can't take her away. That's an infraction of my constitutional rights."

"Actually," Tim said, "Gonzales overturned the right to keep your battered girlfriend within arm's length at all times."

"I ain't *battered*," Jenna said.

"Don't you fucking take her out of my sight." Yves emphasized his words with a stabbing finger that Tim had learned generally presaged violence. Not wanting a carpet dance, he pretended to let his own temper flare to back Yves down.

"Relax, assfuck. Let me treat her eye so it doesn't get infected, and you won't have to waste your precious fucking time driving her to the hospital."

As Tim reached the door with Jenna, he heard a chuckle behind him. "Assfuck," Yves repeated to himself, amused.

Tim sat Jenna on the curb, still in flex-cuffs. He returned from Bear's rig with a first-aid kit, but she jerked her head away from him.

"Just lemme do it myself later. Y'all always screw it up anyhow."

"Okay." Tim knelt, bringing himself to eye level. "We think your boyfriend's going to be involved with a hit on Walker Jameson. I want some information from you, right now, or I'm gonna go in there and arrest him and say it was on your word."

Fear widened her eyes. Tim was surprised by his easy cruelty, but also, oddly, reassured.

"You can't do that."

Tim just stared at her.

"He don't do wet work. Not no more. Wet work comes outta Vegas."

"No shit. Can you give me a name?"

"If I wanna end up on the wrong side of the dirt."

Tim walked her back inside and handed her off to Bear, who cut off her flex-cuffs and sat her on the couch. Tim's Nextel vibrated, and he signaled Bear to give him a second and stepped outside again.

Guerrera's voice came quick and excited. "I found one of Walker's platoon-mates, right here in the VA in Westwood. Medical discharge. They shipped him home from Germany, but he had to go back into the hospital due to complications."

Tim jotted down the name. "Great. And how's it coming with the family?"

"I found a birth certificate so I could track down the parents. His mom's doing a slow fade in some home up in Sylmar—"

"Dying mom's good," Tim mused.

"—and I'm still looking for the father."

"Get a local unmarked, preferably females, to sit on the Sylmar nursing home in case Walker pays Mom a visit before Bear and I can get there." Tim signed off and dialed Ian Summer, a friend who'd recently transferred to the Vegas office. He caught Ian on a stakeout and therefore eager to talk.

"Yeah, we got good intel on the AB chapter out here," Ian said, "especially through the task force."

Tim and Bear had worked closely with the Service-sponsored Vegas Task Force in the past, having Ian track down collateral leads for them in Nevada. He and Bear had returned enough favors to consider Ian a long-distance partner. "I heard these guys use hit men from the Vegas chapter. Do you know who the enforcers there are?"

"No, but a couple of the Metro PD guys have been keeping up files. I'll dig into the intel this afternoon, keep an eye out, and throw you a heads-up if we catch wind of any movement. If it's for the over-the-fence you're dealing with, I'm sure the chief'll be happy to toss some man-hours your way."

Tim thanked him and headed back inside. Her legs tucked under her, Jenna sat beside Yves on the couch, leaning on him and teasing his hair with her fingernails. Yves looked vaguely worried, focused on Bear, who was bent over the Doberman in the corner. The dog still hadn't roused. Tim put two and two together when Bear shook his head, tensing his mouth. "What happened to the dog?"

Yves's eyes were gleaming. "Died of old age."

Bear's gaze lingered on the dog's caved ribs, and then his jaw set, dangerously. "You think this is funny, motherfucker? You lose your temper, hit your woman, kick your dog." He started sharply for Yves, causing him to recoil, but veered instead and headed out the door.

Tim started after him, then stopped. "Look, I have to ask. Do you want to press charges?"

Jenna went on rubbing Yves's bare chest. "For what?"

He'd seen enough domestic violence to know that these two would probably continue to fight it out until one gave the other a street divorce, served by the business end of a .45.

Offering her a resigned nod, he left them to their marital bliss.

Chapter 21

A stray dog licked the necks of soda bottles in the recycle bin at the curb, paws pressed into the extra black bags piled beside the garbage cans. Walker looked up and down the street, then crossed to the tract house. Within a moment of his ringing, a man in his late sixties appeared at the door wearing a barbecue apron that read DON'T *&^%# WITH THE CHEF! Dense chestnut hair powdered with white capped a square-hewn face. Age loosened the skin of his powerful forearms just slightly enough to add texture, and his hands hung like lifeless slabs. The hazel eyes took in Walker with a single sweep.

"Come 'round back." The door closed.

Walker reached across the side gate to raise the latch, then stumbled over a golden retriever all the way to the back deck, where the man awaited him at a picnic table. Wisps spiraled out of holes in the closed barbecue as it self-cleaned. Through a picture window, Walker saw two kids chasing each other in circles around a plush denim couch while an attractive woman in her forties sealed leftover chicken into neat Ziplocs. Pierce threw a rubber chew toy onto the lawn, and the dog sailed after it.

Walker sat down opposite his father. "You don't look surprised."

"I thought you just might be dumb enough, yeah."

"Can't take up a trail a year and a half later."

"No, you can't." Pierce gave a dead grin. "So I guess you did what you had to do."

Walker cast a gaze around the spacious backyard. "Nice house."

"Real estate development. Easy gig." Pierce didn't smile, but the muscles of his face tensed to show amusement. "And it's legal, mostly."

"I'm hungry."

"I bet." His hand pivoted off his wrist to give an abbreviated flare of the fingers.

Constance came out, tugging her sandalwood-colored hair back into a ponytail. She spoke in a lowered voice, though the kids were inside. "Hi, Walk. I didn't know you were out."

"I'm not."

The surprise froze her face for an instant, but she covered with a flat smile. "Can I bring you something?"

"He's fine." Pierce kept his eyes on Walker, eager to pick back up.

She withdrew, pulling the door closed behind her. She whispered something to the kids, who'd been staring out the window, and they went back to running circles.

"You got yourself in the position you're in," Pierce said, as if Walker had just finished moaning about his unjust fate. "You had a fine family. Didn't give her any kids. Didn't build shit. Look at me. I got out—did something else for a change. These children." He shook his head, overcome by his good fortune.

"They got names?" Walker asked, mostly to break up the taped lecture.

"Bronson and Bronwyn." He smoothed a rough palm over the wooden surface of the table, clearing the slate for the conversation at hand. "This thing. Why you're here. It isn't what it looked like."

"You looked into it?"

"Course I looked into it. But I can't do more than that. I'm on the straight and narrow now. Too much at stake. Morg poked around—he can give you a start. Talk to him."

"Where do I find him?"

"He'll find you. What are you gonna do?"

"What do you think I'm gonna do? I need a safe house."

"I got a complex going off Sepulveda, by the dump. Half built, tied up in litigation."

"What for?"

"The shit you care? We had to shut down construction. You can go live in there. Water and electricity to the model unit should work. Hell, there's a security truck and everything. Your very own gated community. Never let it be said I don't take care of my own." Pierce waited for Walker to challenge the claim, but he said nothing. "You good for gear?"

"Always."

"Good, 'cause I can't help you there. Not no more."

"Lend me a shirt, though?"

"Got some shit going to Salvation Army. Trash bags by the curb. Go on and dig through them." Pierce pulled a rubber-banded roll of hundreds from the front pocket of his apron and tossed it across the table. It bounced off Walker's shoulder and rolled on the deck. "You owe her."

"We all owe her." Walker dipped a shoulder and swept the roll of bills from the fine-stained wood. He studied it before shoving it into a pocket. "I can't sit at your table, but I can do your dirty work."

"That's right. *Our* dirty work."

"Why? You never cared about Tess."

"I cared about you both until you turned into the total fuckups your mother raised while I was away. Still, it's a point of principle. Tess was my blood. You don't let your blood get fucked with. Something you could stand to learn."

The cash bulged uncomfortably in Walker's pocket. "Three grand. Tess needed just three grand to move states with the kid. Why didn't you help?"

"What do you think? I'm still in the game?" He ran his tongue across his teeth, bulging his upper lip. "Tess never was an ace with a checkbook. You start a family, you gotta have your priorities. Save your money in case maybe a kid gets sick. Instead she blows it on her hair-trigger brother in the clink."

"What do you mean?"

"Your appeals, the attorney. You didn't think it was free?" A smile cracked his face. "Oh, you didn't know. You didn't *want* to know."

Finally Walker said, "She said you paid."

Pierce was grinning, his face vibrant from the realization. "She put every cent she had and a few she didn't into your defense lawyer's pocket. That's why she couldn't afford a new liver for Spanky. So don't come bitchin' to me like I'm the March of Dimes."

Walker studied the red and blue plastic toys littering the sandbox by the steps, the Wacky Wiggle hose laying limp on the rich green strips of rolled sod.

Pierce kept carrying on the argument alone. "Yeah, well, guess what you win when you complain?" He held up his hand, thumb and fingers forming a zero. "It wasn't my job to do a damn thing. Not with where I was with my career then. Your mother and I worked it out. That woman never kept her word. Not a day in her life. The queen martyr. Only woman I've ever known who'd rather open a vein than fry a fuckin' egg." He stood, tapped a fist on the table like a judge dismissing a case. "I'll get you the keys."

Walker waited for his face to stop burning, but on it went. He kept an impassive expression in place, heavy like a welder's mask. And then, slowly, gradually, he started to believe the mask.

"Who are you?" The boy stood in the threshold, tugging the sliding door so it knocked against him at intervals. Fair hair, light blue eyes, pug nose—the kid looked like a JCPenney model.

Walker studied him, then cleared his throat. "I'm—"

"An old friend," Pierce said, appearing behind Bronson and ushering him inside, large hands encompassing the narrow shoulders. Walker stood and caught the airborne keys. The circle tag of the key ring had an address scrawled in black ink. Walker memorized it and left the incriminating tag on the picnic table. Pierce had already vanished into the house, and somewhere one of the kids started banging "Frère Jacques" on a piano.

At Walker's approach, the scruffy dog retreated across the driveway, where it crouched at the neighbor's mailbox, longingly regarding the plunder he'd been forced to abandon. Walker rustled in the curbside bags and dug out a few shirts and one of his father's outmoded court-appearance suits. Even as he drove off, the mutt remained at bay, skinny and trembling.

Chapter 22

The stumps of Marcel Deron's arms waved in circles as he laughed. The left, which flapped like a vestigial wing, terminated midbiceps, the right two inches below the elbow, so its narrow tip squirmed above the joint like a sightless head. The medical ward at the VA Hospital, sectioned by vinyl sheets to accord each bed a four-foot buffer, housed about twenty patients, most of them grizzled survivors of wars well past. Marcel and his buddy, currently being changed by a burly orderly behind a drawn curtain, were the youngest vets Tim and Bear had encountered on the VA grounds by a good two decades. Judging from the black orbs of Marcel's eyes and the drawl of the friend's complaints one bed over, both soldiers had been easing their pain with a steady stream of morphine. The sheets, strung on overhead tracks like massive shower curtains, offered an illusion of privacy, but the various patients' smells and sounds pervaded the ward.

"You think that was a *war*?" Marcel answered Bear with a snicker. "That was a corporate action. Look at me." Wearing a mock kung fu expression, he arranged his stumps into a martial arts pose, then chuckled. "Half of me's still MIA. And what for? Liberating Fallujah. Is it even liberated? Hey, Mikey? Is Fallujah liberated yet?"

"Fuck if I know," a voice returned from the far side of the partition sheet, picking up the well-worn routine. "But Nafar ain't."

"Nafar? Why you talkin' 'bout Nafar?"

"That's where I left *my* fucking leg."

Marcel joined Mike's braying laughter, writhing on his sheets. Dirty fingernails, sweat-glazed skin, grown-out hair like an Afro that couldn't get up momentum—it wasn't a stretch for Tim to envision Marcel pushing a shopping cart and mumbling to himself like one of the Vietnam vets camped out on the surrounding blocks.

Tim rephrased the question. "You served with Walker Jameson."

"Yessir. I was enlisted. SAW-gunner Deron." Marcel raised his arm in a salute, though there was no forearm and hand to finish the job. No matter how many times Tim had seen it, the abbreviated movement of a stump was always shocking, always grotesque. Marcel continued, "Saw the world with Walkman." With pride he added, "The Corps's been there longer than anyone else. We were the first boots on the sand, you know. Year and a half I served in Iraq, till I caught a rocket-propelled grenade. Something comes at you like that, it's instinct." The blunt ends of his arms tapped together once, twice, Bill Buckner reliving the passed grounder. Marcel caught himself, mounting a carefree grin and a mouthy follow-up. "Oh, yeah, I stuck around Iraqtown. You got your duty extensions, your stop-loss programs. Six months, 'nuther six months, 'nuther six months. Shit, Rummy keep pluggin' quarters into this motherfucker. Game continued. Game continued. Game continued."

"The phrase 'the left side' mean anything to you? About Walker or anything else?"

Marcel shook his head. "What's a sniper like you doin' *Dragnet* for anyhow?" Raised voice: "How 'bout *that,* Mikey? The cops here are Rangers, but we got leathernecks playin' *po*-lice in Baghdad. Upside-down world. Go fuckin' figure."

"Can you tell me anything about Walker that we might not learn from his SRB?"

"Walkman? Uu-*ee*. Like they say in the NFL, he had good motor. You could cut off both legs and the boy'd keep on giving. Or one." He flung back the sheet and wormed a bandage-capped knee around, clearly enjoying Bear's discomfort. "He's a dangerous mofo, Walkman. Goju-Ryu karate or some shit. Knew every pressure point on the body, and that's a fact." His right arm shot out, catching Bear above the wrist, the nub jackknifing. Bear dropped his weight quickly, sitting on the floor before twisting his arm free of Marcel's elbow joint. Quickly finding his feet, Bear rubbed the meat of his forearm and scowled, clearly displeased at the prospect of retaliating against a triple amputee.

"Who says you can't teach a crippled-ass dog new tricks?" Marcel said.

"You pull that shit again," Bear said, "I'll nail you to the wall."

"I wish I had my old form back to make it a fair fight," Marcel said, without a hint of animosity. He warmed again to his story. "Walkman would sneak off when we'd put into port, come back bruised with wads of cash stuffed in his pockets. Finally I cornered him. Turns out he was tracking down underground street-fighting circuits. 'Keeping up skills,' he called it. Homeboy kicked ass in Phuket, Bahrain, Abu Dhabi. . . ."

A coldness overtook Tim's stomach. His adversary's credentials—already more impressive than those of anyone Tim had tracked—continued to mount. Seven years younger than Tim, Walker was more fit physically and tactically, and practiced in the next generation of war toys and techniques. Tim pictured himself coming off Afghanistan—cocksure, skills honed from day-in, day-out soldiering—and figured he wouldn't want to meet his former self now in a mano a mano. For the first time in recent memory, he wondered how he'd fare against a fugitive, and he could tell from Bear's restless shifting that his partner felt the same way.

"And that was just extracurricular," Marcel continued. "Walkman killed hajjis by the bagful. Right up until he got the shaft. *Dishonorable.* Ouch ouch ouch. No pension, no health care, no *fine* VA benefits. Walkman got *nu-thin'.* He ain't here to enjoy the *gour*-met cooking. Orange roughy Sundays. None of it."

"Why'd he get court-martialed?"

"Well, as you may have read in your *USA Today,* they didn't send us over so well equipped."

A surprisingly smooth baritone issued through the curtain: "Dubya sent in 'Merica's *trooops.* Said he'd armor us head to *booots.* Family back home, ain't they the *best*? Mama done pass the hat for a bulletproof *vess.*"

Mikey's chanting provided accompaniment as Marcel continued. "We rolled out in unarmored Humvees—thinskins. Patrolled in flimsy-ass flak jackets couldn't stop an AK round if someone threw it at you. We didn't like it, but we did it. Like most of us dumb-asses, Walkman thought the war was . . . What's that term, Mikey?"

The song abruptly stopped. "*Boo*-shit."

"That's right. And this one LT, Lieutenant Lefferts—I ever tell you about Lieutenant Lefferts, Mikey?"

" 'I'm beset by the undisciplined and the foolish,' " quoth Mikey from the privacy of his bed.

"I had the privilege of speaking to Lefferts this afternoon," Tim said.

Marcel's grin widened. "So you know. Silver-spoon Academy family. Well, us enlisted swine, we'd do what we do for a few days, then LT would get it in his head to put his own special touch on our mission plans. He'd read up on base intel, mix in a bit of that classroom magic they taught him at Annapolis, and retrace our patrols, routing us through dead spots or hot spots, wherever the pencil drew. And when you're light on armor, you get tired playing bullet sponge for a legacy ring-knocker. Walkman let him know. Not directly, but he, you know, body-languaged his displeasure. One night Lefferts personalizes our patrol right through an urban ambush, we near get our asses shot off. We scatter, regroup, and limp in some twelve hours later, minus one. We pass LT just inside the base checkpoint, wearing his pressed garrison fatigues. Walkman don't salute. And LT's like, 'Didn't they teach you to salute in boot camp, Marine?' Still Walkman don't salute. LT get up in his face, saliva and shit flying, says, 'I'm talking to you, Marine.' Walkman still don't move. Not an inch. Starts to walk away. So LT grabs him by the equipment harness, spins him around so hard his helmet falls off, starts finger-pokin' him in the chest."

A dramatic pause. Mikey swept the curtain aside so he could take in Marcel's face.

"With just a single thumb, Walkman strikes him. Once. Like this." The stub of an arm corkscrewed up from the sheets. "Right up under the rib cage. LT went *down,* was sucking dirt for ten minutes. Shit himself, even. Paramedics and all."

The SRB's tailored vagueness and Lefferts's defensiveness on the phone were all the clearer now, though Tim doubted that Walker had broken out of prison now to go after a shithead lieutenant. Tim considered the conviction that had landed Walker in TI—stockpiling frag grenades after being fired from a job. Maybe he'd been looking for a cause, and finally, in the prison chow hall, he'd found one. But what?

When Tim refocused, Mikey had again drawn his privacy curtain and Bear had just put another question to Marcel.

"What did we do?" Marcel repeated. "What *didn't* we do? We were an Advance Force Recon Team. When I was with Walkman, we spent a lot of time in the Anbar province and Sadr City, working in support of infantry operations. A lot of scouting, mountainous navigation, sure. But more night ops." His eyes took on a soulless gleam that Tim recognized immediately as the detachment required for routinized killing, so ingrained it emerged even in recollection. Marcel's voice had gone cold and humorless, and it was clear he wasn't going to stop talking anytime soon. "We broke off into hunter-killer teams. Sometimes we'd parachute in under cover of night to clear a landing zone. Pick off unfriendlies, secure the area for helicopters to unload the main body in the A.M. Sometimes it was urban settings—reconning enemy positions, sniping targets of opportunity. That was a different game. We'd take fixed positions at elevated sites so the rags couldn't determine the base of fire. We could knock 'em down from eighteen hundred yards. Symbolic shots, too, oh, yeah."

Tim, a former sniper with the Rangers who'd neutralized targets on three continents, was intimately familiar with the expression, but Bear asked, "Symbolic shots?"

"Through the spine." Marcel's truncated arm stabbed the air. He wore an unrecognizable smile. "Leave the target alive but in a location where rescue ain't gonna happen. Let his cries work on the opposition for an hour or two. Sometimes we'd go for a more immediate effect, like if we spotted an enemy mortar position. We'd snipe the Head Freds in command simultaneously. Three headshots, three towelheads hit the sand, one echo rolls back from the foothills. Get the cronies scared, get 'em running. Flush 'em onto open ground. Then Walkman would take target practice. No tremor in that trigger finger, I can tell you that." His onyx eyes met Tim's. "You wouldn't believe how good Walkman was unless you saw it. You just wouldn't believe it."

His right arm poked around under the sheets and came up with a clicker for the morphine drip. His nub moved over the button and tensed, and then he settled back on his pillows and closed his eyes. Within seconds his breathing took on a rasp.

As Tim and Bear threaded through the web of curtains to the exit, a dopey rendition of the Marines' Hymn followed them out: *"From the halls of Montezu-u-ma to the shores of Tripoli . . ."*

Tim listened for irony in Mikey's robust voice but found he'd momentarily lost his perspective.

Chapter 23

Soiled with a fringe of water stain and an excessive smattering of bird shit, the billboard proclaimed SUNNYSLOPE FAMILY HOMES—OVER 30% SOLD! A healthy family—Caucasian, shiny teeth—gathered around a nicely set wooden table in a light-suffused kitchen, eagerly waiting for Mom to portion salad from a transparent bowl.

Walker nosed the car around the circular entry below, paved with beiged cinder blocks, and fitted the cylindrical key into the pad mounted on the abandoned guard booth. The mechanical gate topped with anti-climb serrated spikes opened, then rumbled shut behind the Accord. The permanent fence—mock adobe to match the pavers—extended a mere fifteen feet from the guard booth before terminating abruptly, a few blocks still floating in their mortar grips like offset Legos. Left-behind supplies still overloaded their pallets, though sun exposure had baked the lettering off the bags and crates. Picking up where the wall ended and encircling the rest of the complex was a transportable chain-link fence. Rising crookedly from occasional concrete bases, it was topped with three strips of barbed wire. Walker would feel right at home.

As promised, a security truck was parked in the partial shelter between a stack of lowboy Dumpsters and a toolshed. Walker hid the Honda behind the truck, out of view from the gate, shouldered his duffel bag, and climbed out. The stench of sewage intensified—rich, waterlogged, fetid—seeming to emanate from the ground itself.

The development was tucked into the Santa Monicas at the terminus of a quarter-mile private road that intercepted Sepulveda about midway up its tortuous run from Sunset to Mulholland. The stand-alone units, uppity town homes that had outgrown shared walls, remained in various stages of incompletion. A hammer lay on a garage overhang, a trickle of dried rust staining the brief run of shingles below it. A blind hung crooked from a second-floor window. A fluttering tarp stretched across a roofless first story. A shipment of squat palm trees, their bulbous bottoms still wrapped in burlap, sat clustered in a common patch of dirt, leaning sickly in all directions like an old-timer baseball lineup.

Though generic, the houses stayed well spaced as they climbed the slope, their driveway tributaries connecting to a haphazard loop of dirt-blown thoroughfare. The model stood out easily for its finished touches, which imbued the house with artificial coziness. Brushed-nickel numbers on the mailbox. Painted gutters. A valance puffed into view behind fake plantation shutters. Walker crossed the grounds, stepping over a stalled tumbleweed. The place looked like a ghost town from a cheap apocalypse flick.

Pausing outside the house, he kicked in some of the lattice surrounding the porch, then fell to a sniper position and had a quick look at the crawl space. His nose wrinkled against the smell, more pronounced this close to the dirt.

The third key on the ring fit the khaki front door, and Walker stepped inside. A film of sawdust moved as a piece against the draft. He hit the light switch, but nothing happened. A scattering of flyers on the floor broke down unit numbers and prices. North of a mil for a petite house in a gulch filled with emissions. Walker slid his hand along the curve of decorative railing, then stepped down into the sunken family room. Built-in shelves housed what proved to be fake book spines and empty CD cases. The house felt barren, though it was embellished with on-the-nose furnishings—a sectional with a loose-fit twill slipcover, an oversize marble planter housing a dying fern, even a TV in the entertainment built-in that occupied the east wall. Walker dumped his duffel by the stone hearth.

LAST SHOT

A stingy hall led to the master bedroom decorated preciously in a samurai-sushi-bar motif. A framed photograph of a robe was mounted on the wall. A two-fold shoji screened a teak-stained bureau. *Memoirs of a Geisha* sat on a bamboo nightstand. The silk duvet cover flipped back to reveal a bare mattress and a raised bed frame on wheels. Save those seven items, the room was empty. Walker worked the north-facing window open. A half mile of chaparral rolled upslope before hitting the shoddy fence line. Near the chain link, fumes curled the air above an offset sewer grate, left bare in the ground beside a few protruding pipes. He turned to the bamboo nightstand, picked up *Memoirs*. The book slid out from the too-big dust jacket to reveal *The 7 Habits of Highly Effective People*. With a smirk he returned it to its place.

The upstairs featured a den cramped by two rooms for imaginary kids, one done up with pink curtains and a vanity, the other with a race-car bed mismatched with a spaceship comforter. The ceiling hatch in the hall tugged down to disgorge a spring-loaded ladder. Walker took a climb up and crouched in the sweltering heat. Ankle deep in pink insulation, he noted the locations of the various vents. Hundreds of flies speckled the wooden beams; he didn't realize they were dead until he shuffled to lean on a four-by-four, brushing a few dryly from their perches.

He returned to the family room and sat on the couch, which slid back a few inches on the hardwood floor. Just another guy coming home from a long day's work.

He removed Tess's weekly planner from the duffel. A strip of photo-booth pictures fluttered out. Tess and Sam. The first had caught them unaware, still facing each other, probably plotting their poses. The others featured the obligatory faces—tongues out, cheeks puffed, crossed eyes. Sam's mouth was stained blue from some candy and his hair stuck up on one side like he hadn't brushed it since waking. He'd set his glasses crooked in the last, and Tess was laughing so hard she looked unattractive, which was a helluva feat. Studying the first pic, Walker flashed on another photo strip, from another decade. He and Tess used to ride the same wavelength that way, consulting on everything. What flavor ice cream to buy. What to name the puppy. How to mug for the camera.

Walker stared at the browning fiddleheads on the fern, then rooted around in the kitchen until he found a coffee mug in the bare cupboard.

He filled it at the sink, watered the fern, and sat back down. Opening Tess's planner, he located her final entry. June 1. Seven P.M. *Vector Party, The Ivy—Bev Hills.*

Walker worked a 7-Eleven bag from the duffel and upended it on the cushion next to him. Five prepaid disposable cell phones fell out. He called information, waited to be connected after hearing the number for Vector in 310, and asked for Human Resources.

"Yeah, hi. I'm calling to check on my job application. My name's Jess Jameson." He waited while the disaffected HR assistant flipped through some files.

"We have nothing under that name, sir."

"Sometimes it accidentally gets keyed in as *Tess* Jameson," Walker said.

"We have no applications on file from any Jameson."

He hung up and stared at the cheap plastic phone. "What did you get yourself into Tess?" He dialed again, his fingers tracing the familiar pattern across the keypad.

To the boy's high-pitched inquiry, Walker said, "This is Larry Fedder." He waited, listening to receding footsteps and the tinkling of the piano. When Pierce picked up, Walker asked, "What's The Ivy?"

"Some fancy restaurant. Actors and directors, Jap businessmen. Broads buying lunch for their decorator."

"Why would Tess go there?"

"She wouldn't."

"What do you mean?"

"They wouldn't let someone like her past the front door at a place like that." A background shout from one of the trendily named children momentarily distracted Pierce. Then he said, "Don't call me here."

Walker listened to the dial tone for a moment, studying the photos of Tess and Sam. Then he threw them aside.

His step was charged. The door slammed behind him.

Chapter 24

Tim flipped through the visitor log as he and Bear followed the head nurse down the scrubbed tile corridor.

Bear cupped a photo of Walker in his palm. "Seen him?" She shook her head, and he extended the picture to her, and his card. "Would you mind showing this to the staff and patients?"

"Not at all." The picture disappeared into a white pocket at her waist. She signaled them to wait, knocked once at a door, and cracked it. "You have some visitors." She nodded at the muffled reply, then stepped back, letting them enter.

Bev Jameson's frail body left a well-delineated imprint in the thin sheets. Concave cheeks, ash-colored skin, and recessed eyes made clear death had her in its sights. Her gown was open at the throat. The wrinkles clustered and quickened, forming a sagging web before disappearing beneath the collar.

As Bear introduced them, Tim took note of the drawings taped to her walls. "Your grandson?"

Her stiff hair rasped against the pillow as she nodded.

"I'm sorry for your loss."

"Which one?" Cigarettes had taken the veneer off her voice.

"Your daughter. And I suppose your son."

"My daughter is dead. So unless you're here to tell me my boy is, too . . . ?" A cocked eyebrow. Tim shook his head. She exhaled through her nose, a short burst of disdain. "I know people like you—*proper people*—might just as soon have a son dead as in prison, but don't you *dare* offer me your condolences."

"I didn't mean it that way."

"You're not fit to lick my boy's boots."

Bear, stuck for once in the good-cop position, said gently, "We're sorry to barge in on you. We'd like to ask you a few questions, and then we'll be on our way."

"Dottie? Stop pestering me, Dot." Bev glanced at the empty bedside chair, her lips quivering.

Bear and Tim exchanged a puzzled glance.

"Are you aware that your son broke out of prison?" Tim asked.

"Not my boy. My boy's in the marines." She hollered into the imaginary other room. "Isn't that right, Dot?"

Tim did his best, but questioning Bev was like eating a soup sandwich. Bear spent the first few minutes writing down the names of Bev's imaginary friends but soon gave up. He seemed relieved when his cell rang. He glanced up from the caller ID screen and mouthed "CSI" to Tim before stepping out into the hall.

Tim again found himself trying to win Bev's attention back from Dot when Bear reentered, his face serious. "That was Aaronson. He wants us at the lab."

Bev didn't register Tim's farewell. He and Bear jogged to the Ram. They were pulling out of the parking lot when another nurse ran out, flagging them down. The brakes squealed their displeasure, and Tim rolled down his window.

The nurse held Walker's photo. "I saw this man. Beverly's son? He was here this morning."

Tim's voice came louder than intended. "This *morning*? What time?"

"Right around the start of my shift. I'd say seven-thirty, maybe."

"Did you see him arrive? What was he wearing?"

She looked slightly flustered. "I don't really remember. I just came in the room and he was there, and I came back and he was gone. Why don't you ask Beverly?"

"She's a bit out to lunch, no?"

A furrow drew her eyebrows together. "What are you talking about?"

"Senile dementia? Alzheimer's, maybe?"

The nurse's arms wove themselves together across her chest. "Beverly Jameson is perfectly lucid."

Bear lowered his forehead to the steering wheel and let out a guffaw. Dotty indeed. Tim got out, leaving Bear to question the nurse.

A smile pulled at Bev's mouth when Tim entered.

"Nice selective-incompetence routine. Use it myself sometimes."

"I bet you're more convincing, too," she said with sudden clarity.

Tim couldn't stop his smile. "Maybe so." He and Bear had to regroup and rethink. Walker had been out only one night and half a day, but he was moving quickly, hitting his marks, while they'd spent the morning chasing the wrong leads. They had to anticipate, not chase. Tim hoped whatever Aaronson had waiting for them would give them a jump.

He withdrew, feeling Bev's keen stare on his back. At the door he heard the flat, gravelly voice behind him. "I'm never going to see my son again."

When he turned, her head was rolled away, her eyes on the window and the gray-blue sky beyond.

Chapter 25

This time, despite the broken latch, Walker knocked on the back sliding door.

"Come in!"

Sam sat in the living room plugged in to a PlayStation, his legs frogged out. He took no note of Walker's entrance.

"Where's Kaitlin?"

"Work." Sam's eyes didn't leave the game. He took his simulated motorcycle down a fire escape, ran over a bystander, and blazed through a police station.

Walker headed back to Tess's room. The laminated Vector visitor's pass still hung on her closet doorknob. He lifted it and walked out, wrapping the lanyard around his hand like a rosary. Sam continued zooming and blasting away on the TV. Walker was halfway out the sliding glass door when Sam said, "I have a bad gene."

Walker stopped. Regarded the back of Sam's head. "How do you know?"

"I just do." The motorcycle reared up, jumping over a carload of baddies. "I'm gonna die, prob'ly."

Walker took a half step back from the threshold. "Me, too."

"I mean, soon."

"Thems the breaks."

"I'm never even gonna have a girlfriend first."

"Girls don't like you?"

Sam's head swiveled at last. He granted Walker a slack-jawed glance that acknowledged the stupidity of the question and said flatly, "I have *yellow eyes*." He turned back to the game.

For the first time, Walker bothered to take Sam in. Jaundiced skin. Swollen legs folded back under him. Mussed hair. A series of bruises dotting his forearm. He scratched at his shoulder; his skin was bothering him. Walker could barely make out his face in the reflection of the screen.

"Why you taking Mom's card?"

Observant little fucker. "I need it."

"For what?"

"A job. It's for your mother."

"Can I help?"

"No."

"It's not your card."

"You'll have it back when I'm done."

"Done what?" Sam's hands were a flurry of movement around the controller. Levers, dials, and about ten action buttons sprouted from the calculator-size unit, spread along the top, sides, and bottom. Walker recalled his own first video-game experience—Space Invaders, joystick, one red button. He marveled at the kid's hand-eye coordination; he would've put Sam on loader duty in a Bradley before half the shaved-scalp jackasses he'd served with.

Walker said, "What are those marks on your forearm?"

"I bruise easy."

"And."

"This one kid, he hits me in the arm. To watch the bruise. He started a competition at the park. Like who could spray the best graffiti. He calls me Piss-Eyes. I don't tell Kaitlin. She's got enough to worry about. I make things hard. Or my gene does. The one I don't have. I don't wanna wear her out like I did Mom." Sam scratched his head, then his arm, then his head. His sleeve stayed hiked up, revealing a Magic Markered yin above his right biceps.

"The hell is that?"

Sam's eyes clicked over, noting Walker's focus on his fake prison tattoo. He worked at his thigh for a moment with his fingernails but didn't answer.

"Wash it off," Walker said. "It makes you look stupid."

Sam skidded out, his fallen motorcycle throwing up a beautifully animated shower of sparks. In seconds he was reset on a new bike, revving up an alley.

"It used to make her sad. Mom. She'd cry sometimes when we left the hospital. She'd turn her head toward the window so I wouldn't see, but I could still hear her." Sam's voice remained as matter-of-fact as always. "Mom changed my name back, just before she, ya know. I guess she was mad at my dad for not helping. I was Sam Hardy. Now I'm Sam Jameson, just like you."

Walker became acutely aware of his breathing as he did just before a fight. "Don't make me into something I'm not."

"Whatever. I'm just telling you my name."

"Your mother bought me a cross one time, made out of titanium. You know what that is?"

"Like the strongest metal ever."

"She said she had to get it for me in titanium because I break everything."

"Do you?"

"I've ruined my share of stuff, yeah. Didn't stick around to put it back together."

"She should talk."

Walker crossed the room in a single giant stride. Sam yelped, and the controller hit the carpet. "Your mother was a *saint*."

"You're hurting my arm."

"She raised me."

Sam jerked his bruised arm free. "Wish she stuck around to raise me, too." He picked up the controller, checked it for damage, and started a new game.

Walker went outside and got halfway across the patio before he stopped. His head tilted back, mouth set with frustration. Deep breath. He cursed to himself and returned to the living room. He'd grown accustomed to talking to Sam's back and shoulders. "You want a job?" The amplified roar of the motorcycle was the only reply. "Here. Put this in the coffee tin." Walker peeled two hundred-dollar bills from the roll in his pocket and set them on the coffee table next to the label maker, still sporting the red bow. "Don't tell Kaitlin."

Sam glanced at the bills solemnly, twirled a finger in the air in mock excitement, then turned to the game again. "You gonna come back?"

"Why would I come back?" The sound of burning rubber and screeching brakes followed Walker's exit.

Chapter 26

An attractive redhead sat behind a curved shield of a reception booth, elevated as if on a captain's chair, punching phone buttons and speaking silkily into her headset. A frosted-glass sign stood out from the anodized aluminum frame of the console, exhibiting the company logo—a *V* with an arrow rising from the second upstroke.

Feeling stiff in his father's old suit, Walker flashed Tess's laminated visitor card. Workers streamed past—lunch break in full swing.

"I'm slotted for the investors' twelve o'clock walk-through," Walker said. Five bucks at an Internet café had bought him enough buzzwords from Vector's Web site to bluff and jive. "Running late—we sat on the tarmac for a good half hour."

The receptionist tipped down the phone mouthpiece and whispered over her call, "Straight back. Go catch the group."

Walker waited for the electronic click, then moved forward through the doors. A fresh-faced researcher in a white lab coat stood before a door at the end of the corridor, her bearing that of a Disney attraction guide. As Walker neared enough to hear velvety voice-over murmuring within, she leaned forward and mouthed, "Here for the tour?"

At his nod she opened the door. Walker brushed past, surreptitiously lifting the access card clipped to her coat pocket. The rows of mesh swivel chairs in the auditorium were curved to face a projection screen descended from the ceiling. Walker saw now that the room, which could have accommodated a couple hundred people, ran the length of the corridor he'd just passed—a big space that came out of nowhere, like a hotel ballroom. The narrow casement windows set high in either corner of the east wall were cracked for air, but the room smelled of paint and upholstery, and the pale outside light that the tinted panes allowed through was barely enough to dent the darkness.

The thirty or so people inside were captivated by the video. Surround-sound speakers poured the Vector spokesman's voice into the room: *". . . the leading genetic cause of liver transplants in children. It's also a leading cause of death. Why?"*

Walker slid into a chair by the aisle, upsetting the carefully placed stack of glossy corporate literature.

"Because children are born without a proper gene. It's a horrible—but now treatable—disorder." Accompanied by funereal music, a montage of children waxed and waned on-screen, each ethnicity represented by a model specimen—large sad eyes, smooth skin, hair mussed just so. Like Sam looked in the photo-booth pictures, before his condition worsened. *"How does it harm the liver? Well, the faulty gene produces abnormal proteins that amass in the liver, a process called 'pathological polymerization.'"* It dawned on Walker that his GED might not have armed him with enough arrows in this particular quiver, but he did his best to follow along. *"These variant proteins get trapped in the liver, and eventually—tragically—impede its functioning."*

Walker scooped a brochure from the floor, titled *Xedral to the Rescue!* As he tried to make sense of the bullet points, the omnipresent voice asked, *"What are viral vectors? They're the vehicles used in gene therapy to transfer the gene of interest to the target cells, which will then go on to express the therapeutic protein encoded by the transgene."*

The folks at Vector seemed awfully fond of answering their own questions.

Taking advantage of the darkness, Walker removed a digital scanner, about the size of a cigarette holder, from his pocket. Inserting in the slot the stolen access-control card, he activated the reader, setting the miniaturized row of lights blinking. Then he refocused on the screen.

"—freeze-dried storage in five-millimeter vials. And there's no need for

IV infusion or any fancy procedures or surgeries. A few drops of sterile water reconstitute Xedral to a solution, and it can be injected into the arm like a basic vaccine." Jerky 1950s newsreel footage of kids hopping onto exam tables and baring their arms elicited a few titters from the viewers. A musical theme, five upbeat chimes of a xylophone, punctuated a pan across a community of children, gathered together now and apparently happy at their prospects. *"A lifetime of change . . ."*—the image pulled to the northwest quadrant of the TV, the other sections depicting Vector's high-tech labs and scientists in industrious motion—*" . . . in a simple shot."* A distinguished pause and then a smoothly cadenced afterthought: *"Vector Biogenics. The human touch."*

When the lights came up, the presenter thanked Walker for joining the group and made a few closing remarks about Xedral's market potential, his voice echoing off the high ceiling. Walker perused the other tour members, guessing most of them to be scientists, graduate students, or heavy-hitter investors. An Asian doctor entered and tugged importantly at the sleeves of his white coat.

The presenter smiled at the group. "I'm delighted to see that Dr. Huang, our study director, can join us for a few minutes of our laboratory tour."

Hanging to the rear of the group, Walker shuffled out behind two bearded men discussing commodities futures. At the doorway Walker smiled at the researcher, letting her access card drop secretly down the side of his leg. It was important that she find her card and not report it missing.

Fielding questions magnanimously, Huang led them up a corridor that ran alongside the laboratory's various suites, generous windows affording aquarium vantages. Walker jogged his dated tie and listened to a few of the grad students natter on about some famous gene-therapy trial where the subjects came down with leukemia.

Huang fielded each question magnanimously, playing the old pro by catching the nonscientists up. "We've got that covered three ways." Point number one bent back his thumb: "We've engineered Xedral to insert into a nonfunctioning section of DNA." Index finger: "We've flanked our transgene with starting and stopping codons so it won't disrupt neighboring genes." And the fuck-you finger: "We've employed a temporary model that eliminates long-term complications by requiring a booster every month to keep transgene expression active."

They moved along the corridor, spying in on a room walled with vast, glass-fronted refrigerators filled with Xedral vials. A scientist unpacked jars from an ice-packed Styrofoam shipping cooler, taking no note of the observers.

One of the investor types, a wizened man in a leisure suit, chimed in, "Aren't you worried about using a deadly virus to carry this new gene?"

"Push up your sleeve, sir," Huang said. "No, your left. That's it. Your smallpox vaccination scar. We use an attenuated strain of poxvirus, like the one you had injected there. It *can't* cause infection."

They passed one end of the test-subject suite, the tour-group participants cooing cloyingly and waving at the monkeys. A woman with jangly earrings proudly claimed, "I have issues with animal cruelty," in a voice not quite loud enough to draw a remark from Huang.

Walker fell even farther back from the crowd, and when the group passed around the corner, he held the digital scanner to an access pad beside a metal door, testing if it had captured the frequency from the card. A low-register hum and the door came uneven from the wall. Walker pulled it open and peered down another hall, this one appearing to house executive offices. The sound of an argument carried to him.

"Of course not, Dolan. You read the preclinical reports—it just wasn't working." A beat. "Why would you even say that? What are you insinuating?"

Another male voice answered, glumly. "Nothing. I just want to see *all* the raw data, and I'm not waiting until—"

Walker slipped into the hall, shoes silent on the expensive carpet. He followed the raised voices. A door opened behind him, and he froze, but the two young executives headed in the opposite direction, cuffing their sleeves, not seeing him.

"You going tonight?" one asked.

"Bel Air? I'd go just to see the mansion."

That they didn't turn around seemed a good indication that raised voices from the far end of the hall were not an uncommon occurrence. Walker passed a stretch of corkboard, mounted between light sconces.

The top pushpinned flyer, importantly titled *Interoffice Memo,* announced, *S-1 Filing Celebration. 7:30 at the Kagan Estate, tonight. Formal. All staff and spouses welcome. No uninvited guests, please.* Printed below was a Bel Air address.

Walker continued down the hall, matching the names on the metal plates to recalled Web site bios.

The discussion continued.

"Listen, D, data is—I know, *are*—the whole problem. You've got a study director who has to cover the stuff you've missed, because you're busy trying to micromanage him. And me."

The comment was met with silence.

"You wanted a company, not just a lab. This is how a company has to work. We're about to have stockholders. Ten thousand or more. Are you gonna be the one accountable to them?"

Walker reached the threshold of the office from which the voices issued. The nameplate read CHASE KAGAN, CEO.

The same voice continued, softer, "I thought not. Now. I want to give you some advice out of this morning's meeting, if you're open to it. You slouch when you sit. It shows you lack confidence."

"I slouch?"

Angled blinds mostly blocked a hall-facing window. Walker rose on his tiptoes to see through the gaps. Spacious corner office. Darkened and soundproofed exterior windows overlooked muted traffic. A broad desk, cherry with gold handles, held neat stacks of papers. Journals and business books lined the shelves, and on a low-lying table rested an illustrated *Art of War.* One man sat on a leather-and-chrome love seat; the other leaned ass to desk, arms propped behind him, a mauve linen shirt hanging loosely around his muscular frame. Though their coloring and bearing were nearly opposite, Walker pegged them immediately as brothers.

"Tight hamstrings," the man at the desk said, in the voice Walker recognized as the aggressor's. "They make your pelvis tilt, accentuating the arch of your back. It's a common posture pitfall. You really ought to get to the gym, do some stretching. Or if you're tied up here, I'll send Harper—she's a *genius.*"

Dolan was darker, a few years older, and more thinly built—Chase's charitable suggestions aside, Dolan *did* need to log some gym time.

A woman exited her office across the hall, her office overheads back-lighting Walker against the blinds. He jerked back, but too late—Chase's pale eyes had already pulled to the window.

Chase strode across the office and threw open the door. He called after Walker. "Who are you? Ex*cuse* me?" As Walker slipped out into the main corridor, he heard Chase's voice again. "Call security."

Walker pressed through the doors into the lobby. He moved briskly past the receptionist and several well-dressed lobby occupants. Outside, lunchtime foot traffic was flowing past the dark-tinted lobby windows in clogs and streams, massing at the intersections.

As security was converging on the hall outside Chase Kagan's office, Walker floated through the revolving door and disappeared into the midday Los Angeles blaze.

Chapter 27

I need to be clear on this matter: I'm going to have to destroy the evidence." Aaronson's rectangular glasses dangled from a ball-chain clasp, hung up in the collar of his ironed Izod.

The L.A. County Sheriff's CSI lab, divided into cubicles with distinct blacktop benches, smelled pervasively of bleach. Since the Marshals had no in-house forensics, they relied on Sheriff's criminalists. Aaronson, Tim's go-to guy, was a narrow, fussy man with methodical diction and a punctilious eye. He was brilliant, and he made it look hard.

The fresh spread of butcher paper, which covered his bench to collect trace materials, threw Tess's *Littlerock Weekly* obituary, taken from Walker's cell, into relief. Aaronson had rested the torn strip of newsprint—folded along its original lines—atop a plain business envelope, positioned to show how it might have picked up impressions from a pen writing a return address.

The three men stared at the faint indentations in the clipping's upper left corner, ballooned into close-up through the boom-mounted eight-power lens. In the background, Sports Talk radio bemoaned Kobe Bryant's continuing underperformance.

"I dusted it, sprinkled graphite, but newsprint gives poor resolution," Aaronson said. "I even put it under a fiber-optic, used oblique lighting, the stereo zoom, digital photos—to no avail. There's just no high-tech way of doing this yielding." Bear reached for the paper, and Aaronson put in his trademark line: "Don't touch that, please."

"So you have to . . . what?" Tim asked.

"I want your approval for the old-fashioned method. We'll only get one shot at it, and if it doesn't work, the specimen's spoiled." Aaronson withdrew a number-two pencil from the overloaded breast pocket of his lab coat and a narrow X-Acto knife from his top drawer. Pressing firmly, the tip of his tongue poking into view at the corner of his mouth, he halved the pencil lengthwise and held up one of the two resulting sticks, showing off the exposed run of graphite at the core. "We swipe it across the obit, hope it brings up the contrast."

Tim and Bear looked at each other for a moment, then shrugged in unison. Bear said, "What the hell."

Aaronson drew the split pencil evenly across the newsprint. Leaning over, he blew the graphite dust clear. Untouched by the charcoal swath, the faintly sunken numbers and letters of an address showed, fading where the pen pressure had lightened.

3328 Sand

Canyon C

"Canyon Country?" Bear pointed at the mention of the community in the obituary proper—the dentist's office where Tess had worked. "It's up the 14, on the way to Littlerock, where Tess lived and Walker grew up."

Aaronson's quiet-touch keyboard purred under the fluid motion of his fingers. He filled in the blank fields on the database screen, punched "return" with a satisfied flourish, and waited as the hourglass icon tinkled sand. It didn't take long before two matching Canyon Country addresses popped up—*3328 Sanders Avenue #5* and *3328 Sand Canyon Road.* Annoyed with Bear's and Tim's craning around the monitor, Aaronson glared at them disapprovingly and angled the screen farther in his direction.

"Can you get us names?" Tim asked.

"Of course." A few wiggles of the mouse and Aaronson said, "In the first we have a Chellee Meehleis."

"And in the second?" Bear asked impatiently.

Front teeth pinching his thin lower lip, Aaronson right-clicked several times, and then his scalp shifted back, wrinkling his forehead. "Pierce Jameson," he said.

Chapter 28

Walker stepped down quietly into the model home's family room and aimed his Redhawk at the back of the man who was urinating into his fireplace. After spotting the blue Plymouth with a bent hood pulled into the neighboring—and doorless—garage, he'd entered the house silently through the master window, which he'd left open for precisely such contingencies. He waited patiently as the man hummed to himself and rocked on the heels of his Ropers. The man finished, bouncing at the knees to augment his shake, then turned around.

Morgenstein. As Walker's father had promised.

He jokingly raised his hands, letting himself dangle. Walker tucked the revolver back into his waistband, tight against his right kidney.

"Toilets don't work, you know." Morg zipped himself up.

"Yeah," Walker said. "They do."

"Oh. The problems must just be downpipe." He grinned at the wet stain in the fireplace. "Sorry 'bout that." He'd aged badly in the years since Walker had seen him—more jowly, burst capillaries in both cheeks, scalp glinting through thinning hair. His dress slacks were worn thin at the knees, and a dribble marked his button-up at intervals down the right side. He laughed. "It was the worst of times, it was the worst of times." He tucked in his shirt self-consciously, his voice rife with bitterness. "Money's tight now that your old man went straight. He wouldn't use me as a foreman here, wouldn't even let me run security." His chin

138

jerked in the direction of the front door, indicating the grounds beyond. "New truck and all. How's it drive?"

"Dunno."

"He gave you the key, right?" Morg realized Walker wasn't going to answer and chuckled off the question like he didn't care. "Now that he's moved on, he can't afford to deal much with the likes of me. Guess we're in the same boat that way, you and me."

"You'll get by."

"Yeah, well. Not all of us fit his hand-me-downs."

Walker sloughed Pierce's jacket and tugged off the tie. The room darkened a few shades in a single lurch—the mountains had caught the setting sun. Surprisingly crisp air offered a preview of good sleeping weather; thirty-four eventful waking hours had left him tired. He hadn't used a proper mattress in two and a half years, but he had a few more rocks to kick over before lying down. "Electricity's off."

"I'll get it turned on."

A breeze blew through the screen in the kitchen, wrinkling both of their noses. "The fuck went on here?" Walker asked.

"Sewage issue, case you hadn't figured that out. The construction manager cut corners—no Porta-Potties—had a twenty-five-man work crew taking dumps in the one functional toilet"—a nod down the hall—"shift after shift. The drain field backed up, but your old man still wasn't about to spring for a proper system. Department of Health brought down the hammer. Your old man had the plumbing rerouted to the storm-drain channels—fucking genius—while he waits to slide a bribe through. The cool air'll tamp down the odor in the winter. He'll sell off the units, then reconnect to the old shitty system." Morg tapped the cardboard box on the hearth with the tip of his cowboy boot. "Brought you some food." He tossed something, and Walker caught it in front of his face. A can opener. "Not exactly Wolpgang Fuck, but as your old man says, 'Guess what you win when you complain?' "

Walker pried a hand between the overlapping flaps of the box and yanked out a can. Turkey chili. Crouching, he popped the lid with a few hurried twists of the opener and poured out a mouthful, swallowed without chewing. Then another. Morg was watching him like something on Animal Planet, but Walker didn't care.

"Your father wants it clear that he has no idea you're staying here."

Walker set the empty can on the floor. "How 'bout you tell me something useful?"

Morg said, conversationally, "Tessy caught the short end, that's for sure. Your father, he was your age, he wouldn't have stood for it."

"*Useful,* Morg."

"I nosed around the edges, got mostly, you know, vagaries, but I dug up one baton to hand off. I caught word that on June sixth a contract got paid through Game. Know it?" He palmed some sweat off his shiny forehead. "Of course you don't. It's a paintball course. With a twist."

"What kind of twist?"

Morg worked a wad of keys from his pocket and headed out. "You'll see."

He stepped up into the entry and turned. Walker still stood studying him, arms crossed.

"What?"

Walker said, "Can I trust you, Morg?"

Hand resting on the ornamental banister, he looked old and frail. "Thirty-five years in with your old man," he said, reaching for the door. "Yeah, you can trust me."

Chapter 29

The denim couch seemed to sink around Pierce Jameson's weight, the cushions tilting up on either side of him. His broad arms spread across the fabric, ensuring he occupied the entire piece of furniture. A man at leisure. The needlepoint pillow beside him, a wifely touch that inadvertently undercut his tough-guy posturing, stated, IF YOU CAN READ THIS, THANK A TEACHER. SINCE IT'S IN ENGLISH, THANK A SOLDIER.

Pierce's resemblance to his son was evident only in his sturdy frame and the shape of his head. His features were rougher, more craggy—he could have been a longshoreman.

Not having been asked to sit, Tim and Bear remained on their feet at the edge of the living room rug. Pierce's second wife—who seemed far too lovely to have married him—and their two children had retreated to the kitchen, heeding Pierce's pointed glance.

"Nope," Pierce said, "haven't seen hide nor hair for years."

Tim's mouth twisted—con men got under his skin in a hurry.

"Have you talked to him or had contact in any way?" Bear asked. It had been less than twenty-four hours since Walker's escape, but given how quickly he'd gotten to his mother, Tim and Bear were rushing through their contact list.

Pierce shook his head and—again—eyed his watch. The smell of baking biscuits floated through the closed kitchen door.

Tim's irritation flared, and Bear shot him a glance to gauge him. Pierce watched their noninteraction with suspicion.

"Can we have a word with your kids?" Bear asked.

"No."

Tim repeated, *"No?"*

"They don't need to know they have a jailbird half-brother. Maybe in your family, Deputy . . . uh, Rackley—right?—that's no big deal. Around here it is." Pierce hefted himself grandly from the couch and strode to the front door, which he jerked open. "Dinnertime with my family is important to me."

Tim stayed his tongue, and he and Bear exited, Pierce closing the door behind them. They sat in Bear's rig out front, watching through a picture window as Pierce joined his family at the table. Pierce looked out at them and twisted the blinds shut.

Guerrera had taken a run through Pierce's rap sheet and relayed his findings—fraud counts all too familiar to Tim. The scams and rackets Pierce had been charged for showed a range as impressive as Tim's father's, though with greater returns, but evidently Pierce had gone straight in his old age. Not a single arrest in ten years.

Tim caught himself wondering if his own father would pull it together before spending his golden years in an orange jumpsuit. Tim had been three when his mother decided she'd had her fill of his father's schemes and infidelities. She'd fled, sacrificing Tim along with the dour house, and he'd spent his childhood being a supporting player in his father's serial cons. The aid beneficiary, the tantrum-throwing diversion maker, the delivery boy—he'd played them all, but from the time he was school age he'd sought the straight and narrow the way other kids sought drugs and bad company. In retrospect his upbringing had been great on-the-job training for undercover and interrogation work. Despite his not speaking to his father since their latest falling-out more than three years ago, Tim couldn't deny that he owed a number of his acuities to him.

"Work on the poker face," Bear said.

"No shit, huh?" Tim ran his hands over his face. "Sorry."

"It's okay. He's lying. He knows we know he's lying. That's good. Let's tell local PD to keep an eye on the house. If Sonny pops by for some quality family time, we nail him."

"Pierce is too smart for that."

"You never know."

"I do." Tim's phone chirped, and he checked caller ID—*Shrff's Plm-dale Station.* Probably Dray having tracked down her former colleague and the crime report on Tess Jameson's suicide. He flipped open the Nextel. "How's it going with Elliott?"

"I'm with him now, making headway. I'll meet you at the office in an hour, fill you in then. Listen, have Guerrera track down Tess's autopsy report."

"It was a suicide by gunshot. Why would they do an autopsy?"

Dray's sigh, through the phone, sounded like static. "Because she was pregnant."

Chapter 30

A '72 Olds Cutlass Supreme held down the VIP space beside the entrance canopy's awning, the license plate asking, RUGAME? The muscle car's powder blue coat had been recently sprayed, the white soft top restored, the chrome hubcaps and bumpers buffed to a mirror shine. The stand-alone building fronted an enormous mesh-enclosed preserve, like a butterfly pavilion, a bite of maybe fifteen acres from Playa Vista's Ballona Wetlands. A gravel road carved through the marshy ground, widening into a parking lot. Frogs and crickets shrilled. To the west the concrete-clad Ballona Creek moved slow and steady, pulled along like a strip of black fabric. The wetlands between were a surprising sprawl of nature within eyeshot of Lincoln Boulevard.

The last few customers trickled out, paintball guns holstered or dangling from slings, their store-crisp camo getups looking like Halloween costumes. Monday nights, Walker guessed, were slow when it came to war games.

He caught the solid oak door on its backswing and entered the spacious front room. With its wall-mounted weapons, framed *Soldier of Fortune* covers, and wooden bar complete with thatch canopy, tiki torches, elk heads, and twining plants, the lounge was part tropical-themed frat house, part movie-villain lair. The lights had been turned off, though a desk lamp remained on in the connecting room, illuminating brackets of guns and video equipment, clipboards hanging from pegs, and a row of lockers. To the side of a service counter, a wide ass barely accommodated by board shorts jutted into view, its owner rustling in the cabinets below.

Walker moved silently through the lounge toward the office, passing a curtained entrance to the enclosed preserve. Humid air breathed through the olive drab gauze, smelling of greenhouse. A camo tarpaulin banner secured by twine arced across the threshold between the two rooms, red letters offering what Walker assumed was the corporate tagline: GAME: SEXUALITY DISTILLED. Catching the drift, his eyes pulled to a routed-wood sign nailed to a door: GIRLS' CHANGING-OUT-OF ROOM—NO ENTRY!!!

An obese tabby hopped up on the counter, sending a paintball gun into a rasping rotation. A high-pitched man's voice issued from below. "Be *careful*, Elektra."

The cat took note of Walker's shadowy presence, hissing with alarming ferocity. A moment later a pink-faced man hoisted himself into view. A line of perspiration twinkled across a baby-smooth upper lip. Breast mounds bulged out a Hawaiian shirt. Around his neck hung a badge: PAINTBALL COMMANDER. FOUR-TIME COURSE CHAMPION. Walker remembered similar custom-made badges marketed in law-enforcement catalogs, advertised as "real nickel."

The man spoke with unexpected confidence. "Sorry, pal. Closed for the night."

Walker stayed a few steps back in the shadows. The man grew wary of his silence. "Listen, pal. I'm the owner, and I'm tired of the bullshit. Write an angry letter to the editor or something, but get the hell out. *Now.*"

Still Walker didn't respond. The man's hand rustled under the counter, but then his arm froze. "That's not a paintball gun."

The wall-cut light of the desk lamp went no farther than Walker's wrist, illuminating the Redhawk and little more. "No."

The tabby judiciously retreated from the countertop, taking up residence on a row of binders lining a rear shelf. The window looked out over the parking lot, empty save for the beloved Olds.

The Mickey Mouse voice lost some of its confidence. "I'm the four-time course champion. You don't want to tangle with me, pal. All right?"

Walker stepped forward, letting the light fall across his face. He nodded at the man's hidden hand. "Pick it up. Go on."

"Umm . . ."

"Pick it up."

"I don't really want to."

Walker cocked the hammer, and the man cringed and slowly withdrew his hand from beneath the counter, careful to keep the SIG Sauer aimed away.

"Point it at me," Walker said.

The pistol trembled in the man's grip. "Do I have to?"

"Yes."

It took him an eternity to fight his hand north, to place Walker in the sights.

"Open your eyes," Walker said. The man was cringing, sweat beading at the band of forehead beneath his receding hairline. Walker waited until the terrified pupils came into sight. He stared down the barrel of the SIG. "You have no idea how little I have to lose."

"Probably not. Can I put the gun down now?"

Walker nodded, and the pistol clattered into a drawer. "You're going to answer all my questions, and you're going to do so immediately. I will not ask a question twice. Understand?"

The double chin jerked up, then puddled.

"What's your full name?"

"Wesley Aloysius Dieter."

"A contract deal came through here on Wednesday, June sixth. Do you know anything about it?"

"Swear to God no."

"Do you have hidden cameras?"

"Uh-uh. It makes guys nervous. Say the press or a guy's wife gets ahold of some footage. We had a state assembly rep in here last week, ya know?"

Walker's eyes ticked toward the video equipment. "But you film them?"

"Sometimes. But it's just the one tape, shipped to an address they designate." Wes tapped a contract underlying the counter's scratch guard. "We don't keep a master, nothing." He exaggerated showing Walker his hands before pulling a ChapStick from his pocket and moistening his lips. "I had a closed-circuit in for a while, some lenses in the preserve to keep an eye on the girls, but some of my customers are pretty paranoid. They like their privacy." He added, with an element of pride, "We get a lot of tough guys, former operators, ya know?"

"You keep a log?"

"Yeah, but it won't do you any good. Guys use fake names or tags, mostly." Wes wiped the sweat from his cheeks. His voice was less fearful. He seemed to be enjoying himself, playing a role in a real-life dangerous plot.

Walker put a charge back into him, circling the counter and pressing the point of the Redhawk to his greasy cheek. "Get it."

Wes recoiled, then dug through some binders behind the desk and produced an appointment sheet—names marked by the start times. Walker glanced through the list—nothing he recognized, though he wasn't sure what he was expecting.

"Tell me something useful."

"Okay," Wes's voice ratcheted even higher. He snatched up the page, his fingers snapping nervously as he perused the names. "Mostly my regulars here. That was the day Cheetah Runner twisted her ankle. I remember it." Wes's eyes darted around the page, and then he made a strangled noise of excitement. "This guy." He tapped the page excitedly. "Sickle Moon. Rookie mission. He had a silver briefcase. I remember because he had to rent two lockers, one for it, one to fit his clothes and gear. Look right here." Beside the name was scribbled an abbreviation that Walker took to be the locker-rental code.

"Did he take the briefcase with him when he left?"

"I didn't see."

Walker pointed at another handwritten mark: *L13ov.* "What's that mean?"

"He kept one locker overnight."

"And that didn't make you suspicious? A cash drop?"

"Like I said, this is a meeting ground for all types of guys. A lot leave their gear overnight if they book again for the next day. I'd never think it was for a *contract*. At most I thought he was buying guns. Guys do that here, now and then, get around the bullshit waiting-period laws." Wes read Walker's anger, and his face started to quiver. "It's just for fun, really. Guys who want to shoot up at the ranges in the hills, ya know?

Targets on boards, maybe an out-of-season deer or two. Nothing big. Who's that hurt?"

"What'd he do when he was here?"

Wes spoke rapidly, placating. "Normal appointment. One-hour hunt. Minimum requirement if you wanna rent a locker."

In order to locker the cash, Sickle Moon, the bag man for the deal, had to partake of the action.

Walker noted the credit-card swiper beside the computer on the rear desk. "How'd he pay?"

Wes checked the scrawl on the appointment sheet again. "Cash. Most of 'em do."

"Did he order a video?"

"Uh-uh."

"Get on your knees."

Wes blurted out, "I have an address."

"An address? Why the hell you have an address all of a sudden?"

"I always do. Look, this is a high-ticket, high-risk operation. One in five customers invites a girl out. One time in three, she goes. We gotta know who with. Believe what you want, but I know some of these girls years now. I don't want to see anything happen to one. So we shoot digitals of the clients' license plates. I got a pal on the force gives us addresses, so if a girl goes out and stays out too long, we know where to start looking. That's all. I don't tell anyone—I *can't* tell anyone—or that'd be the end of this place. And probably me."

"Get it."

Wes dug through a cabinet. With trembling fingers he aligned the combo on a lockbox, then dug through laser-print close-ups of license plates. He pulled one, handed it to Walker.

Walker glanced at the handwritten name above the address on the back: *Ted Sands.*

He slid the photo in his pocket. "On your knees."

"Oh, God." Wes let out a strident moan. "Come on, pal, I helped you as best I could. I don't know anything."

"Lace your hands behind your neck." Walker stood behind him, pressing the barrel to the wispy hair above his collar.

LAST SHOT

Wes was keening now, voice choked with snot. "I'm just a business-man. I talk a game, that's all. I talk a game, but I'm not really a player. I just like being around them. Please. Please."

Walker pulled the trigger, the hammer clicking over an empty cham-ber. "You're not worth the bullet."

He left Wes collapsed on the floor behind the counter, Elektra groom-ing herself indifferently by his head.

Chapter 31

We're past the twenty-four-hour mark." Tannino leaned into the squad room, arms hooked on either side of the door frame so his shoulder pads, worn to supplement his five feet seven inches, jogged up on either side of his face. "What gives?"

"He's smart," Tim said.

"And?"

"Well-trained, proficient. Covers his tracks like a professional."

From across the room, Thomas called out, "Want to take him to a movie, Rack?" Assorted snickers, most of them good-natured.

"You think he's lying low?" Tannino asked.

"We'll hear from him again," Tim said. "Soon. Any chance I could talk you into that task force? We're juggling enough locations of interest that we could use the manpower."

"We could *always* use more manpower."

"Yeah, but we can't just pick up Jameson's trail like with Joe Fugitive. He's too strategic. He'll keep us chasing our tails. We need to work out where the trail leads and meet him there. And we need more resources to get there. Quickly."

Tannino swept a gaze across the deputies working away at their various desks. "He's one fugitive."

"No, he's a former Recon marine on a mission. And he has one big advantage over us: He knows what the mission is."

150

Tannino made a disgruntled noise and shoved back from the door, disappearing.

Guerrera said, " 'Twenty-four-hour mark.' Think the marshal's watching too much *Law & Order?*"

Tim turned his attention back to the mess of field files before him, piled higher than his head. He'd just gotten back to the office and was trying to get an eye on the latest memos before calling an Escape Team powwow.

Bear snorted his derision at the report he was reading and tossed it atop the stack, his other hand groping blindly inside the Krispy Kreme carton for the last doughnut, which he'd eaten five minutes ago. Tim, Bear, and Guerrera had shoved their desks together, though whether the limited synergy was worth the cost of Bear's secretarial skills was doubtful. Guerrera had stepped into Miller's office, hovering over the fax machine. Tim caught his eye through the blinds and waved him over, but he held up his index finger.

"Okay, guys," Tim said. "Can I borrow your brains again?" He waited for the other deputies to gather around the union of the desks. "Pierce Jameson knows more than he's letting on. We want to dig up everything we can on his current activities. He's a businessman—Freed, we could use your eyes unraveling his finances, properties, tax records, anything that might shed light. Can you take point on that?"

"Sure. How about the mom? We could have one of the nurses put out that she had a stroke or something and needs familial consent for an operation. See if we can bait Jameson to go to the hospital and sign off. Nab him there."

"He's too sharp for the ruse."

Thomas said, "His file did say he was Mensa."

No one laughed this time. Even Freed, Thomas's partner, looked uncomfortable. Thomas withdrew from the circle of deputies, heading back to his desk. "This isn't a military command. Not everyone has to drop everything when the Troubleshooter decides he's got a hot lead."

"The marshal designated Jameson a major case," Bear said. "Or did you go off the payroll?"

"Oh, is that a designation now? 'Major case'? Where's that fall in the hierarchy—not Shit Yer Pants but above Damn Serious? Walker Jameson isn't a Top Fifteen—"

"If we don't catch him soon," Tim said, "he will be."

"—so why's he highest priority? Because Rack's working the case?"

"Over-the-walls always take precedence," Bear said.

"Jowalski, I'd think you'd be tired of carrying Rack's bags by now."

Bear crumpled up the doughnut carton and heaved it straight past Thomas and into the trash can beside his desk—not a touch of rim. "Does it ever occur to you, with your aviator sunglasses and your mini-van and golden retriever, that more and more we have to go after fugitives who are better equipped than we are? Hell, better equipped than the Israeli army. Are you the one who's trained to do that?"

Guerrera hustled back out of Miller's office, handing Tim a warm fax. "Word back on stolen cars near the dump. Two vehicles were taken from the area that night. An Escalade and a Camry." As Tim glanced at the makes, models, and plate numbers, Guerrera said, "You're thinking the Escalade?"

"The Camry. Less conspicuous."

Tim handed the fax to Maybeck, who said, "Not if he's on the West Side."

"Would you get this to Dispatch, have them put out a BOLO on both vehicles? Did you get us an address for Walker's ex?"

Guerrera said, "Zim's on it."

Zimmer nodded. "Kaitlin Jameson. Sorry, got tied up with that DEA fugitive out of Georgia. I'll pull you an address right now."

"Did you talk to Tess's boss?"

"Dentist?" Guerrera said. "Nice woman, couldn't offer much. She said Tess had been on edge, but she chalked it up to her kid. I guess she had a sick son."

"Tess's kid?" A one-second lag as Tim cast his mind back to the name in Tess's letter. "*Sammy.* Where is he now?"

"Don't know."

"Can we find out? And what happened with Tess's shrink?"

"The usual," Guerrera said. "I reached a couple of counseling centers in the area, patient confidentiality, blah blah blah. That nut ain't worth the cracking time, *socio*."

"Did you get Tess's autopsy?"

"He handed the job off to me." In his best Billy Bob Thornton, Denley added, "Ah like them purty pictures, mm-hm." He scurried off. "Lemme grab the file."

The door banged open, and Dray strode in, Tyler koala-hooked to a hip, her other arm pinning down an investigation file.

"You got it?" Tim asked.

"I got more than that." Dray set Tyler down, slapping fives and exchanging hugs with some of the guys. Ty promptly crawled over and undid Bear's shoelaces.

Denley watched Tyler with a smile. "How is the little man?"

"Handful." Dray snatched the autopsy report from Denley. "What's this?" She started to thumb through it as Tyler sat on Tim's shoe, affixing himself to his leg.

One of the transfers—a mustached kid out of the Cincinnati office—said, "That contains some pretty gruesome photos, ma'am."

She looked up from the open file. A few of the deputies chuckled. Denley raised his eyebrows and stepped back from the line of fire.

"During both of my C-sections, I had my bladder in my lap," Dray said. "Don't tell me about gruesome."

Zimmer whispered something to the newcomer, who flushed and got busy on a nearby phone. The deputies dispersed, and Dray rolled a chair over, facing Tim, Bear, and Guerrera and executing a behind-the-back blind snatch of the pencil that Tyler's teeth were about to clamp down on.

"The good thing is," she said, "there was an investigation into Tess's death, however superficial, before the suicide ruling closed the matter. Elliott worked the intro between me and the case detective, and so I got a thorough background. First, about the victim: Tess was single—divorced—no relationship to speak of, not much money. She had a very ill seven-year-old son, some kind of genetic disorder. Bad news. She picked up an accounting degree online after he was diagnosed and went from a waitress gig to running a dentist's office. If I were prone to drawing conclusions, I might say she was seeking ways to maximize her income to pay for the kid's medical treatment. And if I were a chauvinist, I might point out that there are some money-generating activities that can lead to pregnancy, but then I'd have to offend myself, so I won't."

Bear said, "Not married, knocked up, broke, desperate, sick kid—it adds up to a convincing suicide."

"Convincing?" Guerrera said. "I don't believe a woman who was pregnant would commit suicide." His accent got stronger with the machismo.

"How many times you been pregnant?" Dray asked. "Not as much fun as it looks. Now, the good news is the pregnancy bought us a more thorough investigation, as we see here." She tapped the autopsy file with her short-trimmed nails. "The detective dotted his *i*'s, wanting to keep anyone from crying Laci. It was an early-term, seven weeks, so Tess likely knew about it, though from interviews on file, no one else did. Obviously, if we could find the—and I use the term in its strict zoological sense—'father,' we'd be in good shape, but the detective got nowhere on that either, so for now I'll put it on my wish list next to 'Footage of Suicide.' "

One of Zimmer's prostitute informants hustled past them toward his desk.

"Lady haff short dress," Tyler observed.

Bear craned his neck. "She sure does."

Dray said, "You know what else he likes? Bourbon and unfiltered Luckies." Bear shrugged apologetically, and she continued, "Blood-flow pattern shows she was alive at the time of the shooting, so it's either what it looks like or someone knew what they were doing. She did have gunshot residue on her left hand. As Bear pointed out, there's a good case to be made for a suicide. But here's what I *don't* like. One: no suicide note. As we all know, women—*especially* women with kids—leave notes. If only to register their final complaints."

Tyler held out his arms, and when Tim hoisted him into his lap, he rested his soft, warm head in the hollow of Tim's neck and curled a tiny fist around Tim's thumb. Tim tipped his nose to the downy white hair, caught the scent of no-tears shampoo.

Dray continued, "Problem two: She seemed to have a very close rela-tionship with her son, but she left her body for him to find. She made some arrangements for the night of—he was at a sleepover up the street—so why let him walk home and see the aftermath?"

"Maybe it was a fuck-you to the kid," Denley called out from his desk. "His condition's wearing her down or something."

"Like that metalhead in Calabasas," Bear added. "Shot himself in front of the Christmas tree."

"That's right—more male," Dray said. "Females tend more passive-aggressive and considerate. They prefer the rented motel room, the laid-down shower curtain, even, so no one has to clean up after them."

Tyler started fussing, straddling Tim's thigh and sliding around like a boneless chicken. Tim set him down. "Was the gun she used regis-tered to her?"

"I'm not done counting yet," Dray said. "Three: slightly odd angle for the shot. Judging from the spatter and the drainage, her head had to have been turned so her chin was parallel to her shoulder. Not impossible cer-tainly, but why?" Tyler squirmed on the floor, babbling something, and she replied, "I know, baby, I'm hungry, too. We'll have some Goldfishies in a minute. Four: The detective found a red smudge at the curb outside her house above a sewer grate. Bright red." She moved some stacks to the floor, clearing space on the workstation, and then set down the investiga-tion file and produced a few crime-scene photos. A splotch of vivid red stood out against the white concrete. Perspective shots located the mark at the curbside edge of the neighbor's house, in front of a stand of juni-per. A good lurking site.

"Looks like model paint, almost," Tim said.

"They took it to the lab on the off chance it proved to be blood. The results were weird. It contained, among other things, food ingredients"—biting her lip, she flipped through some pages, using her leg to shield Tyler from crawling under her chair—"sweetener and gelatin. It was still wet the night of. The detective thought whatever it was, it might have come from the shooter's vehicle. The neighbor remembered a car parked there, but nothing more. She just saw shadows and a big hood orna-ment."

"A Rolls?" Tim offered. "Jag, maybe? What?"

"Dunno. She said *bigger* than normal ornaments, like the size of a bowling ball. But she's about a hundred and eighteen years old, so I'm not too excited about her account."

"Where's the evidence?"

"In the storage locker at the lab."

"We'll get Aaronson on the stain, see if he can pull a rabbit for us. Now, the gun—"

"Yes, it was registered to her. A Glock 19."

"I'd expect her to have a revolver. Easier."

Bear nodded at Tim's Smith & Wesson wheel gun, snug in the holster. "Not everyone's stuck in the 1860s, Rack."

"She's a gun gal," Dray said. "Which means the gunshot-residue analysis on her hand is inconclusive. She had an ammo card for the Littlerock Canyon Gun Club, which showed she'd shot there just the day before. In his statement the range operator there said she's pretty good, learned from her brother in the marines."

Guerrera finished with the autopsy glossies and passed them to Tim. A pale version of the face Tim had first seen gummed to the wall of Walker's cell. Strong residual powder burns and a star-shaped hole at the left temple indicated that the muzzle had been touching the flesh. Her features had been pressed out of shape by the explosion—nothing obvious, but a subtle shifting of the position of the nose, the levelness of the eyes, the cant of the mouth—a minuscule yet grotesque reskewing that spoke to the destruction beneath.

Tim set down the close-up of the entry wound as if dealing a card. " 'The left side.' "

Bear shrugged, unimpressed. "Maybe. What would that tell Walker, though?"

Tim flashed on Tess's Swatch in her photo, ringing her right wrist. The smudged handwriting on the letter she'd sent to Walker. The criminalist had confirmed that she was left-handed, the entry wound unremarkable in that regard. "Nothing, I guess."

Tess's voice had come through in her letter to her brother; she'd impressed Tim as a decent, struggling woman saddled with responsibilities and trying to carve out a niche for her son and herself. He felt a welling of sadness as he studied the close-ups, the tiny details that composed her. Hair died in a streak pattern, amber against chestnut. Dark roots. Gray threads at the hairline. Slender nose, slightly concave on either side. The fingernail of her right index finger was shorter than the others, a break that she'd taken care to file the edge off. Bare feet. A varicose vein touching the ankle.

Zimmer's voice broke him out of his reverie. "I got you that address for Kaitlin Jameson." He slid a piece of notebook paper over Tim's shoulder.

Tim glanced at it. The background noise dimmed, crowded out by his sudden focus. He set the notebook sheet down beside the top page of Tess's investigation file, looked from one to the other, then turned them to face Dray and Bear.

The address in Zimmer's hand was identical to the one on the crime-scene report.

Chapter 32

Wearing a light cotton Tommy Bahama camp shirt against the balmy August night and a pair of leather slide huaraches, Ted Sands whistled through his teeth as he strolled from his Cheviot Hills house en route to his eight o'clock poker game. His third child, an '88 Bronco geared for off-roading and rock crawling, waited in the driveway. With its custom geared-down axles, widened rims kicking out the tread a few inches on either side, hybrid suspension with three inches of lift, and flared wheel wells accommodating thirty-five-inch Mud Terrain tires, the Bronco was too wide to fit in the garage with his wife's Chrysler Pacifica.

Stopping on the walk, Ted picked up a melted army man and a discarded Barbie sundress and tossed them back at the front step. He had the type of gym-enhanced build common in L.A., heavy on biceps and quads, with more muscle definition than could be achieved without kidney-straining supplements. As a third-string quarterback at a Division One college, he'd learned the art of physical upkeep without having to endure the rigors of injury. The sole nondoctor, -lawyer, or –studio exec on his tree-lined block, he moved across his front lawn with confidence, the erect stride of the proud homeowner.

He pressed the "unlock" button on his key chain, and the Bronco greeted him with a friendly chirp. Spinning the keys around his finger, he paused a few feet from the truck. A folded note fluttered from the tinted driver's window, Scotch-taped, his name rendered in red ink.

He turned a quick circle, laughing in anticipation of a practical joke, but his front yard and the street were empty. A neighbor passed in a Lexus with a tooted greeting, and he waved before returning his attention to the note. He took a step forward, plucked it from the window, and opened it.

Puzzled, he stared down at the blank interior.

A pair of hands shot out from beneath the truck, the left clamping over the top of his foot, the right, which held an unfolded knife, hooking around the heel. Before Ted could move, the blade drew back toward the undercarriage shadows, carving around the rear of his ankle and severing the Achilles tendon. Spurting blood made a soft tapping noise against the driveway. Ted bent, hands shoved to his thighs, emitting a breathy, incredulous moan. The blank note fluttered to the concrete, blood soaking through it in spots. Ted turned to run toward the house, but his right leg didn't respond, and he fell flat on his chest, still unable to find his voice. The hands seized him around both calves, dragging him beneath the Bronco. Limbs rattled against the oil pan.

The brief struggle ended with a thud.

Propped in an uncomfortable sitting position, a cramp vise-gripping his lower back, Ted came to in a dank room. A thickness had seized his legs, which were extended before him, and his head throbbed. He groaned and struggled to move his arms. A lamp hooked to a workbench ten feet away provided meager lighting. Scattered tools, a bundle of antique rifles, a few powdery bags of rapid-set concrete. He strained to look behind him; his body wouldn't obey, but he managed to twist his neck. A roll-up door had been raised, revealing the silhouette of his beloved Bronco outside. The spare tire swing-arm carrier had been released, the tailgate laid open. Two strips of aluminum formed a loading ramp, extending down from the truck's well-advertised cargo space.

A clicking jerked him back around. A form crouched just past his feet, where moments before there had been mere darkness. His night vision was starting to kick in, enough for him to make out the glint of a knife. With a thumb and forefinger, the figure raised the folding steel blade from its handle, then let it snap back into place. The knife, a wicked-looking compression-lock Spyderco, featured a hollow-ground blade, hump-spined with a thumb hole, and a precision-drilled titanium handle, multiperforated for lightness and balance. Ted had come across similar models in some of his shady "security" dealings, generally in the hands of word-of-mouth referrals with extensive unspecified training. The man holding him was the real deal, not like the tough-guy producers, playboy entrepreneurs, and gun-waving pseudogangstas–cum–record producers who generally paid his mortgage. He looked down and saw the reason he couldn't move his legs or feet.

They were sunk into concrete.

The block encased him to the waist, as if he were sitting in a half-filled bath. He shouted and jerked his arms, but his hands had also been immersed in the gray mass, the ragged mouths of the entries cutting into his wrists. Oddly, he and the block rolled a few inches back before striking something that halted their motion. Recollection crashed in on him—the bite at his ankle, his fingernails snapping as he was pulled backward across the driveway, devoured by the shadows beneath the truck. When he refocused, the man was down on a knee, winding black tape around the laces of one boot. The man picked up a hand mallet and hammer and advanced on him. Ted strained and thrashed but could barely rock his powerful torso. The mallet clinked into position. Ted closed his eyes and bellowed.

A bang. A clatter of wood on the floor.

Tentatively, he took a glimpse. The man had knocked free one of the forming boards from around the concrete block. A few steps and the man disappeared behind him. Another bang shocked Ted upright, and a second board fell free. He tried to talk, to reason, but his throat had chalked up, issuing only rasps. The man proceeded with his quiet, measured pacing and hammering until only the block and Ted remained, centered on what he now saw was a carpeted dolly.

Frantic, he sought the man in the darkness. He was crouched again, just beyond Ted's immobilized feet, wrapping what appeared to be heavy-test fishing line around a spool as if he were drawing in a kite.

"Wh . . ." Ted panted a few times, as if readying for a charge. "Who are you?"

The voice—deep and maddeningly calm: "Walker Jameson. Ring a bell?"

"No. Not really."

Walker focused on his task, continuing to take up the fishing line. "Jameson," he said. "Think hard."

Rising heat set Ted's cheeks tingling. "I'll tell you everything."

"Yeah," Walker said, "you will."

Chapter 33

Kaitlin opened the door, smoothing down a poof of bed head and yawning. Bizarrely, her face was labeled with rectangular stickers— CHEEK on her cheek and HARELINE pasted to her upper forehead. She glanced at Tim in the dim porch light, started, then clutched the rumpled fabric of her waitstaff vest above her heart. "Sorry. You look like someone I—"

She caught herself, ignoring Tim's questioning gaze. She glanced at her watch, digital glow reading 9:34 P.M. "I, uh, dozed off."

Bear stepped from behind Tim, holding his star apologetically at his hip as if brandishing a weapon he was loath to use. "We're deputy marshals, ma'am, and—"

The label on the back of her hand, which read, predictably, BACK OF HAND, caught her attention, and she said quietly, "*Oh,* no. Are there . . . ?"

Tim and Bear nodded, and her hand rose to her face, finding the labels and peeling them off with a grimace that suggested smarting. She pivoted. *"Sammy!"* she yelled.

The interior was dark, but a boy's voice muttered something from the ratty couch. She stepped back from the door, leaving it ajar in implicit invitation, and they entered. Kaitlin made exasperated noises as she took in the labels covering most objects in sight. REFRIGARATOR. TABLE. PICKURE FRAME. Tim stared at the floor to hide his smile. FLOOR! it proclaimed.

He and Bear stood awkwardly by the door while Kaitlin spoke with annoyance to Sam. Tim heard him reply, "But it shows I *liked* it."

Tim glanced around the tiny walk-through kitchen to their right. The new fridge seemed out of place given the peeling starburst linoleum and the aluminum foil pressed to the window seams to hold the heat. A browning chrysanthemum on the tiled window ledge drooped in its plastic pot, a pitchforked note reading, *To Tess, the* best *office manager.* A coffee-cup ring had worn through the small table's varnish. Reminders of the dead, everywhere. Tim recalled the first year after Ginny's murder, how he ran into her in every room, how the step stool by her sink or a Krazy straw in a kitchen drawer would pull him up short.

He and Bear ought to be able to uncover more here than they'd gleaned from the elderly neighbor. Millie Kensington had reiterated her memory of the car, glimpsed at night through the junipers outside her bedroom. Low-rider. Bowling-ball hood ornament. It had been a hot night—her hip acting up—so her window had been open, or she wouldn't even have heard it pull up. When Tim had asked what kind of car, she'd replied, "Why, gasoline, I'd imagine." Afterward Tim had bent over the curb between houses, his flashlight picking up the last faded blush of the red spot on the concrete. A calling card? A mark the shooter left behind?

Kaitlin, who'd grown less stern in the face of Sam's contrition, called Tim and Bear into the living room. She clicked on a light, revealing the thin form curled up on the cushions. Despite Sam's yellow sclera and jaundiced skin, Tim placed the features immediately—Vector's AAT deficiency poster child. "Hey. I recognize you from TV."

Sam's breathing was raspy, his voice lethargic. "I'm huge in Germany."

Tim laughed. "I bet. Was it fun? Shooting a commercial?"

Sam, weathered veteran of moderate fame, shrugged listlessly. "It was pretty cool. We got to ride in a limo and everything."

Bear cleared his throat and addressed Kaitlin. "I'm sorry to bring up what may be a tough topic, but—"

"I saw he escaped last night," Kaitlin said.

"Yes, and we thought maybe we could talk to you alone for—"

Sam shoved himself upright on the couch, eyes fixed on Tim's holster. "That a Smith & Wesson?"

"Yup."

Bear, to Kaitlin: "Have you seen or heard from him?"

She shook her head.

Again, from the couch: "Why don't you have a semiauto?"

Tim went into his rote explanation. "Only four rounds are exchanged on average in a gunfight, and since I'm more comfortable with the weighting—" He saw Bear looking at him: Do you need to be medicated?

Bear, flustered and evidently unaware of the hour, tried an inane tack. "Wanna play outside, give us a chance to talk to your mom?"

Sam said, "She's not my mom."

"Right. Can we talk to her anyway?"

Together Tim and Kaitlin said, "It's late."

"Sammy, why don't you go play video games?" Kaitlin offered.

A sigh and a slide from the couch. Sam blew his overgrown bangs from his eyes. "*Aa*-right."

"Eat something," she said, then quoted him even as he replied: "I'm not hungry." He giggled, and she added, "I know. Drink a Pediasure."

"Sick of 'em."

"Have a bowl of cereal. And add MCT."

He trudged off to the kitchen cartoonishly, shoulders slumped.

Kaitlin cast an awkward glance at Tim and Bear. "It's an oil we have to put in his food to give it more calories."

Tim said, "From his commercial it sounds like Vector's doing great stuff."

"For other kids," Kaitlin said. "They dropped Sammy from the trial group. Downsized him."

Tim felt Bear's eyes pull to him, but he kept his gaze on Kaitlin. "When?"

Her hand tapped the pager at her waist, checking it, a nervous habit. "A couple months ago. Then, a week later, his mother killed herself. I think he's doing okay for all that."

Again Bear shot Tim a glance from over the top of his notepad.

Tim asked, "You're his guardian?"

Kaitlin nodded. Down the hall a door thumped shut. Emotion or exhaustion seemed to catch up to her at that moment. "He's a special kid, such a special kid, and I'm in charge of him. Because no one else was around to do it. Not one family member was clamoring, so I got okayed. Me, with my credentials." Her voice dropped to a hoarse, almost scared whisper. "But it's a lot of work."

"Tess didn't have any other family?"

An unmistakable hint of anger—"None she trusted, I guess." Kaitlin seemed made uncomfortable by the silence, so she continued, "We'd stayed in touch a bit, and then regularly after Sammy was diagnosed. Sammy and I . . . well, I guess we took to each other."

"He's lucky."

"I'm not able to . . ." She shook off the thought, then looked down the hall toward Sam's room, her face warming through the sadness. "*I'm* lucky."

"When's the last time you saw Walker?" Bear asked.

"Not in years. We separated."

"Not divorced? How'd it happen?"

"He went to Iraq and came back but never really came back. You know? It was different than his other stints, Iraq. He never took the armor off after that." A faint laugh. "The stint in Leavenworth off the incoming flight didn't much help matters."

"I'm sorry to pry, but was there any domestic violence?" Tim asked.

"Walk never hit me, no. Drank some. Got ugly from time to time—words, you know how it gets—but he never laid a hand."

"Did he know Sam?"

"No. Walk and Tess drifted some after Tess got married, then he was gone most always. Deployed. I doubt Walker'd even recognize Sammy if you put 'em in the same room."

"Do you mind if we take a look at her room? Maybe ask Sam a question or two?"

She looked briefly worried, a mother's protectiveness. "One or two. Don't push him—he's got an active imagination. Tess's room is the last one on the left. Go ahead. I'm just gonna straighten up out here some." With a wry grin, she added, "Peel some labels."

Sam had created a sign for his door with crayons and construction paper. SAMS ROOM. PRIVATE PRIVATE PRIVATE. NOONE ALLOWED WITHOUT NOCKING. Tim heeded the warning, rapping his knuckles against the flimsy wood.

"Come in." Sam sat on the floor, face tilted back to take in the TV on his bureau. The bowl of cereal sat to one side, the milk all but absorbed. On-screen, a would-be sleazeball took a Bonnie and Clyde fusillade to his critical mass. Game cartridges littered the floor. Champions of Norrath. WWF Smackdown. Devil May Cry 3.

"I've got a few questions for you, Sam," Tim said. "Is that okay?"

Sam paused the game, a feature Tim wished they'd had on Frogger back in the day. Bear hung back in the hall as Tim showed Sam Walker's photo.

"Do you know who this guy is?" Sam studied it, then shook his head. Tim said, "It's your uncle. We need to know if you've seen him."

Sam's eyes went to Tim's gun. "You're gonna kill him."

"Not if I can help it."

Bear opened Tess's door up the hall, and Sam's features shifted. "Are you going in Mom's room?"

"Yeah, but we'll be respectful of her stuff." It took a moment for Tim to decipher the apprehension on Sam's face. "Would you like us to keep the door closed while we're in there?"

Sam nodded, relieved. Tim headed into the next room, securing the door behind him. Bear was standing before a patch of bleached carpet, looking at a scrubbed blob of wall. A dark eye stared out from the dry-wall where a criminalist had dug out the slug. The smell of cleaning chemicals burned the back of Tim's throat. Sam's scared look had been sudden, acute, traumatized. He was living with more than just a potentially fatal illness. The headboard of his bed backed on the wall that had once borne his mother's brain spatter.

The plastic underwear drawers, spread-out toiletries, and photos shoved into the mirror frame reminded Tim of a dorm room. The folding closet doors were permanently laid open, broken in the tracks. Clothes seemed to bulge out of the shoulder-wide space. A rack held a collection of exhausted footwear, and Tim could see where Tess had used Magic Marker to touch up her shoes. Atop a world-weary Converse sat the empty holster the cops had left behind.

Tim zeroed in on the rickety bookcase right away, looking for materials from the company that had dropped Walker's nephew. Medical books crowded the shelves, journal articles cramming the gaps. Beneath a well-thumbed dictionary of medical terminology were some stray letters, including one in which Tess requested information from Vector's study director. She'd sought out the company, it seemed, as a last-ditch treatment option for her son.

One shelf down Tim found a report, its cover featuring the familiar Vector logo, a *V* with an arrow capping the second vertical like a directive to scale the evolutionary ladder. Onward and upward. Tim showed off the fancy print job.

Bear said, "We connect Walker to Vector, we've got some traction."

Inside, Tim found a report on something called Xedral, a "viral vector," Tess's notes painstakingly written in the narrow margins. *X4-AAT unknown side effects? Why Lentidra fall off map? Outliers included in stats?* Clearly she'd poured her energy into researching the treatment. She must've been devastated when Vector eliminated Sam from the trial—another possible suicide motive. Among the stray papers stuffed into the report, Tim found no notification of Sam's termination.

Pulling books, Tim checked the scraps of paper she'd used as bookmarks. After coming across a few magazine subscription cards and a torn grocery list, Tim hit upon a business card, used to mark a page in a primer on liver disease. CHAISSON KAGAN. CEO. VECTOR BIOGENICS. A Westwood address and a 310 area code. Another number handwritten on the back.

The videotape beside the primer had a KCOM spine sticker. Sam's sloppy hand labeled the tape, *My News Segmint.* Tim slid it out and walked to the next room, disrupting Sam's video game once again. "This is yours, right? Mind if I borrow it?"

"Go ahead. It's just a copy. They sent me a couple to give to other kids without a gene. But I don't know any."

"I'll get it back to you as soon as we're done."

"'Kay. Thanks. For asking, I mean. Other people just do whatever they want."

"Other people?"

"The cops, I mean. Right after."

Tim looked at him. A moment's pause.

Sam said, "What are you guys doing anyways?"

"Just getting some more information about your mom's death."

"Two months later?"

"That's right." Tim returned to Tess's room, again closing the door behind him.

A triangular desk in the corner held an antique computer monitor and a cordless phone. The drawers contained Tess's receipts and bills, which were clearly if not logically organized. Tim pulled the file holding the phone bills and set it aside on the bed—they'd ask Guerrera to start following up on the numbers she'd called in the months before her death. A checkbook showed an account that scraped the double digits several times a month.

Tim wandered into the bathroom. The ledge above the sink held a roll-on Lady Mitchum, a bottle of folic acid tablets, and a well-wrung tube of Aquafresh. Taking the bottle of pills, he went back over to the desk and sat in the tiny rolling chair, the ovoid wooden backrest of which doubled as a belt rack. He dug through the envelope stuffed with receipts from June, then moved on to May. Near the top he found a Sav-On receipt that contained what he was looking for. *May 28. Folic acid—$12.99.*

The bottle advertised a hundred 400-microgram tablets. He spilled those remaining on the bedspread and counted them. For both of Dray's pregnancies, she'd taken folic acid every day of her first term. Tim counted the pills. Eighty-eight remained, which meant that she'd likely taken one a day, including the morning of June 8 when she'd died. Not necessarily the sort of long-term planning one would expect from a woman about to put a bullet through her skull.

He called Bear over and explained the incongruity to him while Bear poked at a tablet in his sweaty palm, regarding the prenatal supplement uncomfortably, as he might a feminine napkin.

"Okay, but we don't really bank on the presuicidal to act rationally. Or to plan in advance. Especially, I'd guess, pregnant presuicides." Bear sank thoughtfully into the tiny rolling chair, which gave off a moribund creak and collapsed. He fell back, arm striking the desk, bouncing the keyboard in the air and turning on the computer. As he rose and made a big show of dusting himself off with reserved dignity, Tim stifled his laughter, knowing how inappropriate it would sound emanating from Tess's room.

Bear said, "Hang on."

"I'm trying."

"No, check this out." Bear gestured him over to the monitor. Save a hard-drive icon, the screen was blank. Bear double-clicked the icon, opening an empty file. No programs, no documents, no applications. He thunked to his knees on the tangle of belts, examining the computer tower jammed beneath the desk. He ran his thumb across a row of tiny scratches on the beige plastic. "Clever fucker replaced the hard drive." He moved to withdraw, banging his head, and then managed to reverse his broad frame from the cramped space. "Someone purged the computer but left it. Couldn't steal it because that would've raised robbery-murder suspicions."

Despite his excitement Tim played devil's advocate. "Unless she had the hard drive replaced herself."

Bear lumbered toward the door. "I'll ask the kid."

In the quiet of the empty room, Tim sat where Tess had sat when the bullet had entered her head.

The left side.

He turned, getting his body position correct to match the spatter from the crime-scene photos. A bit awkward but, as Dray had noted, certainly possible. He turned his head another inch and raised an imaginary pistol to his left temple. His attention snagged on one of the belts Bear had knocked to the carpet. Two distinct indentations about three inches apart notched the width of the brown leather.

He froze, staring at the familiar grooves. Standing, he went to the closet, picked up the empty holster. He pulled his own holster off his belt and slid Tess's on. The spring clip clamped down on his belt, matching the indentations.

Tess's bloodless hand in the autopsy photo had shown a filed nail on the right index finger, shorter than the rest. It wasn't a repaired break, as he'd thought; Tess kept it cut, as Dray did hers, so it wouldn't catch in the trigger guard.

Knowing of Tess's left-handedness, the killer had made the logical—and incorrect—assumption. Three words—"the left side"—had told Walker all he'd needed to know. A right-handed shooter would not leave a suicide bullet wound in her left temple.

The image of Tess at gunpoint, being posed suicide style by her killer, brought forth in Tim a familiar wrath. What had the killer threatened her with to get her to sit still? To hold her position? What thoughts had run through her head in her final seconds of life once she'd grasped the inevitable?

Bear returned. "The kid says she used that computer every day, and there were no repairs—" He halted in the doorway, taking in the empty holster fastened to Tim's belt. He blinked twice, the cogs meshing. *"No,"* he said. "Really?"

Tim held up a hand, still aligning the remaining pieces. Walker's First Force Recon photo, his rifle slung right to left. The effortless right-hand stab into Boss's neck.

Bear yanked the door shut behind him. "But Tess was left-handed. Why would she shoot right?"

"Because her right-handed brother taught her to shoot."

Bear's whistle dropped from high to low. "We'll get it reopened as a homicide."

"Looks like someone already beat us to the punch."

"Yup. Great." Bear ran his hand over his weary face, tugging his jowls even lower. "So what's next?"

Chapter 34

Lights killed, the oversize Bronco idled beneath an overhang of pepper tree branches, Ted Sands's complaints from the cargo area muffled by a gag. Walker had taken care to dress Ted's visible half appropriately—dinner jacket, bow tie, starched shirt, even a white handkerchief teased into view. Important to observe proper etiquette. Sounds of the party trickled up the unreasonably broad street, reaching Walker at the steering wheel. Of all the Bel Air estates he'd passed, the Kagan mansion had the grandest setback, a rambling garden decorated with stone walls, trickling fountains, koi-stocked ponds, and a leisurely walk that diverged into loops before widening into a circular, bench-fringed patio about ten yards from the imposing front door of the main house.

It was a quarter past ten, and from the jazzish tunes and conversational hum pouring over the house with the glow of strung Asian lanterns, the backyard party was in full swing. The valets remained around the corner, their station positioned before the south entrance's adorned gates that led to the bash. Deliveries to the rear kitchen off the service road appeared to have slowed. The house front, a classic two-story rise, didn't seem of a particular style. Like its neighbors, it just seemed mansiony.

And right now it seemed quiet.

Keeping the Bronco's lights off, Walker accelerated up the dark street, braking sharply at the top of the walk. He got out, his slamming door renewing Ted's stifled pleas. Moving briskly, efficiently, Walker swung out the carrier and opened the tailgate, leaning the two aluminum strips into place. Encased in his concrete block atop the flatbed dolly, Ted jounced down the ramp. Hands on his shoulders, Walker pushed him, jerking in his mold and yelling into a mouthful of balled cotton, up the front walk. At the circular patio, Walker dumped the block off the dolly, the weight of it cracking the flagstone.

He stood over Ted, wide-stanced. A jerk of his wrist and the steel blade flicked out from the handle. "Hold this." Walker spun the knife, reclaimed it in a fist, and punched it down into the dense muscle of Ted's shoulder. Bellowing, veins raised in his flushed neck, Ted fought to free his hands but succeeded only in rebreaking the scabs ringing his wrists.

Walker pulled a grenade from one of his many cargo pockets, and the whites of Ted's eyes seemed to dilate. Ted fought desperately to say something. Walker pulled out his gag. Before Ted could scream, Walker rammed the grenade in his mouth and secured it with electrical tape, which he double-wound around Ted's head. Ted was screaming now, the noise no louder than the distant beat of the swing number struck up by the band.

Walker jogged up the wide steps to the massive porch. Dark strips of plexi-coating showed at the edges of the windowpanes—they were bullet-resistant. He saw deep into the house, past the dark front rooms. In the kitchen an imperious catering captain paced before her cowed waitstaff, barking orders, Patton gone gourmet. A plastered guest loosed his cummerbund and headed into a restroom.

Unspooling a few feet of fishing line, Walker tied an improvised clinch knot around the well-polished brass door handle and rang the bell. An exclamation from within.

The monofilament let out with a zip as he moved swiftly back down the walk. Ted stopped fighting the block once Walker slipped a finger through the grenade pin sticking up above the band of electrical tape. He tugged the knife from Ted's shoulder, freeing a blood flow that saturated the ivory polyester of the dinner jacket. Cutting the fishing line from the spool, he tied the end to the grenade ring.

A shrill, barely audible voice from the house: "Edwin, I don't know why, but someone's arrived at the *front* door."

Walker set his full weight behind a boot and shoved the block back a few screeching inches, bringing the line taut. Ted leaned forward as far as the concrete would allow, but still Walker could've strummed a high C on the razor-straight line.

Ted hyperventilated in pained grunts, snot flaring from his nostrils, eyes fixed on the burgundy front door.

From inside came the officious approach of heels on marble.

Walker nudged Ted's bow tie straight, drew himself up, and stared down at Ted's contorted form. "In ten seconds your head will explode."

He flashed off, his jungle boots slapping the flagstone.

Chapter 35

Tim crouched over the blown-wide mass of flesh protruding from the neck. A chunk clung to a strip of seared electrical tape. "We ain't getting a dental."

Bear flipped back the tattered jacket, worked free a slim leather bill-fold, and laid it open. "Ted Sands, if we believe this."

They'd blocked off the street, but at the cordon the TV-crew lights made it look like dawn. The tux- and gown-clad guests had made a mass exodus, swarming the valets by the south gates like penguins jockeying for cliff position above shark-infested waters. Roped through metal eyelets to the gnarled oak overlooking the black-bottomed pool, a huge vinyl sign featuring the ubiquitous Vector *V* had commanded Tim and Bear's attention as they'd helped usher the guests from the backyard.

The connection between their fugitive and the biogenics firm looked clear, a line that ran through the ailing liver of a seven-year-old boy. Walker had clearly uncovered some link between Tess's murder and Vector. But how did the pregnancy fit, if at all? And the missing hard drive?

It had taken a few tries for Tim and Bear to find a Kagan underling able to forgo buzzwords and talk in layman's terms. The party had been a celebration for the filing of Vector's S-1, they'd learned, which meant that the SEC-required prospectus for the stock issuance had been approved, putting Vector on the fast track to going public. Dean remained

174

holed up in the main house with his sons and security chief. Tim and Bear had yet to make his acquaintance.

Tannino headed up the front walk, still ruffled from running the media gauntlet at the cordon. Word of Walker's involvement had leaked. A high-profile murder by a high-profile fugitive at a high-sticker-price house in Bel Air—the incident combined all that was lurid and worth holding an audience's attention between commercials. The press explosion, Tim knew from experience, only heralded grander coverage to come. Tannino waved off Guerrera and Denley, both approaching with requests, and paused over Tim and Bear, taking in the remains of the day with the expression of irritated disgust he generally reserved for the inedible sack lunches his wife devoutly packed for him.

"Spitting distance from the Playboy mansion and Aaron Spelling's estate," Tannino pronounced. "Can you imagine the VIP phone calls I'm gonna have to field? For the love of Mary." He debated spitting but caught himself, refocusing on the flesh-and-concrete sculpture that had been Ted Sands. "That his jaw?"

"No," Bear said. "Here. I think."

Tannino's dark eyes shifted to observe Tim. "We jumped him to a Top Fifteen and set up a task force. Your command post is on the third floor. Say 'I told you so' and I'll stick you on court duty and put Thomas in charge."

Tim raised a hand, a silent, appreciative wave, and Tannino headed back to the tungsten-halogen lights at the cordon, muttering to himself about vultures. Bear finished rooting through Ted Sands's wallet but came up with nothing except a stack of crisp twenties and a few credit cards.

Aaronson scurried over, gripping two chisels of different sizes. "Please let us process that first, George."

Bear sighed and dropped the wallet into Ted's concrete lap. "Sure thing."

Aaronson frowned, then peeled something off Tim's back and handed it to him. Tim looked at the familiar label-maker lettering—DEPUTY MARSHILL—and couldn't suppress a half grin.

Aaronson shrugged at him and returned his attention to the sullied wallet. LAPD's Homicide would catch the murderer, but, for consistency's sake, Tim had pulled some strings to grant Aaronson's team from Sheriff's the crime scene. Tim's first move back at the command post would be to assimilate Aaronson into the task force to get around any future jurisdictional jockeying. Tim touched the criminalist's thin arm and asked, "Did you reprocess that evidence from Tess Jameson's suicide that wasn't a suicide?" Aaronson still seemed distracted by the wallet Bear had tainted, so Tim gave his arm a little shake.

"In the past two hours? Yeah, right after I repainted the Hollywood sign. Come on, Rack. We've obviously hooked into a whale on this one—we need time to do it right. Now, let me free Galatea here." Aaronson settled down with his tools, ignoring Tim's questioning glance.

Tim crossed to Bear and Guerrera in a huddle on the shadowy fringe of the crime scene. "Who's Galatea?"

"I think a midfielder for Real Madrid," Guerrera said.

Bear watched the criminalists work, his lips rolled forward over his teeth. A chisel stroke went awry, landing wetly. "He's got a base somewhere," he said. "This took planning and privacy. Equipment."

"Looks like your boy found his cause," Guerrera said.

Tim watched the bustle of deputies, the stressed-out house staff at the windows, the flying chips of concrete. "He's gonna kill the shooter and anyone else—like maybe Sands—who was on scene to help. If it was a hit, he's gonna kill the guy who paid and the guy who transferred the money. Then he's gonna kill the guy who made the phone call and the guys in the room when he did it."

Bear was regarding him warily. Guerrera asked, "How do you know?"

Tim just looked at him.

"Right." Guerrera bobbed his head in a faint nod.

"Thomas done with the guy who made the positive ID?" Tim asked.

"Yeah, he's holding him so we can firsthand it." He rested a hand on Tim's back and steered him toward the front door.

One of the bartenders who'd gone to an upstairs balcony for a smoke had gotten a good look at Walker when he'd passed under the porch light to ring the doorbell. The witness couldn't see Sands because some branches blocked his view, but he'd heard the explosion.

"You keep him separate from everyone else?"

"Course, *socio*. Kagan's security man was playing Andy Sipowicz before you got here, so Thomas didn't let him near the witness."

Due to all the foot traffic, the front door had been left unlocked. They passed into a grandiose foyer, and Tim took in the furnishings. A classic Bel Air Norma Desmond, complete with curving banister. California Spanish by way of old-line Boston—an odd, May-December relationship. He and Bear followed Guerrera up to the second floor, through a library and two gauzy curtains to a front-facing balcony that seemed to float among the tree branches. Under Thomas's watchful gaze, a kid worked his way through a cigarette before adding it to a mound on the coaster precariously balanced on the railing.

"This is Speedy," Thomas said flatly.

In his early twenties, Speedy had dark blue eyes set in well-tanned skin—Caucasian with a flare of something darker. He was ridiculously handsome, no doubt the best-looking kid in the history of whatever high school he'd graduated from before heeding the siren call of Hollywood and running aground on the rocks of L.A.'s bloated service industry.

Eager to get to Dean Kagan, Tim spoke quickly. "You're positive that's the guy."

Speedy stared at the photo, dwarfed by Bear's hand. "Hundred percent."

"What'd you see?"

"Like I told him"—the head jerk indicated that Speedy and Thomas had not embarked on a cozy friendship in the past fifteen minutes—"just him jogging onto the porch and then away. He wore dark clothes, baggy, like army pants or something. T-shirt, too. I also saw him drive off through the patch in the trees there. An SUV, kinda jacked up—"

"A black Bronco, late eighties?"

Speedy studied Tim with surprise. "Yeah, fits the description. How . . . ?"

"There's one parked a half block that way, along the blind side of the house." Tim pointed north from the balcony at a stretch of visible street. "We passed it coming here. Thomas, can you run over and check a plate for us?"

Thomas gladly left the balcony, the curtains drifting around his vanishing form like a magic-trick effect.

Tim asked, "You work for the catering company?"

"No, I'm full-time here. I'm usually in charge of the cars, you know? But they have a party, I help out. Pays me good and leaves me free for auditions."

Bingo. "You see some other car come from that direction?"

Speedy lit up another cigarette and discharged a cloud of smoke off the balcony. "Just you guys."

"Us guys?"

"A security truck, you know?"

"Not sure I do. Bel Air Patrol? LAPD? What?"

"I don't know, I'm not so hot on security. I just notice the decals and watch my posture." A laugh that didn't get returned. "It was a pickup, like, for one of those shitty family communities out in, say, the West Valley. Shady Hills. Pleasantview. You know the type. I thought it was gonna give pursuit or whatever, but it just kept going all slow."

Tim turned to Guerrera. "Contact all local law enforcement and security companies, see if we get a bite."

"It was kinda weird. I mean, I saw the truck, but then no cops showed up for, like, another ten minutes."

"That's because it was probably this guy"—Bear brandished Walker's scowling booking photo again—"after he switched vehicles around the corner."

Speedy let out a stoned laugh. "No *way*. Smart dude."

The curtains snapped and disgorged a rounded yet powerful man in his late fifties. Chest hair overflowed the notched collar of an expensive Hawaiian shirt, and a faint sunburn colored his cheeks and the flat end of his nose. An East Asian ideogram was tattooed in faded blue on his forearm. The wind wafted a blend of cinnamon and rum off him, cologne-strong, and pressed his shirt to his distended belly, outlining a pistol handle.

He offered Tim a firm grip. "Percy Keating, head of security. We're glad you're here. If you have a minute, Dean Kagan wanted to thank you in person."

They followed him down the sweep of the stairs, up a dim wainscoted corridor decked with dour oils in frames stained to match the molding, and into a study with mallard green walls, a pair of distressed leather club chairs, and knotted slab desk. Percy made introductions from the doorway as if announcing titled nobility at a ball, and no one exchanged salutations beyond slight nods.

Even under the circumstances, Dean Kagan was impeccably put together, the thirty-two-tooth CEO smile, every hair fixed in place despite the rotor blades overhead. "I wanted to let you know we appreciate your quick response, and I give you my assurance that we'd like to cooperate in every way."

"Thanks, that'll help," Tim said. "Can I get your contact information?" The three Kagans produced business cards in short order. "If you wouldn't mind writing your home and cell numbers on the back?"

As Tim collected the cards, Bear asked, "Do any of you know this man?" He handed off Walker's photo to Dolan, who stiffened and passed it to Chase, who finally glanced up from his BlackBerry.

Of the two brothers, Chaisson was more at home, leaning back in his club chair. "This is the guy who—"

Dean's smile firmed.

Chase glanced over the top of the picture next to Percy, who gave a nearly imperceptible nod. "This guy broke into our lab offices today."

Tim knew better than to be surprised. "What happened?"

Chase filled them in. Dolan offered a few embellishments to the story but largely deferred to his brother's version.

"Do you have security footage?"

"In the lobby, yes," Dean said. "But not within the lab. A damn fine idea, though." He nodded at Percy to look into it. So the guy wasn't just house detective after all.

Dolan tipped the photograph to the light. "Who is this guy?"

"Walker Jameson," Tim said. "He broke out of prison last night."

"I read about that," Chase said.

"Do you know Tess Jameson?"

"Doesn't ring a bell."

"You might go through your records." Tim pulled an ivory business card from his pocket. "She had your business card in her bedroom."

"I give away hundreds of business cards a week."

Tim flipped it over. "With your home number written on the back?" He fanned out from behind it the matching card Chase had just jotted on. "In your handwriting?" From the corner of his eye, he saw Kagan the Elder's gaze intensify.

Chase's lips seemed stuck to his smile, but then his hand raised and clapped to a knee. "What can I say? I meet a lot of people, and I don't always remember names."

"How about you, Dolan? Ring a bell?"

"She's the mother of a kid we were going to use in our trial."

Chase snapped his fingers. "That's right. She had a different last name than the kid."

"Had?" Bear asked. "Not has?"

"Killed herself," Dolan said.

"Hold on," Bear said, "you don't remember this woman, but you remember that she killed herself?"

"Walker's her husband?" Dean Kagan broke in.

"Brother."

Dolan was flushed, but the other Kagans' milder reactions of surprise seemed feigned.

"You mentioned her son," Tim said. "Sam Hardy. You used him in your commercials, a KCOM news segment. Why did his name leave the trial list?"

"Ours is the only trial in the world this year for children suffering from AAT deficiency," Dean said. "Every AAT parent wanted in. We had over eight thousand applicants. Sadly, we could only accept a small percentage of the kids."

"But the Vector poster boy?" Tim asked.

Dean pursed his lips thoughtfully. "The selection of trial participants is scientific, Deputy." He paused. "I wish public relations were as well, but it's not."

Tim pressed forward. "Do you know Ted Sands?"

Dean's eyebrows quivered contemplatively, and he looked at Percy.

"He was a former Beacon-Kagan security worker," Percy said. "I hired him myself. He left about a year ago to pursue freelance options."

Dean asked, "Is he the mess in my front yard?" At Bear's nod he said to Percy, "Get to the bottom of this. And quickly. These officers will need all the specifics of his employment with Beacon-Kagan and anything else on him you can assemble."

Already on the job, Percy moved to the door, earnestly but awkwardly poking a handheld.

"A fugitive and a former security guard?" Chase said. "Why's this ending up here?"

Bear said, "We were hoping to defer to your greater knowledge."

"I haven't the damnedest," Dean said. "I run an international conglomerate. That's a lot of employees, and each one of them steps on some toes for the bottom line now and again. I've had threats originating from every state in the union, and quite a few not of this union. Percy can acquaint you with our file of disgruntleds, if you'd like."

"We'd like," Tim said. "And we'd also like the guest list for the party."

"We need to proceed with discretion. To protect the company—and my guests. We're about to launch a product that's a major breakthrough for tens of thousands of kids. It's lifesaving. I don't want us to do anything to threaten it."

"So that's a . . . ?"

Dean smiled. "A gentle no. I don't know about this killer, but our guests are not connected to him. There were some important people here this evening."

Tim and Bear looked at each other. Tim nodded. Bear cleared his throat and said, "In addition to being a deputy marshal, I've been admitted to the bar. So let me explain, since your own legal staff are not in attendance, the legalities of where we're at: Your house, while a private and sumptuous residence, is also a crime scene that figures in a federal investigation. You, your family, and your companies are going to cooperate with that investigation. Your choice—the Marshal can make a phone call, and a federal judge can explain why, in writing. Your attorneys can call their contacts at the office of the attorney general, and we're off to the cock fights. Or we can just get to work. Together. It's timing, really—a matter of wising up before someone else gets turned into folk art on your porch."

"You make a convincing case, Counselor. Change that to a reluctant yes." Dean's unflappable grin remained. "It's a red herring, but you'll get the list. Now, it's been a long night, and this is clearly a topic requiring our alert attention. Why don't you come by the office tomorrow. Noon. I'll have the boys there. The list. And whatever you'll need from Percy's files." He gestured to the door, a man used to directing human traffic. "Anything else?"

"Just that guest list." Tim handed a Service card to Dolan, since he was closest, and said, "Call if anything else goes bump in the night."

An actual butler, who'd been waiting fussily in the wings helplessly regarding the legion of trespassers, saw them out. He closed the door behind them without a farewell, seemingly glad to be sealed back within his domain. Tim and Bear paused at the edge of the porch, surveying the scene. Most of the deputies had cleared out, and the media crowd at the cordon had thinned considerably, leaving the diehards and the paparazzi.

It took four criminalists to lift Ted Sands into the CSI van. Though they'd made some headway with the chisels, Ted still remained in the block, a frozen tobogganer.

The blotch on the flagstones looked like an oil stain.

"Helluva statement," Bear said.

"This isn't a statement," Tim said. "It's an introduction."

They threaded through the remaining cops at the cordon and climbed into Tim's Explorer.

"Of course the old man's gonna be cooperative," Tim said once both doors had shut. "And every button on every phone in that house is lit up right now."

Bear hummed two notes of agreement. "Dispatching flunkies to purge the files at Vector."

"By noon tomorrow they'll have already cleaned house. We can't wait."

"Right. So call Tannino. Get him to wake up some judge."

"I'm driving, you call him."

Bear, looking righteous but increasingly uneasy, got Tannino on the phone and asked for clearance for the subpoena request.

From the driver's seat, Tim could hear the Marshal's voice. "Listen, is the High Plains Drifter with you, or is this your own two A.M. brainstorm?"

"Yeah, Rackley's here."

"You got hands-free?" Bear snapped his Nextel into the speaker cradle as Tannino continued without a pause. "If not, just repeat this as

I go. The judiciary do not construe their role as making our job easier. Sorry—less difficult. The bench sees its duty, vis-à-vis us, thanks to the attorney general and his buddy Chertoff, as defending the rights of citizens. The rights of *certain* citizens have always been particularly fiercely defended. The people you guys just left are not merely rich. They don't just put people in office. They decide who stays in office. And how far forward on the gravy train the officeholders ride. I've already had three calls *at this hour*—one from Sacramento, two from our nation's capital: Houston, Texas—regarding the little speechifying you did in Kagan's study, improvised from your law degree taken at Camarillo Veterinary College. The people calling me are shocked—*shocked*—that we appear to be taking the victims of such a heinous crime into a back room of their own modestly decorated middle-class home and beating them with a rubber hose. The callers assume they can make our lives unpleasant. So the fuck what? Our lives *are* unpleasant. But they can make it nigh on impossible for us to do our jobs."

Bear said, "So that's a no, then?"

"We wouldn't even get to hear a judge *say* no. The AUSA would run circles around us with probable cause. And because the old man's playing it all smiley, Your Honor'll say, 'If he quits cooperating . . .' " Tannino muttered something to his stirring wife, then said, "Don't pick fights you can't win. Until you can win them."

Dial tone.

Bear disconnected the call, looked at Tim. "Thanks. Set up by my partner. Explains why animals always react to you with instinctive hostility."

They passed a few blocks in silence, and then Bear said, "I knew I should've driven."

Chapter 36

Ortiz got off a solid blow, and Kenny Shamrock's nose exploded in red mist. Chase whooped and raised the volume on the plasma as the Ultimate Fighting Championship surged into the fifth round. He sat in the embrace of a soft leather couch in the sunken TV pit, picking absentmindedly at his Gibson—natural finish, spruce top, mahogany sides, rosewood fingerboard, nickel frets, and abalone inlays. A bottle of Johnnie Walker Blue pinned down a magazine on the coffee table on which he propped his feet. His eyes and nostrils had gone pink around the rims, pronounced flares of color against his fair skin.

Dolan paced frenetically behind him in the game room proper, circling the pool table and knocking balls off one another. The spacious area, a converted drawing room on the second floor of the south wing, had been redone in the style of an architectural loft. Composed of a bar, a panel kitchen, a game area, and the conversation pit–cum–lounge, the sleek room joined the brothers' childhood bedroom suites.

Dean had waited until late in life to have children, and Dolan had been the recipient of four years of undivided domestic attention before Dean's long-suffering wife, Mary, had died giving birth to a second son. In a rare touch of sentimentality, Dean gave the baby her maiden name, Chaisson.

With relief Dean had recognized his second son's intensity and charisma and sought to cultivate them further. Chase was strong-willed, daring, at ease in his own body. Slamming doors. Skin lifted at the knuckles. Girls climbing through his window. Over the years Dean managed to keep Chase on course without reining him in. Riding the momentum of a strategically timed Kagan-endowed Business Department chair, Chase had entered USC. In the fall semester of his sophomore year, he'd switched his major from sociology to finance. Dean had overseen the transition, supplying a team of tutors, including a former adviser to the state treasury. Within months, Chase had hit his stride, as Dean always claimed he would. There'd been no slowing him since.

Though tonight was a hell of a shock for them all. After the grenade on the front walk had designated Ted Sands as proxy target, Dean had insisted—with little resistance—that Chase and Dolan move back behind the gates. Concentrating resources had been a mantra of the old man's since back when Beacon was still in the picture.

A plexi-coated bulletproof window (all the better to ease Dean's paranoia) looked out over the back pool. Dolan had undone its various locks and cracked it a few inches, hoping the breeze would evaporate his panic sweat. Honeysuckle had worked its way up the lattice outside, framing the window, the bobbing white flowers scenting the cool inrush of air.

"Did you know Ted Sands?" Dolan asked.

Chase strummed the first four notes of the Fifth with bored irony. "I remember him, sure. Nice guy. Good head on his shoulders." Chase finally turned around. "Oh, come on, that was funny." He whipped a coaster at Dolan, narrowly missing. "Have a drink or something. Christ. It's not good to stress this late at night, D. Especially after dinner. All you're doing is stewing in unused fatty acids."

"Not my predominant concern at the moment."

"Right. Your health pales as a priority next to the boogeyman." Chase feinted a few jabs, leaning with the defending champ though he'd watched the recorded fight at least ten times and knew that Ortiz would finish him with an armlock in the next round. "Listen. The Dean's having Perce beef up security. Jameson does it again, he'll get his nuts shot off." Abruptly, Chase turned off the TV and rose.

"Where you going?"

185

Chase brushed past him, sliding the window open farther and swinging a leg over the sill. "Girl." He waited for the patrolling guard to disappear around the corner below.

"Percy said—"

"Yeah, but Percy doesn't put out." Chase got a toehold in the sturdy lattice, then looked up and grinned. "Old times, huh?" His flexed arm pulled out of view, leaving Dolan to watch the honeysuckle buds shaking with his brother's continued momentum.

Chapter 37

You're not safe here." Kaitlin followed Walker down the hall, over a dozen or so floor-adhered labels reading CARPIT. She grabbed his arm, spinning him around outside Tess's door, speaking an urgent whisper. "There was a deputy poking around."

She produced a card, and Walker paused to take a look. TIM RACKLEY. DEPUTY U.S. MARSHAL. Vaguely familiar name.

"I'll be fine," he said.

"Yeah, well, bravo, but we *won't*. You're all over the news. I get an aiding-and-abetting, what happens to Sammy?" She returned his silent stare, her eyes surprisingly pretty in their anger. They'd always been; it was as though the rust flecks around the pupils glowed with the intensity. "He won't be safe until you're . . ."

"Until I'm what?"

Her gaze dropped; she released his arm. The fire had dissipated as quickly as it had flared. "Gone," she said.

Walker set his mouth, nodded. He turned the corner into Tess's room and began loading up an army knapsack with all the Vector materials he could find. Kaitlin watched him from the doorway, arms crossed. He stopped, hand tapping a bookshelf. "There was another tape. Kid's writing. Where'd it go?"

"I think Sam said the deputy took it. Wait a minute, Walker, don't wake him—"

Walker brushed past her and into Sam's room. Sam scrambled up from the floor, smacked the TV to turn it off, and dove into bed.

Kaitlin's anger shifted, heat-seeking the new target. "You're supposed to have been asleep *two hours* ago."

"I couldn't. Too itchy."

"There's a tape missing from Tess's room," Walker said. "Did the cop take it?"

"He's a deputy U.S. marshal," Sam said. "That makes him a fed, not a cop."

"Did he take it?"

"Don't spaz. I have another." Sam bugged his eyes at Kaitlin. "Am I al*lowed* to get out of bed now?"

She waved a defeated hand. He dug in the closet, rubber T. rexes, comic books, and orphaned board-game figurines taking flight over his shoulder. He handed Walker a duplicate, except MY NEWS SEGMINT was now rendered in label-print.

Eyes on the tape, Walker headed out swiftly. He heard Sam call after him, "You're *welcome*."

Walker lowered himself to the living room carpet and plugged the tape into the VCR. That annoying local reporter, Melissa Yueh, led the way to the house in which Walker now sat. A shot of Sam sacrificing army men to an ant hill in the front yard, then a clip from his Vector commercial. All the while, Yueh's honey-sweet voice singsonged on, detailing the magic of gene therapy and Sam's "tragic" condition. Some inserts from the Vector lab featured Dolan answering Yueh's questions awkwardly, until Chase, clearly the more charismatic of the brothers, took over.

Next the segment cut to Tess, the archetypal Troubled Mother, sitting at the tiny Formica-topped table wedged in the corner of the kitchen. She leaned over her coffee, her wrist and hand curled around the mug the way they always did. Despite her evident exhaustion and the widened span of her crow's feet, which had begun incursions on her upper cheeks, she still had that inner life pouring out of her. God only knew the source—it certainly wasn't inherited, and it was more than the sum of her looks. Men homed in on it at a glance, crossing movie theaters, pursuing her at shopping malls; when she used to take him for walks around the park, she'd actually stop cars. Girls were wary—they either steered clear or went submissive like bellied-up dogs. Women hated her, blindly and irrationally. "Spirit," some people called it, though to Walker the word had been worn useless by repetition, like "miracle" or "values." Or "tragic," for that matter. Whatever Tess had, she drew hotshots who wanted to possess it, older men who fed on it, and tough guys who were afraid of it, but she always skipped on, unscathed, until an unplanned pregnancy ensnared her with a wedding band. The sight of her now—her captured aliveness—was disorienting, like a déjà vu that retrieves a segment of dream.

". . . I got a new job," she was saying, "so we got health insurance in place now. Group coverage, so they had to take preexisting. And I'm—me and Sammy are—so grateful to Vector, which has given us some real hope."

Yueh enumerated Tess and Sam's "struggles" that led them to Vector, adding, "You were at the end of your rope. How many people were ahead of Sam on the transplant list?"

Tess made a popping sound with her lips. "Sixty-seven."

"And how long would that take?"

Tess watched the steam rise from her coffee. "Too long."

Yueh looked on, lips pursed with camera-friendly empathy. "So Xedral is your only hope," she said, in full movie-trailer-voice-over glory.

A scene worthy of a talk show followed, Dolan entering the house as the scientist-savior, appreciation and humility offered up like cheap goods. The usual staged interaction—Dolan playing Dungeons & Dragons with Sam—as Yueh v.o.'d "the hopes of an ailing community."

The segment ended with a zoom on Tess. Walker could see her age more clearly now. Sound quality was slightly lacking, the soft crackle of the mike pinned to Tess's lapel lending the moment a genuineness absent from the previous footage. Yueh doled out a classic human-interest-story question, vicious in its kind concern. "If you could wish for anything, what would it be?"

A ripple passed through Tess's face, a sob put down in its infancy, and her toughness reasserted itself over her features. Her voice wavered slightly with conviction. "The *only* thing I want is for Sammy to be well enough. To live a life. That's all."

Walker rewound the tape and watched her again closely, her face, the tremor, the still-unblemished skin at her left temple. He missed her as he hadn't yet, and it struck him for not the first time that anger gave him access to grief instead of vice versa.

He heard Kaitlin's soft footfall on the carpet behind him. "You want to dig into this, Walk? Well then, you get this mess. The *whole* mess. The pain and the pager and the wait list. You want it?"

"No."

"That's the problem with you. You never got the 'for better or for worse' stuff." Kaitlin looked as though she'd expected him to fight back; her weight was even forward, like someone who'd swung and missed.

"How much time does he have?" Walker asked.

"If he doesn't get the liver? Months. Weeks. Maybe not even. That's one of the torments of this thing—there's no road map. He just fades and fades, and then all of a sudden there'll be the final downturn." She checked the pager again, a little ritual she must have repeated a hundred times a day, but this time she caught herself. She brought the pager level to her eyes, confronting it on its own terms. "You find yourself hoping for some kind soul to get run over or drop dead." The desperation in her voice made Walker want to cringe, and it called up in him an anger toward her that he didn't understand. "You wait and you watch the pager. I've been doing it since the minute I got him." She laughed, and he noticed that the lines around her mouth, like Tess's, had grown more pronounced. "You get Sammy, you get the pager. That's just how that goes."

"Is he gonna get a liver?" He gestured for the TV. "They say—"

"I *know* what they say." She covered her mouth, then looked away, and her hair fell across her eyes. A sob creaked out of her. "I can't save him. I can't do anything. Except help him to die." The VCR signaled that the tape had reached its end and clicked over to regular programming, Paul Newman popping eggs into his mouth, one after another. Kaitlin jerked the hair from her eyes. "Why am I bothering? You don't get it. You've never done a goddamned thing for anyone but yourself."

"Then why did you marry me?"

"Because I was stupid and self-destructive."

He laughed, and a moment later a grudging smile replaced her frown.

Sweatshirt sleeve pulled over her fist, she swiped at her tears like she was aggravated with them.

"I thought you forgot how to smile," he said.

The thumping of feet as Sam beelined down the hall. "I'm on TV! I'm on TV!" He stopped. Twisted a finger until the knuckle cracked. His commercial ran in the background, the poor-me orphan shot. He drew a rattling breath. "I didn't know you were still here."

If Kaitlin's voice were any more weary, it would have been inaudible. "You're supposed to be asleep."

"I'm sorry." He cocked his head slightly, trying to see her face. "You okay, Kaitlin?"

"Yeah. Just go to your room, kiddo."

His eyes shifted to Walker. "Don't make her cry."

Walker held out his hands: *Whatever you say, boss.*

"He's not making me cry, Sammy."

"Am *I?*" Sam asked.

Kaitlin pressed her lips together for a moment to still them. "No. Of course not. Go to your room. I'll come tuck you in."

Sam shuffled off, bouncing his head side to side and murmuring the theme song to one of his video games. Walker extracted the tape from the VCR and stuffed it into his knapsack.

Kaitlin said, "The night Sammy was diagnosed, I came over and sat with Tess. She was furious she was type B. She said if she could've cut out her liver and given it to him, she would have." She studied Walker, no longer angry, though her tone was cool, judgmental. "Do you know what it's like to have that kind of love?"

"Yes."

"*Yes?* How?"

Walker shouldered the knapsack and turned for the door. "From her."

Chapter 38

The command post took shape as it usually did, around an enormous conference table on the third floor, the Top Fifteen designation buying the Escape Team a two-story promotion, court security officer admin backup, and a few loose hands from Probation/Parole. It was just the second dawn since Walker's escape, but already the paperwork had claimed most surface areas in the room. The false sightings were rolling into the phone banks, Walker Jameson popping up everywhere from the Griffith Park Zoo's reptile house to the Ferris wheel at the Santa Monica Pier.

Tim lifted his notepad, the page now more ink than white. Ignoring the palimpsest effect from Tyler's purple crayon—in toasting an English muffin, he'd left the young artist unattended—he reviewed the updates on the checklist he'd jotted at the breakfast table. No word back from Aaronson yet on the red stain with the odd sweetener and gelatin composition. No information on Aryan Brotherhood hit men from Ian Summer and the Vegas Task Force.

The Bronco had indeed traced to Ted Sands. He'd been taken in a front-yard snatch, the dried rivulet of blood and snapped fingernail on the driveway saying it hadn't been gentle. Since Walker had driven Ted off in Ted's own vehicle, Guerrera was running down taxi records to Cheviot Hills around the time of the kidnapping—Walker had to have gotten there somehow. The cab companies that were actually organized enough to keep records had produced logs too numerous to be helpful, and there were enough other transportation scenarios—accomplice, bus, cached car—to irritate Guerrera about doing likely dead-end work.

Thomas had spent the morning looking into Dean's head of security. Percy Keating, who'd done two tours in Vietnam, lived in the Kagan guesthouse with his Bangkok mail-order bride. He'd been investigated for a handful of indiscretions over the years—everything from illegal wiretapping to criminal threats—though he'd never been formally charged.

Working a vast range of mostly inherited business and IRS contacts, Freed was still gathering background on Dean Kagan's corporate doings. When Tim had arrived a little before seven, Freed was at his desk downstairs, slaving away, wearing the same suit he'd had on the day before. He'd waved Tim off; Freed wasn't ready to talk until he was ready to talk.

Haines and Denley reviewed Sam's news segment on the wall-mounted TV in the corner. Tim had watched it through several times last night, his somber mood prompting Dray to recommend that he incorporate SpongeBob into his Netflix queue. Tess's moving declaration—"The *only* thing I want is for Sammy to be well enough. To live a life. That's all."—was tearjerked into cheapness by Melissa Yueh's sobering coda: "We can *all* hope that treatment for young people like Sam Hardy . . . may not be far away. For KCOM News, I'm—"

"Believe me, lady," Denley said, "we know who you are."

Chewing his pen cap flat, Tim swiveled to take in Yueh's windblown image outside Tess and Sam's house. "Hey, Denley. Will you contact Yueh, see if you can get the raw footage? Unedited?"

"Can I wear earplugs?"

"I'd recommend a condom, too, *socio*," Guerrera said.

Freed entered, soft briefcase swollen, Armani wire-frames low on his thin nose. With aplomb he kicked aside the rolling chair at the head of the table and began removing and organizing his notes. Everyone silenced. Tim caught sight of a cover of *Forbes* magazine, Dean Kagan astride a golf cart with Jack Welch, looking tanned and pleased with himself.

"Dean Kagan," Freed said, displaying an impressive grasp of dramatics, "was a legend in the barter trade in the seventies and early eighties, dealing primarily with the Soviet Union. He made tens of millions in the commodities market, walking the line between free trade and private profiteering, raping the USSR of their natural resources."

"Poor commies," Denley said.

Freed continued, "He set up a shell corp in Australia to get around Our Country 'Tis of Thee's more stringent regulations."

"What kind of product?" Bear asked.

"He bartered copy machines, shoes, TVs, jeans, toilet paper, that kind of shit, for copper, tin, steel, fertilizer. He'd acquire enough tonnage to resell at up to a two *thousand* percent return to, say, China, even before having to fork out for the acquisition. His activities engendered more investigations than I could count, but he was never charged. In some of those years, he paid seven figures in legal fees. It wasn't until the late seventies he made the move to pharmaceuticals."

"Why'd he go legit?" Zimmer asked.

In a rare instance of inelegance, Freed released a guffaw. "Yeah, legit. There's a reason Kagan, with his *From Russia with Love* skill set, saw an opening in Big Pharma. Greener pastures, zero downside. The Rx T. rexes are a step ahead of clowns like Kozlowski, Lay, and other relatively honest, hardworking corporate looters. They don't *have to* do anything illegal—they bought the three branches and retooled the laws instead. Big Pharma has the largest lobby in Washington—more members than *Congress*—and a revolving-door employee policy that would make Dick Cheney dizzy. We, the humble taxpayers, get hit twice: First we foot the research bill, then we pay marked-up prices for the drugs generated by the research *our* money funded.

"And guess who was a prime mover behind the reengineering of the FDA and American patent law to work in Big Pharma's favor? In 1980 our very own Dean Kagan helped ram through the Bayh-Dole Act, solidifying technology-transfer laws and granting exclusive licenses for NIH research to drug companies for a royalty arrangement that in any other sector would be mythical. In '84, at Mr. Kagan and his competitors' prompting, our unparalleled Congress passed an act that extended monopoly rights for brand-name drugs to the point of preposterousness. Another piece of chicanery Mr. Kagan helped tug the marionette strings on: tax credits for 'orphan drugs.' These kick in if a pharm company bothers to tackle a disease with a smaller patient population—an unprecedented congressional *guarantee* that they'll profit on every product. Not that they don't manipulate the classification system anyway to get tax breaks on money *earners*. Beacon-Kagan has proven masterful at dodging kickback laws, too, offering prescribers—I mean *physicians*—paid consultancies, speaker-bureau gigs, advisory-board positions, and various other tits to slurp on the sow belly. Meanwhile those lobbyist dollars keep paying off in spades. The Medicare Bill of 2003 actually *prohibits* the government from negotiating prices with pharmaceutical companies. You couldn't make this shit up."

Freed took a breath—his first?—then continued. "If they have trouble marketing a drug for a disease, they'll market a disease to sell the drug. Ever notice all the new disorders that pop up every year? Well, new, for-profit companies carry out trials or crunch the data from trials the pharmaceuticals run in-house. They're called contract research organizations—CROs. And guess who owns them?"

Denley, bored by his own cynicism, said, "Big Pharma."

"Worse." Freed smiled, a wan, bitter shaping of his mouth. "The advertising agencies *employed* by the pharmaceuticals. In some cases the ad execs are closer to the test tubes than the scientists."

Tim had never seen Freed—a laissez-faire, highest-tax-bracket, fiscal Republican who'd worked landmark corruption and embezzlement cases—so fired up.

Guerrera, channeling his past, naïve self, said, "That can't be true."

"There's a lot at stake," Tim mused, "in Dean Kagan's empire."

Freed glanced at him. "You're thinking if you've gone legit to the tune of a 4.7 billion annual gross, you don't risk it by offing some broad in a glorified trailer home."

"No. You wouldn't."

Thomas added, "Not without a very compelling reason."

Slumped in his chair, Bear livened up at the switch of topic. "Did you get any information on Pierce?"

"I looked into it a bit," Freed said, "but got sidetracked with this stuff. I can say this, though—the guy may be a smaller fish than Kagan, but he's just as slippery. He's got corporations spun out of corporations. Not an easy trail."

Bear stood, hoisting his pants in a manner that wouldn't have looked out of place in a western. "I think whatever Tess had on her computer got her killed. As far as I'm concerned, the case turns on that missing hard drive. Guerrera, how are you making out with her phone records?"

"Whole lotta nada. But me and Haines found a red flag in her financials. Her bank statement shows she retained a lawyer on May twenty-eighth."

Eleven days before her murder.

Tim snatched the bank statement across the table. The buzz of conversation in the room stopped at once.

Guerrera held up his hands. "But we don't know what for."

"May twenty-eighth is the same day she bought folic acid pills for the pregnancy," Tim said. "Maybe she'd just found out."

"And hired an attorney," Bear mused.

"We just got off with the lawyer, and he won't budge on discussing it," Guerrera said. "Client-attorney privilege, no way around it."

"We gotta pay him a visit," Bear said.

Haines said, "You'd be wasting your time. I promise. We have no legal standing here, and the guy knows it."

Bear said, "Get him on the phone for me."

"I'm telling you—"

"Just get him for me."

Guerrera muttered something in Spanish, dialed, and flopped his wrist, offering Bear the cordless and a smart-ass introduction: "Esteban Martinez, Esquire."

Bear introduced himself as a deputy marshal and fellow attorney-at-law. Tim joined Guerrera in slipping on a headset, just in time to hear Martinez express his exasperation.

"I just explained to your colleague, I will not under *any circumstances* divulge the nature of confidential conversations I had with my client." His English was clipped slightly by the cadence of his accent.

Bear asked, "Even if she may have been murdered as a result of them?"

"Yes. Even if that. What would it mean to the security of future clients? To my reputation? I'm sorry, sir, and *believe* me I'm sorry about what happened to Ms. Jameson, but it simply is not an option." The regret in his voice was palpable, but also his resolve.

"Will you at least tell me how many times you met?" Bear asked. A long pause, during which Tim could hear Martinez tapping his pencil against his desk. "As far as I know," Bear added, "there's nothing confidential about dates."

"Only twice."

"May twenty-eighth when she retained you. When was the second?"

"June one."

"That Friday? Seems like a quick job . . . ?" Bear waited, hoping to get something back. Guerrera flicked his chin, his youthful features pulled tight in a told-you-so scowl. Keeping the phone pressed to his ear, Bear resisted additional prodding, sensing, as did Tim, that Martinez was not the kind of man who responded well to pressure. They listened to the sound of Martinez's breathing, banking on that note of regret that had found its way into Martinez's voice. A full minute passed—an eternity of silence.

Finally Martinez said, "If you must know, she discharged me."

"She spent two hundred and fifty dollars to fire you?"

"It was a decision we arrived at together."

"Why?"

"Don't push your luck, Deputy."

Bear rolled his lips over his teeth, then popped them back out. "Might I ask if the subject discussed *wasn't* . . . General Foods?"

"I can assure you it wasn't."

"Was it not . . . Hughes Aircraft?"

"It was not."

"Was it not . . . Vector Biogenics?"

"I'll neither confirm nor deny that," Martinez said, leaving them with a click and the hum of the dial tone.

Chapter 39

The churning of the roller bottles in combination with the moist warmth of the incubator augmented Dolan's stress hangover. He sped his pace through the passage, his skin reflecting back the red tint thrown from the hundreds of quarts of gently spinning growth fluid. The events of last night, from the party to the explosion's aftermath to the hum of the crime-scene cleaners' machinery, had left him so wired and rattled that he'd lain in bed agitated for hours after Chase disappeared out the window. He'd awakened with a sourness in his mouth to match the toxic thoughts that had pervaded his broken sleep.

He passed through the airlock into the test suite, the screeches of the monkeys making him smile for the first time in days. Huang wasn't at his desk, but on his chair, as promised, were the PowerPoint slides that Dolan needed for his talk at Friday's pre-IPO presentation. The magnifications depicted the stages of poxvirus's transformation into Xedral. Always a crowd pleaser.

The macaques settled from the excitement of Dolan's entrance, emphasizing the emptiness of the suite. Tuesday morning's departmental stratcom had drawn Huang's team into the conference room on the south corridor.

Grabbing the slides and turning to go, Dolan extended his arm to receive Grizabella's high five. His hand whiffed through air.

The cage was gone.

Dolan stood dumbly, regarding the blank space.

Across the suite the storage-closet door sucked open from an unfelt breeze, the latch bolt tapping back against the plate. Before the door a janitor's mop protruded from an abandoned rolling bucket.

Uneasy from the sudden calm of the monkeys, Dolan set down the slides. He crossed the lab and toed the bucket. It rolled to the side on squeaky wheels. He gripped the door handle and pulled.

An empty cage sat centered on the closet floor, Grizabella's name and ID number rendered on the affixed plaque.

Two men in generic Beacon-Kagan lab coats entered. They nodded, and then the burlier of the two breezed past Dolan, claiming Grizabella's cage.

"Where is this test subject?" Dolan asked.

"We don't know. We were just told to clean up."

"What do you mean? What happened to the test subject?" The men didn't slow, so Dolan followed them. "Was she in the cage when you started?"

The other said, "She was removed from the study." They were maddeningly uninterested, unhalting in their progress toward the doors.

"This is part of my experiment," Dolan said. "Who gave you permission to remove this test subject?"

"I'm sorry, Dr. Kagan. We're just following instructions. Isn't this Dr. Huang's section of the lab?"

The sliding doors opened with a hiss, and they passed through.

"Who authorized this?" Dolan shouted after them.

The doors sealed with a vacuum slurp. A few of the monkeys tittered, in on a private joke. Dolan fell into Huang's chair, rolled a few inches.

Huang's screen saver bounced around. A monkey striking the pose of Rodin's *Thinker.* Witty.

Dolan allowed his pinkie to graze the keyboard. The screen saver vanished, revealing a Windows desktop. Huang was still logged in.

Alone in the suite, no approaching footsteps on the hallway tile.

Dolan did a search/find using Grizabella's subject ID number, calling up a number of documents. The most recently changed was a spreadsheet titled *Subject log—X3-AAT thru X5-AAT.*

He stared at the Excel icon for a very long time, the chatter of monkeys echoing around the sterile walls.

Then he double-clicked on it.

Chapter 40

I said no *lime*." The paunchy gentleman waved off the waiter with a flare of his manicured fingers.

"I'm sorry. Let me bring you a new glass."

"Why don't you bring me a new bottle."

The kid backed up, cheeks flushed, bottle of Pellegrino tilted in both hands, still on display. Below his server's apron protruded scuffed Converse low-tops, an Ohio State Buckeye tattooed on the bare strip of ankle. "Right away."

The lingering patrons awaiting the maître d's nod made it easy for Walker to loiter as he inventoried the waiters. He didn't exactly blend in in his father's suit jacket and a T-shirt, but a few Armenians going *Miami Vice* casual put him more at ease. On its framed menu, The Ivy announced itself as country cottage, but Walker thought it was to a cottage what Restoration Hardware was to Home Depot. A white picket fence hugged the perimeter of a raised patio framed with ivy. Someone had put a lot of time into the wood to make it look distressed. It wasn't *too* distressed, though; it looked pretty content watching the slender European types slither past in tight dresses to eat scallops among the so-called rustic antiques.

Robertson Boulevard's perennial congestion put the valet off the main street. The narrow mouth of the driveway disgorged foreign-make SUVs, each larger than the last. There was a break in cashmere, and Walker eased forward, catching the maître d's attention.

"Excuse me, I called in earlier? My employer believes she left a purse here the night of June first?"

The maître d's phony British accent amped up a few watts. "That's a long time ago."

"She's a very busy woman."

"No one's left a purse here."

"Maybe I should tell her to call the manager herself?"

A prissy down-the-nose glance. "June first was a"—his nail tapped a few beats on a tiny square calendar taped to the stand—"Friday. Victor works Friday nights." He whistled over the last waiter Walker had inventoried.

Victor came quickly, putting a jog into his step.

"Please see to this gentleman's questions," the maître d' said.

Walker drew Victor away from the cluster of people. "Uptight crowd, huh?"

"You're telling me."

"I thought you were gonna pop that asshole about the lime thing."

"You saw that?" He shook his head. "I know, huh. What are you gonna do?"

"Listen, I was hoping you could do me a favor. I just moved out here from Columbus—"

"No shit? I went to school there."

"Fellow Buckeye? All right. Anyways, I been trying to make my way in journalism, freelance, but it can be tough. You know how that is."

"Hell, yeah. I'm a musician myself."

"So I'm writing a story on Vector, that biology firm. They had a dinner party here on June first?"

"Sure, I remember. They rented the whole place out." Victor nodded emphatically, thumb dusting his first two fingers. "It was a celebration. They got some patent approved or something, had people making speeches."

"I was wondering if I could ask you a few questions for my story?" Walker pulled out a photograph of Tess. "Was this woman there that night?"

"Yeah, I remember her." A smirk. "Past her prime, but still pretty smokin'. She's a photographer or former model or something."

"Is she? How do you know that?"

"Well, she got into a discussion with this other guy over here by the valet—"

"Show me."

Victor walked him a few paces down the sidewalk. "I remember because there was some kind of valet mix-up, caused a little commotion."

Walker noted a dark portal in the restaurant's side, overlooking the valet stand. "What'd the guy look like?"

"I don't really remember. I remember the chick better, right? I was circling with chardonnay, and I heard him say something about what happened in the limo at the shoot. He was sorta, I guess, apologetic without really being apologetic. I remember thinking, The problems these rich folks have, right? Like the guy probably packed Cristal instead of Dom Perignon or something."

"Did you hear anything else?"

"Naw, I was busy."

"You guys have a security camera or anything?"

"Yeah. See that little window?" He pointed, and Walker feigned surprise. "The security director keeps a valet cam, ever since some has-been TV star sued because someone stole personal photos from his glove box. They won't tell us who—part of the settlement, I guess."

"Do you think you could get ahold of the security tape for me from that night?"

"I wish I could. But no way. *Especially* not for press. The security director would have my ass."

"Maybe he'd let me take a look?"

"No, he's kind of a dick. Actually, scratch the 'kind of.' Plus, they store like three *years* of the old shit at the security company, in case a lawsuit pops up down the line. It's a hassle to retrieve it. I know because one of the valets got accused of emptying an ashtray full of change my second week. You're not gonna get old footage easy."

The maître d's head poked above the crowd, swiveled, and found Victor. His conveyance of inconvenience was no less than epic.

"Gotta go. Sorry I couldn't be more help."

Walker smiled and returned the handshake. "You been plenty."

Chapter 41

Dean barely glanced up when Tim and Bear entered. His office was surprisingly small and unpretentious, save the desk's almost wall-to-wall breadth and the expansive window framing his broad build. From the twenty-sixth-floor perspective, his shoulders ranged from the neat rows of granite marking the dead in the veteran's cemetery to the old Fox Village tower, long subsumed by Mann's of Chinese Theatre fame.

Gripping a beautiful guitar by the neck and looking stylishly disheveled in a baggy grosgrain-ribbon button-up, deck shoes, and linen khakis, Chase went to the trouble to meet them at the door. A stack of copies sat neatly centered on a side table. Dean gestured to Tim and Bear, indicating that they should sit, but they remained on their feet, picking through the offerings. The so-called file of disgruntleds. Beacon-Kagan's employment records for Ted Sands included the basic facts, nothing more. A pamphlet on Human Resources guidelines. A few pages on test-subject selection read as if they'd come out of the marketing department. The party guest list Tim knew, by its inclusion, to be as sanitized and inessential as the other documents. He flipped the final folder closed, unimpressed.

"I hope that's a help," Chase said. "Everything you asked for."

"Not everything," Bear said.

"I've got a very busy day."

"Yeah"—Bear nodded to the unplugged Gibson acoustic—"you look pretty wrapped up here in high-level corporate affairs. We'll try not to inconvenience you too greatly."

"On Friday we have our pre-IPO presentation to investors and management. Which means . . ." Chase's lips pressed thin. "My staff at Vector and I have three days to prepare to receive a hundred of Wall Street's top money managers here in the auditorium on our first floor. Not to mention a raft of business reporters and various other members of the media. So as for inconveniencing us? You haven't. But Mr. Jameson has. And you seem a lot more interested in harassing our company than in apprehending him. Why is that?"

Dean continued alternating between the various lines feeding his headset and the countless stacks positioned at even intervals along the vast run of oak. He paused to offer his son a patient warning: *"Chase."*

Bear answered the question. "Because you've turned over what looks to be an embarrassment of riches from your PR department, but not much that'll shed light on why Walker Jameson is out to wreck you. Until we can find some answers, we'll keep coming back to you with the same questions." He shifted his attention to Dean. "Where's Dolan?"

A raised report covered Dean's eyes. "Any second." An assistant entered with a question about where to house a hedge-fund group winging in for the presentation, and Dean said, "Four Seasons. The whole team. But rooms—not suites."

"Okay." Chase sat on an arm of the leather couch, set his guitar across the cushions, and busied himself on his BlackBerry. "I'll play along. What more do you need?"

Bear said, "We need you to answer some questions."

"Like."

"Why did your former employee get killed in front of your house?"

"Haven't the foggiest."

"Coincidence, maybe?"

"A lot of power forwards at that party. So. Maybe it had to do with one of them."

"As we suggested—but your father's pretty sure the guest list is not the motive. And it *was* his flagstone that got stained."

"Indeed it was." Chase lowered his BlackBerry and offered an intentionally insincere smile.

"Listen," Tim said, "maybe we got off on the wrong foot. We know how valuable your time is, but you're giving the impression it's routine for brutal killings to happen on your doorstep. If that's the case, you can understand our deepening interest in you."

Chase put down his BlackBerry and slid his guitar onto his lap. "My company is about to launch its first product. It's not a video game or a hair conditioner. It's a viral-vectored genetic enhancement that will save the lives of a hundred thousand children in this country alone in the coming year. So as for the relative importance of Ted Sands, who seems to have been exactly the kind of sleazeball you think he was . . . ?" He twanged the opening notes of "Taps" on his guitar.

Dean removed his glasses and tossed them on his desktop. "Knock it off, Chaisson."

Chase stopped immediately. At Dean's glare he set down the guitar altogether.

Dolan came in, slightly winded, nervous energy twisting his hands around each other. "Sorry I'm late."

"Sit down," Dean said from behind the report.

Dolan dutifully moved to the couch as Dean mumbled his displeasure at whatever he was reading, then turned his focus to Tim and Bear. "What are you after? Tess Jameson, family connection with Sands's killer. What about her?"

Tim said, "You were looking into why you dropped her son from the trial."

"The specifics on that are proving harder to retrieve than we thought—there are so many applicant subjects," Chase said. "We're still digging. But my guess? Since there's nothing specific, it means he was disqualified for the same reason ninety-six percent were: didn't meet the criteria."

"What were the criteria?"

"Well. There are a lot of medical variables when it comes to—"

"Because I took much of last night to read your corporate Web site—very impressive, by the way—and I found out that what's so great about

Xedral is . . ." A considered pause as Tim patted his pockets, withdrew his notepad, licked a thumb, and found the page. "Here we are. 'Xedral is unique in its broad applicability and effectiveness. Preliminary tests project an eighty-six percent success rate in treating anyone from infants to adults afflicted with ATT.' "

Dolan seemed suddenly to realize that his father and brother were both waiting on him to speak, and he said, "The inclusion criteria for the Phase I subjects are very strict. The issue isn't scientific, though. Medical records are confidential. Our preclinical analyses are part of the private data on these subjects, so discussing them with you would be illegal."

Tim picked up the stack of folders and fanned them. "Some of your records seem to be more confidential than others."

Dean rolled back his chair and pulled himself upright. For the first time since Tim and Bear had entered, they had his full attention. "I don't like where this started, and I don't like where it's headed. We're doing our best to work with you, and we're even willing to put the operation of two companies on hold to do it. But everything about your approach—and the entire . . . worldview of your oversize friend here— would suggest that perhaps you should be dealing with our lawyers, since you have somehow converted this into a grudge match between yourself and Vector. Which it may be, for all I know. But if so, it's one in which you will not prevail. I will match my resources against those of the Justice Department anytime. And have. If you want cooperation, stop making ludicrous, poorly veiled accusations. We all know that the murder at my house last night is, in all likelihood, unrelated to me, my sons, or this corporation."

Tim said, "The victim was a former security employee of Beacon-Kagan. The perpetrator, the uncle of a kid discontinued in a Vector trial. Unrelated? Not even you can sell that, Mr. Kagan. Why else would you add a two-man security detail to the house as of this morning?"

"Caution, of course."

"You sure you don't know something we don't?"

"I'm quite sure I know *many* things you don't, Deputy." Dean's hand raised from the desktop, tilting toward the door. "Now unless there's something else . . . ?"

———

The door closed behind the deputies, leaving the three Kagan men in uneasy silence. Dolan started to say something, but Dean held up a hand, pausing him until the elevator doors dinged shut in the hall.

Dolan said, "Walker Jameson blames us for his sister's death."

"Come *on*," Chase said.

"He's after something else," Dean said. "Ted Sands hasn't worked for this corporation for over a year—he certainly had nothing to do with Tess or her son. And besides, what could we possibly be at fault for?"

"We drove Tess Jameson to her suicide." Hearing it aloud, even from his own mouth, sent a wash of acid through Dolan's stomach. Months ago Dolan had been informed of Sam's discharge in a closed-door meeting with his father, brother, and Chris Huang, his protests quickly dissolved into silent complicity (what was that adage about good men doing nothing?).

"No one drives anyone to suicide," Dean said. "If you think so, you're a fool."

"She was hanging on by her fingernails for that kid when she came to us, sir."

Biting his lip and sliding his hand up the neck to the tenth fret, Chase played the opening phrase from "Don't Cry for Me Argentina," bending the last note into a whiny vibrato.

"We've been over this," Dean said. "We didn't have a choice."

"We knew Sam. We used him. I visited him in his own room. And we pulled the rug out on his last option."

"Right," Chase said. "And now some other fucking kid will live and not the one you played checkers with on the local news. We can't save everyone. Not until we have this product approved. And don't forget, *she* brought this on. Not us."

Dolan said, "It didn't look that way when I came into the parking garage."

Dean laughed—the dry chuckle that had made Dolan's palms sweat for more than three decades. "This isn't test tubes and Bunsen burners.

This is the real world." He jogged a finger back and forth, indicating himself and Chase. "Where we live. Wise up, son. And don't lecture me about options."

"If the Xedral trial goes as smoothly as we think it will," Chase said, "who's to say it won't be to market in time to save the kid?"

Dolan smoothed the wrinkles at his thighs. "His liver's deteriorating faster than our business plan's progressing."

"You're so wrapped up in that kid that you're keeping tabs?" Dean shook his head. "Guilt is an indulgence, Dolan. It tangles you in the past. Science is forward-looking. Likewise our business. We have a sound product that will save millions of lives. If you have confidence in Xedral—"

"One of the monkeys is missing," Dolan said. "From the longitudinal safety study. She just disappeared."

Dean settled back in his chair. Same dry chuckle. "Test subjects don't just disappear."

"Well, this one did."

"You watch your tone."

"I'm sorry, sir." Dolan moistened his lips nervously. "The thing is, this isn't the only monkey that disappeared. I checked the safety study trial data, and we also lost two subjects in X3 trials and one in X4s that aren't accounted for. I now *require* the Lentidra data—not reports, not summaries, but all of it, in raw form—so I can gauge the comparison—"

"Trust me," Dean said. "The data's sound."

"Sir"—Dolan took a moment to still his voice—"you're not . . ."

"I'm not *what*? A scientist? Qualified to assess data? No. I'm an entrepreneur who's done approximately forty *billion* dollars of business in pharmaceuticals. I believe that I—and your CEO—can be trusted to know if there's a problem with some standard data."

Dolan kept his hands together in his lap, his gaze on the union of his knuckles. He couldn't push any further, but he also didn't want to capitulate. He heard some rustling and figured that Chase and Dean were exchanging glances—puzzlement, contempt—and then Dean said, "Jesus Christ," and snatched up the phone. "Get me Huang. Upstairs. Now." He turned his attention to Dolan. "I'll tell you what. If there is, in fact, a problem with Huang's numbers as you claim, we'll get you anything you need. If not, can we stop this endless cycling through old data on discontinued products?"

By the time Huang had arrived and Dean had impatiently brought him up to speed on the impasse, Dolan had settled his nerves enough to remain calm and—he hoped—confident on the couch.

Huang turned to him with evident irritation and said, "Yes, we took a hit in X3 animal trials, two subjects gone. And one in X4. And their deaths aren't noted in the main body of data."

Dolan shifted to the edge of the couch.

Huang held the pause, stoking Dolan's anticipation. "It was simian hemorrhagic fever, Dolan. Not a conspiracy. This shouldn't be news to you. You know we lost two subjects to it at the outset of our X5s."

"Now three. If you count Grizabella."

"Grizabella reached through her cage and drank a beaker of sodium hypochlorite last night. I don't think that cause of death figures prominently in our areas of concern. Nor does SHF, which is why it's not factored into the stats for transgene effectiveness."

"Okay. Fine." Dolan caught himself backpedaling. "That begs the issue—"

"Which is?" Chase asked impatiently.

"Which is *not* that monkeys are dying—fourteen percent of our Xedral monkeys die—it's that they're disappearing from the subject suite and the staff refuse to tell me how."

"What is going on in that test-subject suite downstairs will reverberate around the world," Huang said, "both medically and financially. I hold my team to the highest level of confidentiality. They clear *everything* through me. That they won't answer the random questions of a scientist from another department—"

"I am the principal investigator and senior scientist of Vector Biogenics. I started this goddamned company, Chris. You're my employee. And your employees are my employees." Dolan felt his face growing hot. "I'll ask whatever questions and take whatever data I require to advance our work."

Huang glanced at Dean, and Dean offered him a patient tip of his head. "Of course you can. And of course you will," Huang said. "But you, like me, have to answer to a board. And adhere to corporate policies for internal communication. I would've been happy to tell you about Grizabella and the other test subjects we lost if you'd simply come to me and asked." A pause, and then Huang pressed on, "How did you get that data from earlier trials anyway?"

Dolan polished his glasses to give his hands something to do. "I pulled it off your computer."

Dean made a soft noise low in his throat, and Huang sank back in his chair.

"Well," Huang said after a measured pause, "I'll be sure to log off my computer every time I leave my station. Any more questions, or can I get back to my work?"

The door swung shut behind his angry exit. Dean ruffled papers at his desk, and Chase strummed a few chords before his cell phone chimed, summoning him into a Net meeting with investors in Asia.

After a few minutes, Dolan rose, mildly unsteady on his feet, and walked out.

Chapter 42

Tim screeched his Explorer around overburdened gardener trucks clogging Wilshire's left lane. With a swipe of his hand, Bear pulled the loose skin of his face into a droop, no doubt shoring up his enduring argument that himself at the wheel was the better default setting.

Tim screwed his cell phone's earpiece in another half turn, as if transmission were the problem. "You *gotta* be kidding me."

Denley's voice hid an element of amusement. "She will only do it in exchange for an exclusive interview with you."

"No way."

"She promised us the B-roll."

"I don't even know what that is."

"Neither did I, but now I like saying it. It's the tape that has all the background stuff for the segment or 'package' "—Denley's rustling, Tim figured, was his squiggling air quotation marks—"anything that might be a story element. In other words, lots of footage that may have wound up on the cutting room floor. Connective clips of Tess, with the kid, the Vector guy. Pretty critical nexus, that segment. I don't know that we can afford to pass it up."

Ever since Ginny's murder and Tim's highly publicized ouster from—and then reentry to—the Service, KCOM's Melissa Yueh had been determined to interview him. At various significant periods during the past four and a half years, she'd left him messages, FedExed written requests, even stooped to dating the Service's public information officer in an attempt to bring bureaucratic pressure to bear.

"Give me her goddamned number." Tim wrote it down angrily at a stoplight, the pressure of his notepad against the horn causing it to honk. His call-waiting was going, so he signed off and clicked over.

Dray's voice asked, "How attached were you to that vase on the coffee table?"

"Not very attached?"

"Good answer. Ty knocked it over." A pause. "With the *other* vase."

"We need to declaw him."

"I'll get some quotes. What gives with the case?"

He gave her the rundown. When he got to Melissa Yueh's request, his vehemence even drew Bear's interest from the UCLA girls bobbing on elliptical trainers behind LA Fitness's comprehensive windows. Tim waited for Dray to express her disbelief—which he presumed would caption Bear's expression—but instead she said, "Not a bad idea."

"I'm sorry, is my wife there, please?"

"Listen, Timmy"—she only led with the hated nickname when she knew she was charging uphill—"think of this as an opportunity."

"Come again?"

"Yueh's a ratings slut like the rest of the meat puppets. She wants a scoop and she wants your ass in her guest chair—that's all. Now, Walker's a strategist, as you pointed out. Put yourself on the board. You've got more pawns at your disposal. And rooks. And horses."

"Knights."

"Them, too. Get Walker to contact you. You've got information he wants. Use Yueh's show to tease him with it. Put out a phone number. Go through the command-post switchboard and use some detailed questions about the escape to screen out the wannabes. Use yourself as bait."

In the background he heard Tyler say, "Fishie bait! Fishie bait!"

Tim said, "It scares me that our child spends his whole day alone with a mind like yours."

"Me, too."

"What about all the *National Enquirer* shit she's gonna dredge up?"

"Set boundaries with her. It'll only up the wattage of her crush on you."

"You think Melissa Yueh has a crush on me?"

"Jesus. While we're at it, maybe I should point out that Freed owns the complete boxed set of *Will & Grace*."

"Freed is gay?"

"Aren't people in your line of work supposed to be observant?"

"But Freed was *married*," Bear said, straightening Tim's collar as they sat on the plush maroon couches of KCOM's third-floor lobby. Having already called in the Vector party's guest list to the command post, Bear had toted along the Beacon-Kagan files to ensure that they were as useless as they appeared.

Plasma TVs hung on the walls like works of art, offering best-of eye bites, the weeks' news strained through KCOM's yellow filter and abbreviated by flash cuts. A basketball brawl took to the—. A columnist at the Gray Lady under inspection for falsifying—. Four adult-film stars tested positive for—. Each tale conveyed with wild-eyed drama, thundering moral indignation, bereft pauses. The Endgame of Western Values. The Demise of America as We Like to Believe We Knew It. And viewers, tuning in from households with grown children on deployment and dying parents and windows overlooking homeless people foraging in trash cans, shook their heads and tut-tutted at all that packaged heartbreak.

Tim threw Bear's hands away. "Would you knock it off! And just because Dray says Freed's gay doesn't mean he's gay. Not that I care if he *is* gay."

"C'mon, Seinfeld. When's Dray been wrong about anything?"

In the dismayed pause that ensued, a voluptuous assistant with a clipboard and a radio entered and said, "Tim Rackley." At Tim's weak nod, she added, "Ready for makeup?"

"I don't need makeup."

"Freed," Bear said, "might beg to differ."

Tim followed the young woman's trail of perfume back through a tangle of cords and control rooms, heeding her silent example. She knocked briskly at an office door and stepped aside. Melissa Yueh glanced up from her call script, the ravenous touch of her eyes augmented by blush sharpening the rise of her cheeks. A paper collar stippled with foundation dust ringed her neck. Eye shadow picked up the hues of her plum-colored suit, and her sienna eyes reminded Tim, as always, of a cat's.

Her hand moved into her purse in her lap, and her shoulder tensed.

"Turn it off," Tim said. "Understand?"

Her arm flexed again, and a muffled click issued from the confines of her purse. "Understand." Without embarrassment she rose and breezed past him, smelling of hair spray. Her suit seemed impossibly pinched at the belt line. As he followed her, an entourage developed swiftly around them, underlings rotating forward to powder her face, proffer scripts for her perusal, hold mirrors for her approval. Not once did she slow her charge to the studio. At a break in the action, she cast a flirtatious glance over her shoulder. "I spoke with Tess Jameson three days before she died, you know."

"I didn't."

"I was in Baghdad. Did you see my coverage?"

"Missed it."

"I was embedded with the First Marine Division, saw some spectacular firefights."

"Spectacular," Tim repeated.

"Do you want to know what she wanted?" Yueh didn't bother to wait for a reply. "Well, I'd like to know what's going on with Vector and the murder at the Kagan estate. The unauthorized account."

"I'm not talking now."

"I'd like to help this woman if there's more to her suicide . . . ?"

"I think she's past help, but your empathy is genuinely moving."

"Will you take care of me later? When you do talk?"

"That depends on how well you take care of me."

She half turned so he could catch the gleam of her smile. "She wanted to see me. She said she had something to show me."

Tim did his best to downplay his reaction, not wanting Yueh to home in on it. But they both knew the obvious implications of Tess's seeking out an appointment with a reporter a few days before her suicide—assisted or otherwise.

"I told her I'd meet with her on my return," Yueh continued, "but I got back the day after her death."

"Any idea what she had? Did it have to do with Vector?"

"Something she was too nervous to discuss over the phone. Granted, I was in Iraq and fairly rushed. The generator by my barracks made my sat phone blink in and out." She halted abruptly, and the minions around them bumped into one another. "If those Vector guys wind up being assholes, I'm gonna be *furious*. I was really pulling for them, this new technology. My goddaughter has cystic fibrosis."

"So that's a yes. Did you seek them out? For the interview?"

She resumed her pace, the crew lurching back into motion. "No, it came from the top down. Their daddy company books twenty million dollars of airtime with the network annually. I wasn't forced to do the story, certainly, but it was suggested." She added quickly, "And it was a *strong* story."

She strode across the set, cameramen and producers silencing like students when the teacher returns from a bathroom break. For interviews, Yueh forwent the anchor's desk for Charlie Rose seating at a wooden table, the background dressed with a few broad-leafed plants. They sat, and an audio tech threaded a mike through Tim's shirt.

"We'll be live, the lead story for the five o' clock. And we'll reair on prime time and for the morning shows." She practiced her on-air smile, her cheeks dimpling just so. "Ready to do this?"

"Remember our terms."

"Sometimes an interview takes its own shape, and past events become relevant—"

"We know how this is played. I give to get. Respect the balance. If you don't . . ."

Yueh cocked her head at an angle generally reserved for spaniels and Playmates, as if debating whether to call his bluff.

A producer shouted, "Live in four, three, two—"

Tim said, "I'll make sure all future exclusives from the Marshal's office go to Fox."

Yueh's expression of dismay clicked into a perfect mask of welcome.

"Tim Rackley, known as the Troubleshooter due to his high-profile antics—"

Tim gave her a bland look.

"—is joining us. And tonight he'd like to deliver a message to the prison escapee who's been terrorizing the Los Angeles community."

In the darkness of a vacant office, with the bustle of ceaseless KCOM staff and equipment thumping past in the hall beyond the drawn blinds, Tim and Bear reviewed the spoils of Tim's encounter—the B-roll. They'd suffered through ten minutes of establishing shots of Tess's house and on-site pickups, Yueh jabbering between takes about lighting and flattering angles. A pewter Mercedes Gelaendewagen rolled up to the curb, seemingly impervious to the dust. Dolan stepped out and headed toward Yueh in greeting before the take ended. The next resumed with them waiting, now impatiently, at the curb. An assistant clicked a light meter around Yueh's face until she knocked it away.

"Where the hell *is* this woman?"

"We're twenty minutes early, Melissa," an off-screen producer said. "Keep your pantsuit on."

Bear leaned forward, excitedly jabbing a finger in the corner of the screen at what Tim had already noted: Chase Kagan. Leaning against the G-Wagen, he regarded the run-down neighborhood with something like delight. The aired segment had shown only Dolan at the house, but clearly Chase, as the more polished Vector mouthpiece, had accompanied his brother to oversee him. Chase's temporary amnesia when presented with Tess's name now seemed even more likely feigned.

The take ended. The next began with Yueh practicing her lead-ins, variations on a theme: "A young boy *stricken* with a disorder . . ." "A *boy* stricken with a disorder in his youth . . ." "A young boy *courageously* fighting a genetic disorder . . ."

In the background Chase sat on the tailgate of the G-Wagen, guitar across his seersucker shorts, playing "Dueling Banjos"—a joke no one registered.

A prolonged blackness. A shot of asphalt as someone adjusted the camera. Then Dolan's voice: "Here she is. Here she is."

"*Fi*nally."

A beat-up Mazda clattered up into the driveway, Sam waving from the backseat. When Tess climbed out and shook her blond hair loose from a pink Dodgers cap, Chase lowered his guitar. His gaze stayed fixed on her as she unbuckled Sam from the back.

"You guys got here early." Tess hefted a grocery bag from the trunk. "I wanted to have some things to welcome you."

"Let's get the crew set," Yueh said.

The next shot was in the kitchen. Tess had unpacked some clear plastic wineglasses from the bag and arranged them on the chipped kitchen table. Chase popped the bottom off one and held the top like a cup; Dolan's fell apart in his hand. She was setting up dip and generic-brand crackers when Chase said, in a surprisingly charitable tone, "You know what? Let's clear this. We don't want it to look like a celebration or anything."

Tess dipped her chin. "Okay, right." She tucked her hair behind her ear and smiled with a hint of embarrassment.

A few outtakes followed of Yueh teaching Sam some basics about being on air. She dealt with him sweetly; when he didn't smile on cue, she set her fists on her hips in mock anger to make him laugh. Tess looked on with beaming maternal pride, Chase at her side, taking in her profile.

"Don't worry, sweetie," Yueh said, "we'll shoot some footage of you, and you can watch it right here in this screen till you're comfortable. Okay?"

Some takes ensued—Sam hooking fingers into his mouth to pull his cheeks wide; Sam pretending to descend stairs, lowering his torso by increments from the lens's view; Sam hamming it up with a ballplayer's "hey momz."

Back to static, then an establishing shot as two PAs arranged pillows on the couch and the sound engineer fussed with a boom mike. To the side, only half in the frame, Tess finally turned and met Chase's stare.

Her voice, far from the mike, was barely audible. "Help you?"

Chase manufactured a blush. "Your husband must adore you."

"He kept the TV. I kept the ring."

The exchange was tough to make out over the foreground noise.

Bear raised the volume in time to catch Chase's reply: "Why do you wear it?"

"It keeps jerks from bothering me."

"Am I bothering you?"

"Not yet."

Tim and Bear watched the rest of the B-roll for more of this daytime drama, but other than Yueh's further warming to Sam and Tess, it depicted little of value.

Bear popped the tape and thrust it into an immense jacket pocket. "You know who we gotta talk to now."

Chapter 43

Sam ground a stick into the top of the anthill, leaving it protruding like a flag. He squatted, fists in the dirt, elbows bracing his knees. Tiny red motion set the stick alive. A neighbor kid about two years younger aped Sam's stance, casting sideways glances and making minute corrections to his foot position. The sun had dropped from view behind the roof, bathing the front yard in a gray swath, a precursor to shadow. When the wind shifted, it brought laughter from the children in the park at the street's end.

Sam reached tentatively for the stick, finally snatching it and shaking off the ants while his little friend watched with wonderment. Pulled to the opposing curb, waiting for Bear to finish his check-in with the LAPD homicide detective working the Ted Sands murder, Tim watched Sam play.

Ginny came to mind, sitting on a park bench regarding her nemesis, the monkey bars, her swinging legs too short for her sneakers to scrape tanbark. No concern greater than if she was at last going to make her way across the metal bars. No knowledge of what was in store for her at the end of her brief life. No premonition of Roger Kindell. Kindell of the tall forehead, the sloppy mouth, the uncomprehending gaze.

Roger Kindell of the garage shack and the hacksaw.

The pain came, but it was duller these days. Maybe after a time, some of the nerves in a well-pried wound finally burned out. Or maybe a part of Tim had capitulated, had gratefully traded a memory sensation or two for numbness. Either way, Sam at the anthill brought Tim back over familiar terrain. Another seven-year-old on the brink of death. The difference was, Sam knew it.

Despite the fate hanging over him, he seemed like any other boy. Tim didn't know what he expected—someone more maudlin, more tragic, more precocious—but Sam was just a kid poking at insects. Tim couldn't help but reflect on his own trivial parental concerns. Someday while he worried about Tyler choking on a cashew or slipping on just-washed tile, one of the billion parts that made up his son's tiny, splendid body could malfunction, and then Tim or Dray would be the one wearing a pager. With all the resources and love that get poured into a child, year after year, there were no guarantees. A weakened artery wall. A renegade mole. A malfunctioning gene. Watching Sam issue bossy directives to his sidekick, Tim mulled over what he'd learned about Sam's stage of illness. He was a sweet kid on a slow-motion descent, a little worse every day. And there was not a thing anyone could do for him. Except Vector, and Chase had made clear the clinical trials were closed.

Tim became conscious of Bear's staring at him. Tim's focus on Sam, the comparison with Ginny—it was all embarrassingly apparent. He wondered if he felt so much for Sam because it was a way *not* to identify with Walker, a commando avenger so obviously like himself. Tim reined in his emotions, refocused on his job. He couldn't lose sight of Sam as a key link in an investigation.

Sam dropped his stick abruptly and ran inside. A few seconds later a burly kid on a Huffy dirt bike jumped the curb, coasting across the front yard. He hopped off his bicycle, running beside it, then letting it fall, and confronted Sam's cowed little friend.

"Where's Piss-Eyes?"

Still in his petite imitative crouch, the younger boy shrugged.

The kid kicked over the anthill, hopped on his bike, and rode off. A moment later the little boy rose, dusted off his knees, and trudged up the street, presumably to his house. Bear finished jotting some notes, hung up, and followed Tim to the house.

Tim knocked at the screen, and Kaitlin called for them to come in. She was occupied with Sam in the living room. He was curled up on the couch, listlessly flipping channels. Tim and Bear's intrusion brought a certain level of awkwardness to the domestic scene.

"What is it?" she asked.

Sam said, "*Nothing*, Kaitlin."

"Is it Dylan again, that little shit?"

"No. It wasn't anyone. I'm just sick of playing outside."

Kaitlin looked at Tim, and then Sam, waiting to see if Tim was going to rat him out. Tim shrugged. Seemingly exasperated with both of them, Kaitlin stormed outside.

Sam pulled himself from the couch and slumped toward the kitchen. He wore a T-shirt with a demented jester face and green lettering that said *Foot killer*. "Tommy gets scared when the ants come out."

"He's little," Tim said.

Sam doled out a hunk of rice from a cooker and sprinkled it with MCT oil. "Yeah, well, kids my age don't play with me."

Tim almost asked why not, but he looked at Sam's weary, world-wise face and didn't want to put him through the paces. Instead he said, "That must suck."

Sam stopped his sprinkling. He met Tim's eyes. "You get used to it."

"Listen, Sam, we gotta talk."

"So talk."

"I watched your news segment. With those guys from Vector . . ."

Sam's face brightened. "Dolan and Chase."

"Right. Did your mom spend any time with them?"

"Sure. When they came here for the TV story, then after during the commercial shoot. They paid me, you know. For the commercial. I wanted the PlayStation Portable, but Mom bought the dumb fridge instead."

"Did she hang out with them any other times?"

"She went to Vector for meetings sometimes. Brought me in for some testing and stuff. But she never, like"—his face screwed up with disgust—"*dated* them or went bowling with them or anything."

"Anyone else she saw that was, say, new?" Tim asked. "In the days before she . . . ?"

"Killed herself? Well, that's what she did. You might as well say it."

"Okay. Before she killed herself."

"A lawyer guy. I heard her on the phone with him once. She said she was gonna go see him at his office."

"Do you know what it was about?"

"No, but when I went in the living room after, there was some stuff from Vector—like brochures? papers and stuff?—out on the couch. So maybe it had to do with that."

"Do you remember anything about the papers? Were they letters? Did they look like research?"

Sam shrugged. "That stuff's kinda boring to me."

Bear firmed his mouth, lips bunching. Tim knew the look—Bear was all for squeezing the attorney until the only privilege he considered would be having Bear out of his office. Bear's hand rustled in his pocket, and he produced a picture of Ted Sands. "Did you ever meet this guy?" Bear waited until Sam shook his head. "How 'bout this guy?" Dean's photo elicited another head shake.

Tim asked, "Do you like Dolan and Chase?"

"Yeah. Chase had a cool guitar, and he could play, like, *anything.* Dolan was nice, but he sucked at Dungeons & Dragons." Sam added thoughtfully, "I'm not sure what I did wrong."

"What do you mean?"

"Why they didn't pick me."

From Bear's face it was clear the comment had caught him as off guard as it had Tim. A severe pause ensued, Sam looking at them with wide, curious eyes, awaiting an answer that might help him make sense of it. Tim's Nextel vibrated at his hip. Bear crouched down, his broad knees cracking, to mumble an answer to Sam so Tim could step away and take the call.

"The shooter used a silencer."

Tim held the phone away from his face, checking the caller ID. "Aaronson?"

"I took a look at the slug that killed Tess Jameson."

"I thought you couldn't tell from a slug if a silencer was used."

"Usually. But this silencer was rifled, with a different number of lands than the gun barrel. There were two sets of grooves on the projectile—one just barely offset from the other. I picked it up under the stereoscope and cast the marks in Microsil."

"Why wasn't this checked before?"

"Because most silencers we see are the smoothbore homemade variety. And most criminalists aren't as good as I am."

"I won't argue with that."

"And you shouldn't. Because I sourced the red stain for you, too."

Bear glanced up at Tim's expression, excited by proxy. Sam had wrangled away his badge and was busy flashing it from various poses.

"It's paintball fill," Aaronson continued. "The photo of the mark on the sidewalk outside Tess's house suggests it was squashed—stepped on, not fired. So I'm thinking you're right that it may have rolled out of the shooter's car, gotten crunched."

"He would've left more marks if it had gotten on the sole of his shoe."

"Not if he stepped up onto the grass to circle the house for a rear break-in. You said the back slider's missing a latch?"

"But then they'd have seen marks on the—"

"Sprinklers. June was dry as usual." Aaronson took a well-earned moment to be impressed with himself, then said, "More good news: It's a custom paintball, called the Bunny Bopper, designed to reduce bounces. It's got a brittle shell and easy-to-wipe fill. And it's made exclusively for a place called Game. Because they require easy-to-wipe fill and a softer, brittle shell."

"Why?" Tim asked.

Aaronson laughed, a nasal stutter. "Because the targets are naked."

Tim hung up and said to Bear, "We gotta go."

With reluctance Sam relinquished the five-point star, and they thanked him and stepped out into the brisk air. Her shoulders rounded, Kaitlin was on her knees by the kicked-over anthill, facing away. She didn't acknowledge them as they approached. A breeze parted her hair at her neck.

"I always wanted kids." She watched the red ants scurrying over the avalanched side of their home, set into unthinking motion. Endless repair work, one dirt speck at a time. "But I couldn't hold a pregnancy. Not past a few months. Walk didn't care so much, but me . . ." A listless shrug. "And now this."

"What can you do?" Bear said, rhetorically.

"I can wash his clothes and drive him to the hospital and pet his head at night," she said. "And if I'm lucky, we can do it over again."

She rose and walked past them into the house, the screen door banging behind her. After a moment Tim and Bear headed to the Explorer. The SUV pulled away from the curb, its taillights fading in the dusk.

The stand of juniper at the property line rustled and released Walker Jameson into the yard.

Chapter 44

Kaitlin looked up from the pot on the stove and started, dropping the wooden spoon.

Walker stood in the doorway. He said, "Sorry."

"You just—" She pointed to the front door.

"That's the guy?"

"Yeah. The one who—"

"Looks like me. Right." He ran a hand across his mouth, his palm rasping over the scruff. "You were right. I won't come back here anymore." He removed a disposable cell phone from his pocket and set it on the chipped table. "I want to leave this."

She stirred the sauce, pausing twice like she had something to say. Finally she cleared her throat, knuckled her nose awkwardly. "I'm sorry. What I said. About you never doing anything for anyone but yourself. I haven't forgotten the ways you were good to me."

He stepped once and hooked a hand behind her neck, pulled her forward on her tiptoes so their foreheads touched. She reached to press her hands to his chest but then didn't. They stayed like that for a moment, frozen, breathing the same air, her hands raised either to feel him or shove him away.

"I am Hrothgar of the Tree People! Fear my rat!" Sam guarded the hall, cracked plastic light saber raised, Viking helmet loose on his head.

Kaitlin settled back flat on her feet. "I think you mean 'wrath.' "

"Hrothgar of the Tree People might have a rat," Walker said.

Sam grabbed a plastic horn and shoved the oversize helmet back out of his eyes. His was an awkward face, years short of growing into itself, but something in his smile pulled his features into line, made the nose bow slightly, the chin firm. It made him, briefly, handsome.

"This is true," Kaitlin conceded.

Sam's stare still had not left Walker. "Why are you here?"

"To talk to you."

"I'm important today." Sam ran back down the hall, fending off imaginary villains with the Force.

Walker followed, finding him sitting on his bed, a lump beneath the comforter. A fluorescent length of light saber protruded like a tail. "The stuff that could've cured me is a syrup, like chocolate syrup," the lump said. "Except instead of chocolate, it's filled with the gene I need. I just had to take it in a shot once a month, and the other kids'd even be jealous because I got to have chocolate syrup and not them. But then they said I couldn't have it. The chocolate syrup. Why not?"

"Prob'ly because we can't pay for it."

"We?"

"Tess. Kaitlin. Whoever. It's too expensive's my guess. Look, I can't be here long and I need some answers."

Sam tugged at the comforter so it slid down over his head, leaving his hair mussed and his glasses pitched left. With a few wiggles of his cheeks and a nose scrunch, he righted the frames without raising his hands. "If I help you, can I get my gene?"

Walker looked away, but the kid's reflection was waiting in the mirrored closet door and then in the dark window. "Sure."

Sam's hopefulness forced a smile. "Promise?"

Walker said, "At the commercial shoot, you rode in a limo, right? Who was there?"

"Dolan, Chase, a bunch of camera guys. Oh—and that guy with the *Magnum, P.I.* shirts. Mr. Keating."

"What was the limo company called?"

Sam scrambled out of bed. "The driver gave me a card. He said I could call him if I ever needed a limousine." He dug in a drawer and handed a glossy card to Walker—ELITE CHAUFFEUR SERVICE, no driver name.

"I was gonna call him for Mom's birthday. She was gonna be thirty-nine, you know, and . . . darn it . . . darn it." He returned to the mattress and pulled the comforter back over his head, and then Walker heard him snuffling.

"Take that thing off your head."

Sam tugged it off. He pulled off his glasses and rubbed his eyes, then wiped his nose on his shirt.

"Was your mom with you the whole time?"

"Except when she left once in the middle to get her jacket from the limo. I was nervous, but she said she'd be right back, but then she wasn't. Not until they smeared off the makeup and stuff from my face—not girl makeup but TV makeup that even guys are supposed to wear. Then she was all weird when she came back."

"Weird how?"

"On the drive home, I thought she'd be all happy, but she wasn't. She had her jacket on, zipped up all the way, but it was hot."

Walker felt his skin get taut, as in a cool breeze.

The words of Victor the incompetent waiter returned, now sharpened with meaning. *I heard him say something about what happened in the limo at the shoot. He was sorta, I guess, apologetic without really being apologetic. I remember thinking, The problems these rich folks have, right?*

"Come here." He walked out, Sam at his heels, and shoved open the door to Tess's room.

Walker reached the mass of clothes crowding the closet. Some of the items he recognized from his childhood. Tess had never been any good at giving away old clothes. Too many years being broke, too many times coming up short for a date, a job interview, an outing with a new friend. Some of her clothes from her teenage years had cycled back into style once or twice already, and some never would.

Walker turned, expecting Sam at his side, but Sam stood in the hall, two feet back from the threshold. "Come on. Come in here."

Sam's face was red, maybe from crying or maybe because he was going to again. He didn't move.

From the kitchen Kaitlin yelled, "Dinner in fifteen, Sammy!"

"Get over here," Walker said.

His lips trembling, Sam regarded the white patch of carpet, the neatly made bed. He took a cautious step forward, one shoulder raised nearly to his chin, half cowering. He kept his eyes on the floor and stepped quickly to Walker's side. His hand reached out and grabbed at one of the cargo pocket flaps on Walker's pants. He twisted, pulling at the fabric.

Walker pointed at the virtual wall of fabric. "What did she wear to the shoot?"

Sam raised a quaking hand and scratched his shoulder. "A yellow one, but it's not here."

Walker caught a haze of yellow through the window of a garment bag. He tugged the bag free, unzipped it, and laid it open, exposing a run of fabric. "This one?"

A nod.

"Okay. Get outta here."

Sam ran from the room. Walker pulled the sundress free. One thin cornflower blue strap had been torn. A rip extended the side slit.

Had Tess been raped in this dress? Just mauled? He thought of his sister, like all those skinny, scared kids hauled to Boss's cell.

The assailant had lent her the car to get home. Gentlemanly. She'd ridden away from the shoot, jacket zipped to her chin so Sam wouldn't know. And then, ever mindful, she'd stored the evidence, readying for a counterattack she hadn't lived to make.

Walker shouldered against one of the broken closet doors, clutching the puddle of fabric in both hands. His head hummed, the sound the power lines give off over a desert road where nobody lives important enough to complain.

He balled the dress and stuffed it back into the closet. It took his legs a moment to respond, and then he walked out.

For once Sam's TV was dark. He sat on the floor, knees poked up into his T-shirt like he was cold. Walker paused at his doorway. Looked back. Gave him a little nod.

Sam nodded back.

Chapter 45

Through the humid night air, Tim and Bear could hear the popping of ammo and the strained shouts of hunters stalking prey. Darkness had settled over the Ballona Wetlands, the largest habitat of its kind in Los Angeles. A decades-old struggle between developers and environmentalists had resolved for the time being with the city relinquishing a few scattered parcels to environmentally friendly businesses. Industry's encroachment was nothing new; the Spruce Goose had been constructed on these very wetlands back when Howard Hughes held the deed.

An Olds Cutlass Supreme from the seventies was parked by the awning, looking postcard pristine with its broad, smooth hood, a sparkling powder blue coat, and a restored white soft top devoid of bird shit—no small feat in the wetlands. The license plate inquired provocatively, RUGAME?

Behind the building, green netting enclosed the fifteen-acre preserve. Tim and Bear walked along the perimeter, peering in, their shoes sinking in mud. The hunt-zone motif was Disneyland jungle—wide fronds, pump waterfalls, mud wallows, camo-splattered boxing heavy bags feathered with leaves and swinging like mini-golf distractions. Tim caught a flash of flesh deep in the foliage, the frenzied run of the out-gunned, and then the chuffing of four men, hunting in pairs, closing the distance.

By the time he and Bear retraced their steps to the entrance, his cuffs clung wetly to his ankles. They stepped into the lounge and took a moment getting their bearings, Bear readjusting the star on his belt like an old-school deppity. The roomful of men hummed with the locker-room and private-club glee of the unsupervised. A focused gentleman at the bar practiced a spin move into the holster, dropped his paintball gun, and patiently set up for another try. Thumbtacked to the bamboo wainscoting were flyers advertising used equipment, martial arts classes, and car pools to gun shows and paintball tournaments.

"Car pools?" Tim read incredulously.

Bear said, "Hard to get around when you live with your mom."

Three middle-aged guys with aggressive sideburns were oohing and aahing over a new scope, ignoring the woman with porn-star dimensions nestling into the lap of a self-satisfied gentleman. Evidently hard feelings didn't persist after the pursuit. Not when there was recompense for making nice.

One of the lap dancee's clean-cut cohorts did a double take at Tim.

Tim offered him a curt nod. "Your Honor."

The justice hastened for the exit, reseating his tie and frowning severely as if on to weighty matters. Tim and Bear pressed on past the tiki zone. An undulating gauze curtain led back to the preserve. In the rear office, which doubled as a staging area, a group of eager weeknight warriors, tacked up from camo socks to face paint, endured an orientation; their group hunt was about to kick off.

Someone was streaming an MPEG from Iraq on his PalmPilot, sharing the footage with a cluster of onlookers. Tim recognized the distinctive percussion of twenty mike-mike rounds, the whooping blades of either an Apache attack helo or a Cobra Gunship. "Check it out," the ringleader said. "The terrorist pops back into view and"—assorted cries and exclamations drowned him out—"just *disintegrates*."

From all sides carried snatches of other conversations, rife with buzzwords.

"—got a new Violent bolt for his Intimidator. The bad boy's Teflon, so the internal diameter stays nice and smooth—"

One voice, notable for its high tenor, stood out from the cacophony. The hefty presenter in the staging area paced in front of the rookie shooters like a drill sergeant. "No shooting under five meters. No head shots. Don't aim for the genitalia. Bouncers don't count—only bursts. Everyone sign your waivers?"

A price board behind the counter announced the fifteen-hundred-dollar entry fee. To the side a video tech gone bulky with elbow and knee pads adjusted the settings on his digital camera.

Tim knew before he saw the name on the speaker's nickel badge. Wes Dieter's discerning gaze snagged on one of his charges. "Get your barrel plug in, pal. This isn't a game."

Bear couldn't stifle a guffaw, and five pairs of night-vision goggles swiveled toward them. "Hey, man," one of the paintballers said, gesturing at Tim, "it's the Troubleshooter." A few of the guys offered waves, and one chucked Tim's shoulder. Tim caught Wes staring, too—that odd blend of reverence and disquiet.

Good to know his fame had reached such rarefied circles.

Wes returned his focus to the men before him. "You boys ready to hunt some pussy?" A chorus of cheers. "Candy Racer, you're on!"

A side door banged open, and out paraded an Asian woman with flawless tanned skin and breasts too high and hard to have been factory equipment. She wore goggles, low-cut tennis socks with lime-green poofs at the heels, black Pumas, and that was it.

Bear's mouth finally got the better of him. "Can't you at least give the girl a helmet?"

Wes cast a know-it-all gaze in his direction. "Deers don't wear helmets, do they?"

"I believe it's 'deer.'"

"What?"

"The plural of 'deer' is 'deer.'"

"I *said* 'deer.'"

A couple of the men nodded in agreement, eager to get on the range. Bear looked to Tim, and Tim shrugged. Bear pretended to be peeved, blowing a jet of air where his bangs would be if he didn't have cropped Polish hair.

Wes walked over and stroked Candy Racer's well-toned flank, then administered it a jockey's smack. To whoops and cheers, she sprinted off into the preserve, the gauze curtain whistling around her. "Remember, boys, she gets a two-minute lead."

"Last I checked," Bear said, as it became increasingly clear who was going to have to play good cop this round, "deer don't wear goggles either."

"You're a perceptive guy *and* a shrewd grammarian," Wes said, minding his stopwatch. "But city business services came down on me. We used to be able to shoot the girls anywhere on their bods, too, but then we had to add regs. We still do our best to simulate natural conditions."

"Of what?" Bear said. "Berserking Vikings in the Amazon Basin?"

"We're an environmentally sound business."

"Jungle orchids being indigenous to the Ballona Wetlands."

"Hey, they like green, they got green." Wes clicked his stopwatch ahead of schedule and said, with a tough-guy delivery, *"Game on."* He waved on the paintballers, who shuffled eagerly off into the preserve, barking code words. "It's bad enough the fuckin' Christians are cracking down. I don't need Johnny Law harassing me in front of my clients. You here on official business, or just to express your personal views on the morality of leisure?"

Before Bear decided to wax poetic with synonyms for "clients," Tim said, "We're working a murder investigation that points here." He flashed a picture of Tess without asking a follow-up question, just to see what he could read in Wes's face.

Wes's eyes snagged on the photograph an instant, and then he shuffled back behind the counter and plugged a few paintball guns into an automatic washer, seating the water nozzles into the gun barrels. A fat tabby leapt up from a hidden crouch, purring and parading across his shoulders. *"What* pointed you here?"

"Paint. My guy traced it to your place. You make your own paintballs?"

"Have 'em made, sure. I need to, place like this, bare flesh and all. Besides, hard-shell mishaps can get expensive. A paintball ricochets around enough, it hits the guy with the most expensive lawyer."

The cat's face spread in a hiss that made Bear take a step back. Wes smiled and glanced down at his clipboard. He clicked on a loudspeaker, and his high-pitched voice echoed through the building: "Santa Monica Blood Warriors on deck. Start suiting up at the half hour. Tunnel Rat, you're in the hole." He hefted himself onto a barstool, the cat taking flight to the back counter.

Mounted above a computer monitor was a trophy shot of Wes in the preserve. One boot rested on the sweat-slick rump of a naked, prostrate black woman Tim recognized from semipro beach volleyball tournaments sometimes aired on the local sports channels. The blatant misogyny and—accidental?—racist overtones must have brought an inadvertent scowl to Tim's face, because Wes looked at him, a touch self-conscious in the face of the Troubleshooter's judgment, and said, "Hey, man, these chicks take home three hundo a run, a cool half grand if they don't get hit. Beats waitressing for tips."

"Socially responsible of you to keep them off the mean streets," Bear said.

"I provide people with a little diversion, and a very good income to some just-about-unemployable women. And—unlike your jobs—it's fun. You see, in here I'm king. Four-time course champion. I can hit an ace of spades with a nine mil at twenty yards."

"That's great if you get attacked by a bridge club."

Tim wheeled on Bear. "Take out the tampon, Jowalski. If some dumb broad wants to get shot in the tits for three hundred bucks a pop, who gives a shit?"

Bear raised his hands—a classic *What do I need it for?*—and walked out.

After the front door slammed, drawing giggles from two of the quarry-turned-strippers, Tim pivoted back to the counter. "Sorry 'bout that. He's a former bull cop. Old dog, old tricks. He hasn't figured out that when you need answers from people, you don't bust their balls first. We're dependent on guys like you to make headway, you know? We're not writing speeding tickets here. Jesus *Christ*."

"Hey, whatever. Don't worry about it. I'm used to dealing with assholes."

"I bet you see all kinds through here."

Wes said, "Believe me."

" 'Nam vets?"

"Oh, yeah. Now and then. Old guys, but *man,* are they mean. Former law enforcement, too. Rich college kids—mostly USC. Lotta Persians. We get some guys training for tourneys, like the squad that just deployed to the preserve."

Tim leaned over the counter conspiratorially, setting his weight on his elbow. "Anyone . . . *shadier?*" The pause was a beat too long, giving Wes too much time from brain to mouth, so Tim offered his hand. "Tim Rackley."

"I know who you are." Wes thumbed out his badge from his shirt so Tim could read his name. "And I'd be happy to help a stand-up dude like yourself."

"Look, Wes, you're the owner. A guy like you, a big shot here, well liked—you got your finger on the pulse. Who comes through here?"

Wes cast a glance around, then lowered his voice to match Tim's. "We get some *Soldier of Fortune* types, sure. A lotta whispered conversations at the bar. This place is the real deal. A place to get stuff, ya know? But I got a good thing here—count those guys. Each one is paying fifteen hundo. Overhead, dick. I walk out with forty, fifty K a week. Your partner would call me a less-than-model citizen—but I'm paying my taxes and putting it away, not jeopardizing my retirement just to know what deals get made here."

"No fuckin' way. Not with hard-core operators moving through. That'd be like making me responsible for what every guy in my platoon did on liberty."

"*Exactly.* I can't see every inch of this operation. I make sure I don't. But you know, a guy's been around, like me, a guy hears things. Whispers."

"Right. Like maybe one of these boys"—a wave at the crowded lounge—"takes his hunting to the next level?"

Wes glanced around, having a hard time keeping the glint of pride from showing in his eyes. "I've heard hits come through here. I think it's all bullshit. What have you been told?"

Tim held a poker face. "We've got solid evidence implicating Game."

Wes took this in with a regretful nod. "Maybe a money drop got set up here—the jury's still out. That guy Sands all over the news—got his head blown off in Bel Air?" He hesitated a moment. "He was in here.

June sixth. Rented two lockers. Left a briefcase in one overnight. Maybe he was the cash courier, maybe not. Maybe someone came in here after, picked up the cash and the contract."

"Who?"

"I'm a computer guy at heart, so I bounced through the right chat rooms for a little follow-up."

"Which sites?"

"The usual BS. Mercenary forums. Silencer chat rooms. Militia sites, you know." Wes jotted down several URLs, and Tim pocketed the slip of paper, knowing that Guerrera would likely surf around and find little more than wannabes jawing off behind the protection of virile screen names. "The topic's in the wind, all right," Wes continued. "People giving theories anonymously."

"What name's being bandied about?"

Wes actually looked both directions before leaning across the counter and putting his mouth inches from Tim's ear. He smelled of coconut lotion. "The Piper." He settled back on the barstool, the cat jumping into his lap. "No one knows who the guy is. I coulda seen him here like every week and not known it. The guy's stone cold, I heard. Stays remote, can only be contacted through the Internet. The chat rooms I gave you? Like those, but ones that guys like us can't even find."

"Is that all you know?"

"Like I said, I don't *know* anything. That's what's in the wind."

Tim showed Wes a photo of Walker. "Seen *this* guy?" He watched Wes closely, but he remained impassive. "Uh-uh."

"Let me know if you do." Tim pocketed the picture. "I'll need a list of your employees and clients. We won't let leak that you slipped it to us."

Wes's face reddened. "Employees, sure, but you think we keep a client list here? Not with this business. I'd be finished."

"You knew Ted Sands by name, and I doubt he ambled up with his briefcase full of cash and gave his driver's license as collateral to reserve the lockers. Can't exactly recognize him from the picture the *Times* ran either. Even if the names your clients sign on your waivers are bullshit—which I'm sure they are—and even if the occasional credit card you run traces to an offshore account or a shell corp—which it might—I know you keep different records for when you need blackmail leverage on a powerful client or for when the girls rent out after hours. If not, you'd be a fool and an incompetent pimp, and we both know you're neither."

"I don't have shit." Some of Wes's swagger was returning, along with the first premonition that he might have been duped. "And if you serve on me, you won't get anything either. There's nothing to get."

Tim straightened up. "Listen to me closely, Wes. You're gonna get me those names, and you're going to do it right now while I wait. And I'm not waiting long."

Wes affected a casual sneer, but his voice came out higher than usual. "Or else?"

"We will tear apart every square foot of your operation, and we'll do so with vigor and pleasure. I will call my buddy at the IRS, my brother-in-law who's a comer in the Office of Finance, and my niece who's a lesbian feminist in the U.S. Attorney's Office looking to make a name. We will write you up, tie you up, and drag you into court for nuances of the law you've never heard of, right down to the missing side view on your Oldsmobile out front. I will post federal agents outside your property to tip their hats to all the ministers and judges who come in here to shoot naked girls' flanks. By the time the news crews catch wind, there won't be space for their vans to park. You think that'll go over swell with your 'clientele'? Look at me." Tim snapped his fingers, terminating the drift of Wes's dismayed eyes. "I will ruin your life. I will eat you for lunch and come back for seconds. There is a murder investigation we have traced here, and I will see the law do right by that victim if I have to burn you and every other woman-hating shitheel who's plunked down a dime in this fuckhole."

Wes's mouth had creaked slightly open. A line of sweat glistened in the strands of his scraggly mustache. Tim's voice had not raised a notch.

Tim said, "I will be patient until I leave this room. Now, you give me those names to make me go away happy or your carefree life ends in"—he reached over the counter and retrieved Wes's stopwatch—"five minutes."

Thirty-seven seconds passed, and then Wes slid off the barstool, falling onto his feet. He fussed at the computer with the lethargic motions of the chronically depressed and printed an employee list, then retrieved a lockbox from a cabinet and removed a mound of license-plate photos, some with names and addresses written flash-card style on the backs. He dumped the pictures into a plastic bag with the spread-sheet and handed them over at exactly 4:23.

Tim tossed him the stopwatch and left, nodding politely to the ladies at the bar on his way out the door. As he pulled in his first lungful of fresh wetland air, Bear eased the Explorer around, meeting him under the awning like a well-trained valet.

Chapter 46

At half past nine in the morning, the electricity kicked back on. The TV blared; the cheap chandelier over the kitchen nook flickered to life; a square worker's fan by the garage door revved up so fast it blew itself over.

At the commotion Walker had sprung from the floor up over the couch into the best position of cover the family room afforded; he found himself in a high-kneel shooting stance, his Redhawk trained on the front door. He returned his revolver to the back of his jeans and rose.

He unplugged the fan, which was rattling its death throes against the floorboards, then turned off the lights and the garbage disposal, which was roaring its waterless displeasure. He couldn't locate a remote, so he thumbed down the volume on the TV itself, leaving the morning anchor to murmur in the background about Gaza settlements.

The disposable cell remained on the arm of the sofa where he'd left it, resting atop Tess's tiny bound calendar. He picked it up, hit "redial," and waited for the same answering machine he'd gotten the previous nine tries.

This time a woman answered. "Elite Chauffeur Service."

"Yes, hi, I'm calling from the billing department at Vector Biogenics, and I'm showing an outstanding invoice from April nineteen."

"Just a minute, sir." She hammered on a ridiculously loud keyboard. "Yes, here it is. I show that it's been paid in full."

"This was the trip to the studio?"

"Yes, Quixote Studios. The limousine was booked through Mr. Kagan's office."

On the TV, Walker's booking photo appeared in the graphics box above the newscaster's shoulder. He walked over and clicked the volume back up. "That's the one. Apologies—I must have my records crossed."

"No problem, sir."

An attractive Asian reporter had filled the screen. "Tim Rackley, known as the Troubleshooter—"

"Oh, and one more thing," Walker said. "The driver we used last time, Mr. Kagan liked quite a bit. What was his name?"

"Chuck Hannigan."

He asked her to spell the last name, then asked, "Is Mr. Hannigan available today?"

"Oh, no. He's quite busy. He's available after six?"

Walker declined, thanked her, and hung up.

Looking a touch uncomfortable under the studio lighting, Tim Rackley spoke directly to the camera. He seemed to stare into the model house's family room and address Walker alone. *"—message for Walker Jameson. I understand that you believe firmly in what you're doing. I have shared your motivation. We have information about your sister that impacts what you're trying to do."*

To Tim's side the newslady couldn't contain her surprise—hot damn, a scoop unfolding right before her. Walker would bet his own face held an equal measure of shock.

The exploitation of Tess Jameson, take two.

Tim said, *"I want you to contact me at the number below, anytime, day or night."*

A 213 number popped on-screen like a telethon prompt.

Walker stepped in front of the TV, going face-to-face with the Troubleshooter. He might have been looking into a mirror.

"Careful what you wish for," he said.

Chapter 47

A **young security** guard led Tim and Bear down the shiny warehouse corridor. Storage racks, bolted to the concrete floor, stretched up to the forty-foot ceiling, assiduously labeled boxes and crates filling each shelf. Industrial rolling ladders with handrails were parked at intervals like well-tended vehicles. In the dirt yard outside, the spike-collared Doberman kept protesting the deputies' intrusion. Barks and growls reached through the high windows, echoing around the bare walls of the vast building. Even Bear, nicknamed the Dog Whisperer around the Arrest Response Team for his preternatural rapport with the explosive-detection canines, had failed to settle him as he and Tim had strode to the long-term-storage warehouse's entrance.

Tim checked the lettering on the storage containers looming overhead. MARCONE. MARDEL. And at last a raft of MARTINEZes. The common surname continued around the corner to the next aisle before Tim encountered a run of legal-width cardboard boxes stamped ESTEBAN MARTINEZ, ATTORNEY-AT-LAW. The file boxes, organized roughly by date, carried stickers in hazard-warning orange—CONFIDENTIAL: LAWYER-CLIENT MATERIALS.

Tim rolled a ladder over and put his foot on the bottom rung to begin his ascent. The guard rested a hand on his forearm, halting him, and turned to Bear, whom he figured for the heavy. "Listen, you can check out whatever, but I know you're not supposed to *open* anything without a warrant."

Bear quelled the kid's concerns with a Godfather-like patting of the air. "Like we said, we're just following up on a trademark infringement. If there's no knockoff logo on the outside of the box, we're out of here. If there is, we'll come back with paper."

Tim scaled the ladder, reaching this year's June dates on the third shelf up. He located the box from the last week of the month, grabbed it by a punched-out handle, and jogged it loose, letting the shelf support the far end. Barely pulled into view, a typed label filled the index square on the lid's side flap. Tim scanned the names, none of them familiar, then tried again with the neighboring box from mid-July. *Will Newell. Fred Marcussen. Theresa Jameson.*

The box Tim held propped before his face contained the legal records of Tess's meetings with her attorney on a matter likely involving Vector Biogenics. Meetings that had taken place days before her murder.

And Tim couldn't so much as crack the lid.

Bear regarded the box reverently. Tim squirmed his hand around through the punched-out handle, fingertips brushing papers. He let the tiny metal device fall inside, nodded at Bear—mission accomplished—then said, with feigned exasperation, "No logo. Struck out," and shoved the file box back into its slot among the others.

He descended the ladder, and he and Bear headed out, leaving Tess's files behind.

Chapter 48

The scent of brine, damp wood, and seaweed brought Walker
back to exotic ports of missions past and made him crave the burn of
tobacco in his lungs. Crouched at the dark brink of land, he kept his
gaze fixed way at the end of the floating dock, where a houseboat
rocked in its slip. The sole point of living movement, a man stooped and
shuffled, waxing his deck with hand-slip brushes. Unseen crabs scuttled on the throw of black rocks at the water's edge. The slips were dotted with weekend sailboats, Bayliner cruisers, and motor yachts too
spit-polished to be more than vanity possessions. A quiet place to live,
undisturbed among the playthings of the rich.

The dock was well positioned at the edge of the two-mile channel off
the harbor that gave Marina del Rey its name, a good distance up from
Fisherman's Village with its rip-off New England buildings, cobblestone
paths, and landlubber tourists wielding ice cream cones. The village's
boutiques were long closed, but the eateries still threw wobbly streaks of
light across the black water. When the wind shifted just so, it carried a
few rueful notes from the seafood restaurant's bad string quartet. A
plane rumbled overhead, three dots of light blurred by the thin August
clouds, still climbing from the LAX runway it had left behind five miles
south.

The strip-planked houseboat was good and light, with enough salt
in its wounds to lend it a cranky, rustic character. A white life preserver,

243

flaked into a mosaic on the pilothouse wall, announced *The Jeeves*—a dead giveaway. As was its owner's air of strained dignity; he was a service-industry lackey if Walker had ever seen one.

An afternoon intel-gathering trip to an Internet café had yielded a wealth of data, including the address of the mail drop in the boatyard deckhouse ten yards from Walker's back. There between the laundry room and coin-accessed showers for the live-aboards was the name Walker sought, rendered on a blue sticky band cranked out of an old twist-top label maker.

The man rose from all fours, stretched his back with a hands-on-hips arch, and settled on a bench with an Amstel and a cigarette.

Walker headed for the boat, minding the bob of the dock beneath his feet. The man watched him as he passed through one spill of lamplight and then another.

Walker stopped on the dock at the edge of the thirty-five-foot slip, the man rocking out of time with his own rise and fall. The trusty ropes creaked, straining against their moorings. The man took a pull from his beer, not yet fearful.

"Chuck Hannigan?"

"That's right."

Walker stepped up onto the houseboat.

Hannigan set down his beer and rose quickly. "You're supposed to ask permission to come aboard."

Walker strode to the triangular hatch at the bow. The just-waxed deck was slick. No grime, no oxidation. Chuck Hannigan made a fine swabbie.

Walker pulled the anchor onto the deck, throwing the toggle so the windlass fed chain out into a puddle at his feet. He dragged the anchor to the prow, the crown raising peels of epoxy varnish, the chain rattling behind. Hannigan looked scared now, his body bladed to hide one arm. Walker dropped the anchor at Hannigan's feet and was not surprised to look up into the barrel of a flare gun.

Walker's hands blurred, and then both of Hannigan's arms were twisted back on themselves, the muzzle pressed into the soft pouch of flesh beneath his chin. Walker's face was inches from Hannigan's, so close he felt the heat of the cigarette cherry against his cheek. He nodded, and then Hannigan nodded, and Walker pried the flare gun free and released him. Hannigan let out a shaky breath. Walker tossed the flare gun overboard, then kicked open the rail gate. Removing a pair of handcuffs from his back pocket, Walker secured one end to the anchor chain, the other to Hannigan's ankle. Hannigan looked down, eyes glazed, just now seeming to comprehend that Walker had cuffed him to the anchor. The cigarette, now long on ash, dangled from the corner of his mouth.

"You know who I am?"

Hannigan said, "I just figured it out."

Walker toed the anchor toward the open rail gate, and it coasted a few inches on the waxy deck. Some water lapped up, beading on the wood.

Hannigan said, "Don't."

A trilevel yacht drifted past, couples twirling with champagne glasses on the upper deck. It passed swiftly, trailing laughter and the smell of weed, and the wake rocked *The Jeeves,* causing the anchor to slide about a foot toward the rail gate. Hannigan let out a little cry, ash falling across his chest.

Walker held up the handcuff key between his thumb and forefinger like a photo slide.

"If I tell you everything, will you let me live?"

Walker gave a nod.

"I've been waiting to tell someone. Waiting for someone to come, I guess. Hell, maybe I was waiting for you." Hannigan flicked his butt overboard and tapped the pack in his pocket, waiting for Walker's approval before he removed and lit another cigarette. "It was at this commercial shoot, right? I'd picked up your sister and your—I guess it'd be your nephew?—at their house. Nice lady, your sister. I really liked her. Mr. Kagan—"

"Chase?"

"That's right. He was in the limo, too. I drove them to the shoot and waited in the limo bay in the garage. It's an underground garage, real private, you know? No one was there." His voice grew strained. "I stay with the car always, right? So Ms. Jameson comes out to get something—her purse, maybe—and Chase followed. He ducked inside. Started flirting heavy. She didn't want any. A nice lady, like I said. So he, you know . . ."

"He what?"

Hannigan's lips quivered. A drop of sweat rolled down his right cheek, staining his shirt. "He forced himself on her."

"Who was there?"

"Just Mr. Kagan—Chaisson Kagan. But this other fellow came out— Hawaiian shirt?—to check on things. The windows were tinted, but he must've heard . . ."

Walker nodded him on.

". . . something. He knocked on the window, then Chase rolled it down a bit, and . . . well, then the guy sort of stood guard."

Walker started to talk but had to clear his throat. "Anyone else?"

"Dolan Kagan came out also. He saw from a distance, maybe. I don't know what he saw. The other guy told him to go away."

"So Chase could finish."

Hannigan wiped his cheek. "I guess so."

"And you sat there."

"I did. I sat there." A defeated pause, and then Hannigan rallied to his own defense. "I'm not a bad man. I've not slept, barely, since it happened. Like I said, she was a nice lady. But what was I gonna do? Look, guys like that, they pay my rent, right? I can barely afford to live out here on this square of water. They got fancy lawyers and press agents and publicists in their back pocket. I'm gonna . . . what? Press charges?" Hannigan wept silently into the fold of his hand. "I've had all order of things happen when I'm up front, behind the divider, but never anything like that. Never anything like that. Never."

"You were in the car. The whole time."

"I was," Hannigan said. "I was."

Walker stared out at the world's largest man-made marina. Then he kicked the anchor off the boat. It plunked into the water, the chain grinding across the deck's edge as it paid out, kicking up chips and splinters.

Hannigan's voice came high with disbelief. "You said you wouldn't kill me if I told you!"

"Changed my mind."

"Give me the key! Please, God, give it to me!"

Walker flipped the key in the water. He and Hannigan stared at each other, and then the chain pulled tight and Hannigan slammed to the deck and skidded off into the water with a splash. His cigarette, still lit, remained behind on the deck where it had been jerked from his mouth or he from it.

His churning was barely audible among the groan of the boats, the slap of water against the pilings, the cry of the night birds; he was just a few feet below the surface. After a minute or so, Walker sensed only the regular sigh and heave of the sea.

He picked up Hannigan's cigarette, placed it in his mouth, and headed along the dock for land, the orange dot moving through the mist like a firefly.

Chapter 49

Tim's head throbbed from too much caffeine and from squinting at online databases. He threw down one of the few license-plate photos lacking a name on its back and rubbed his eyes. To catch Walker they had to get a step ahead of him, to locate his next target before he did.

Using a hit man to lure a fugitive was ambitious, but Tim knew, if the lead was accurate, that Walker would be gunning for the Piper sooner or later. The Service would have to find him sooner. Set up surveillance. And wait.

Thomas had been playing Ma Bell all afternoon, gathering word on the Piper from Service offices around the country. In the meantime Tim, Bear, and Guerrera had split up the flash-card IDs of Game's esteemed clientele, double-checking the addresses on the backs and finding Wes's intel surprisingly accurate. The list was like a who's who of rich scumbags. A surgeon with a felony for selling meds. A studio VP who went down for a handgun in his Porsche. A failure-to-appear. More businessmen with embezzlement and fraud charges than Tim could count. The clean ones were almost more troubling. Despite the varied degrees of shadiness, no one was an obvious choice for the Piper. Guerrera had red-flagged a few top contenders, but Tim was skeptical that any of them were extracurricular hit men.

The Piper was a professional, which meant that even if one of the flash-card leads panned, they'd probably wind up with a link in a longer chain—a Hertz rental, a stolen car, a fake plate. Or maybe the Piper rode Yellow Cab, in which case they were shit out of luck. Unless Thomas came through with something that rang the cherries.

On the corner TV, Maybeck was reviewing the footage of Walker's brief passage through the Vector lobby. For the fifth time, Tim watched Walker disappear into the spokes of the revolving doors. Nothing new gleaned from the tape. Likewise no sightings of the Camry that had been stolen by the San Pedro landfill the night of Walker's escape. Freed continued pursuing the trails of Pierce's financials, so far with limited success.

Thomas racked the phone, finally, and ran both hands through his hair. It took a moment before he seemed to pick up that everyone was waiting on him, and then he said, "Still low resolution. The Piper's a professional, rumored to operate out of Los Angeles and Phoenix. He does some wet work for Chicago, may have been used by the Asian Triad in Houston and locally by the Russians. Hell, Rack, you should pick up this lead yourself. It's right in your area of expertise."

Tim ignored the dig. "Do we have a name?"

"Leslie Cardover." Thomas nodded at the gallery of photos spread across the table. "Not one of our Gameboys. If it's fake is another question."

Tim wondered if Leslie Cardover drove a low-rider with a hood ornament the size of a bowling ball. "If we're gonna use him, we'd better get to him before Walker turns him into ground beef."

"Or vice versa."

"My money's on Walker."

"Seems to be." Thomas cleared his throat hard into a fist, then swept the remains of his lunchtime burrito from desktop to trash can. "My hook at the Bureau said the Piper's been keeping his name off the boards for a while. He may have been feeling the heat after this Aspen job he allegedly did in January. A launderer for the Colombians."

"That'll do it," Bear remarked.

"So he flies to L.A. and takes out a single mom," Guerrera said. "Safer prey."

Bear noted Tim's troubled expression. "What's bugging you?"

"The hit on Tess *was* highly competent"—Tim took a breath, held it a moment—"but not meticulous. If this guy's a high-end contract player, why the left-side entry wound? The neighbor sighting? And the paint?"

"The car the hundred-year-old neighbor claimed to see?" Guerrera said. "Who knows if that's real? As for the entry wound, shit, *socio*, that's a pretty tiny detail, something even a pro could overlook. I mean, Tess Jameson *was* left-handed."

"Maybe so," Tim said. "Either way, we need more on the Piper, and we need it in a hurry."

Bear asked the room at large, "Any movement from the Vegas Task Force on the Aryan Brotherhood hit men?"

Zimmer said, "I been on it with Summer. They're watching the AB chapter, but there's been no unusual activity."

A court security officer ran in, the door banging against the wall. His neck was flushed. Tim cringed, anticipating another bad phone lead or interview request. "Rack, there's a call you're gonna want to take on line three. *Now.*"

Tim glanced at the phone unit centered on the broad conference table. The red light flashed rapidly, as if to announce a malfunction. "Who is it?"

The officer gestured for him to hurry up. "Walker Jameson."

Chapter 50

There's a pay phone on the northwest corner of Baldwin and Huntington in Arcadia. It'll ring in thirty minutes." Slung in the fork of a sturdy oak, Walker clicked off his cell phone and refocused his tactical binoculars on the main house, which the laser range finder put at 105 meters away. The binocs were night-vision equipped, though he didn't need the feature since the lit interiors provided clear visibility. Through a front window, he could see the two hired security hands still sitting detail in the foyer, playing chess, handguns and walkie-talkies bulging their blazers. The Spectra Shield vest beneath Walker's shirt was flexible, a starchier version of a wetsuit top, the ballistic composite lighter and thinner than its woven Kevlar counterpart.

Walker let the binocs drift south. A Pathfinder with dealer plates slowed as it approached the rear gate. The tinted driver's window rolled down, and Percy Keating waved an access card at the pad. The gate rumbled open, and he pulled through and parked beside the guest-house, a four-room stand-alone in the far corner of the estate. Through an abundance of windows, Walker watched an attractive Asian woman greet Percy inside, then lead him through a beaded curtain into a candlelit room where a low massage table dressed with towels awaited. Percy peeled off his shirt, a pale yellow number rife with fronds and daiquiris. His wife crossed to the window and lowered the bamboo shade.

Walker slid from the tree and began his approach.

———

The woman drifted musically through the beaded curtain, replenishing her hands with lotion from the pump on the shelf beside the sleeping Buddha carved in soapstone. Her slippered feet jerked off the ground—kicking noiselessly—the moist rag clamped over her mouth, and a few seconds later Walker set her limp form down on the tile.

Over the hypnotic twanging of Eastern instruments, Percy's muffled voice called, "Hurry, *tee ruk*."

Walker slipped through the curtain, the beads rattling soothingly. Percy remained on his stomach, naked, his face sunk to the ears in the crescent headrest. Acupuncture needles of various lengths stood up from his back like spines. When he shifted, they rippled like the coat of an animal. The needles' placement grew denser at the base of his back, a few even straying to the ruddy hump of his ass. An incense cone teased a string of spicy smoke into the air. Percy's clothes, neatly folded, were on the silk cushion of a rattan chair, a walkie-talkie and a Colt .45 pinning them down.

Walker circled the table and Percy moaned, anticipating pleasure. Gray hairs were scattered across the mass of his shoulders. "Whaddaya say you free me from those needles so I can turn over?"

"Not just yet," Walker said.

Percy lurched up, and Walker struck him across the face, feeling the bones of his knuckles connect with the hard ledge of Percy's jaw like the skin between them was bedsheet-thin. Percy flew off the table and hammered into the wall, crying out as the needles dug into him and snapped off, the broken heads pinging on the floor. He reared up, but Walker hit him again, fist to sternum, sending him reeling back into an embroidered silk hanging. The whimper that rose from Percy seemed to be leaking out around the penetrating steel. As he deflated, he keeled forward, leaving bloody streaks on the wall, the heads of sunken needles stubbling his lower back. His jaw hung off kilter. It made him look quizzical.

"You set up the contract," Walker said.

"No." The word, blurred to Down syndrome proportion by the unhinged jaw, forced a crimson bubble at Percy's lips.

"That's not what Ted Sands told me."

Percy was hard to understand. "Within a week you'll be dead or getting your ass rented in prison." He tried to move, but his back brushed the wall and his legs straightened like he'd been electrocuted.

Walker withdrew his revolver and held it at his side. "Your wife is alive in the next room. Unconscious, but still alive."

Slid low so the wall forced his head forward into a painful nod, Percy registered the threat, his pupils straining upward.

"Who'd you hire?" Walker waited a moment, then aimed at Percy's head.

"The Piper."

"What's his real name?"

"I don't know. No one knows. You don't get more with these guys."

"Who paid him? Who paid the Piper?"

Percy's laugh was a moist wheeze. "Witty."

Walker put a boot on his chest. A needle broke against the floor.

Percy howled, his chin awash in blood. "Who the fuck you think paid him?"

"Was it the old man? Was he in on it?"

A dark grimace. "The old man is in on everything."

The radio on the rattan chair burst to life. *"Base One to Big Brother. Mr. Kagan wants to see you."*

Percy looked up from his painful slump, breaths rattling in his chest. Walker shifted his weight forward onto his boot. Percy's face contorted, and popping sounds came out of his mouth. Walker pressed down once, hard, 190 pounds of fuck you, and there was a terminal crackle and a shudder of flesh, and then there weren't any more popping sounds.

"Big Brother? Big Brother come in?"

Walker picked up the walkie-talkie, thumbing the side button as he headed for the door. "Be right there."

The security guard hunched over the chessboard. His partner leaned back on the metal folding chair, releasing an impatient sigh that carried up the staircase curve to the ceiling and echoed back, a ghostly whisper. An ancient housekeeper bused their empty glasses, muttering Polish to herself and adjusting her box-pleated maid's cap.

The guard's radio chimed, and he pulled it from his belt, keeping his eyes on the board. "Base One."

"Rook to A-five."

"What?"

"Rook to A-five. Or he's got your queen cornered."

The guard released the button and stood, his blazer rasping against the chair. He and his partner shifted their anxious gazes around the night-shrouded windows. They were about to break for the intercom system when the mail slot lid clanked open and a grenade scuttled across the floor, spinning to a halt at their feet. They sprinted for cover, getting no more than a few steps when an explosion, originating across the room from the grenade, bounced the foundation. Pebbles of ballistic glass rained across the floorboards.

A muzzle blazed from outside, and the first guard grabbed his thigh and collapsed. Walker stepped through the manhole-size breach in the window, cutting through the airborne particles and wisps of smoke. The second guard popped up from behind an upholstered bench by the parlor threshold, and Walker shot off a good chunk of his gun hand. The man screamed and collapsed out of view, his pistol clattering off into a corner. The housekeeper stood on sturdy white-stockinged legs, her mouth ajar, her cap blown off by the explosion.

Walker crouched over the grenade, its pin still intact, and calmly pocketed it.

In the various rooms around him, the intercoms came to life, slightly out of sync. A robust voice—probably Dean Kagan's: *"To the safe room. Now."*

The first guard scraped on the floor, moaning and gripping his leg with both hands. He barely took note when Walker claimed his still-holstered pistol. The other guard had crawled behind the chesterfield when Walker caught up to him. He'd located a slab of his hand and was trying to press it back into place. His uniform sleeve was matted to the elbow. Walker picked up the fallen handgun and turned for the foyer but paused above the cowering man, straight-arming the Redhawk so the sights aligned on his forehead.

Walker nodded at the wound. "That enough to keep you occupied?"

A vehement nod.

Walker lowered his gun and headed for the stairs. The housekeeper still had not moved. As he passed, he picked up her cap and handed it to her. She took it with unsteady hands. "Where's the safe room?" he asked quietly.

With a trembling finger, she pointed through the north wall.

Walker coasted up the stairs and reached the landing. One of the four facing doors swung inward—someone had spotted him and withdrawn. He charged through the door to its left, flying silently through an empty bedroom, an adjoining chamber, another bedroom. A rustle behind the bathroom door. A flash of light hair through the hinges.

Chase.

Walker flattened against the wall and waited.

A highball glass lay on its side on the master suite's floor, ice cubes nesting in the plush deep-pile; someone had retreated in a hurry. The space seemed too wide to be a bedroom, but the California king, stranded on a plain of carpet, said otherwise. Walker moved around the corner to the enormous dressing suite. A hardened-steel fire door had lowered over the walk-in closet's doorway, sealing it like a vault.

Walker knocked the wall. Impressive. Judging from the sound, at least five inches of steel lay beneath the coat of paint. Too thick for the explosives distributed through his various cargo pockets. He could blast down and in through the roof, but he wouldn't have the time.

He glanced at the mounted security camera on the safe room's outer wall, then dragged over a vanity chair and stood on it. A few tugs loosened the camera on its housing. From his thigh pocket, he removed a digital camera with a fiber-optic minicam cable wrapped around it. He fed the cable into the wiring assembly behind the security camera. Using the image on the screen, he guided the peeper through the pencil-thin conduit between the outgoing video and audio lines and the power cable. It traveled about two feet before threading through the O-ring seal and poking out into the safe room on the other end, giving him a fish-eye view of the interior.

Inside the safe room stood Dean and Dolan Kagan. A wall-mounted monitor showed Walker staring at an image of them staring at their monitor. At the minicam's sprouting from the ceiling, Dolan took a step back, tripped, and sat abruptly on a padded chair. Dean remained stoically upright, turning to face the camera, Hannibal Lecter gone corporate. His arms were crossed, his legs shoulder width to suggest an unshakable foundation, like he was waiting to be bronzed. His face was so white it could have been powdered. An alarm panel inset on the wall beside the shoe rack blinked. There wasn't much time.

Walker nodded at the setup, impressed. "Good work."

Dean said, "What do you want?"

"Just following the Piper." Walker headed out and returned dragging Chase's body. Bands of electrical tape bound his ankles and wrists, but there was no gag. Walker needed to make use of his sounds.

Chase was stammering about offshore accounts. Walker pulled his Redhawk out from the back of his jeans and aimed it down at Chase's knee. "Open the door."

Dean stared into the camera unflinchingly. "No."

Walker fired without dropping his gaze. The dull impact of bullet to kneecap. Chase's howl rode up an octave, like a baying coyote's. Walker reached down, yanking Chase's wrists away from his torso. Embedding a boot in his armpit, he held Chase's arms in flexed-biceps position against the carpet. He aimed at the top elbow. "Open."

"No."

Walker pulled the trigger. The bullet pierced both aligned limbs. Bone shards glittered in the carpet. Chase's sobbing shifted in quality. Now it sounded like maniacal laughter.

Dolan was screaming—"Open it! You *have* to open it!" He rose, eyeing the panel on the wall, but Dean fixed him with a stare that shriveled him back onto the bench.

Dean said, "It's one of us dead or three of us dead. That's the only choice."

"Open," Walker said.

Chase was whimpering and pleaded in what sounded like a Middle Eastern tongue.

Dean said, "No."

Walker moved the muzzle a half inch, never breaking his stare-down with Dean, and fired again. Chase's shoulder gave way. The thin wail of approaching sirens came audible.

Walker let the gun sweep north over Chase's head.

His voice shaking, Dean said, "No."

Chase's yell, now more anger than pain, raised the veins in his neck. It was terminated with the final bullet.

Dean's knees buckled, but he caught himself with a little half step. The sirens were louder now, maybe within a few blocks. Dolan stayed twisted on the bench, face turned away. Dean leaned against the wall, fighting off a faint, then straightened up.

Walker flicked out the cylinder and tapped the extraction rod, the spent casings popping out. The new bullets, held by the speedloader, nosed into place, reloading the wheel with a single titanium thrust. "You can run," he said, "but you'll just die tired."

Walker slid the Redhawk into the waistband of his jeans and strode from the room. Dean again set his weight forward against the door, his lips cracked. Behind him Dolan wept quietly.

Less than a minute passed before the house shuddered with boots and shouted commands. Dean punched the code into the panel, and the shield slid upward, disappearing into the ceiling. Unsteadily, he walked out and kneeled over his favored son. He closed the corpse's eyelids, then leaned and kissed the forehead, still unblemished above the entrance wound.

Removing the BlackBerry from Chase's pocket, he slid it into his own.

Chapter 51

The pay phone rang, and Tim snatched it off the hook, hunching to the concrete wall of the liquor store and plugging one ear to muffle the traffic. He nodded at Bear, sitting an admittedly conspicuous shotgun in the Electronic Surveillance Unit van across the parking lot. Bear turned around to confer with Roger Frisk, the ESU deputy in the back. Frisk had opted for a straight tap off the junction box at the pole to cut interference.

Tim pressed the phone to his ear, but instead of Walker Jameson, it was Thomas from the command post, his words coming hard and fast.

Tim stood in the hydrangeas, staring into the hole blown in the ballistic glass of the front window. He had his hands full—Percy Keating's perforated body in the guesthouse, a sobbing Thai widow trying to convey useless facts in broken English, Chase's gray matter caking the carpet upstairs, and two ER-bound security guards who'd recounted Walker's appearance as if he'd descended from Valhalla on a phantom steed. The first phone call—which had led Tim and Bear to Arcadia, where they'd waited, holding their dicks while Walker mounted a full-frontal assault on the Kagan estate—Walker had managed to route through the Vector switchboard, icing Tim's embarrassment. The news crews massed at the resurrected cordon had it over European soccer fans for vehement persistence, and judging from the questions battering Tim on his approach, the next round of media portraits were to be—deservedly—none too flattering for the Troubleshooter.

Aaronson had teamed up with Maybeck, breacher for ART and for the Service's national Special Operations Group, to assess the explosive residue. As Tim suspected, the front window had been blown through with a linear shape charge, its firing assembly consisting of a blasting cap, a shock tube, and an initiator. The lab would need time to determine further specifics, but Tim already knew how the rest had played. To minimize on-site prepping, Walker would have prefabbed the charge, adhering a ring of the taffylike explosive cutting tape to an oval of cardboard. In about two seconds, he could've thunked the self-sticking charge onto the window, paid out the shock tube to a good standoff distance, and clicked the detonator. The distraction of the grenade had prevented the guards from redirecting their attention when Walker slapped the charge onto the ballistic pane. Walker had engineered the device with military precision, using exactly the right amount of ECT, the mark of a skilled breacher. The components were relatively common; none would be traceable.

Precisely how Tim would have made the assault.

Walker had reconned from a distance, waited for Keating's return. Then he'd taken him out—strong man first—extracted information, and moved on the main house. He'd been geared up for the raid, but the girth of the safe room's walls had come as a surprise, requiring a higher net explosive weight than he—or Tim—would've thought to lug along given binoc surveillance.

Picking through the aftermath of a Spec Ops attack launched on a house felt eerie and unsettling. It was something that generally happened in the Third World, not in Bel Air. A taste of Kandahar, right here in L.A.'s backyard.

The jagged edge of the glass had been caramelized. Tim tested the dark brown flakes with the tip of his finger. Freed paused on his way out the front door, Thomas at his side.

"He should've killed the guards," Tim said, mostly to himself. "Easier, more secure. It's not like he's concerned with his sentence."

Freed asked, "So why didn't he?"

"He's only killing those he considers guilty."

Thomas said, "Fugitive after your own heart." He gave Freed a little shove, moving them down the walk before Tim could respond.

Tannino stormed by, his feathers and dated Italian Afro ruffled from navigating the camera zone. He pressed his cell phone to his side, the barking voice on the other end muffled by one of the love handles that had softened his frame in the past year or so. "I got you your god-damned task force, Rackley. Now find me this fucker."

He, too, breezed by, leaving Tim with the hole in the house. Edwin the butler appeared at the front door, holding a cordless phone in two honest-to-God white gloves, regarding Tim in the flower bed with a look of reserved contempt that he must have rehearsed to perfection in but-ler school. "Mr. Rackley. Telephone."

Tim stepped up onto the porch, splitting the stream of criminalists, paramedics, cops, and deputies, and took the phone. "Rackley."

"Sorry I stood you up."

Tim looked around. The movement continued, every worker bent to a task. Tannino was arguing with Aaronson over by the guesthouse. They were not set up for a tap on Dean Kagan's phone, and Walker knew it.

Tim keyed the radio freq of his Nextel, sending Bear a double-chime and a *911* text message. "Come by, let's talk it over. I'm sure we could work out a way for me to forgive you."

Bear came jogging around the corner. Tim pointed to the phone, mouthing Walker's name. Bear snapped open his phone, got Frisk on the line, then pointed inside. If they could get a verbal from Dean, Frisk would be able to jockey the phone line at its entry point to the house and save the time of shinnying up the pole.

A chuckle from Walker. "Escape offense. Multiple homicide. Put the coffee on. I'll be there in five."

"In the meantime . . ." Tim said, moving swiftly up the walk, heading inside. The foyer was full of criminalists who sounded off like birds when Tim passed through the crime scene.

Frisk met him in the hall and mouthed, "What?"

"In the meantime?" Walker repeated.

Tim thought about Walker on the line, a rare opportunity to talk to his fugitive one-on-one. Being on an untapped line presented him a narrow window of opportunity he didn't want to squander by tracing a throw-away phone that was gonna be ditched within a few minutes anyway.

Tim shook his head, waved Frisk off. Frisk shrugged and headed out to his van.

Tim said quietly, "There's no reason we can't share information."

"Until you bust my ass."

"Until I bust your ass."

"Or until I kill someone else."

"You're not gonna kill anyone else."

"Why?"

"Because we'll get you before that."

Another chuckle, then: "You were a Ranger."

"That's right."

"'If you are brave and bold, you, too, may wear the black and gold.'"

"Something like that." Tim started down the hall. "The safe-room steel caught you off guard. No time to go up through the floor?"

"I was thinking the roof down to get the drop, but yeah."

"Solid entry downstairs. And I bet you got some good information from Percy. But I think you fucked up killing Chase. You could've gotten more answers out of him."

"Are there more answers to get?"

"Why else you calling me?"

"What do you know about my sister? Or was that just bullshit for the news?"

"You might have to give to get."

"Why should I tell you anything?"

"Because you need me. For *your* investigation."

A long pause. Tim strained to hear anything in the background, but there was just the crackle of the line.

"She was raped at the kid's commercial shoot," Walker said. "Chase Kagan. Percy Keating and Dolan Kagan were witnesses."

A scenario came into rapid focus—the rape, the pregnancy, the lawyer, Tess's execution. Tim halted, his momentum carrying him to the threshold of Dean's study. Amid a bustle of subordinates, Dean issued directives.

"Dean had Percy take out a hit on Tess," Walker said.

Dean paused, homing in on Tim across the room. Their eyes met. Two men frozen in the midst of disorderly human movement.

"They were worried she'd press charges," Walker said. "Or she threatened them with blackmail—Tess was tough if she was anything. Percy ran the cash through Ted Sands, who set the drop at Game."

Phone to his ear, Tim withdrew from the doorway and Dean's stare, moving back toward the foyer.

"You got a name for this hit man?"

The line hummed for maybe a second. "Not yet," Walker said, but his pause was a poker tell. He would've pressed the Piper's tag name out of Percy, and his not giving it up now confirmed Tim's suspicion that the hit man was high on his list. "Now," Walker said. "Something you have that I'm missing?"

Tim hesitated, but not long. "For one, Tess was pregnant."

The silence stretched until Tim feared that Walker had hung up. Finally the rough voice came, so low Tim could barely hear it. "Adds up. What else?"

The evidence wasn't sitting right with Tim. The facts he and Walker had pieced together formed too neat a tale. Lacking were the rough edges, the chance reversals, and the dead ends that violent cases, once fully reconstructed, inevitably prove to have.

Walker again, a touch impatiently: "You think there's more to it?"

"Yup."

"Why? It's a clear picture."

"That's the problem. Plus, if you think Dean Kagan is going to risk going to San Quentin to avoid a he-said/she-said rape prosecution for his son, you're less intelligent than I've been trying to convince everyone you are." Tim pictured the blank screen on Tess's computer monitor, the missing hard drive. "Tess must have been coming at them with something different—and more threatening—than a rape and a pregnancy."

"I'm not following."

"You underestimate her."

Walker's anger was palpable during the pause. "I doubt that."

"Then you're a shitty investigator. Because the one guy who really knows what we want has his brains all over the master bedroom."

"For good reason. Now, what else can you tell me?"

Through the hole of the front window, Tim saw the marshal, now pacing in circles, talking into his Nextel, and gesturing apologetically. "A lot. But you're not as useful to me as I thought you'd be. So you'll have to work with me." In the silence on the line, Tim could hear Dray, his perennial voice of reason—*What, Timothy, playing loose cannon didn't land you in deep* enough *shit last time around?* He asked himself if he dared take a gamble this big, though he knew he'd already made up his mind that morning in the warehouse. Given Tess's rape, he needed the information more than ever. But was he willing to put his ass on the line to get it? And, maybe even more critically, was he willing to let his desire to nail Walker pull him out of bounds again? He strolled back outside.

He started cautiously. "Here's a sample: Your sister met with a lawyer the week before she was killed. She dropped him four days later—maybe she was threatened. Between a rape and a pregnancy inconvenient for at least one party, we can both use our imaginations as to what that was about. But the lawyer refuses to break confidentiality. If we want to know what *else* they may have covered in their meetings . . ."

"We do."

Tim pressed his lips together, a last-minute deliberation before the point of no return. "The files are in boxes at Richco Long-Term Storage in Van Nuys, under Esteban Martinez. Just sitting there. The problem is, there's nothing *I* can do about it. They're beyond subpoena."

"This *is* a problem." Walker clicked his tongue. "Only problem *I* have is I show up, maybe someone's waiting."

"You were with First Force Recon. I'm assuming you're not gonna stroll up and knock on the door. Besides, it would be a criminal conspiracy for me to suggest that you do anything like what you seem to be inferring. Blow my whole case."

"While I'm mulling that over, maybe you should check out the valet-drop security footage from The Ivy in Beverly Hills," Walker said. "Night of June first. It's archived off site, so call over and have them pull it."

Tim sat on a bench by the koi pond. "What is it?"

"Take a look. You'll recognize a couple people. The perpetrator refers to the rape in that conversation. Maybe we get a read on their body language. She makes a blackmail threat, he gets angry. Whatever. Maybe Chase's brother and father make a guest appearance."

"Okay, I'll call now. If you're playing straight, I'll nail these guys."

"Sure, rape prosecution with a deceased victim—and attacker—should be a breeze. Maybe you could get that broad from the Kobe Bryant trial to fly out, cinch things up."

"We don't need the rape. The murder case is reopened."

"Took what? A prison break to get that done? No one gave a shit to look into it until someone rich got killed. Tell me that ain't the truth." Walker snickered, an ugly, one-note laugh. "Don't fault me for not trusting the Establishment to handle it. Guys like this, you'll never hang 'em on the murder."

"Then I'll hang them on something else."

"Campaign promise. And besides, pardner, I'm gonna do it for you first."

"Listen—"

"Now's when you tell me I can't take the law into my own hands, right, Troubleshooter?" Walker chuckled.

A click, and the line disconnected.

Chapter 52

Tim turned off the phone, sat on the garden bench, and watched the fat, mottled fish wobble through the algaed water. Next he got The Ivy and put in a request for the footage, combating a snotty manager to get the information passed on to the security company. He gave his name and the comm center's callback number so his ID could be confirmed.

Guerrera came around the bend and whistled Bear over. Setting a boot on the bench, Bear leaned across one knee as Tim brought them up to speed, keeping his voice low so the deputies gathered behind the garden's stone wall wouldn't overhear.

"Something doesn't add up on motive," Bear said. "As far as we know, there's no rape kit anywhere. No hard evidence. A broke divorcée against a rich golden boy—she didn't stand a chance. With the Kagans' money, they could've hired O.J.'s dream team twice over."

"She was pregnant," Guerrera said. "A DNA test could've put Chase on the hook."

"So why wouldn't they just pay her off?"

"Rich people are assholes?" Guerrera offered.

"The prosecution rests."

"Didn't Freed mention that Chase was engaged?"

"Yeah, but still. You'd think you'd rather get caught with your dick wet than face a murder one."

"So maybe there *was* evidence. Maybe that's what they stole her hard drive for. Scanned photos or something."

Bear looked skeptical. He used his thumb to flick dirt from under a fingernail.

Tim said, "That hard drive housed something with more bite. Remember, Sam's participation in that drug study got Tess a full-frontal of Vector."

"Yeah," Bear said, "she had to have something that would make their *shareholders* pucker." He gestured at the mansion behind them. "Dean ain't risking all this to avoid a rape trial for his boy."

Guerrera took in the span of the massive house. "You think Walker'll strike here again?"

Tim said, "Not with the security Dean'll have in place here come tonight. He'll wait them out. They won't hide in their compound forever."

"Funeral?"

" 'The Kagans aren't big on personal ceremonies,' " Tim quoted dutifully, " 'nor public displays of private emotion.' "

"So where?"

They stood eyeing the ripples in the pond, and then Guerrera spit in the flowers, said, "Catch you at the post," and headed to his car.

Tim and Bear moved single file to cut through the workers still dissecting the crime scene. Dean was in his study where Tim had left him, but now he sat alone, the inevitable banker's lamp lending a nauseous tint to the dimness. Behind the desk a framed poster showed the miracle cure in a vial, floating through space. XEDRAL. THE FUTURE HAS ARRIVED. THIRTY DAYS AT A TIME. For once Dean had no paperwork, no phone calls, no assistants. Just a tired man sitting in the dark.

Tim said, "We'd like to assign some men to stay. For your protection."

"We can handle our own security."

"I understand that, sir, but we've spent a lot of time guarding judges and—"

"And I've spent fifty-plus years running businesses. To say I trust private sector over public servants would be an understatement."

Bear said, "I'm sure Keating would be flattered."

Dean took in Bear with an irritated sweep of the eyes before returning his focus to Tim. "Why do you think he's coming after me?"

266

Tim said, "We suspect you know why already. If you'd tell us, we could do a better job of apprehending him."

"You seemed awfully cozy when you spoke to him on my phone. You sure he didn't mention something?"

"Quite," Tim said. "I think you should stay holed up here for a while. With Dolan."

"I can't. We have our pre-IPO presentation in two days. Chase would've wanted us to see it through."

"That's where Jameson is most likely to make his next attempt. It's certainly where I would."

"Would you close down your whole operation in fear of some . . . terrorist, Deputy?" Dean waved his hand in a terse dismissal.

Tim debated asking where Dolan was but didn't want to put the old man on alert. Instead he nodded at Bear, and they left the study with the assertion Tim had gone there to get—the dog and pony show for investors would go on, hell or high water. Finally a point of reentry for Walker they could count on.

In one of the dark halls, they bumped into Speedy, the worker they'd interviewed after Walker's first assault on the house. Tapping down a pack of Marlboros, he told them how to get to Chase's and Dolan's former rooms on the second floor of the south wing. The directions involved more turns and half flights of stairs than seemed possible for a residence.

After twice getting lost and having to be redirected by various workers, available at every turn, they entered the immense game room. Bear leaned back on his heels, whistling as he regarded the high ceiling. The doors to both bedroom suites were ajar. Tim called out Dolan's name but, hearing no response, entered the room to the left. King bed, satin sheets, a walk-in closet deeper than some trailer homes Tim had kick-entried. A shaky penned dedication split a framed photo of the Greatest himself—*To Chaisson, Sting like a bee.* On a drawerless desk rested a laptop, a roaming James Bond Walther barrel as the screen saver. Cables snaked off to various peripherals. A line of glass cubes formed the mantel over the vast fireplace. Centered on it was an urn, *Mary Chaisson* etched in scrolled letters. Tim stepped up onto the hearth and raised the burnished silver lid. Cocktail napkins and glossy matchbooks filled the inside. Tim pulled out the top matchbook and flipped it open. *Jenni. 451–1215.* Peering in, he saw where ink had bled through the napkins—more telephone numbers rendered on the paper between beer-company logos and condensation rings.

Tim returned Mary to her rightful post and nosed through the night-stand drawers. The top held a variety of condoms and lubricants and a tray filled with single earrings. Tim wondered if whatever house Chase shared with his fiancée was as well stocked. A leather-bound notebook in the second drawer held an anthropological accounting that might have put Kinsey to shame. *Silver-dollar areolas. Landing-strip trim. Faint blond down across lower back.* Tim flipped through May and June searching for one name. No mention of Tess. Was Chase too smart? Did she not make the best-of reel?

When Tim glanced up, Bear was standing before the swung-open doors of the armoire, regarding a wall of gift-wrapped boxes. Pulling out the top package, he tilted it to show Tim the Frederick's of Hollywood logo on the paper. Lingerie. Outcall party favors?

Below, a carved see-no-evil monkey served as a bookend to a row of generic DVDs, his two simian cronies bracing similar collections on the shelves below.

Bear plucked out a DVD and plugged it into the player underlying a massive plasma screen. Chase's naked ass bobbing up and down, the limbs of a woman crabbing up around him. Bear regarded the footage as if considering Chase's form, ready to hold up a judging card. The woman's face popped into view over Chase's shoulder, her mouth open in a moan, but the DVD seemed muted. Bear raised the volume, but the bars already stretched across half the screen. Tim backtracked the camera angle to a wall-mounted mirror. He pressed his fingertips to the glass. No separation between his nails and their reflection. "One-way," he said.

"There goes the obvious motive." Bear ejected the disk. "I don't think Chase was worried about news of Tess leaking to his fiancée. Nor do I think a knocked-up broad from the high desert would throw his world into Puritan uproar."

"No, he doesn't strike one as the most discreet individual." Tim looked from the urn to the DVD in Bear's hand and thought someone could probably write a treatise on the psychology stretching between them. "Can we take the DVDs as evidence?"

Bear stared at the seventy or so unlabeled DVDs. "You're thinking Tess makes a guest appearance?"

Though the notion of enduring a review of Chase's humping through the twelve seasons was less than palatable, Tim nodded. "It'll give Guerrera something to do while his café cubano congeals."

"If there *was* footage, I doubt Chase would be reckless enough to keep it after Tess was killed," Bear said. "We can talk to the AUSA, but even at Camarillo Vet-n-Law, we know prosecutors won't green-light a warrant for the DVDs anyway. Not with the Kagan lawyers and various elected allies weighing in from around the country. Think ahead to how appalled—*appalled*—they'll be about the way our pursuit of unrelated sensitive materials undermines the murder victim's dignity."

"Unless the tapes themselves are illegal," Tim said. "Then we could seize them *and* avoid an ass chewing from Tannino." Bear shrugged. Also unfamiliar with state statutes, Tim flicked open his Nextel and dialed home. "Is it illegal to videotape yourself having sex with someone without their consent?"

Dray said, "Babe, all you have to do is ask."

Tim laughed, then said, "Seriously."

"That's one of those laws that makes you wonder what they're smoking in Sacramento. Video without consent is perfectly okay in California, but audio without consent is illegal."

"Clever prick kept the sound off," Tim said.

"Who's this clever prick you've been cheating on me with?"

Edwin floated into view at Bear's shoulder, and Tim muttered, "Gotta go."

"You seem to have lost your way en route to the door?" Edwin suggested.

Bear slotted the DVD back into the row and closed the armoire. "We need to speak with Dolan."

"He's quite upset."

"Us, too. Distraught, even." Bear took a step forward, forcing Edwin's head to tilt back until his Adam's apple bulged out. But if Edwin was intimidated, he didn't show it. A man practiced at contending with the whims of plutocrats didn't scare easy.

"Mr. Kagan has gone to the indoor pool."

"Where's that?"

"I'll be happy to escort you." The impeccable white glove unfurled toward the door, and for not the first time, Tim wondered if Edwin might be holographic. L.A.'s rich loved their musty props, but even for the town that produced *Citizen Kane,* Edwin seemed a stretch.

Bear and Tim hung back on one of the endless halls that conveyed them soundlessly across the mansion.

"What kind of idiot has an indoor pool in Los Angeles?" Bear whispered.

"The kind of idiot who has an outdoor one already."

They arrived at an unimposing door off a dank corridor, and Edwin rapped on it once and pushed it open. Diffuse green light undulated around the dark walls like sheets of gauze. Dolan's form streaked through the water, swimming laps with punishing exertion. When he came up for air at the near end and spotted them, he was gasping.

Tim and Bear stepped down onto the tile, and Bear thanked Edwin and shoved the door closed in his face. They'd have limited time before Edwin's situation report would bring Dean's interference.

Dolan swiped his thin brown hair out of his face and squinted, handicapped without his glasses. "Hi."

Tim reached the edge of the pool and crouched, looking almost directly down into Dolan's face. "We know about the rape in the limo. We know everything. Your brother's dead. You can't protect him anymore. We want to hear your side of what happened—it's Jameson's motive, but it's also what makes you an accessory."

Dolan's chest was still heaving from the laps. For a moment it seemed he might cry, but then he slapped the water with both arms and sank down so his head bobbed on the surface. "Chase keyed to Tess the minute he saw her. Sitting outside her house with his stupid guitar. He likes older women. Milfs, he calls them. He told me Tess turned him on even more since she had"—he blushed at the memory—"a fuck trophy."

Resting on the poolside towel, a cell phone put out a classical-music ring—Bach's haunted-castle organ riff shrilling off the hard tile. Dolan tensed. Tim looked down at the hot-orange caller ID screen. *DadStudy.*

"I program rings for certain people." Dolan's face said the rest.

Eager to get him back on track, Tim said, "And 'fuck trophy' would be slang for . . . ?"

"A kid."

Bear gave Dolan the stare he'd perfected from years of playing bad cop in interrogation rooms.

"Look, Chase was Chase. He was a dick. But he was charming when he wanted to be. He was my brother, but I didn't . . . No one could . . ." Dolan trailed off, staring at the rippling water. When he spoke again, his words were pressured, almost eager. "I didn't see much at the shoot. He'd followed Tess out to the garage. I went to get him because he was supposed to be overseeing the producer. I could . . . I could hear some banging from the limo, but I thought . . . I don't know what I thought. Percy was there, outside, like he was standing guard. I started for the limo. I wasn't sure what I was going to do. When I got close, Percy squared himself toward me, said, 'Let's give a man his space.' " Dolan made a faint sound of disgust. His face was wet from the pool water; Tim couldn't distinguish tears on it. "I heard her . . . kicking on the window, you know, then her hand, fingers spread. I could see it even through the tint, the shadow of her hand. Banging." Dolan raised a dripping arm and imitated the gesture, perhaps unknowingly. "You know when you freeze?"

Tim wanted to say no but opted for silence.

"I'm not like them. I never know what to do." Dolan looked shrunken and feeble in the pool. "So I left." His gaze dropped again to the water. "I left. I waited around the corner by the elevator. A few minutes later, I heard the door open. I peeked around the corner. I saw her bloody mouth in the crack of the door before it closed. Chase straightened his shirt. The front pocket, the monogrammed one, was ripped. The driver rolled down the window and said, 'She okay?' and Chase said, 'She's fine. I'll get her son as soon as we wrap. Then you can take her home.' And he thumped the roof like a pit-crew guy sending off a race car. I went upstairs before he reached me and pretended like nothing had happened."

"And Tess threatened to prosecute?"

"I can't—how did you . . . ?—I can't discuss that. I can't discuss anything involving the trials."

"Trials?" Bear was mystified. "What trials? The *drug* trials?"

A boom startled Tim upright and jerked Bear 180 degrees. The door vibrated on its hinges, stunned, where it had struck the tile wall. Backlit by the light of the corridor and centered in the doorway was Dean's silhouette, somehow conveying the strength of a man with enormous power at his disposal, a man assured of his place on the planet.

"Gentlemen, it's already been a very long night, and I need to ask you to continue your questioning in the morning," Dean said. "My surviving son has a great deal of work ahead of him."

"What did you talk to them about?"

Dolan turned toward his open locker, searching for privacy but finding none. Now that he'd actually dredged up the memory and cast it in words, he realized that what he *hadn't* told the deputies seemed almost as vivid. Chase's air of exuberance when he'd returned to the commercial shoot, as if he'd just stepped off a harrowing roller coaster. Chase's sullen face days later when the chickens had come home to roost. How Chase had gone directly into Dean's study and seemed to disappear, swallowed up by the high-backed leather chair. Though Dolan had walked with him to their father's door, he'd held in the hall, knowing himself to be an outsider in matters such as these. As Percy swung the door shut, Dolan heard his brother's disembodied voice, finally confessing to the old man—*We've got a problem here.*

"Nothing, really," Dolan said. "Just the same details we covered earlier."

"Did you talk about the business?"

"Of course not." Dolan cast a glance over his shoulder. Dean's eyes were still boring through him. Dolan hooked his towel loosely around his waist before shucking his trunks, and he held it in place until he'd managed to pull on his boxers. From what he knew, Dean had never changed him, bathed him, or dressed him. Aside from a few vague recollections of his mother (scented powder, dangling ringlets, stern vertical lines etching the lips), Dolan mostly remembered nannies. Being naked in front of his father now was more uncomfortable than the prospect of stripping in public.

"For security purposes, we're ending all outside access to the office and lab," Dean said. "No tours, no visitors. You'll be transported with armed guards to and from work. After Friday's presentation we're decamping to the London office until this blows over. We are the family now. I won't have you at risk."

"Did you say *after* the presentation? Chase just—" Dolan buckled his belt with an unnecessarily hard pull. "How can we do the presentation without him?"

"It's taken nearly five years to maneuver your company into position. If we show weakness now, in this marketplace, it'll be a death sentence. Plus, it'll be giving Jameson what he seems to be after. Vector is strong, but there are worthy competitors. If we pull back now, we'll miss our window of competitive advantage. You want to let this son of a bitch take that away from you? From your shareholders?"

"From the patients who could benefit?"

Dean ignored the sardonic edge in his son's rejoinder voice. "Of course. Them most of all. We have responsibilities bigger than ourselves, Dolan."

"Sir, I think we should consider working more closely with the deputies."

"You let me deal with the police."

The humidity of the room was starting to get to Dolan, making him light-headed. "The guy ate Percy for lunch."

"You're taking your brother's death hard. You're in shock, which is understandable." Dean rose from the bench. "Don't worry about this bullshit. Go back to your lab. Leave this in my hands."

Dean padded through the doorless arch that led to the pool, the underwater light's refractions playing across the back of his charcoal suit, making the fabric swim. Dolan smoothed his wet hair and watched his father make his way across the tiles.

As Dean reached the exit, Dolan called out, "Dad? Sir?"

His father turned, the flickers having a dizzying camouflage effect. He was a specter, there and not there at the same time.

"Who's the Piper? Walker Jameson mentioned the Piper."

His father's voice came back reverb-enhanced by the hard walls, each word trailed by the edge of an echo. "I don't know." He mounted the three concrete steps, the door closing heavily behind him.

Chapter 53

A lingering party remained at a back table inside the long-closed restaurant, bathed in golden light. Tim and Bear stood shoulder to shoulder on the Beverly Hills patio, waiting for a worker to come to the locked door.

"We'll never beat him," Bear said.

"Walker?"

"Dean Kagan. Guys like that, they don't get beat."

The Ivy's point man arrived. "Sorry, gentlemen, we closed hours ago."

Bear's gaze shifted to the VIPs drinking red wine in the rear corner. "Uh-huh."

"Deputy Rackley." Tim showed his badge and creds. "I spoke with a manager on the phone earlier, asked for some security footage for a federal investigation?"

The manager wore an expression of mild irritation that Tim would've bet occupied his face with some frequency. "That was me. Your guy already came and picked up the footage."

"When was . . . ?" It hit Tim, and he lowered his head and laughed with stunned respect.

A moment later Bear shook his head. "That's a ruse worthy of . . ."

"What?"

"Worthy of you, Rack."

The basics they pried from the bemused manager fit Walker perfectly.

Eager to help, The Ivy had surrendered the original security footage, and there was no backup copy.

They climbed back into Bear's double-parked Ram. Bear had left the Marshals placard on the dash to fend off the tow-truck drivers who circled L.A.'s affluent communities, clanking scavengers with sharp night vision.

Of course it would be Thomas who fielded Tim's call to the command post. When he didn't bother to gloat, Tim knew that something was wrong.

"Esteban Martinez just called here and chewed on my ass," Thomas said. "There was a break-in tonight at the warehouse that stores his legal files, and the box containing his case information on Tess Jameson was the only thing taken. He said one of the guards claimed you were by earlier, casing out the joint. Anything you want to come clean on?"

Tim tried to open the glove box, but like everything else on Bear's truck, it was broken. "Walker stole the files."

"How do you know?"

Tim gestured excitedly, and Bear finally clued in. "We thought he might," Tim said.

"And you didn't post men?"

Bear banged the dash in a particular spot, and the glove box fell open.

"Not on site. He would've seen them." Tim rooted around among Burger King wrappers and retrieved the GPS handheld he'd put in there this morning.

"Why are you protecting this guy, Rack? Whose side are you on? Walker Jameson's playing you. And you're letting him."

The GPS unit whirred to life, throwing a blue glow across Tim's face. "That might be true if I hadn't—" Tim's call-waiting beeped, and he checked the screen: *Electronic Surveillance Unit.*

"If you hadn't *what?*"

Bear screeched across the corner of someone's lawn, winging the mailbox with his remaining sideview mirror and revving down the residential street as Tim said, "No, *left.* Your *other* left."

His head knocked the window as Bear screeched into a U-turn, and it took him a moment to relocate the RF pulse of the digital transmitter on the network of streets rendered schematically on the GPS readout. Along with four other task-force cars, they'd been chasing Walker—more specifically, the transmitter Tim had dropped into the legal file box Walker had stolen—around the neighborhood. His evasive maneuvers were so keen it seemed he was invisible. Bear kept circling the same route, Richco Storage flying by on their right like scenery in a Saturday-morning cartoon. Frisk droned on the primary channel of the dashboard Motorola, along with the other ESU units that had been in the area for hours, waiting for the file box to leave the warehouse.

Tim watched the dots of the Marshal vehicles converge on the blinking red light.

"We got him boxed in." Frisk's voice was just shy of a shout. *"Thomas and Freed, take your hard left. Denley—slant-park and throw up a road-block. Bear, where the hell are you?"*

"Look up." Bear squealed to the four-way intersection, meeting the other vehicles penning in the stretch of asphalt. The GPS unit showed Walker right in their midst, moving slowly.

Shouts came through from the various cars on a slight radio delay; Tim could see the speakers arrayed around the four stop signs, mouths moving behind windshields.

"The fuck is he?"

"You got your left?"

The ring of headlights caught wisps of vapor and little else. Thomas was out of his car in the fork of the open door, Glock drawn and aimed at nothing. Tim and Bear shoved free of the Ram, Bear gripping his Remington shotgun.

A pattering approach, something clicking across the asphalt. A faint jingling—coins in a pocket? About ten firearms swung to aim at the darkness behind Denley's car.

A Doberman padded into view, looking humorously intimidated.

The guard dog from the storage facility.

He sat in the middle of the ring and licked his chops self-consciously, then scratched behind the red band of his collar. The bouncing ID tags jingled again.

Too humiliated to lose his temper, Tim closed his eyes and cursed softly. The guns lowered, but the men behind them remained frozen. The dog, suddenly wary, bared his teeth.

Bear approached, hand held low, and the dog lay down and nuzzled his palm. Twisting the collar, Bear plucked free the digital transmitter from where Walker had taped it by the tags.

Thomas seated his gun in his shoulder holster. "Great work, Rack. You buy Jameson a one-way ticket to the Caymans, too?"

Chapter 54

What were you thinking?" Dray set a plate down on the open file in front of Tim. "What if Walker had gone after the lawyer?"

"He wouldn't. Esteban Martinez was trying to help Tess, not hurt her."

"And you were willing to gamble his life on your intuition? How about if Walker went to Martinez and he wasn't cooperative?" She pointed at the reheated chicken and mashed potatoes. "You need to start thinking straight. So eat something."

It was past midnight, and Tim hadn't had a bite since breakfast, but his stomach was churning, and putting food into it seemed like a bad idea. He pushed the plate over next to a mound of field files and continued reviewing the break-in report from Richco warehouse security. "It was a ploy to catch him."

"*And* you wanted your hands on those legal files. When you made the arrest. So you could take it from there against the Kagans. A ploy. So was swallowing the spider to catch the fly." She waited, arms crossed. Tim knew she would take his silence as an affirmation, and she'd be right. She said, "You're too clever by half. Walker is *not* a colleague."

Tim stayed his quickest reaction—defensiveness—as he tried to do when his wife was right, which was most of the time. "I know that," he said evenly.

"Do you?" Dray wiped her hands on a dish towel and threw it on the counter. She nudged the plate back before him. "Eat. Or I'm gonna throw it at you."

Coverage of the second assault on the Kagan compound was playing on every news channel, blown tabloid-wide with speculation. Dean had wasted no time retaining a crisis-management PR firm, the just-flown-in spokeswoman for Vector and Beacon-Kagan insisting, on a slate of station-hopping spot interviews, that the threat was limited and it would be business as usual come morning.

The phone banks at the command post had lit up like Christmas, the media requests so heavy that Tannino had to designate a second public information officer to share the load. A former B-list director had called in hysterically when a corpse, illuminated by the running lights of his motor yacht in the waters of the Marina, had disrupted a late-night cruise with a *Penthouse* Pet. While Tim and Bear, along with half the task force, had been chasing a Doberman in circles, Haines had responded to the Marina, bringing back copies of the crime-scene photos. Chuck Hannigan, Chase's limo driver, had been suspended underwater, his bloated arms bobbing overhead, knuckles nearly breaching the surface. Melissa Yueh had gotten ahold of the murder and run with it. KCOM's panicky coverage left the impression that Walker was littering the city with bodies, which Tim conceded was accurate. No question as to how Walker was getting his information. His methods certainly lent credence to Dray's concerns.

Tim picked at a drumstick with a tine of his fork. "Chase Kagan raped Walker's sister, then his rich daddy probably had her whacked when she turned up pregnant. So yes, that possibility grinds at me, and if I'm working Tess's case also, that's my prerogative."

"Since when? You're a federal deputy, and your jurisdiction doesn't get anywhere near Tess Jameson's murder. Your attention—your *professional* attention—is in the wrong place. Dean Kagan did not kill an inmate and break out of Terminal Island. Tess's murder doesn't concern you."

"It concerns me to the extent it drives this case. And it's getting clearer every hour that it *is* driving this case. The evidence trail from that murder has been the only way to track Walker."

"Fine. But you're turning it upside down. Again. Chase Kagan is a *victim* in your investigation."

"And probably a rapist."

"Right, Timothy, but we don't have the death penalty for rape, not before a trial and certainly not before charges are brought. Don't use what happened to that woman as a pretext for snapping into loose-cannon mode."

"For Christ's sake, Andrea. Back off. I didn't kill Chase. I did *every-thing* to warn them. But dealing with the Kagans is like punching sand."

"Look. These guys are assholes, sure, and they're up to shady, rich-white-man bullshit. I get it. And Walker's had some crappy breaks and a dick lieutenant who screwed him over, and his dad's a smug asshole who reminds you of your own father."

"Where the hell did *that* come from?"

Dray's look answered that, and she continued unimpeded, "You got a sick kid with Disney orphan eyes and an attractive ex, and no one on that side of the fence has caught a break in their lives, but that's all ex-actly irrelevant to the job. Walker Jameson has killed a prisoner and four civilians, and he's gonna keep on killing unless your task force stops him."

"I *know*!" Tim knocked his plate with his hand. It flipped over, bouncing on the floor, mashed potatoes splattering against the refrigerator.

Unfazed, Dray continued wiping the counter, her bare feet dodging the blotches of potato stuck to the linoleum.

He watched her back for a few minutes. Then he said, "The thing is . . ."

Dray paused, half turned. "What?"

"I like him."

Dray came over, bearing a fresh plate of food and a mop. She placed the plate before Tim, leaning the mop against the table to his side. "Of course you do." She ruffled his hair, kissed him on the forehead, and headed back to the bedroom.

He sat a moment before rising and scooping up the chicken and clumps of mashed potato. Smirking at himself, he wiped off the fridge door and mopped the floor.

Sitting back before his collection of reports and vivid photos, Tim clicked open the wheel of his Smith & Wesson, thumbed it hard, and watched the brass spin. With a jerk of his wrist, he snapped it shut.

His Nextel vibrated, dancing across a photo of Chuck Hannigan's suspended corpse.

Over the din of the command post, Freed's weary voice said, "I've been running down info on Pierce Jameson since nine 'o clock."

Reading Freed's tone, Tim leaned forward, on point. "And?"

"One of his holding companies owns a portfolio company that owns a housing development called Sunnyslope Family Homes. It's tied up in litigation, shut down by the Department of Health. But this morning? Someone had the power turned back on. In just one unit."

Tim's mind went to the description Speedy had given of the security truck he'd spotted by the Kagan estate's perimeter the night of Ted Sands's murder. His recollection of the name on the decal had been hazy: *one of those shitty family communities out in, say, the West Valley. Shady Hills. Pleasantview.*

Or Sunnyslope.

Tim was on his feet, halfway to the garage. "Scramble the squad."

Chapter 55

The ground stank of sewage, and the night canyon fog wasn't helping any. To the right of the complex gate and its supporting stand of adobe-block wall, Maybeck had offset two segments of the transportable chain link, creating a gap through which the other ART members silently whisked in their olive drab flight suits. Subdued gray flags and Service patches decorated the sleeves. The ARTists held their MP5s, set to three-round bursts, at high-ready. Having come from home, Tim alone wore civilian clothes—jeans, T-shirt. His hip-holstered .357 also made him stand out; the others wore .40 Glocks slung at the thigh. Even bulkier in his tactical vest, Bear clutched his cut-down twelve-gauge Remington in a hand made invisible by darkness and a black glove. Tim breezed through the gap in the fence, and Bear came a moment later, looking wary but popping his broad frame through.

Maybeck cocked a finger at the one house that was clearly completed, and the eight deputies jogged in a silent single-file approach, the odor thickening. Freed had discovered that the parcel hadn't passed the perc test for a septic drain field. Too much clay and rock, not enough subsoil to take the runoff. After an inspection determined that the information previously given about the land's absorbency was falsified, the Department of Health had pulled the permit and the Building Department had issued a cease-and-desist order. Pierce was countersuing, a move Tim knew—thanks to a primary education at his father's school of shenanigans—was a stall tactic until an understanding could be reached with the right city official.

Tim caught sight of the security pickup, hidden between two Dumpsters. No sign of another vehicle—he still held out hopes for the Camry that had been stolen near the landfill. If Walker had another vehicle, he would've stashed it elsewhere, establishing a motor pool for strategic switches.

Thumbing down the volume on their radios, the deputies reconvened at the end of the walk. They'd met briefly down the hill at the staging point with the chief and Tannino, who'd gladly slipped out of an extended-family engagement. Tim had pressed for an unorthodox entry plan to take into account Walker's unorthodox skills. They were going after a soldier trained to lead assaults of the kind they were trying to use against him. Walker could anticipate just about every angle. And probably had. He would've planned a number of escape routes from the house, maybe even leaving booby traps at the doors, windows, and halls. Rather than having the team barrel into a potential clusterfuck, Tim would slip in alone, move tactically through the house, and try to kill Walker or flush him out. The others would take positions of cover around the perimeter and wait for Tim's signal.

A few gestures and the deputies spread noiselessly around the house, their dull-toned flight suits blending into the darkness. Tim stood alone in the darkness before the silent house. A tingling at his fingertips signaled his nervousness. He tapped his belt, making sure the Mag-Lite slotted through the ring didn't give off a jangle.

He moved swiftly to the front door and worked the lock with his pick set, giving up little more than a click as he eased inside. The closing door shut out the moon, leaving him in the pitch-black interior. Crouching with his .357 drawn, he waited maybe a full minute, breathing the faint scent of smoke and blinking frequently to stimulate his night vision. The flashlight would only broadcast his position.

He rose to search the family room, moving with excruciating slowness, stepping over a few boxes and an unzipped duffel bag. By the fireplace he found a collection of cans. Beans, mini hot dogs, tuna. He ran a finger along the inside of an opened can, and it came away wet. A heap of ashes, when stoked, hid a dying ember. A hobo camp pitched in an upscale family room.

Down the dark hall, Tim heard a thump, then the resistance of unseasoned floorboards.

Straight-arming his .357, Tim pivoted around corners, making his way to the master bedroom. He slipped through the doorway, his back to the inside wall, sweeping with his revolver. Empty, save a translucent Japanese screen, a nightstand, and a bed centered on the bare floor. The window looked out on moonless, starless sky, so Tim sensed the furniture only as shadows within shadows. He'd just cleared the adjoining bathroom when he heard an undeniable creak behind him.

He swung, gun aimed at the darkness.

Under the bed.

He had to check beneath the raised bed frame, a move that wanted a partner to cover the space from the doorway. Another sound—scuffling, faint, but no question—cemented Tim's sense that he was in the room with Walker. Tim pulled his Mag-Lite from his belt, set it silently on the sawdust-powdered floorboards. Straightening up, he clicked it on by stepping on the button. A circle of light formed on the far wall. With his boot, Tim pushed the flashlight into a roll. It purred across the floorboards, parallel to the bed, drawing with it a twirling disk of light along the far wall.

As the flashlight passed beside the bed, a shadow stood out clearly against the opposite wall, cut from the beam of light passing beneath the frame. A man's silhouette, enlarged by the angle and the scrolling illumination. Boots pointed, frogged legs, and, finally, the alarmingly clear curve of nose and lips. When the screen of the wall passed into darkness, Tim heard a whoosh as fabric slid across floor, but Walker didn't pop up into his sights. The flashlight continued spinning past the bed, striking the far wall and rolling back, now wobbly, to reveal the suddenly empty space beneath the bed.

Tim stared, stunned at the magic trick, until the roaming yellow circle threw a barely raised ledge into relief—an offset square of floor.

The portable was at his lips: "He's on the loose. Repeat: He's on the loose, under the house. Rear left quadrant. Let him slip past." Grabbing the flashlight, Tim dove under the bed, sliding so his head and shoulders dipped into the recently buzzsawed hatch. He caught an upside-down view of a scrambling form moving like an ape through the cramped space. He aimed, but there were too many support posts and cross-beams severing the diminishing form.

Tim jerked himself back up and ran down the hall, wrists crossed so he could point gun and flashlight simultaneously. He flew through the kitchen door into the backyard. Caught off guard, a dark form pivoted, blocking out the low moon, legs braced and hips sunk in submachine-gun-wielding posture. "Drop the gun! Drop the *fucking* gun!"

Through his surging heartbeat, Tim recognized the voice as Thomas's, and he realized he wasn't going to be blown to bits on the back porch. He held his revolver to the side. "It's me."

"Drop the gun. Now!"

The flashlight, Tim realized, was blinding Thomas. Tim dropped it and his revolver. "Thomas, it's me. Rackley."

In the background he saw a form streak past. He wanted to grab his radio but knew better given the razor edge that separated him from friendly fire. Thomas lowered his MP5, squinted, and raised it again, pointing at Tim's chest. "Show me your fucking hands."

Tim spread his hands farther. "Thomas, it's Tim Rackley. Walker just slipped through. I gotta give the go command. Put your light on my face. Come on."

With one hand Thomas retrieved a Mag-Lite from his belt, his head never rotating. He clicked it on, shined it on Tim's face, and then his muscles loosened. "Jesus. Sorry."

Tim snatched the radio from his belt. "Okay, he's through. Fall in behind and run him to the fence." He grabbed his .357 and the light and sprinted upslope.

The others had already folded in behind Walker, a line of MP5s trained at his back as he labored up the hill, fifty yards ahead. Bear shouted after him, but he kept moving.

Walker was ten yards from the fence.

Tim raised the radio to his lips. *"Now!"*

The ground vibrated, and then two LAPD helicopters flew up from the canyon beyond the fence, giant in their sudden proximity. Walker froze, trapped in the spotlights, raising an arm to shield his eyes. A sniper in each chopper, kneeling on one knee, viewed Walker down the length of a rifle. Tim could see the red dots pinning Walker, catching his arm, his face, his chest as he shifted, reeling under blasts of air. The deputies fanned to a half circle, keeping a good distance.

A voice boomed from the chopper bullhorn: *"Hands on top of your head!"*

Walker spread his arms wide, brought his hands together over his head, laced his fingers. Wind shoved his hair on end and snapped his T-shirt. He staggered a few steps to the right, then a few steps more.

Tim started forward, picking his way up the vast rise of chaparral, Bear doing the same fifteen yards to his right. The helicopters hovered just over the fence line.

Walker turned slowly to face Tim, his front shadowed, the spotlights blazing around him. Gun steady in both hands, Tim tried to shout at him over the sound of the rotors to stop moving.

Keeping his hands laced above his neck, Walker dipped his head as if in acknowledgment of the shouted commands. He raised a boot and took a final step. A clang and he dropped from sight, disappearing into the earth, an upended grate popping into view.

The deputies sprinted up the hill, Tim in the lead. He kicked the grate aside and swung his gun barrel and flashlight over the black hole. A fifteen-foot drop, walled in concrete, a hot reek of sewage and nothing else. The other deputies huffed up behind him.

Bear recoiled from the stench. "He jumped into the fucking sewage system?"

"You gonna go down there?" Maybeck asked, also yelling over the choppers.

"Not if I don't want to land on his gun barrel," Tim shouted. "I think it's a closed system. I want a schema of all the grates."

Freed raised his phone and stepped away.

"Let's start getting bloodhounds and more men up here, just in case there's an outlet," Tim said to the small huddle. "He's trained in mountain nav, so we need to move. Maybeck—guard this hole. Let's sweep the property and see if there are any other pipes he could crawl out of."

Freed was yelling into the phone with more animation than seemed necessary to be heard above the rotors' whomping. He slapped the phone shut and ran back over. "The contractor said they fucking routed the sewer system to the storm-drain channels."

"God*damn* it," Bear said.

"Do we sweep the hills?" Maybeck asked.

"We can't cover that kind of ground," Tim said. "There are drains and runoff channels all through these canyons. He can crawl out anywhere. Get more choppers in the air—that's our only shot."

Maybeck was bent, hands on his knees. "He's a First Force Recon marine. By the time more choppers get here, he'll be sipping margaritas in Mazatlán."

Tim reached Tannino at the staging point and told him to have police block off the surrounding roads. The marshal's grunt said it all—the Santa Monicas stretched long and far, touching countless streets and spilling out into numerous communities. The storm-drain network ran from beneath their feet all the way to the ocean.

It would be like trying to trap water in a fist.

Within ten minutes LAPD SWAT arrived in force, providing support and keeping watch over the various grates on the property. The deputies reconvened in the model unit and started picking through Walker's possessions. One of the helos had peeled off to recon the surrounding gullies, but Tim could see the other through the windows, a giant predatory insect, tilting forward as if tethered to the mountainside by the leash of its spotlight. A few minutes later, it was joined by two more.

To the chagrin of the overworked criminalists, cops and Service brass clomped through the house. They were hot on the trail at last, and preservation had to bend to the exigency of a fast search.

The legal file box in the corner haunted Tim's peripheral vision despite his efforts to focus elsewhere. Bear regarded it with a canine absorption usually reserved for In-N-Out Double-Doubles, toeing it just above the ESTEBAN MARTINEZ stamp. Standing with his arms crossed so his jacket bunched at his compact shoulders, Tannino alternated his attention among Tim, Bear, and the box, slowly piecing matters together. "Bear," he finally said, "why don't you go put that in your truck so you can deliver it *promptly* back to Counselor Martinez in the morning?"

"Right," Bear said, hefting it into the crook of an elbow. "Good idea."

Denley puzzled over a new answering machine by the fireplace. It had been removed from its box but still appeared unused, ensconced in bubble wrap. "No phone line, so what the fuck's he want with this?" he asked nobody in particular.

Thomas's face stayed drawn and bloodless, and he apologized to Tim at intervals. "I'm sorry, Rack. I thought you were him, you know, a ruse. Jesus, I almost . . ."

After dispensing another "Don't worry about it" that he hoped would have a longer shelf life than the two prior, Tim dug through the duffel bag, impressed with the range of equipment Walker had managed to accumulate. In his brief break between crime scenes, Aaronson had pegged Walker's bullets as homemade. The slugs were composed of an alloy containing titanium—titanium!—which would have required sophisticated equipment not present even at this most finished of Sunnyslope homes. Which raised the possibility of a cache elsewhere—a cache from which Walker, when he slipped through LAPD's net, could replenish. The disposable cell phone—another terrorist advance recently appropriated by fugitives—on the mantel was so cheap it didn't have a call-history feature. A single key beside it fit the front door.

Bear, crouching over the duffel as if regarding a picnic basket, said, "Looky here." He withdrew a DVD case and showed Tim the label. JUNE 1. As Bear stepped off to argue Aaronson into a laptop loan, the chief tapped Tim's shoulder with his cell phone. "Pierce Jameson wants to talk to you. They transferred his call from the command post."

Tim pressed the phone to his ear to hear Pierce say, "The hell's going on down there? My lawyer's en route."

"Wise choice." Tim let the silence stretch out an extra beat. "Your son was here."

"Ain't that something."

"Funny—he had the key, too."

"Well, we left the site as it was. Someone must've left a key behind."

"And you know what else is odd?"

"What's that?"

"You turned the electricity on in the model unit again, just this morning."

"I don't actually oversee the electrical for all of my companies, Deputy. There are quite a few of them. Companies. On that particular site, you might have heard that we had some problems with sewerage? 'Nuther round of testing coming up next week, the guys need somewhere to plug in their gear."

"I thought there would be a simple explanation."

"There usually is. Adios, 'migo."

"Wait a sec. About the 'sewerage'—"

"My contractor just informed me that our system accidentally got routed into the storm drains. I'm furious. With what this'll cost me to fix, heads are gonna roll."

"Yes," Tim said, "they will."

By the time Tim handed off the phone to the chief, Bear had the security footage paused at the appropriate frame on Aaronson's laptop.

The image unfroze to show Tess waiting in The Ivy's side drive as Porsches and Ferraris rolled through the valet. She wore a cocktail dress, staying hunched as if cold, her hands tucked under her bare arms. She held a ticket out to a valet, explaining something—Tim could read the words "purse" and "car" on her lips. The valet handed her a set of keys, then jogged off to retrieve another car. Tess glanced around, then climbed into the Mercedes Gelaendewagen positioned in the prize front spot.

"Wait a minute," Bear said. "Isn't that . . . ?"

Tess leaned over to the driver's side and dug through the jacket hung over the seat. She came up with something and tilted it in her hands.

Chase's BlackBerry.

Tim chuckled with a kind of awed respect.

Tess worked furiously on the tiny keypad, glancing at intervals back at the restaurant. Her focus grew more intense, and she punched another flurry of buttons. The face of the BlackBerry was visible—given digital enhancement and a miracle, they might be able to discern what she'd typed. She did a double take as the valet taxied a Carrera back through the drive, and then she returned the BlackBerry to the jacket pocket and hopped out while the valet was distracted with the Porsche handoff.

She held up the ticket and explained something, gesticulating her confusion.

"Poor thing," Bear said. "They switched her and Chase's valet stubs."

"Inconvenient."

The valet puzzled over her ticket, then ran off. A moment later he returned with Chase, who smiled at Tess, clearly uncomfortable. Tess greeted him with poise, shaking his hand. Chase retrieved his own valet stub, and they compared them, then the keys, and then they and the valets shared a strained laugh. Chase waited with her while the valet ran off to get her car. They stood side by side, looking out at the street in parallel rather than at each other. Chase smoothed his suit jacket and spoke, his expression indicating he was offering a few words of apology or contrite explanation.

The valet rattled up with Tess's car. She nodded good-bye to Chase, even squeezed his arm, climbed in, and drove off.

"Home girl's got *moves,*" Bear said. He was popping the DVD out from the laptop when the disposable phone on the mantel rang. Everyone in the room froze. Down the hall Denley's hoarse Brooklyn-accented voice continued until someone hushed him harshly.

Tim stood before the plastic phone, watching it rattle against the wood. After the third ring, he answered, keeping his voice gruff. "Yeah."

"Not bad, Troubleshooter. Payback for the stunt I pulled with your digital transmitter and the Doberman. That was nice."

If Walker already felt safe enough to make time for a chat, they'd lost their opportunity at him. Tim guessed he'd have needed a car—the Camry, strategically hidden?—to put that kind of comfort distance between himself and the house so quickly after he'd washed out through the culvert. Knowing Walker, he'd stashed fresh clothes and equipment in the trunk, a kit bag that'd help him roll right into the next phase of his plan.

"I could have killed you," Walker continued. "Tonight."

"So why didn't you?"

"You're more useful alive. For now. Remember that. You live because of me."

Tim kept the phone against his face until the dial tone turned to a hiccup.

"Two phone calls, one day," Tannino said. "This guy might come after you."

"Rack's not a target." Bear pocketed the DVD. "He's his idol."

"Or vice versa," the marshal said wryly. "But I'm not complaining. That's the one goddamned thing we have going for us."

Chapter 56

ESTEBAN MARTINEZ, ATTORNEY-AT-LAW. Tim, Bear, and Dray sat on the couch back, their feet on the cushions, regarding the verboten file box centered on the throw rug before them.

Frisk and his ESU team had doggedly backtracked the records from the disposable cell phone company. They'd managed to source Walker's incoming call, only to learn that Walker had anticipated them and left a customized taunt, routing the connection—again—through the Vector switchboard. The trail before that was impossible to trace.

The early-morning light at the windows was sufficient that they didn't need the lamps in the living room. Dray shifted her weight impatiently.

"Confidentiality is still attached," she said. "You crack that box, you lose those files as evidence."

"We don't have them as evidence to lose," Tim said.

"Maybe the box spills," Bear said. "Maybe the files fall out and they're not clearly marked."

Dray eyeballed the fluorescent orange labels. CONFIDENTIAL: LAWYER-CLIENT MATERIALS. "That's bullshit."

"Yeah," Bear said. "Sure is."

"The AUSA'll have your ass," Dray said, "but it might be worth it. Then again, if the box contains the only solid evidence you get, since Walker is nicely killing the roster of prosecution witnesses, you could blow any possible case against the Kagans and Vector." She added quickly, "Not that you're pursuing one."

A few minutes passed, their focus intensifying. Finally Bear lumbered off the couch, popped the lid from the box. He chuckled and raised a sheet of paper with a handwritten note: *Thought you could make better use of this than I could.*

Bear set aside the paper and started rooting inside. Tim joined him. Dray mumbled to herself a few moments before sliding down and circling the box, peering in at first, then finally settling between them. There wasn't much inside on Tess's case—the only paperwork detailed Esteban's hiring and firing and the dates and times of the two visits. Esteban had been her attorney for four days, not long enough to get past preliminary discussions or generate much paperwork. Tess met with and retained him May 28. But why had she discharged him the same week? No clear answers. After all they'd staked on the confidential files, they hadn't yielded much.

Bear ran a thumb across a rectangular indentation in the manila folder that housed Tess's thin sheaf of documents. Something had been stored there that had fallen out or been taken. Bear dug around the bottom of the box, past the other clients' files, and came up with a microcassette. He held it up, matching it to the indentation. "I suppose this explains the answering machine at the safe house. Walker must've been getting ready to use it when we stormed his ass."

Dray went to search for the microcassette recorder she used to take statements in her deputy days; once she set it on the coffee table, they huddled around like kids listening to a game on a transistor radio.

Rustling. Background voices. The clink of silverware. After a few moments, Bear grew impatient and fast-forwarded a few bursts.

Dean Kagan's voice: *"Hello, Ms. Jameson. Thank you for agreeing to meet me."* The sound of a chair pulling in and then, *"Pellegrino, please. No ice."*

Tess said something inaudible, the recorder—buried in her purse?—rubbing against fabric.

Dean said, *"You threatened my son yesterday. I think this is going in the wrong direction."*

"It seems like a lot of things are."

"He should have known not to try to handle this himself. He's not a bad businessman, but he's a poor negotiator."

"I'm not much of a negotiator, either. Good thing there's nothing to negotiate."

"I suspected I was dealing with a smart woman. A lot smarter than my son, surely." A thoughtful pause. *"Here's the part where I offer you money and you say it's not about money, right?"*

"Right."

"Of course it's not." The jangle of ice cubes against glass. *"No ice, please, as I said."* Pause. *"All of these issues are resolvable without any disruption of your life, ours, or Vector's important work on behalf of those afflicted with AAT. As much as we matter, I'm sure you agree, they matter more. So let me be plain—"*

"Please."

"I've dealt with mobsters and health ministers and other extortionists in more countries than you've heard of, young lady, and I'm certainly not going to be blackmailed by you and whatever attorney you can afford. I could purchase your whole block tomorrow and have it bulldozed. We can do this the wrong way, my playing the asshole CEO, you playing white trash—"

"Don't count out trash."

"—but I suggest you will do much more for your son by continuing your relationship with Vector than by trying to bring out big guns. Our guns are bigger. And our leverage better."

Beside Tim, Dray stiffened.

"I understand, of course, that you want to prosecute Chaisson," Dean continued. *"As I'd guess even your own attorneys would caution you, this is in the line of 'acquaintance rape,' as they put it now, I think. You got into the car willingly, knowing his interest in you. Of course, your attorneys have told you all of this. What they may not have is that Vector, the biomedical firm of which the accused is chairman, cannot expose itself to the liability of actually treating, particularly in the clinical trial of a drug involving risks, a patient who is the accuser's son. If something should go wrong, it would be impossible for Vector to defend itself against the allegation that this was willful malpractice, in some kind of sick revenge."*

Tess released a rush of air. *"Trials start in a few months. I already have a signed agreement for Sammy."*

"Of course you do. Your consent to his involvement. No obligation by Vector is provided, however. That's why I suggest we do nothing to jeopardize our relationship. You love your son. As unlovable as they may be, I love my sons. Let's start over. On the right track. We're having a celebration tomorrow night at The Ivy to commemorate Xedral's patent approval. It won't be complete if you're not a part of it."

Tess sounded calm, but her voice quavered, ever so slightly. *"My dating history with your execs hasn't promoted a lot of trust in your corporate culture."*

Anger edged Dean's voice for the first time, though not directed at Tess. *"Believe me, you won't have any problems."*

"That's good. I'd hate to tear another good dress."

"I like you, Ms. Jameson. Under other circumstances we could do some good work together."

"We still might. For all those AAT-afflicted you lose sleep over."

"I'm not sure I catch your drift." Dean's voice held genuine puzzlement; she'd caught him off guard.

"I mean," Tess said carefully, *"it's nice to have our aims aligned once again."*

"Agreed. I'm afraid I have a meeting that got moved up. But, please, order whatever you'd like. The waiter's already got us on my house account."

The sound of a chair scooting out, and then footsteps tapping away.

Tess's breathing was audible for a moment, and then she made a soft sigh between relief and frustration. There was a rustling, and then the recording abruptly ended.

"Sharp," Dray said. "And given that prick, you gotta give her credit."

"He is smooth," Bear concurred. "He made no illegal threats. Didn't have to—he held all the cards. Tess wasn't gonna let her son get dropped over a rape case. She was boxed in before she got started."

"So the day after this lunch, Tess goes in and plays Esteban the tape," Tim said. "They confer. He concedes that Dean argues a good case. Tess reconsiders her priorities. She leaves the tape in her lawyer's hands—makes sense—then drops the rape case to protect Sam. Even shows up at The Ivy to show she's playing nice. So why'd Vector kick him off the trial list anyway?"

"Whatever she got off Chase's BlackBerry that night . . ." Dray said.

"Of *course,*" Tim said. "The rape was her wedge. Dean offered her a better in with Vector to smooth things over. She used it to dig for whatever she was looking for. Something so Vector couldn't get her over a barrel and drop Sam later."

"You can bet she was rooting through unattended briefcases, poking around the lab on her visits, questioning the scientists," Bear said. "Now, we only met Chase twice, and *we* know that BlackBerry is his lifeline. She saw a chance at it, and she grabbed it. If anything, she was well researched about the Vector information pipeline—either she knew something was due to come downstream or she ran a search-find on his e-mails and hit the jackpot. She wanted more insurance. What she got was too much insurance."

Dray was nodding. "She picked up—as Dean said—'better leverage,' and the old man had to play hardball after all. She sure as hell signaled her extracurricular interest in Vector at the end of their chat here. I bet Dean watched her pretty tight after that."

Bear pulled himself up, grabbed the microcassette, and checked his watch. "We need to make copies now. And we'll need an enhancement of that security footage from The Ivy. But we can't do it at the office."

Tim was already dialing. He got the beep of a pager tone and punched in his and Dray's home number. He'd barely hung up when the phone rang—it seemed impossible that the page could have gone through so quickly. Tim answered.

"What *now,* Rackley?" Pete Krindon sounded rushed, as always. An off-the-books technical security specialist, Pete freelanced for all order of agencies and individuals on both sides of the law. Tim and Bear used him to boldly go where no warrant could take them and to cover technological angles that hadn't yet filtered through FLETC and Quantico classrooms.

"I got some digitally formatted security footage I need you to bring up the resolution on. We gotta make a high-quality copy tonight."

"Tonight? So you have dubious ownership over said footage."

"Precisely. It's taking a brief pit stop here on its way back to its rightful owner. We want it crisp, so I'd like your equipment on it."

"I can make the copy, but there's no way I have time to do an enhancement for you tonight. When you need it by?"

"Aarrhghdfhah!"

"What?"

"Ty!" Tim shouted. "Get off the phone!"

Dray jogged back to corral their son from his late-night expedition.

"Sorry," Tim said. "The sooner the better. Can you do it?"

"What else? Dry cleaning? Baby formula?"

"He's on solids now."

"This wouldn't have to do with that over-the-wall at TI you've been working?"

"How'd ya guess?"

"That boy is relentless," Pete said with admiration, his distinctive half smile detectable in his voice. "Reminds me of you."

A sticky thumb pried Tim's eyelid north, revealing Tyler's face offset by ninety degrees. Already he'd donned the Evel Knievel helmet. "Kaiyer eat beckfest."

It was 6:38 by the alarm clock on Tim's nightstand. He'd dozed off less than an hour ago; the quality of light in the bedroom had yet to change. "Splendid," he said.

He dragged himself from bed, Dray muttering something about sock puppets from a dream stupor. By the time he got Ty dressed, Dray was ready to take over, so Tim ducked into a cool shower to wake himself up. He retrieved his .357 from the gun safe and headed down the hall.

Tyler sat in his booster, Snowball's cage at his elbow. When served oatmeal, he demanded that his hamster eat with him, a rigid adherence to some arcane decree of child logic.

Dray smiled at Tim. "Good morning, sweetie. I'm just cooking you some eggs and bacon."

"Really?"

"No. Are you high?" Dray tossed him a granola bar, then held his face in both hands and planted one on him.

He glanced past her again. Tyler stood, face sneery with exertion, his legs spread as if to muster strength. The engorged bubble of Snowball's head peeked from his fist.

Tim ran over and pried Snowball free. If hamsters could look relieved, Snowball did. Last week Dray had caught Tyler preparing to swing him by his tail. No wonder the little guy ate and slept every chance he got.

"You can't do that, bub. We talked about this."

"Fowball eyes budge."

"Yeah, his eyes bulge. But you'll hurt him. We're gonna have to put him somewhere safe now." Tim inserted Snowball back into his cage and lifted it to the refrigerator top, already crowded with other Typhoon contraband.

Tyler was bawling, again with the huge tears—the horror, the horror of the confiscated hamster. His chubby legs were doing their Wild Things dance, high knees, downward stomps.

"If you're gonna scream, you're gonna have to scream in your room," Tim said. "Your animals may want to hear that, but your mother doesn't. Get going."

Tyler rearranged his features in a cartoon pout and thumped out of the kitchen. Tim wondered which sitter had reinforced that expression, because he was sure Tyler wouldn't get mileage out of Dray on it.

Tim walked over and gave Dray a quick embrace. He'd just turned for the door when a crash from the kitchen startled him. Bathed in the yellow glow of the open refrigerator, Tyler lay on his back amid a head of lettuce, four flaking onions, and several still-rolling oranges. The preceding scene pieced together immediately; Ty had pried open the fridge door and tried to use the interior shelves as ladder rungs to get to Snowball. It took Tim a moment to realize that his son had only feigned a retreat to his bedroom, really circling the living room couch and sneaking back into the kitchen while his parents had been occupied hugging. Confronted with the blunt nature of Tyler's deviousness, Tim found himself encountering as much admiration as anger. Though he rarely admitted it, he used to feel the same watching his father work one of his elaborate deceptions. Determination and cunning—the essential qualities of a good con man. Or a deputy U.S. marshal.

"I got this," Dray said. "Go stamp out crime."

As Dray descended on Tyler, still sheepishly awash in incriminating produce, Tim slipped out and trudged down the walk toward his Explorer, which he'd left at the curb. For once Tad Hartley wasn't up already, mowing his lawn in the FBI windbreaker he'd worn unfailingly since retirement. An anorexic girl wheezed by on the sidewalk, a skittish Chihuahua in a knit sweater fluttering after her. The annoyances of L.A. hipness had recently started to migrate to Moorpark. Attitude poured in with the rising housing market, which Tim figured for a fair trade. Home to the state's largest concentration of law enforcement residents, Moorpark would not have been mistaken for Chihuahua-friendly a mere few years ago.

As Tim chirped the car alarm, a guy in a USC baseball cap stepped around the Explorer, whistling and tossing a football to himself. The football took flight at Tim's chest, and his hands pulled up, instinctively, to catch it.

He felt a tug at his waist as his revolver was lifted from his holster, and then the guy's head tilted back and Walker Jameson stared out from beneath the brim.

Chapter 57

Walker flicked Tim's gun to indicate the front seat, sliding into the back as Tim got behind the wheel. The doors closed, and they were locked behind tinted windows.

"Drop your phone and portable radio over your back. Now cuff yourself to the steering wheel. Attaboy." Walker waited, then emptied Tim's bullets from the cylinder and let the revolver fall over the headrest onto the passenger seat. He settled back, hands out of view in his lap but positioned so Tim knew he was holding a gun. His right T-shirt sleeve was hiked up, revealing what looked like half of a yin-and-yang tattoo.

He studied Tim's reflection in the rearview. "You're softer than I thought you'd be. Married, right?"

"That's right."

"Kids?" Walker returned Tim's nod. "Explains it." He looked out the window at the house.

The venetians were mostly closed, but Tim could make out Dray's figure at the table, serving Tyler breakfast.

"You got the microcassette before I had a chance to listen to it. I want it back."

"You're in luck. I always carry irreplaceable, crucial evidence in my pocket." Tim rolled his right hand over, nudging it against his left, trying to get a stray finger beneath the watch to the handcuff key taped there.

"You do when it's illegal for you to have it."

300

"You got a point there." Out of view, Tim's finger worked against the edge of the hidden key. He sensed anxiety pounding beneath his heartbeat and realized it was due to the proximity of Dray and Tyler. He'd vowed never to let the violence of his work touch his family again. Less than thirty yards away, Dray wiped something off Ty's face.

"My wife's gonna notice the car still sitting here and come check it out. She's a sheriff's deputy." It was all bluff; the tinted windows hid them nicely, and it wasn't unusual for Tim to sit out in the Explorer before starting the commute, reviewing files out of Tyler's earsplitting range.

Walker said, "Retired, isn't she?"

"You want to take that up with her Beretta?" Tim drew the key out from its hiding place and buried it in his fist. "We'd better move before she gets suspicious."

Walker's grip closed like a mechanical claw on the back of Tim's neck, his thumb digging into the pressure point just behind the ear. His voice came right beside Tim's head. "Open your hand."

Tim complied, and Walker reached past him to grab the key. When Walker's fingertips brushed Tim's hand, Tim jerked his head free and snapped it back into Walker's face. A satisfying crunch of bone, and Walker fell away to the cushioned seat. Tim leaned on the horn with his full weight, but it made no sound, and then he heard the gruff tick of Walker's laugh and felt the gun barrel pressed to his neck.

A trickle of blood darkened Walker's upper lip, but it didn't seem he was going to retaliate. Not yet. Tim opened his fist. Empty. Walker had somehow managed to hold on to the handcuff key.

"And let me save us another round." Walker pointed to the dashboard radio. The cord on the push-to-talk mike had been cut. Tim noted the hatched scars on the underside of Walker's forearm—nicks from combat knife kills. Cutting throats from behind took a surge of adrenaline and a well-honed blade. If the knife penetrated too deep into enemy flesh, it wound up slicing your own arm, the one used to brace the head.

"I need you to tell me where that tape is."

"My partner took it last night. Go wrestle him for it."

"You know how the game is played." Walker nodded to the house. "I could go in and have a look."

Tim's heart seemed to hold beatless for a suspended moment. "If you threaten my wife or my boy, I will kill you." He sat upright, bringing his glare within a foot of the mirror. "Look at me. I will kill you."

"You been trying. So far you're not doing real well."

Walker reached for the door. Tim's rage flared, and he thrashed against the cuffs.

When he came to, he felt some good pain through the buzz, his head bent forward across the wheel. It took a moment for him to realize that Walker wasn't pressing the gun to the base of his skull, that the throbbing he felt was the aftereffect of getting pistol-whipped. Walker sat relaxed against the backseat, shuttling the dubbed copy of the microcassette across his knuckles like a casino chip. Tim's badge and wallet were spilled on the seat beside him. The clock showed 7:05; Tim had been out less than a minute. Dray was gone from the kitchen, probably fighting Tyler into his clothes. That could take a while.

A band of shadow darkened Walker's face, but Tim could make out his amused eyes. "Must be something. To feel like that. To have that kind of . . ." He sucked his teeth and looked away. "Most people fake it. Want to give themselves a sense of purpose. Something to do. Some people, though, like you, it's the real deal. Tess was that way. My ex, sure, her, too. Same genes, me and Tess, but I'm not built that way. That's where I have an advantage over you, Rackley: I don't give a fuck."

From what Tim knew of Walker, he rarely spoke, let alone for so long. He wanted to talk. He already had what he'd come for and could've just split while Tim was unconscious.

Straightening himself in his seat, Tim fought through the blur of pain to find a way to keep him engaged. "It's not about giving a fuck. It's instinct. How would you react if I threatened your nephew?"

"I don't give a shit about him. That's what people like you can't get."

"How about your ex-wife? She seems like a hell of a woman. If you don't care about anything, how'd you land her?"

"Even a blind squirrel finds an acorn now and again."

Tim still expected him to bolt with the tape, but he just sat there, studying Tim's house.

Walker said, "You got a nice family." Not a threat. Envy. "You were a killer once. I checked up on your record in the Rangers, too. How do you get from that to this?"

Tim tried to figure out if Walker saw Tim's settling into his life as an advance or a degeneration. Probably both. He stared at Tad Hartley's lawn, wondering why, on this of all mornings, Tad had decided to take a pass on his yard work. No joggers in sight. Living in a cul-de-sac meant no through traffic. "You give up the stuff you think matters the most to you. And you do it before you find out that it never really mattered to you anyway."

Walker made a noise, and his chin dipped in faint acknowledgment. "If you get in my way, I'll kill you. You're a husband. A father. You really want to put your life on the line for these scumbags?"

"Not for them."

"For what, then?"

"For me. It's my job."

"To protect rapists and murderers?"

"My preferences don't figure in here."

"They used to."

"I was foolish and self-righteous and pissed off. Like you."

Walker's face was drawn, menace etched in the squint lines. "Man, you haven't learned a damn thing. People like us get *used*. There are no rules for the policy makers and the baby kissers. There were no weapons of mass destruction in Iraq." A good-natured smirk. "There didn't have to be. We brought our own. Depleted-uranium bullets. Gulf War syndrome—and its sequel—ain't no syndrome. It's low-level radiation poisoning. I got buddies whose wives can't sleep with them no more. Stings when they cum. We pack off on a lie and a flag and come back broken, and nobody gives a shit." He wiped the trickle of blood from his lip. "I was supposed to deploy for six months, wound up in the dirt almost two years. Cost me my marriage. People drift. I sure as hell did. But, hell, I paid the price and I shut up. I even served my time when they put me behind bars for doing the right thing to the wrong person. But meanwhile, back here"—he firmed his mouth, rage overpowering a flicker of something more tender—"back here they can haul your sister into a limo and rape her, then kill her for her troubles. I don't get it.

Maybe you do. You're a guy like me. How come it worked out so much better for you?"

Tim could produce no judicious reply, so he kept his mouth shut.

Walker shifted across the seat toward the door. "Stay the hell out of my way. You might catch a bullet."

"I'm gonna keep coming. You know that."

"Course. That's our ROEs." Walker smiled, genuinely amused. "If there's one thing you are, Rackley, it's dependable. I can count on you. Ain't that right?" He kicked open the door. "You get me in your sights, you'd better shoot straight."

He vanished, jogging around the corner to whatever vehicle he'd stowed unassumingly on the middle-class street. Tim hit the disabled horn again, more from habit than anything else, then sat and watched the empty cul-de-sac. His keys were by the gas pedal, and even if he could retrieve them with his foot, he couldn't get them to his hand. He worked off his left boot, then wedged his heel beside the seat, finally reaching the controls. The driver's seat whirred back until the tracks came visible. And the tip of an antenna. Hunched forward so the metal wouldn't grind at his wrists, he fought his sock off using his other boot, leaving red streaks down his shin. He clutched the antenna with his bare toes, retrieving his portable from beneath the seat. Using the ball of his foot, he depressed the call button.

When the comm center responded, Tim leaned over, talking loudly at the pinned radio. "This is Tim Rackley. Will you call my wife at home and ask her to come outside?"

Chapter 58

The front rooms of the Kagan house, mood-lit for a somberness uncharacteristic of the dearly deceased, were scattered with a gathering of soberly dressed people. A few familiar faces, the inner circle able to be summoned at a day's notice to pay tribute to the dispatched CEO. The curtains were drawn. A spread of fine cheeses on a velvet-draped table. Same caterer, same staff relentlessly clearing and replenishing, different pattern of china. The sparse mourners stood around awkwardly, as if unsure of what they were supposed to do. Dean and Dolan were conspicuously absent, leaving the mourners to fend for themselves or to offer condolences in shifts to Jane Bernard, who circled endlessly like a bride greeting out-of-towners while her daughter, buried in the corner amid a swarm of dark suits, played the part of the grief-stricken fiancée. All signs of yesterday evening's assault had vanished. No scattered glass, no jagged hole in the window, no blood spatter.

Tim and Bear had been screened by guards at checkpoints at the gate, the walk, and the door, but once inside they moved unimpeded. During the command-post debriefing, Tim's headache had dissipated, forgotten, but it returned with a vengeance after he'd had some quiet on the ride over. Bear had returned the file box to an irate Martinez that morning, keeping the second dub that they'd fortunately made the night before. Tim had reached Pete on the drive over, extracting a promise that he'd analyze the security footage from The Ivy within twenty-four hours.

Received stonily by Jane Bernard, Tim and Bear turned the corner, arriving at Dean's study, where a team of suited extras toiled, parked on every available chair and counter. The fax machine whirred, cell phones hummed, laptop keyboards clacked. Tim caught the gist from six angles—final preparations for tomorrow's investor presentation. Never before had he seen so thin a veil between grief and industry. Dolan alone sat still, occupying a club chair, his legs drawn up beside him.

The activity paused at Tim and Bear's entrance.

Bear cleared his throat and announced, grandly, "We've retrieved a tape of you threatening Tess Jameson."

From behind his wooden slab desk, Dean said, "A moment, please, gentlemen." The think-tank suits assembled their paperwork and shuffled out. Looking wan and nauseated, Dolan remained. The door clicked shut, and Dean's eyebrows lifted.

Bear raised Dray's microcassette player from his breast pocket and punched a button. Dean's voice issued forth. Dean listened to himself impassively. As the recorded conversation progressed, Dolan shook his head faintly at intervals in what seemed like private self-reprimand.

The tape ended, and Dean said, "I do not need to remind you that it's illegal to record someone without their consent in the state of California."

"Speaking of illegal," Tim said, "it seems like you had a pretty strong motive to keep an eye on Tess."

"She was one of a thousand problems we deal with on a daily basis. Nothing more."

"I don't know. A high-profile rape trial, lurid stories of a pregnancy, a lawsuit threatening."

"Not 'threatening.' We'd reached an agreement."

"Oh? Then why'd you pull Sam from the Xedral trial?"

"I'm afraid you're mistaken there, Deputy." Dean shoved back from his desk, the chair casters squeaking on the floor. "*She* elected to drop her son from the study, not vice versa."

Dolan emerged from his groggy state, his attention pulling to his father.

"Sure," Bear said. "She's gonna remove her son from the one clinical trial that might save his life?"

"Odd, I know," Dean said. "We questioned it ourselves. But I think we can dispense with the notion that all Ms. Jameson's actions were rational. I have it here in her hand." Without lowering his gaze, he slid open his top desk drawer, removed two sheets of paper, and extended them to Tim.

Dolan pushed down on the chair's arms, almost rising to his feet.

Bear laughed once, in disbelief. Confounded, Tim stepped forward and took the papers. At once he recognized the lavender-tinted stationery and Tess's distinctive handwriting. The second paper was a faxed version of the same letter.

> *4th June*
>
> *To the Vector Biogenics Department of Human Trials:*
> *After some deliberation, I have decided to remove my son,*
> *Samuel Jameson (Samuel Hardy in earlier paperwork),*
> *from the Xedral Phase I and II combined study. Sam's*
> *doctor believes that he has at least a few months, and*
> *we're hopeful we should be able to secure an O-type liver*
> *for transplant in that time. We've elected to pursue this less*
> *uncertain course.*
>
> > *With much thanks for your consideration,*
> > *Tess Jameson*

Dean said, "Apparently she thought it was a choice between a guess and an outright crapshoot."

Wordlessly, Tim handed the letter to Bear, but Dolan snatched it away and read it while Bear occupied himself with the fax copy.

"The agreement requires written notice if a prospective subject decides to drop out," Dean said, "and written notice we received."

"She wrote that under duress," Bear said.

"A handwritten letter? A full page?" Dean shook his head, as if saddened to see Bear clutching at straws. "Send it to your handwriting analysts. They can tell when one has written at gunpoint, if I am to trust my le Carré."

The letter was dated four days before Tess's murder. The day before she'd called Melissa Yueh for an appointment. Maybe she'd discovered something in the three-day interim between firing her lawyer and yanking Sam from the study. Something to do with what she'd seen on Chase's BlackBerry. But they couldn't explore that possibility unless Pete worked magic with the digital enhancement.

Bear was still forging through denial. "The trial starts what? Monday?"

Still regarding the letter, Dolan nodded faintly.

"She fought to get Sam into that study. He was dying, on a clock. She's gonna opt for a liver transplant—that they were *way* down the list for—when they were just two months away from starting gene therapy?" Bear shook his head, aggravated, it seemed, at all of them, Tess included. "I don't buy it. Unless you escalated your threats. Unless you scared her so much she decided to stay away from you."

"At the cost of her son's life?" Dean chuckled. "I assure you—not a woman of that constitution. It was a big decision. She got cold feet. We see it all the time."

"Right," Tim said. "Hysterical, emotional Tess Jameson."

Dean shrugged. "Out of character, perhaps, but consider the stakes. An experimental protocol, a young life on the line. These are not matters to be taken lightly. And bear in mind, once a patient begins gene therapy, he is removed from the organ-donor list."

"It does explain a lot. What it doesn't explain is how a few days ago you maintained no recollection of this woman."

"I never maintained anything of the sort. I fear you're mistaking me for my younger son."

Dolan's hand was trembling; he'd creased the letter. "How could you not tell me? That it was *her* choice?"

"I couldn't see how the *manner* in which this woman opted for euthanasia for her son was relevant to your work," Dean said.

"It would have mattered to me."

Dean leveled his hard, dark eyes at Dolan. Dolan's shoulders lowered, and then he eased back into the club chair.

Bear said, "Tess had better judgment than that."

"Yes." Dean sighed. "But she wasn't well. She committed suicide within the week. Depression is a serious illness"—deadpan—"that must be medicated."

"About that," Bear said. "You might be interested to know Tess Jameson's case has been reopened. As a murder."

Dolan jerked in a deep breath, but Dean just calmly said, "Really?"

Tim said, "So you knew she was killed?"

"Why would I know that?"

"Her brother knows," Bear said, "and he holds you responsible and intends to kill you. And he's willing to literally swim through shit to do it."

"Well, I'm sure that a delusional prison escapee has all the right answers."

Dolan couldn't help himself and broke in. "She was killed? How do you know?"

Tim said, "Tess was left-handed. The entry wound was on the left side of her head. Only problem is, she was a right-handed shooter."

"Couldn't she have used her other hand? Lots of left-handed people are pretty ambidextrous."

"I don't know, Dolan," Bear said. "Gun to temple. Pretty important moment. I think you'd want your shooting hand."

"How . . . ? Who do you think did it?" Dolan asked.

"Sources tell us she was murdered by a contract killer called the Piper," Tim said.

Dolan looked shocked, his Adam's apple vibrating.

Bear said, "But what we're more interested in is who hired the Piper."

"And?" Dolan said.

"Tess was pregnant," Tim said, "with Chase's child." He eyed Dean. "That's a start, though I'm sure there's more to the story."

Dolan sank back in the chair as if he'd lost all strength. "Chase's? You have proof of this?"

"Of course not. Can't do a DNA analysis on cinders, now, can you?" Dean's tone never wavered, but he tugged a handkerchief from his pocket, fluffed it out, and dabbed his forehead. "Now, if you don't mind, I have a son to put into the ground and a presentation to finish for him." He tapped a button on his desk, and the door opened, the executives shuffling in. Briefcase lids snapped up and computers chimed back to life, but no one spoke.

Bear walked out, but Tim lingered a moment, noting the contrast between Dean's reengagement and Dolan's near-catatonic repose.

Dean and his team were back in the swing by the time he slipped out.

Chapter 59

Other kids ran and squealed with after-school exertion, but Sam slumped in the swing, his jaundiced face lax with exhaustion. The swings on either side of him were empty, the only unoccupied pieces of playground equipment in the whole park. The sole trail of footprints across the sand pit was his own.

It took two tries for his hoarse voice to grow loud enough for Kaitlin to hear him over the clanking of the seesaws: *"Push me."*

She rose from the bench and headed toward him, dodging a jump-rope threesome and a swirl of kids hanging from the merry-go-round. Her waitstaff vest was unbuttoned, her dress sleeves cuffed. Though it was just past four, a blanket of clouds blotted the sky, a premature dusk that left their house, a mere block away, blended into gray.

Kaitlin reached Sam and gave him a soft push, getting him going again. "You ready to go home?"

"Ten more minutes."

"We gotta get dinner going."

Together they said, "I'm not hungry." She laughed, and he managed a smile.

Dylan threaded through the playground on his dirt bike. The other kids quieted a bit, noting the older boy's presence. He was only eleven, but thick like a young teenager, and his fake toughness was palpable, precocious.

"What's a matter, Piss-Eyes?" Dylan shouted. "Can't pump your*self*?"

Sam said softly, "Okay. Let's go home."

Dylan popped a wheelie, then rose up, shoving down on the pedals, the bike jerking side to side as he burst from the park. He got about ten yards down the street when a form melted from the sidewalk bushes, stepping in front of him and grabbing his handlebars so he slid forward, racking his nuts on the high bar.

"Ow! What the *hell*!"

"You're gonna leave that kid alone."

The boy yanked his handlebars back, but they didn't budge in Walker's hands. "You're a grown-up. What are *you* gonna do?"

Walker leaned forward over the grips, and here the kid's eyes flickered. "I'm gonna hunt you down, in your bed, while you sleep, and cut out your *fuckin'* heart. That's what I'm gonna do."

He released the handlebars, and the kid jerked back in sudden recoil, tangling in his bike. He scrambled up, running and dragging his bike beside him until he could swing a leg over the seat and pedal furiously away.

Walker continued toward the park's entrance. Kaitlin and Sam stepped through the gate. Sam looked weak, sagging against her side. A noticeable deterioration even from three days ago, when Walker had first seen him at the house.

Walker started toward them, but Sam just stared at him blankly, then looked away. Kaitlin stiffened. Walker stepped to the fence, putting a parked ice cream truck between him and the street. "What?"

Sam spoke quietly and with impressive anger. "You don't care about anything."

Walker said, "That's the first smart thing you've said."

"Like my life doesn't suck enough *already*."

Walker looked at him, feeling a grind deep in his chest. "Guess what you win when you complain?" He held up his hand, fingers and thumb curled to shape a zero.

Sam said, "Screw you," and sulked off toward home.

Kaitlin called after him, "I'll be there in a minute, Sammy." The lightness at her eyes faded when she turned back to Walker. "You told him that he'd get his gene if he helped you? How could you promise him that?"

"I didn't know what to say."

"Yeah, you sure didn't." She crossed her arms, locking down a shudder. "Why are you here?" She nodded at his hesitation, her suspicions confirmed. "You need help."

"Never mind."

"Gladly. We don't want to see you again."

He watched her walk off. She jogged a few steps to catch up to Sam, then slung an arm across his shoulder. The kid was walking slowly, like a windup toy winding down.

Walker strode back to the parallel street where he'd parked the Accord—his home for the time being. When he set his elbow on the console, it struck the microcassette recorder, turning it on.

Dean's voice said, *"Our guns are bigger. And our leverage better."*

The odd ache in Walker's chest returned. It wasn't until he'd hit the freeway and picked up speed that he registered it might not be anger.

Chapter 60

Tim nosed out from behind a moving van and floored it, ignoring Bear, who crossed himself elaborately. Tim leaned forward, speaking loudly into the Nextel speaker-mounted on his dash. "Why don't we have a full rundown on Pierce Jameson?"

Guerrera, from the command post, sounded irritated. "We do."

"Not thorough enough."

"I told you, he's clean now."

"Then run his past associates from when he wasn't. And why the hell can't anyone get anything on the Piper? Or the Aryan Brotherhood hit men?"

Wearing a Mona Lisa smile, Bear ticked a finger at the rearview mirror.

"Shit—gotta go." Tim swore at the flashing blue lights and pulled over onto the shoulder, his aggravation mounting.

No updates of any worth from the task force. Guerrera had used the reverse directory to source the fax number tattooed across the top of Tess's letter. She'd sent it from the dental office she'd managed—no big surprise there, since Tim didn't remember seeing a fax machine in her house.

Tim clicked on his interior light to give the cop good visibility, rolled down his window, and put his hands at the ten and two, his left gripping his badge and creds. The CHP officer was fully decked out—riding gloves,

314

white bulb of a helmet, mirrored glasses despite the hour. "Step out of the car, please, sir."

"I'm a federal officer. Take a look at the badge in my hand."

"Impressive. Now, *out of the car,* pal."

Tim noticed Bear's shoulders heaving silently, so he turned and squinted into the flashlight beam. Pete Krindon chuckled and slid into the backseat, unscrewing his helmet from his mop of fire-red hair. He imitated Tim's tough-guy voice, " 'I'm a federal officer,' " and then he and Bear had another good laugh.

"I oughta haul you in," Tim said. "What the hell are you doing impersonating a cop?"

"Same thing you're doing impersonating one. Only you don't know who authorized me." Pete whipped off his glasses, fogged them with a breath, and polished them on his sleeve. His hand flicked inside his vinyl jacket and withdrew a flat-screen monitor the size of a school notebook.

Bear said, "Cool. I want one."

Pete shifted forward, laying the screen on the console. A paused image of Tess in Chase's G-Wagen outside The Ivy, her head bent over his BlackBerry. Pete tapped around with a stylus, smoothing out the grainy picture in waves as the software compared each pixel to its neighbors and adjusted it accordingly. Once the freeze-frame had been enhanced to sufficient clarity, Pete diminished the window tint and zoomed in on the wireless e-mail device in Tess's hands. "I captured her forwarding one of Chase's e-mails, then deleting the last sent-mail entry."

"So Chase couldn't tell she'd done it?" Tim asked.

"Not from the BlackBerry at least. But what she probably *didn't* know is that there'd still be a record of the forwarded e-mail on Chase's primary computer."

"Which would be at Chase's office. So he could've seen it when he went in to work Monday."

"And it probably got flagged when it hit Vector's server. Digital security at an outfit like that—they don't want to wind up like those bozos at Arthur Andersen."

Tim flipped open his notepad, checking the case chronology. The alignment of dates provided a frame for the other loose facts they'd gathered. They were far from the heart of the matter, but it seemed they were finally circling it. "On Tuesday, Tess drops Sam from the trial. Wednesday she calls Melissa Yueh—a reporter—to tell her she had something to show her. She's killed two days later."

"And her hard drive was stolen," Bear added.

"That's a helluva e-mail," Pete said. "I'm thinking we've got a whistle-blower who drank one too many Vioxx-Celebrex milk shakes or nude JPEGs of Chase in a three-way with Bigfoot and Michael Jackson."

Tim said, "Did you make out what address she forwarded the e-mail *to*?"

Another click set the footage rolling frame by frame as Tess's thumbs worked the mini-keyboard. "Only these forty-seven frames are visible, just a couple seconds plus," Pete said. As Tess continued, her forearm blocked the BlackBerry screen and keypad from view, and then the angle was lost on the unit altogether. "All I could make out was that the address ended with 'azzu-dot-com.'"

"So what do we do with that?" Bear asked.

"*You* don't do anything with that, for you are a mere bumbling deputy. But I do several things with that. The logical domain name was 'pizzazzu-dot-net,' one of those cheap-ass banner-intensive ISPs. Working off the assumption that she forwarded the e-mail to herself—the obvious bet given how she covered her tracks—I tried the typical screen-name variations. They all bounced back undeliverable. So I sat down on my doughnut break and had another look at Ms. Tess. Well-put-together girl, not a lot of money. You see her jeans label?" He reversed Tess out of the Mercedes. A few clicks brought the brand name in question into view above a hip scarf. "*Tarz*. It's Turkish for 'style.' Turkish textiles—great quality and cheap as dirt." Pete regarded Bear's rumpled jacket. "You might consider looking into it. Only one company distributes Tarz in the U.S. They're based in Paterson, New Jersey, and they're online only. So I called, told them I was Tess Jameson's personal assistant and I never received an e-mail receipt for my last order, could they double-check the e-mail they had on record."

Bear said, "And?"

"Tuffnuff-at-pizzazzu-dot-net. Cracking her password wasn't hard: *Sammy*. But here's where I hit a wall. Pizzazzu deactivates an account

316

and clears the mail cache after it's inactive for two months. Hell, she probably set up the account just to receive this e-mail."

"And we're at?"

"Two months and eight days."

"What now?"

Pete shrugged. "I can't recover the e-mail from her computer because the hard drive was—wisely—switched out."

"Maybe she printed the document and it's hidden at her house," Bear offered.

"And the Piper elected to whack her and steal the hard drive but not check under the mattress? If she *did* have a hard copy, you can bet your ass he didn't leave it behind."

Bear looked at Tim as if to say, *A little help here,* but Tim was sorting through Bear's last words. He pictured Tess's cluttered workspace in her bedroom—what was missing from it?

"You're right," Tim said slowly to Bear, "she would've wanted a printed copy of whatever she found in the e-mail to bring to her meeting with Yueh."

"But . . ." Bear circled a pawlike hand, a monkey who'd flipped the script on the organ grinder.

Tim was still putting it together, the thoughts a half step ahead of his words. "She didn't have a fax machine, so she faxed her letter to Vector from work."

"So? What's that give us?"

"No printer either. That's why her letter to Vector was handwritten."

Pete snapped his fingers, coming upright in the backseat. "She would've forwarded the e-mail to her work e-mail address—"

"To print it *there,*" Bear finished triumphantly.

Tim squealed out from the shoulder, throwing Pete back in his seat. "Come with us," Tim said. "You're dressed for it."

A slender woman with clean, pleasing features and maroon-rimmed eyeglasses pushed around some paperwork behind the reception window. On the counter a ceramic tooth held a stack of WESTIN DENTISTRY business cards in caricatured hands.

Tim tapped his knuckles on the glass, and the woman looked up with a smile. A pencil protruded from her dark brown hair above her ear.

"Can we see Dr. Westin, please? We need to ask him a few quick questions."

"That's me." She stood—not far—and offered a hand. "Michelle Westin."

Behind Tim, Bear fake-coughed his amusement.

"My wife would back him on that one," Tim said. "I'm sorry."

"That's okay. I lost my office manager a few months ago, so I'm trying to cover the cracks between temps." Michelle's expression shifted as she took in the Glock at Bear's belt and Pete in his Erik Estrada getup. "What can I help you with?"

She listened intently, troubled, as Tim filled her in. "Follow me back." She let them through, peering up at Bear; she was maybe five-four, and the contrast was humorous. "You are one big guy."

"I'm on the North Beach Diet," Bear said. "Chips and pasta."

Her smile lingered an extra moment, and then they moved down the hall in single file. Flecked tiles, scrubbed clean, squeaked underfoot. The chilled air smelled of latex and the faux-fruit flavorings that enhance fluoride.

The suite accommodated a dentist chair and a desk tucked into the corner.

Michelle regarded the empty chair. "As much as it sounds selfish, I still have a hard time forgiving her."

The injustice again hit Tim—not just that Tess had been dispatched after such deliberate mistreatment but that her place in people's thoughts had been altered as well. From what Tim had learned of her, he knew she'd have been mortified to have the taint of suicide accompany the mention of her name. Not only had she been murdered but her memory doomed to a sort of haunting. She was a specter unavenged, unredeemed, trapped in the rags of false surrender. Alive, she'd seemed vibrant and strong. The face saved from mere prettiness by a thin nose and intelligent eyes. The self-deprecating tone she'd struck in her letter to Walker. The piles of reading she'd accumulated in a quest to save Sam, a son who now knew her as a mother who'd given up on herself, on him, on everything. She'd been reduced by her death in more ways than one.

Michelle slid a rolling chair out from the desk and beckoned for Pete to sit down. "Help yourselves. This was the computer she used."

Pete grimaced at the iMac. "*Great.* Macintosh."

"What did she do?" Tim asked.

"What didn't Tess do? Insurance, billing, scheduling, the books."

Tim said, "You were close?"

"We got to be. I hired her right out of her associate's program. She told me about Sam in her interview, and I admired how she threw herself into it, going back to school, all that. She worked after hours every chance she got. I was glad to pay it. We have one of the best group insurance plans, and it still sucks. It's like blood from a stone these days, but I'm sure you know that. I helped her navigate the billing at first, but soon enough she outpaced *me.* She spent hours every day on the phone with our patients' plans, so she learned how to talk to them. The time came when I'd go to her with questions. Same thing with Sammy's condition. I pointed her in a few directions, a month later it was like she was a geneticist." Her voice warbled, and she paused to recompose herself.

Bear pouched his lips, his eyes pulling to meet Tim's. Tess knew the *science* behind Xedral. Where had that led her?

Pete, no master of tact, paused from banging on the keyboard and said, "Gimme her work e-mail again?"

Glad for the distraction, Michelle dictated it to him. Munching on a sugar-free lollipop he'd requisitioned from a glass jar in the lobby, Pete proceeded.

Bear said, "Sounds like you lost a good friend."

Michelle nodded and patted him affectionately on the arm. Their eyes met and held an extra beat, and for the first time since Tim had known him, Bear colored. He mumbled his condolences, then blushed again and excused himself for the bathroom. Busy at the iMac, Pete snickered into a fist. Bear smacked him on the head as he passed.

With amusement Tim noted Michelle watching Bear's exit.

Pete's hammering rose to a furious pitch—he could work a keyboard so fast Tim sometimes didn't believe he was actually typing. Pete tilted back in the chair with a sigh and spit the hard candy back into its cellophane wrapper. "You deleted the trashed e-mail cache," he said accusatorily.

319

"What?" Michelle looked surprised by his sharp tone.

"You have an autoerase feature set up that deletes trashed e-mails after—guess what?—two months." Pete looked at Tim, his palms flipped skyward.

"That's because any e-mails of substance get filed," Michelle said. "We keep records connecting to patient complaints, claims, litigation even. Everything of relevance should be saved in her e-mail files."

"Not *everything* of relevance," Pete said bitterly.

Bear came in, wiping his hands on his pants. "What?"

"Tess Jameson's old e-mails. They're not on here. I shouldn't be surprised—she probably deleted it herself anyways." Pete rocked forward in the chair and unplugged the computer. "I'm gonna have to take this with me and restore the data."

"Do you mind?" Bear asked.

Michelle shook her head. "Not if it'll help Tess's case. But can you do that? Find data that's been erased?"

"Nothing ever actually gets deleted except the pointers to *find* the data." Pete stood, tucking the iMac under his arm and rapping its side with his knuckles. "That e-mail's in here. Somewhere. It's just a matter of teasing it out."

Chapter 61

The house, when quiet, worried Tim. Tyler's squalling arrival on the premises had ratcheted up the average noise level several decibels, and Tim had grown accustomed to laughter and crying and shouting. Signs of life. The day had started with Tim at gunpoint by his own curb, so his normal unease at the uncharacteristic silence was exacerbated.

Tim had spent a punishing three hours at the command post planning security operations for tomorrow's Vector investment presentation with one of Dean Kagan's innumerable mouthpieces. His headache had largely subsided, but the bruise at the base of his skull remained swollen. It had been painful when he leaned his head back against his chair, which he did, forgot, and did again in a five-minute loop, a Homer Simpson reprise. Finally he'd come home to catch a few hours' sleep before festivities kicked off.

He gently closed the door from the garage, the alarm's quiet chime announcing the breach. He took off his shoes so he could creep soundlessly down the hall. Miraculously, the Typhoon was asleep, spun in his sheets, the Tasmanian devil gone Tutankhamen. Relief unknotted Tim's stomach, and he bent to kiss his son's sweat-moist head. Tyler stirred, his mouth suckling air. Tim patted his back, his arms, his legs, taking comfort in the undeniable physicality of him.

Dray lay flipped with her back to the door, a fall of soft yellow light illuminating her side of the bed. A paperback lay face open on the comforter beside her. Tim thought she was asleep until he heard her uncock the hammer of her Beretta. Her shoulder shifted, and the gun slid out from under her pillow. After Walker's cameo at the house that morning, Tim had renewed his appreciation for housewives who pack heat.

"Hi, babe." Dray handed him her gun, and he secured it in the safe. "How'd it go?"

"Bear has a new girlfriend."

Dray's lips pursed. "She a cop?"

"Dentist."

"Good. Never trust a woman in law enforcement."

Tim slipped into bed, and she rolled over with a faint groan, a sound effect she'd acquired during pregnancy and held on to. She petted his chest lazily while he filled her in.

"She's under your skin," Dray said. "Tess. I get it. But why so much?"

It took Tim a few moments to hit an answer—he was unsure if it was the right one or the complete one, but it felt as if it gave a pretty good shape to his sentiments. "She really turned it around. She came from not much and found herself in a tough place with a sick kid. And she handled it. Got a degree, a new job, therapy, was working hard to cover medical bills. How many times do you see that? I mean, forget the triumph of the human spirit, forget people empowering themselves, forget all the liberal bullshit. How many times does someone, for whatever reason, actually turn their life around? They usually wear down under the weight of it. Give up. But Tess didn't. She struggled and fought and was making it work, and then someone canceled her. And framed her as a failure."

Dray kept petting him, and he let his eyelids droop, though he wasn't tired, not yet. Dray clicked off the light, and they lay there in the still house with the rasp of the baby monitor and the wind rattling the metal catch of the side fence.

He thought Dray had long fallen asleep when she said, "I don't care how much you like him, or how much you think he's right, you gotta take him down when the time comes." Her tone was not combative or stern; if anything, it was sympathetic. "You know that."

Tyler's restless shifting came through the monitor, and then he settled back into silence. Tim stared at the shadows of branches scraping across the dark ceiling. "Yeah," he said.

Clad in boxers, Walker sat on one of two twin beds with sheets so thin they showed off the ticking beneath. A duffel bag, misshapen with the ordnance packed inside, rested next to the jagged hole where years ago a wet-bar minifridge had been ripped from a cabinet during the building's conversion from crappy motel to crappy housing complex. To his right, a fire escape wound down from the second-story window into an alley in which he'd already seen two blow jobs negotiated and executed. Sloppy, stumbling exchanges. He'd closed the blinds on the front window that overlooked the floating walkway and the parking lot. The carpet stank of tequila and lemon freshener, and the toilet in the tiny nook of the bathroom looked to be made of durable plastic. When he'd set foot in the shower, the molded floor had dented down with a thunderclap like sheet metal bending, the noise repeating each time he'd shifted his weight.

His latest cell phone at his ear, the cool stainless steel of the Redhawk pressed to his bare thigh, he let the other end ring and ring. Finally Kaitlin picked up the cell he'd left her, a dreary, half-asleep mutter.

He gave her his location right away, rattling it off before she could hang up.

"And?" she said, deadpan.

So much like Tess. He heard her push herself up in bed, and he could picture her body position exactly, the slouch against the headboard, her hand holding her bangs at bay. "There's a dirt lot four blocks north, behind a Denny's."

"Sounds appealing."

"Bring the kid by. Around eight."

"He's not doing so hot right now, Walk, in case you haven't noticed. He doesn't need to stand around in a dirt lot at night."

"Please." He couldn't remember the last time he'd used the word, and he imagined that's what her stunned silence was about. "I won't ever try to see you again. Or him. Just gimme a shot to explain it to him better. About his mother."

A long silence, just the two of them breathing in the darkness. Again he could see her face, the sleep-softened cheeks, the way her hair got mussed by the pillows so it framed her eyes.

"You owe it to him," he said.

"You're not the best judge of who's owed what." Her anger lingered on the quiet line, and then she said, "Why's it gotta be so late?"

Walker snapped open the gun to eye the six bullets staring out from the chambers, each one containing a piece of Tess's titanium cross. "I got a very full day."

Chapter 62

Given the VIP handling, the carefully negotiated seating, and the dramatically timed arrivals, Tim would've thought he was attending the Academy Awards. The private security firm Beacon-Kagan had hired was surprisingly competent, constituted of former soldiers, a few of whom Tim knew in passing. They'd put up metal detectors just beyond the revolving doors in the building's lobby and a checkpoint at the entrance to the Vector labs. A sentinel at the auditorium door inspected the laminated IDs; he even politely stopped Tim his first time through to radio-check his creds. Every angle had been covered, down to car-bomb-deterrent trash cans hiding metal posts, positioned on the sidewalk outside the corresponding stretch of building.

Though the various hedge-fund honchos, I-bankers, Wall Street journalists, and mutual-fund managers had been told that the precautions were to discourage information leaks—a ruse bolstered by the guards' insistence that cell phones with built-in cameras be turned off—the current of whispered conversation showed that the attendees knew otherwise. The murders of Ted Sands and Chase Kagan were national news, and as much as the Kagan Machine continued to put out that they were by-products of a private, misguided vendetta, they held enough allure and promise of danger to add another layer of excitement to the afternoon's proceedings.

To augment the rising sun's glare through the two thin, tinted casement windows set high in the east wall, well-positioned recessed lights beamed down, lending a reading glow to the pitch books and prospectuses. On the raised dais behind the draped podium sat an enormous glass sculpture of the Vector logo, the ubiquitous *V* capped with an arrow. A fine backdrop for the sanctioned press photographs. Draping the east wall was a giant Xedral poster, the same version Tim had seen in Dean's office, and another captioned THE LIVES WE TOUCHED, with Sam ironically featured in the grid of multiracial children.

A partner at Goldman Sachs made the introductory remarks from the floor, walking among the aisles as he talked like a professor who'd seen too many movies about professors. After hemming and hawing about "the Kagans' recent family tragedy," he claimed that "having lost a beloved CEO, it was important for Vector to push forward for the sake of *others* whose lives can be saved." The strained attempt at emotion caused an awkward halt in the buzz of the audience. The few scripted asides and canned shtick that followed, rather than lightening the mood, struck a bad contrast with the earlier remarks, and to everyone's great relief, Jane Bernard, eleventh-hour appointee as Vector's temporary CEO, formally took the podium. As she launched into an explication of P/E ratios from comparable companies, Tim paced the back of the auditorium, eyes on the entrance, keeping in radio contact with the other task-force members arrayed through the building and outside. After drawing a few glares, Tim settled in a seat. Xedral's twenty-thousand-dollar annual treatment cost drew a gasp, until the CFO revealed that they'd pushed through Medicaid a patient-reimbursement agreement for half of the cost. While Tim got the play-by-play of Bear rousting a homeless guy by the parking garage's gate, she concluded by saying, "This monthly shot—literally a *lifesaving* shot—that has been in the pipeline for years, will roll out with human trials three days from now. A month and a half later, we go wide with Phase IIIs." Greedy applause.

Bear came through again on the primary channel. *"Eyes up, eyes up. White male loitering by the east exit. Baseball cap pulled low so I can't make an ID."* The distinguished businessman in front of Tim turned to offer a censorious look at the interruption.

Thomas's reply sounded strained. *"Exit is sealed."*

Miller came on: *"I got Denley and Maybeck in position. You want to move on him?"*

Tim lowered his mouth to the radio. "Bear and Thomas can take it. Everyone else keep your posts. What kind of hat?"

"Hang on." Bear prompted, *"Turn, motherfucker."* And then: *"USC."*

The hat Walker had worn to Tim's house. "Roust him," Tim said. *"Now."*

Despite the thunderous applause that accompanied his introduction, Dolan looked terrible when he took the podium, almost sickly. At his side, playing the role of the proud father, Dean waved to the crowd like a vice presidential candidate on autopilot.

Tim turned up the volume, pressing the portable to his ear, but he couldn't hear anything except the applause. He rose, hovering over his seat and drawing an insistent shoulder tap from the reporter behind him.

"Come in. Come *in.* Someone tell me what happened."

Sounds of a scuffle. Thomas said, *"Gimme a sec, Rack."*

Up front Dolan cleared his throat. He glanced nervously at the door, then at the back of the room. Finally, off cue, the lights dimmed and a projector screen descended from the ceiling with a whir. Assisted by PowerPoint slides, Dolan began to walk the crowd through the science behind Xedral.

Stepping over people's knees, holding the portable to his ear, Tim tried to keep his voice down. "What's going on?"

"It's not him," Thomas barked. *"Repeat: It is not Walker. Hang on. What? What's he saying?"*

The radio crackled. *"He says . . ."*

Tim was out in the aisle now, heading for the front. *"What?"*

A number of sharp complaints peppered Tim from all sides.

Tim picked up a Frisbee-size circle of light, phasing into existence like a reverse eclipse on the carpet of the dais, just in front of the podium from which Dolan spoke. But the ceiling lights were uniformly dark for the slide show.

Tim jogged down the aisle to get a better look. Dolan broke midsentence, glancing at Tim, then resumed. Dean glared out from the darkness, his face tight with an implicit threat.

Bear's voice now, jockeying in on the primary channel: *"Suspect says a guy gave him the hat and paid him to hang out by the—"*

Tim traced the beam to the darkly tinted casement window. A circle had been excised from the pane with a glass cutter. It completed a pivot out of its flush position on a remote-operated hinge the size of a matchbook.

"He's on the line," Tim said into the radio. "Lock down your buildings."

An event coordinator strode across the front of the auditorium, meeting Tim before the dais. "Sir, I'm sorry, but I'm gonna have to ask you to—"

Tim straight-armed him to the side. He was sprinting now, finally getting a good look through the circle cut into the high pane. Outside, contrasted against the dark wood of the apartment building across the street, a strip of red cloth fluttered from an overhead phone line. A strategically placed, makeshift wind sock.

Tim leapt onstage, hurling aside the podium and tackling Dolan. He felt a buffet of air across his back as a round sliced behind him.

Chapter 63

The glass sculpture behind the podium webbed instantly, thousands of cracks appearing as if thrown on at the instant of the bullet's impact. Dolan reeled back, falling from the dais into the arms of a waiting guard, who dragged him to the secured back exit. Attendees were on their feet, yelling and hastening for the main door, the contagious panic of the corralled. Dean stood frozen as the sculpture finally burst, fragments pattering on the thin carpet. Tim rolled from his stomach, sweeping Dean's legs and bringing him down as another bullet whined past, punching a hole through the projection screen behind the space Dean's head had occupied an instant prior. Tim raked Dean toward him by an ankle, gathering him in like a hockey goalie, and handed him off to three advancing guards. Dean disappeared in their midst, joining the current toward the back exit.

Tim looked up into the sudden warmth, realizing that his uptilted face perfectly captured the circle of light and—likely—Walker's crosshairs, too. As he threw himself off the dais, he registered the stab of a view he'd caught through the window's missing disk—a curtain flickering behind a slid-back door on a fourth-story balcony across the street.

He ran, cutting through the crowd, lips moving against the radio as he coordinated the task-force members to seal off the apartment building. Fleeing bankers had massed at the revolving doors, so Tim cut back up a side hall and kicked out an emergency exit, joining Thomas, Freed, Maybeck, and Bear. Haines and Zimmer, assigned the building from the start, had secured the main entrance from Tim's first lock-down command, swinging four LAPD units into perimeter position sec-onds later. The building, six stories of dilapidation, had somehow dodged the Westwood renovation. From the looks of the passing resi-dents Miller had backed out of the lobby, the place provided shoddy housing to students and some elderly couples, likely hangers-on from when the building was new.

Zimmer waved Tim through, and the deputies fell instinctively into their ART entry stack up the stairwell. They wouldn't have time for bul-letproof vests or MP5s—it would be an improvised raid. They ham-mered up to the fourth floor, the stairwell spitting them out onto a floating corridor on the east side.

Two units down, a door stood open. Tim barely slowed his momen-tum around the turn as they exploded into the cramped space, shout-ing, flooding the galley kitchen, living room, and bedroom, handguns trained at every corner. Bear's kicking into the bathroom took the door clean off its bottom hinge.

No one.

Slicing through the fluttering curtains, Tim caught himself against the balcony railing. He peered down across the street at the ground floor of the towering Beacon-Kagan Building. The excised circle of tinted window provided a narrow vantage into the Vector auditorium, exposing a spot of visible dais—podium, ring of carpet, scattered glass. A clean line of sight, the precise reverse of the one he'd had minutes before from his sprawl on the floor.

"Hey, Rack!" Filling the front jamb, Bear pointed to the triangular stop wedged into place, holding the door open. It had been nailed into the floor. His finger next indicated the pair of saloon doors at the mouth of the living room. Oddly, they'd been pressed flat to the walls and nailed into place.

Tim felt his insides go to ice.

He moved through the permanently open saloon doors and brushed past Bear onto the floating corridor. A sleek, modern high-rise crowded the east side of the apartment building. Two stories up was another balcony, another open slider, another fluttering curtain. Behind the thin cotton drapes stood the outline of a sniper rifle, abandoned on its tripod.

Walker had cleared a path for the bullet's trajectory and shot straight through the building in which the deputies were currently gathered. A trained sniper, he could easily hit his mark from two hundred yards—another building back—especially since he'd cleared all the glass between his muzzle and the target, removing the possibility of bullet deflection or fragmentation. He'd known that the deputies were waiting to storm the closer, more obvious location, buying him extra time for the getaway. He'd anticipated Tim's anticipating him and come out one move ahead.

Tim shouted at the deputies, and they sprinted out, legs aching as they attacked a set of stairs, a stretch of pavement, another set of stairs. Bear radioed in for the broadened perimeter, but Tim knew, even before he kicked through the next door and found himself two floors up and one building over, that Walker would be gone.

Breathing hard, Tim stood before the suspended .300 Remington Mag. Bear, Freed, and Thomas milled behind him. The others had hit the street, helping LAPD canvass the area. Good luck there. The ministampede caused by the shooting had created a broad diversion—town cars, rental-car-ensconced New Yorkers, and masses of pedestrians still blocked the nearby intersections. Without touching the rifle, Tim lowered his right eye to the Leopold variable power scope, the same one he kept mounted on his match-grade M14.

The podium remained centered in the crosshairs.

Walker had seen Tim's face through this very scope, had watched him looking up through the hole in the tinted window from his sprawl across the glass-strewn dais. The magnified view of the site where he could well have lost his life was chilling. Tim wondered if he'd rolled away before Walker could squeeze off another round or if Walker had chosen to spare him. Neither scenario made him feel less incompetent.

Tim's Nextel rang, and he pulled back from the tripod-mounted rifle. Caller ID flashed *L V TSK FRC*.

He answered, and Ian Summer said, "Rack, we flipped a little fish in the Aryan Brotherhood. We nailed him for trafficking, but guess what, he's staring down a career-criminal enhancement, so he's cooperating. You want the good news or the bad news?"

"Whatever."

"The good news is AB *did* dispatch a hit man to track down Walker Jameson, and we have a line on him. Caden Burke."

"The bad?"

"He's already in L.A. We've been monitoring his credit cards, and a charge just dinged at the RestWell Motel in Culver City."

Tim covered the phone. "Bear, we gotta go. Freed, hold down the fort till CSI takes over the scene?" He swung the Nextel back to his mouth and jogged out to the elevator, Bear at his heels. "Can you get me a photograph?"

"I'll have someone dig through our surveillance files, see if they can find a clean shot. I'll have them scan it and send it to your phone."

"Please. Soon."

Tim had almost hung up when Ian said, "Hey, Rack. Someone in your office was looking for intel on the Piper, right?"

"That's right. Same case—high priority. You got something?"

"You might want to call DeSquire in the Albuquerque office."

"Why?"

"Just give him a call. Confidential shit, but I went through FLETC with him."

"Got it. Thanks."

The phone cut out on the elevator, Tim watching the reception bars as he summarized for Bear. The doors dinged open, the lowest bar held, and Tim hit "dial." He had the CSO from comm center dig up a cell number on DeSquire and patch him through. Cars screeched as they ran across Wilshire to Bear's Ram, parked in the outdoor lot off Gayley.

DeSquire picked up on a half ring. Sirens and rattling wheels in the background—the song of the crime scene. He paused when Tim introduced himself, placing the name. "Sure," he said. "The Troubleshooter."

"I'm working the Walker Jameson case, and I caught word you've got something on the Piper."

"I might."

"I understand what you've got might be sensitive till you take it public. I can keep my mouth shut. I just need information."

"How's this involve Walker Jameson?"

"We believe the Piper executed Jameson's sister in June."

"That would be pretty tough."

Tim barely got the door closed before Bear roared off toward Culver City. "Why's that?"

"Because I just found him in the back of an auto-parts garage, pickled in poured concrete. Been dead six months, easy."

Chapter 64

The Nextel felt hot against Tim's cheek; he realized he was pressing it harder than necessary. "How firm," he asked, still reeling from the news, "is the ID?"

"DNA firm," DeSquire said. "The concrete bath? We been seeing it lately from the Colombians. The Piper did a hit on one of their launderers in January."

"I remember." Tim braced himself as Bear veered over the edge of an island to U-turn onto the freeway. If the Piper was dead, then who'd crushed a paintball on the curb outside Tess's house? And if the lowrider with the unusually large hood ornament existed outside the senile haze of the neighbor's mind, who'd driven it? *Someone* had picked up the money Ted Sands had dropped at Game, and the contract for Tess's life that went along with it. "Listen," Tim said, "would you consider keeping this from the press?"

"No way, pal. This is a big find." DeSquire lowered his voice. "Someone's looking to make chief, get his mug in front of the flashing bulbs. I wouldn't mind bumping up to supervisory deputy myself. Why you want a lid on it anyways?"

"If Walker Jameson doesn't know, I'd prefer to keep him chasing after a ghost."

One-handing the wheel at high noon, Bear shot Tim an unamused glance across the meat of his shoulder. "Kinda like us?"

When Bear's boot hit the lock assembly, the entire motel shuddered. The door flew open, knob punching through the drywall. A thin, bald guy leapt off the bed like a goosed cat and crashed to the base of the wall, clutching his wife-beater undershirt at his chest. Bear hauled him up and threw him onto the bed, but the mattress was so bouncy he soared off the other side. Tim frisked him on the floor and sat him on a chair as Bear cleared the closet and bathroom. A Dodgers game blared on in the background until Bear, die-hard Giants fan, smacked the power button, zapping Gagne and the pitcher's mound into blackness. Aside from a pair of sneakers by the door and the open laptop on the opposite twin, the room was empty. Tim stared at the floating aphorism on the screen saver—*If we'd have known it would be this much trouble, we would've picked our own damn cotton*—and resisted an urge to ping-pong the shitheel off the bed a second time.

"You're on Walker Jameson's trail?" Tim said.

The guy scratched his bald pate, fingers flickering as if over piano keys. "Dunno."

Bear looked from the abandoned sneakers—huge and floppy, size thirteens at least—to the lanky guy in the chair. Normal-size feet.

"Wait a minute," Bear said, "this ain't Caden."

The phone shuddered in Tim's pocket, and he opened it to watch a booking photo download on the small screen. Caden Burke was a hulking man, six-three by the markers behind him. His thick chest dwarfed the neckboard. He had a mouth like a seam, no lips, and a pronounced chin that gave the effect that his face was folded around the black slit.

"Hell, no, I ain't Caden. My name's Phil Xavier. I'm just the fucking driver."

"So where's Caden?" Bear stood over Xavier. "Where is he?"

Tim said, "You'd better tell us everything you know, right now, or we'll nail your ass for conspiracy to commit murder." Xavier bunched his mouth, biting the insides of his lips. Tim leaned over him. "Right now, this moment, this is one of those decisions you *don't* want to spend twenty years rethinking at Lompoc."

Sweat streaked down the sides of Xavier's head just behind the ears, lending a sheen to the inked shamrock low on his skull. The tattoo was still scabby—Xavier was a newbie, which meant he wasn't so far in he couldn't see a way out. "And if I tell you?"

Tim made an on-the-spot call for expediency's sake. "Hey, you're just the driver, right?"

Xavier cleared his throat nervously. "Caden's the guy, like I said. I just drive. But I heard him making calls on the way out, pieced together a thing or two."

Bear: *"Like?"*

"After the escape, Jameson made some underground calls checking out a hitter named the Piper. It trickled back to us—we'd put it on the street we wanted any word on Walker Jameson. Turns out the Piper's dead. Jameson found out someone snaked his commission."

"Does Jameson know who? Maybe someone gave him a name?"

Xavier's eyes shifted. "He might have gotten a name, sure, but not us."

"What did you get?"

"A time and place."

"For what?"

"Where Jameson could find the guy."

"The time?"

Xavier pulsed his hands into fists, working out tension. "Right now."

"Where?"

"You guys gonna hurt Caden?"

"If he's going after Jameson, we're probably going to save his life."

"You don't know Caden." Xavier had one of those nervous smiles where the lips touched at the middle but gapped at the sides.

Bear palmed Xavier's head, his massive hands enclosing either side, and forced eye contact. "Where?"

"I swear I don't know. Caden looked something up and took off outta here."

"Looked something up? In what?"

But Tim was already across the room at the laptop. The odious screen saver vanished when he hit the space bar. Explorer was open to Yahoo!'s TV page, the schedule highlighting the Dodgers-Marlins game.

LAST SHOT

Tim clicked the browser's back button, passing a baseball stats page and a news story before a Mapquest page started to load, slowed by the phone-line connection. As the driving directions popped on-screen, one line at a time, Tim tracked them impatiently with his finger.

Caden's route ended at Game.

Chapter 65

Tim had called for backup, but there was no way he and Bear were going to wait. A few minutes past seven, and already the wetlands had come alive with night noise, all order of chirping and scratching insects lending their sounds to the ashy air. A flurry of dusty moths beat against themselves and the lamp by the awning.

The Game lounge was in full swing, its well-heeled clientele drinking and groping happily at the bar. The mood chilled at the sight of Bear prodding Xavier in cuffs through the door. No sign of Walker or Caden. Bear stormed to the back office. The counter was being run by a man with ruddy cheeks and a Scarface T-shirt, the *S* faded off, probably when his mom did his laundry.

"Hey, Carface," Bear said, slapping his badge across the laid-open *Paintball 2 Xtremes* magazine. "Who's in the preserve? Right now." Bear snapped his fingers in front of the guy's face to jerk his focus from their handcuffed sidekick.

"A . . . uh, handful of guys. And Afternoon D-Lite."

"How many guys?"

"I think three."

"You think?" Tim pointed to equipment hanging from pegs near the lockers. "Can you count the missing vests?"

"They brought their own." The worker flipped a binder out from the

338

row and showed Tim three names, none of which meant anything to him.

Xavier spit on the floor. "How 'bout I sit down?"

Bear said, "Believe me, your presence at this moment is no fucking treat for us either."

A movement caught Tim's eye through the side window—Wes Dieter pulling up to his marked space by the entrance. Dressed in pseudo-combat gear, he climbed out of his Cutlass Supreme.

Tim turned back to the worker. "Have you seen this guy?" A head shake at Walker's picture. "How about him?" Tim snapped open his phone and showed the photograph of Caden.

"Yeah, that guy was here a minute ago. At the bar, maybe?"

Tim scanned the lounge again, and then his eyes pulled to the gauze curtain. He said to Bear, "He's in the preserve. Hunting."

Bear unsnapped his holster strap. "Or waiting."

Tim said, "Could he have snuck in without your seeing?"

"Shit, I don't know," the worker said. "I guess someone could cut the net anywhere at the perimeter and slip through, they really wanted to."

Which Walker may well have done earlier to set up for Tess's killer. Tim said, "Let me see the schedule for the rest of the night. *Now.*"

The worker fumbled at the computer. Wes entered to a stir, exchanging high fives with a few zealous clients. He cued to the tense vibe, spotted Tim, Bear, and Xavier, and approached. "Hey guys, what's the 411 here?"

Tim said, "We think whoever killed Tess Jameson is on the premises. We were told he had an appointment here, right now." He didn't add that Tess's murderer might have drawn Walker Jameson on site for the kill, or that an Aryan Brotherhood hit man, in turn, was pursuing Walker.

"I see." Wes rocked on his heels, then said, "Hey, Kenny, I need you to unload the paintball units from my backseat." He aimed his key chain at the window, and, outside, the soft top on his convertible retracted, a custom feature that must have cost thousands. "I'll help these gents."

Kenny offered an annoyed look, then headed out.

Wes said in a fierce whisper. "I thought we had a deal. You can't be hauling perps through here."

Tim said, "We need tonight's schedule."

Wes fought a handkerchief from his pocket and dabbed sweat from his forehead but made no move toward the computer. "Come *on,* guys. Come back after hours, I'll get you whatever you need. But you're freaking my clients. Again."

Outside, Kenny waited for the sluggish soft top to accordion out of his way, then hefted a crate from Wes's car. Wes crossed his arms, ready to cause a scene. Bear shoved past him, stepping around the counter. The tabby stuck her head up from the Cutlass's passenger seat, then jumped up onto the hood, her orange coat rippling.

Wes shook his head at Bear's rudeness, then said, "The schedule's on the clipboard by the preserve entrance." He went to get it, mumbling.

The cat padded across the front of the Cutlass, her breath wisping, then curled at the end of the hood above the warmth of the engine.

The oversize hood ornament.

Bear looked up from the monitor, brow twisted with consternation. "This says the next appointment's a hunt-off. Metal Jacket and—"

The clues aligned at once, pulling together in the instant Tim's hand dove for his Smith & Wesson. The low-rider—the Cutlass with the top peeled back. Wes's own words—*I'm a computer guy at heart.* He'd posed as the Piper in one of the chat rooms—*ones that guys like us can't even find*—and snaked the contract. The hit itself—highly competent but not meticulous, the imperfect work of a well-read and -practiced wannabe.

Before Bear could utter his name, Wes Dieter slipped through the gauze, disappearing into the green-tinted shadows of the preserve. The four-time course champion, trying for a getaway but inadvertently heading into the lion's den. Given the recent fallout from Tess's murder, Tim had to assume that a real gun lurked in one of Wes's innumerable holsters and cargo pockets.

Bear seized Xavier, steering him for the door. Tim ran for the curtain, shouting over his shoulder, "Clear the whole building! When backup gets here, have them seal off the preserve's perimeter!"

He slipped through, dropping low on a knee, his revolver clutched tight in both hands. A muddy trail went a few feet before splitting in three directions. Fronds fluttered. Cottonwood, sagebrush, willow, and coyote bush broke his sight line. A coarse cawing. The silhouette of a great white egret scanned across the roof of the black netting, strobe-flickering against the dark gray sky beyond. The netting encasing the fifteen-acre preserve brought a kind of night-within-night. Tim eased forward, boots shoving into the mud, then stepped off the trail. He turned down the volume on his radio, cutting himself off from his backup. Noises all around.

Tim melded into the imported foliage, listening for the sounds of human movement—headlong progress through brush, metallic clinks, leaves whispering across fabric. He and Walker were like sharks squaring off in a kiddy pool.

Advancing on hands and knees could help him reduce his noise signature, but it would also slow him down. Since concealment options were copious, there was no need to maintain a low-to-ground profile. He was within an enclosed space with three potentially armed men, all of them killers, all of them hunting and being hunted. Time was of the essence if he wanted to play a role in the outcome. And prevent the naked corpse of a well-siliconed woman from making tomorrow's page one. To strike the balance between caution and pursuit, he opted for a slow upright patrol, stop-move-stop.

He paused, getting down on a knee in the tules to listen and feel the air.

Walker likely didn't know that Tim and Caden were present. If he had come, he'd set up to wait for the Piper. If Tim had some luck, Walker didn't realize yet that that meant this nickel-badge-wearing keyboard jockey. What would be the best tactical spot from which to observe, and execute a shot? Tim would have chosen the highest ground. A rise in the northwest quadrant seemed the best bet. Tim started to forge in that direction, through the dark heart of the preserve. If he heard anyone moving, odds were it was Caden, Wes, the girl, or one of the paintballers. Tim's first priority would be to reach the nonsuspects and direct them to safety. Then he'd try to latch on to Caden and trail and outflank him for an ambush, or stalk Wes until he drew Walker from cover.

Someone large lumbered up the trail to Tim's right, and he whipped his gun over, waiting to see who appeared. An excessively camoed man with a beer gut charged around the bend, slipping to a halt. He smiled at Tim, raised his paintball gun. "Pow." His eyes changed when he took in Tim's expression and the steel gleam of the Smith & Wesson. Tim flicked his barrel toward the exit to keep the guy moving; he was only too happy to comply.

In the blackness up ahead, a woman shouted, "Who the hell are *you*?" She yelped, and Tim ducked into the foliage. A few moments later, she ran past, naked and screaming, Afternoon no longer D-Lited.

To his left he heard two bodies startle in the leaves, then move for the exit also, the panicked movements and shouted directives telling him they were the last two paintballers. Bear could deal with them and the girl once they spilled through the curtain.

Moving briskly, Tim closed in on the area of foliage in which the regulars had stumbled upon an uninvited guest. The band of dense, shoulder-high bush crossed the base of the slope where Tim thought Walker might be bedded down. Tim steered clear of the loose rocks composing the waterfall's base, picking quiet footholds around the mud wallow. Another theme-park addition, a camouflaged heavy bag, creaked on its chain, its sway more than the net-blocked wind could have generated. Someone had shouldered it on his way past.

Tim inched upslope, letting the branches bend slowly against him to avoid snaps and backwhips. A stout sprig hung up against his ankle, and he grabbed it, stepping past then carefully releasing the tension. Through the patchwork of underbrush, his eyes picked up the faintest movement against the mud, a dark boot rising out of view. He straightened, but the foliage blotted out any movement ahead.

His stalker's instincts froze him. Someone else moved to his left just a few feet away—Tim sensed a vibration or the heat. With excruciating slowness, he pivoted to face his pursuer, his heels soundless in the mud. He lifted his .357, dodging leaves on the rise. In the silence between the brush of leaves and the scratch of crickets, he heard it.

The faint yet undeniable click of a hammer cocking.

Behind him.

His body reacted before the sound registered as a thought. He spun, and as his own gun jerked in his grip, he saw the flare from a muzzle illuminating Walker's face, floating as if detached among the leaves. The gunshot, compounded, seemed unreasonably loud.

Chapter 66

Before Tim could comprehend that the explosion came in surround sound—from in front of him, behind him, and his own hands—a hot streak ripped his neck. His recoil spun him around to see Caden Burke drop to the mud howling and gripping his shoulder. Walker Jameson grunted—Tim's bullet had struck home—and a Redhawk six-shooter spit from the bushes, knocked loose. Walker's furious retreat sounded like a beast fleeing.

Tim couldn't go after him right away because he still had Caden loose and who he guessed was Wes up ahead. Putting his knee in Caden's back, Tim frisked him, pocketing his Ruger and a quaint switchblade. Walker's shot had missed Tim and embedded in the ball of Caden's shoulder, pulling Caden's shot off center and inadvertently saving Tim's life. When Tim cuffed him, Caden screeched with pain.

Tim scrambled back to reclaim the Redhawk. The stock was still warm and felt familiar somehow, molded to his hand. He stiffened at a sudden footfall, turning to source the noise. With a whooshing of leaves, Wes charged out of the brush—he'd circled during the commotion and come in from the west. Tim went airborne, extended in a sideways dive, using Walker's Redhawk to sight on Wes's substantial critical mass. A slow-motion clarity came over Tim as it often did in a close exchange. He saw the black hole of Wes's mouth looming behind the smaller black hole of a handgun muzzle. The moonlight's sheen on the glossy leaves misted from the waterfall. Caden bucking against the cuffs, snarling with pain and a sort of dumb puzzlement. Tim flashed on Tess, made to sit at gunpoint on her bed, made to wait as Wes Dieter—the man at the receiving end of the Redhawk that Tim now clutched—pressed steel to her temple. Her last-second, turned-head recoil before the shot, when fear turned to dumb instinct. Tim's finger tensed, and the trigger inched back, hammer ready to fall on one of Walker's titanium bullets. At the last instant before he struck mud, Tim moved the barrel three millimeters left and put a bullet through Wes's forearm.

Wes's gun spun from his limp hand, and he shrieked, plopping in the mud wallow, his gun echoing the splash an instant later. Tim retrieved the gun, cinched Wes's good wrist to his ankle with plastic flex-cuffs, and sprinted off after Walker, feeding Bear the update a mile a minute through the radio. Across the dark preserve and through the netting, he could see a line of blue and red lights moving in from the south.

Leaves and thin branches whipped Tim's face. He hurtled over a slope, and the netting appeared, blindsiding him and cradling his full momentum to a stop. Tim could see Bear at the parking lot, shouting at the incoming units to spread out. Working his way along the netting, Tim shoved into it at intervals to test its tension. Finally a shove yielded no resistance and he tumbled through, landing on the flat, sparse wetland outside the preserve. The net had been sliced cleanly through. Within a few acres' sprint lay Lincoln Boulevard and scores of side streets, the freeway a brief stretch beyond. The wind snapped the netting angrily behind Tim.

He focused on the dark sweep of earth, looking for any movement. Its lights off, a car peeled out from the wetlands border, too dark for Tim to discern its make or model. It turned a corner, and Walker was gone. Tim ran his hand along the slit in the netting, and it came away sticky. He raised his fingertips, and the moonlight brought the drops of Walker's blood visible.

He radioed Bear the car's approximate location and told him Walker was wounded. By the time he walked around to the building's entrance, Game had been cleared of clients and the area was swarming with deputies, cops, and ambulances. Thomas and Freed had already retrieved Wes and Caden and turned them over to LAPD, a pair of cops keeping the hit men company in their respective ambulances. Xavier glared at Tim from the back of a departing black-and-white.

Crossing the parking lot, Tim heard a pattering and looked down. Dime-size drops on the asphalt. He touched his fingertips to the ground, and they came up red, his prints marked with his own blood above the smeared stain of Walker's. He patted himself down, searching for the entry wound with no luck until a paramedic clamped a gauze pad to the side of his neck and tried to lead him to the rescue vehicle. Tim took over the pressure clamp and said, "Just a second," breaking toward Tannino and a cluster of deputies. The paramedic followed, voicing his concerns.

Tannino said, "We're spreading out through the area, two choppers en route. The roadblocks are up, but we've got two freeway entrances within blocks. How bad's he injured?"

"Not bad enough that he couldn't haul ass out of there." Tim readjusted the gauze on his neck; it was getting soaked through. The paramedic tugged at his arm, and Tim gestured he needed more time. "But there's enough blood that he'll need some aid and a hole to curl up in. Work the news outlets, the hospitals, the drugstores. I want to know if there's a break-in at a veterinarian's. Our nose is on the trail, we're hot on his ass, and he's injured. We keep charging at him and closing down options until he's cornered. Now is the time to be relentless."

"You got nothing on the vehicle?" Freed asked.

"It's a standard car—Toyota, Honda, something. It could have been that stolen Camry. Remember, he doesn't know we're eyeballing it."

"The Camry just popped up in long-term parking at LAX. The driver's seat was soiled with ash. Word came in just before we left the post." Freed let the disappointment sink in. "Think he was faking that he went out of town?"

"No, he just left the car where we wouldn't find it for a few days so we'd be chasing our tails on the lead. Which of course, we were." Tim bit his lip, tamping down his frustration and pondering his next move. "The parking-lot ticket should be in the car. Check when he pulled in to the lot and see if any other cars were stolen out of there in that time frame."

"Guerrera already handled it. None were. It's a pretty secure lot."

"God*damn* it." Tim hadn't realized how much he'd staked on getting a vehicle ID.

The paramedic quietly urged him, "You need to let me take a look at that."

"Okay." Tim handed Tannino Caden's Ruger and Walker's Redhawk.

Tannino hefted the Redhawk. "Walker's?" He took a look at the wheel and said, "There's three bullets missing. You reported to Bear that he only fired once."

"That leaves one unaccounted for. I fired the bullet that injured Wes Dieter."

Tannino's dark brown eyes peered out beneath his bushy eyebrows. A few of the deputies bristled uncomfortably. "You used Walker's gun on Dieter?"

Tim nodded and let the paramedic lead him over to the rescue vehicle. He sat on the tailgate.

"You are a lucky son of a bitch," the paramedic said after a cursory examination. "You just got grazed. A few stitches, is all. About a centimeter to the right, you'd be geysering."

Tim shouted at Bear to seize Wes's computer as evidence, and the paramedic said, "Can you hold still, please?"

Thomas jogged over from Caden's ambulance, his concern fading once he saw the paramedic readying a needle. "You awright, Rack? Shit, you scared me a moment there."

"You're making me nervous, Thomas."

"What do you mean?"

"Since you gunfaced me." Tim winced against the pinch of the needle. A few seconds' hitch and then numbness spread through the wound. "We don't like each other much, right?"

Thomas's Adam's apple jerked, and he smoothed his mustache and looked away. "No, I guess not."

"For a minute there at Walker's safe house, when you had the MP5 aimed at my head, you thought it would've felt nice. Maybe to pull the trigger."

The paramedic kept stitching. After a moment Thomas nodded. His stare met Tim's in something short of hostility, something akin to intimacy.

Tim said, "That's what you're freaked out about. You caught a glimpse. Don't try to bury it. We all have it. So keep an eye on it and go back to being an asshole."

The crinkles around Thomas's eyes deepened, and for an instant Tim thought he might get angry, but then he laughed and smacked Tim on the shoulder. "You know you're doing your job well when your fugitive saves *your* life."

"There you go."

"Maybe you guys could be a team, get a hit TV show."

"We're on too many already, but thanks."

"You think maybe he missed on purpose? Close shot and all?" Thomas broke off his stare with a smile, offered his hand. "Enemies?"

Tim shook. "Enemies." He watched Thomas disappear back into the mix, a faint grin tensing his mouth.

The paramedic said, "I never understand you guys."

Guerrera, in whispered consultation with Tannino, drew Tim's focus. Guerrera showed the marshal some papers, and Tannino blanched, his tired face drooping with worry. Whatever it was, it was significant enough to pull Guerrera out of the command post, overriding his light-duty sentence.

Tannino pointed at Tim, and Guerrera started over.

Tim felt a knot of barbed wire in his stomach. The paramedic said, "Relax. I'm almost done."

When Guerrera got within range, Tim said, "Tell me."

"I . . . uh, I wanted to come myself." Guerrera's voice sounded funny. "I was checking all of Pierce Jameson's holdings, contacts, everything, like you asked."

Tim shrugged free of the paramedic, the needle dangling from his neck on a length of suture. "And?"

"His past known associates came back. There's one who I think we might be able to leverage." Reluctantly, he offered the top page, what looked like a printout of a rap sheet complete with a booking photo.

Tim took the sheet and stared down at the face of his father.

Chapter 67

Walker left the Accord two blocks away in an alley. Heat stabbed down his side with every step. The bulletproof vest absorbed most of the blood, but at the armhole a wet crescent rimmed his army-green T-shirt. He wouldn't know how bad it was until he got to his room and took a proper look.

He was breathing so heavily he had to pause at the base of the stairs. Each jarring step caused the vest to scrape over the wound. Putting his head down, he almost collided with someone midway up. Kaitlin. She'd made herself up a bit with mascara and a touch of eyeliner. Sam stood at her side, looking bemused and slightly scared by her evident anger.

She said, "The least you could do if you drag us to a dirt fucking lot is show up. I would've left, but Sam insisted we—"

"You shouldn't be here." Walker sagged against the railing. Kaitlin saw the blood and scrambled to his side, purse slapping against her hip, her shoes clattering on the stairs. She fought the apartment key out of Walker's pocket and fumbled it toward Sam, who took it calmly. "Go get the door open. Go on."

She helped Walker upstairs and in. Sam locked the door behind them, then gave a dramatic glance through the closed blinds of the front window. The bed bowed under Walker's weight when he sat. He used his right hand to dig his Spyderco knife out of a pocket. Flipping it open with a jerk, he ran the blade under the front of his T-shirt. Kaitlin helped peel it off.

About four inches down from his armpit, a quarter-size entry hole marred the meat of his lat. The blood welling inside looked like black ink. The bullet had missed the protective ballistic composite by a thumb's width. There was no way, in the nighttime pivot-and-shoot, that Rackley could have seen he was wearing a vest. The bullet had sought flesh as lead often seemed to do.

Kaitlin helped him unsnap the vest. He'd hoped the back fabric would have caught the slug, but no such luck. There was no exit wound.

Kaitlin got a ratty towel from the bathroom, wiped off the blood, and applied pressure. Sam watched with wide eyes.

She seemed light-headed. "This doesn't look good, Walk."

"Seen worse."

Walker took up the pressure so she could sit down. When he withdrew a tweezers from the medic kit in his duffel, she flattened herself over her knees. "I don't think I can."

He inserted the tweezers into the hole but had a tough time getting an angle. The metal tips digging around the swollen flesh was unpleasant. He said, "Kaitlin, just gimme a sec here."

Kaitlin started to stand up but fainted and fell back on the bed.

Walker said, "Well, there you go."

Sam said, "I'll do it."

"I don't think so."

"I hit level forty-four on Champions of Norrath. I think I can find a stupid bullet in a cut." His stomach looked more distended than before, bulging over his thin little-boy belt. He returned Walker's gaze, playing up the apathy.

Walker said, "God, you've got your mother in you."

"And you."

"Nah, not me."

The kid's face went slack with hurt—not an expression Walker had expected. He'd meant it as a compliment, but it was too thorny to explain, and he had a mushroom of lead grinding in his side. He offered Sam the blood-tipped tweezers, and Sam took them. He raised his arm, and the kid went to work with an impressive scientific detachment.

349

Kaitlin stirred, propped herself on her elbows to take in the tableau, and said, nauseously, "There goes my spot on the PTA."

She rose, keeping her eyes averted, and disappeared into the bathroom. A moment later Walker heard the sink running. Inside him metal clinked against metal—he wasn't sure if he heard it or just felt the timbre of the vibration.

Sam said, "Doesn't that hurt?"

"This? Nah." Walker braced himself as the tweezers made another pass at the embedded slug. "Pain's got fear, too. You can scare it outta you."

The bullet came slowly and not without friction. Sam dropped it in Walker's palm. A Troubleshooter special, served hot from a Smith & Wesson.

Sam stared at him with those crazy yellow eyes. "I know about pain."

"I figure. You're smart for an eight-year-old."

"Seven."

"Whatever."

Walker rotated his arm once, testing it. He leaned against the pillows and blinked once, slowly. Sam watched him intently.

Walker said, "I got nothing to offer you. I guess only the example I didn't set. But I can tell you this: Your mom didn't kill herself. Some men had her killed."

All the lines seemed to smooth out of Sam's face, and then tears were on his cheeks, though he didn't seem to be crying. Anger, sure, and some fear, but mostly relief. He sat down, head bowed, scratching at the dry patches on his bruised arms. "So you're gonna what? Kill them all?"

The toilet flushed, and then the sink water turned on again.

"Yup," Walker said.

Chapter 68

Dolan had spent the last hour pacing laps around the pool table, his agitation sprouting more hydra heads than he could keep in sight. His momentum finally flung him off the table on a turn, propelling him through the double doors. A security man wordlessly stood his post outside. He shadowed Dolan down the hall like a bodyguard, his finger raised to his ear, seating the transmitter. His orders being updated? After a few paces, Dolan grew uncomfortable. When he glanced back, the guard dropped his gaze as if granting Dolan privacy. On the way down the stairs, it struck Dolan that the man now seemed more like a stalker than a bodyguard. He tried to convince himself that he was manufacturing the guard's tacit menace, transferring his anxiety onto something concrete.

Dolan stopped short when he entered his father's office and found it blanketed with open manila folders, Dean shoving papers through a shredder with uncharacteristic haste. Edwin abided Dean's pointing finger, retrieving and filing with a stiff-backed posture that infused each menial task with elegant rectitude.

Dean paused, then shot an accusatory glare at the guard, as if he were responsible for Dolan's appearance. Dolan made out the label on the report in his father's hands: X4-AAT SAFETY STUDY. Dean lowered it to the blades. A chuffing disintegrated it into snowflakes.

Dolan moistened his lips, looking around in bewilderment.

Dean said briskly, "Nothing untoward is going on here. There are confidential documents that I don't feel comfortable having at the house. Not with the fallout from this afternoon and the investigation that's grinding forward. Your company's been set back enough by recent events." Dean handed off an expurgated folder to Edwin, who promptly returned it to the file cabinet. "Don't ask questions you don't want the answers to."

"Sir, I *do* want answers. I'm entitled to know what's going on with Xedral. I've given seven years of my life to this."

"And I devoted thirty-five years to building the business that underwrote the lab in which you were working. So why don't we leave *entitlement* out of this? Every test tube you've touched since you were six, I bought."

Dolan felt his outrage transmogrify into adolescent defensiveness. "Not at school."

"Right. A multiyear, seven-figure pledge to UCLA's biology department that commenced the day you matriculated. But the test tubes came out of the professor's pocket."

"I got into UCLA on my grades, not your money." Dolan picked up an empty folder, turned it inside out, and dropped it on the floor. "What happened during the Xedral safety studies?"

A disgusted exhale. "Nothing. Huang spoke to you. He told you himself nothing was out of the ordinary."

"You own Huang."

"I own *everyone*. Including you. Every lab station, every microfuge, every pencil."

Dolan felt beaten down, diminished. "You don't. Not me."

"Oh? Your corporation is behind on its rent, Dolan. Or do you recall that your lease specifies a dollar a year?" Dean scowled at him, a rosy flush rouging his pallid cheeks. "I can have Bernie retroaccount so hard and fast you'll be in debt to Beacon-Kagan until your children's children have children. I will ruin you."

"You're actually thr—"

"I'm saying there is an empire at stake, Dolan. This—" Dean gestured to the loose papers, though there were few left; while they'd been arguing, Edwin had tidied up, even spraying sanitizer on and wiping the wooden surfaces. "This is the mess and sweat of a corporation. You don't want this. You have a sinecure and unlimited funding. Few would complain in your situation. Tinker with your petri dishes and leave the business to us."

"I've always been willing to leave the business to you. Just not the science."

"It's the same thing," Dean said with slow exasperation.

Dolan weaved a bit on his feet. The sanitizer's lemon scent coated his throat, soured his stomach. Dean indicated the guard with a flare of his hand, and the guard came off the wall and positioned himself a few feet behind Dolan.

Dean folded his hands at his stomach, the picture of reason. "Here are your choices: You let me handle what needs to be handled, and you return to a top post at your own company poised to make one of the most significant advances medicine has seen in decades. Or you can be stubborn and obtuse and wind up teaching photosynthesis to snotty seventh-graders at Harvard-Westlake."

Dolan's throat clicked drily when he swallowed.

"Now, if you wouldn't mind going upstairs"—Dean nodded at the guard—"I'd like a bit of privacy in my own office."

Chapter 69

The lawn was overgrown. Not a noteworthy observation elsewhere, but Tim had never seen the grass without mow strips aligned as though they'd been measured off. The mailbox—stuffed. Four still-rolled newspapers on the doorstep. An unswept porch. He paused midway up the walk, his first hesitation about choosing to come alone. It wasn't until he rang the doorbell and heard the approaching footsteps that his brain gave voice to the concern that had been lurking beneath his thoughts—that he'd find his father dead in the house.

The doorknob turned, and then his father, a handsome man approaching sixty, peered out from the gap. Behind him the lights were off, the interior projecting gloom. His usually impeccable hair was disheveled, and he was unshaven. His stubble had grown in more white than black, a detail that Tim found inexplicably disconcerting. In his thirty-eight years, Tim had known him only to be immaculately composed. Never a stray hair, a stain on his pants, an unironed shirt.

In a rare show of restraint, Tim's father offered no wisecrack about the half-stitched gash in the side of Tim's neck. Instead he stepped back from the door, letting Tim enter—another break in protocol. He didn't even ask him to remove his shoes. The living room air was stale from thrown-out coffee grounds. The kitchen, normally museum meticulous, was strewn with dirty dishes. His father scooted two sealed VCR boxes over on the couch so Tim could sit, then took his favored La-Z-Boy opposite. All these years later, the picture frames on the mantel still displayed the stock photos they'd come packaged with.

Tim's palms were slick and his stomach roiled. He'd done zero-visibility oxygen jumps from thirty-three thousand feet without breaking a sweat, but his father's proximity still set him on edge. He reminded himself to offer up nothing—if given an inch, his father could unload oceanfront time shares in Wyoming. Tim wiped his hands on his jeans, taking in the boxes and papers piled around the living room. "What's going on here?"

"You've got no right to ask me that." Tim hadn't heard his father's voice in three years; it had picked up some hoarseness around the edges. "What do you want, Timmy?"

"One of our fugitive's fathers, Pierce Jameson, has become a name of interest in our investigation."

"Ah, Pierce. Yes, I've seen Walker's making a run to knock you off the tabloid covers. Is the Troubleshooter feeling neglected by his public? Upstaged as vigilante darling of the masses?"

The old chess match. Playing his part, the stoic straight arrow, Tim maintained an expression of impassivity. "I know you've dealt with Pierce. I need to find some leverage on him. We're having a hard time untangling his finances. If I know you, you did your research before getting into bed with him. I thought you might know enough to give us a way in."

"What about honor among thieves?" Tim's father's lips tensed—they both knew he'd snitched, double-crossed, and back-doored his way out of more jail time and soured deals than either of them could remember. "And what do I get?"

"Nothing."

"A characteristically vain proposition." His father picked a speck of lint from his trousers, crumpled it into a handkerchief, then settled back and crossed his legs. The same regal bearing. A man with more grace than character. To Tim's great surprise, he said, "I'll help you. If there is something to get on Pierce, I know how you can get it." A moment to let his magnanimity sink in. Tim waited for the other shoe to drop, and of course it did. "But. You'll owe me a favor later. I won't disclose what it is now, but I'll tell you it's not illegal."

Tim said, "No."

"It won't have anything to do with using your law enforcement connections improperly to help me."

"No."

His father, who Tim had once seen bluff a table of professional poker players out of a twenty-thousand-dollar pot with a seven deuce in the dark, maintained even eye contact. He looked unconcerned, but Tim sensed—from the state of the house and from the quickness with which he'd offered to help—that he was verging on desperate. Tim made a move to rise, and his father said, "Okay, look, just . . . just sit a minute."

He'd never seen his father capitulate, and he was surprised that the sight of it made him feel bad. Holding all the cards—at last—in an exchange with his father didn't make him feel vindicated or powerful, just vaguely sad. Though his father's face still betrayed nothing, the awkward delay showed he was struggling for words. He'd been many things over the years, but never vulnerable.

Finally he pressed his lips together and said, "I'm going away. I report in a month and change. Monday the twenty-fourth, seven A.M. Not just a three- or six-monther. No deals to be had. No pleading it down. Fifteen years."

Despite all the work Tim had done to get free and clear of his father, despite the fact that he'd always known that one day he'd be having a conversation like this with his father—he'd imagined it, rehearsed it, pictured it taking place in this very room, even—Tim felt dismayed by the notion of his father doing hard time. He couldn't make eye contact. He was unsure what to feel. The thought did occur to him that this could be the introductory act of one of his father's convoluted scams, but Tim had come to him, not vice versa. And through the nearly five decades' worth of ruses Tim had witnessed, never once had his father permitted his house or appearance to lapse. He was genuinely distressed, and Tim was shocked to discover that he was distressed along with him. His father usually pled or bargained, flipped on guys higher up the fraud chain. To Tim's knowledge he'd never served more than a six-month stint at a low-security facility. And now he was staring at fifteen years. Even with good behavior and early parole, he'd be close to seventy when he got out. *If* he got out. Time was hard on the inside, and often it turned into less time.

"Fifteen years? What'd you do?"

"I had an inside man at the DMV." He shook his head faintly—at himself, perhaps. "Never trust an inside man who's a woman." He lifted his impenetrable stare to Tim. "Identity theft. Multiple counts."

"Okay," Tim said, buying time, though for what he didn't know. "Okay."

"I'm getting older, Timmy. What am I gonna do, go on the lam?" He pressed his fingertips together. Tim noticed that his knuckles were white from the pressure, though his tone remained perfectly calm. "I'd like you to take me in."

Tim was well practiced at betraying nothing in front of his father. He waited until the rush of blood at his ears faded, and then he said, "Your deputy marshal son walks you in, maybe you get treated like a VIP?"

"You did some time, you know nobody gets it cushy. Make my transition a little easier, is all. Perhaps we could let the guards know . . ."

Tim had a hard time keeping the disdain from his voice. "What?"

He cleared his throat. "Let them know I have family."

Tim swallowed hard and looked away. The curtains were drawn, leaving him feeling blocked in. "Where are we going?"

"Corcoran." He made an effort to say it evenly.

Roger Kindell's prison. His father in the same lockup as his daughter's killer. Another one in the eye from Fate. Tim supposed it made a perverse kind of sense.

His father's smile gave way to an amused chuckle. "Yeah, it's an irony to savor."

Tim said, "What do you have on Pierce?"

"Pierce." His father settled back into his well-worn chair, seemingly pleased to be back on familiar terrain. "Pierce and I ran some charity scams in the wake of 9/11. Red Cross, victim funds, that kind of thing. He'd cleaned up mostly by then, but it was a boon to business, 9/11. A lot of bacon to go around. Hard to pass up. Back in the day, Pierce had an operations guy named Morgenstein. Hard times now, though, with Pierce getting out of the game altogether. I'd bet the phone doesn't ring for Morg the way it used to. But I'd bet it still rings now and then. See him and lean. He'll cough."

"You got an address?"

"Got a phone number in the other room. Dump by the beach. Tell him you know about the incident at the greyhound track in Corpus Christi."

"What happened there?"

Tim's father smiled—the same impenetrable smile. "That," he said, "is a story for another day."

Saltwater had eroded the staircase leading up from the sand. Tim warned Bear about a cracked step, not wanting to see his well-fed partner put a boot through the soft wood. The wind-battered wreck of a building sat atop a patch of Venice real estate worth more than an average trust fund. Probably owned by a nightgown-wearing widow in her nineties who lacked the patience for upkeep, the energy to remodel, and the nerve to sell.

Bear had met Tim up the block, coming directly from Parker Center, where Wes Dieter had crumbled early into the interrogation. He'd confessed to appropriating the contract intended for the Piper through an elaborately fraudulent Internet communication and to swapping out Tess's hard drive and delivering the original to Ted Sands. Wes had hedged his bets with Sands by making a spare copy of Tess's hard drive, which he'd gladly turned over as an opening concession for plea-bargain negotiations. Bear's preliminary spin through the hard drive had revealed no e-mails—pizzazzu.net was Web-based—but an immense file on Vector that included everything about the company from pipeline projections to early-phase vectors. Though Guerrera was now continuing the search, Bear had found no damning documents about Xedral, certainly nothing to cause a mother to pull her son from the last-ditch trial. Pete Krindon was unreachable, but Bear planned to get him on Tess's hard drive if he couldn't coax the forwarded e-mail from the dental-office computer.

Bear thought that Wes was sincere in his claim that he couldn't source the trail beyond Sands; having copped to a murder one, Wes had little reason to lie about that particular. Most contracts ordered by high-end players were issued through a third party like Sands to preserve plausible deniability, a concept with which Tim presumed the Kagan family was familiar.

A thousand bucks in folded hundreds stiffened Tim's back pocket, cash from the Service's unspecified account generally tapped into for bounty hunters and confidential informants. Tim's father could predict people's actions better than anyone Tim had known. If Morgenstein talked—and Tim was confident he would—he'd need to be set up with some cash to get out of Dodge. It would work out cheaper than protective custody.

All that remained of the apartment numbers were dark outlines on the sun-faded wood. Bear knocked on the appropriate screen door, and it tilted back from where it had been leaned against the frame.

"Come in."

They entered the flop. A futon mattress with no accompanying frame lay on the floor, heaped with trash and dirty clothes. A man sat before a black-and-white TV holding a sagging antenna in position, supporting his extended arm on the prop of his opposite hand. He wore a sport coat with the front pocket ripped off. A bottle of Gordon's gin leaned between his legs.

Tim held up his badge, the cash fanned into view behind it. "Are you Arthur Morgenstein?"

The guy glanced over, thinning hair wreathing a peeling scalp. He smiled, dropping the antenna, and the screen went to fuzz. "About fuckin' time."

Chapter 70

Sam sprawled on the bed, mouth ajar, glasses askew over closed eyes, his breath coming shallow and regular. His olive green T-shirt, still sporting the folds from the store shelf, stretched over his distended belly. Walker sat on the other twin, shoulders propped against the wall where a headboard should have been. A few gauze pads and tightly wound tape had brought the bleeding under control, and he'd zipped into his flexible bulletproof vest to keep pressure on the bandaging. In the alley below, a homeless guy shouted schizophrenically, the latest dose of street theater. The lights were off. Kaitlin sat next to Sam, stroking his head.

Walker listened to the whine of passing traffic. He'd retrieved his backup Redhawk from the duffel, filled it with his last six titanium bullets, and seated it in his rear waistband. With the press of metal against his right kidney, he felt whole again. His heartbeat had finally started to slow, but his head still felt wobbly from the blood loss, and his skin was damp. "You should get out of here."

"His sleeping's been so off, I hate to wake him when he's down."

The yelling from the alley faded, replaced by a bed knocking the neighboring wall and sweet nothings grunted in Spanish. On the verge of laughter, Walker and Kaitlin shared the inside joke across the distance of the room until the predictable climax of *"Ai, papi"*'s gave way to the sounds of a Telemundo talk show and a running shower.

The intervals between Kaitlin's yawns shrank until she switched beds, curling beside Walker and putting her cheek on the ballistic composite plating his chest. Sam murmured something and rolled over, clutching a pillow between his knees.

Walker spoke softly, so as not to wake Sam. "Sometimes we really had fun, me and Tess. We had a Thanksgiving together during our mother's little break. We walked around, watched everyone eating through their windows, these great meals. We went back to the Buick, tried to sleep, but we were too hungry. So Tess had this idea"—a faint smile at the memory—"we were so broke and so hungry we drew pictures of food. Big turkeys. Hams. Mashed potatoes."

Kaitlin looked at him with amused eyes. "Cranberry sauce."

"Why not, huh? I drew mine with a broken pencil on the back of a road map. I wish I had that drawing still. What a great Thanksgiving." On the other bed, Sam mumbled and shifted, and they were quiet until his breathing smoothed out again. Walker said, "I ever tell you that story?"

Kaitlin nodded, her cheek rasping against the vest. "Yeah."

"I never told you about when I got strep throat, though. The next month."

"I thought I knew all those stories."

"It was a few weeks later, when we kept the Buick under the freeway at Griffith Park. The whole back of my throat was white with pus. I wound up spitting into a bag because it hurt too much to swallow." Amusement crept into his voice. "I was a mess. I needed penicillin, but we couldn't go in to see a doctor because we were scared they'd report us and haul my ass off to a kids' home or something. Tess found a guy worked at the drugstore, said he'd filch some pills for us for twenty bucks. But, of course, we didn't have twenty bucks. That night I got bad. Fever, sweating, the whole nine yards. Tess stayed up with me, rubbing ice on my forehead. She told me . . ." Kaitlin looked up, startled, but already he was back in control. His voice, twenty-two years later, still held disbelief. "She said if she could've had it instead of me, the strep throat, she would have. Well, there was this older guy always sniffing around us. Gold Rolex, would come to the park with his wife, push his kids on the swings. He'd always watch Tess. A few times, when he came alone with his kids, he'd take her aside and talk with her. The next day

361

after that night with my fever going, the guy comes by again. He pushes his kids on the swings. Tess goes over and talks to him, and then they go away. I remember thinking it was weird, him leaving his kids playing alone on the swings. Maybe fifteen minutes later, she comes back. She drives me to the drugstore. We get the pills."

Kaitlin was propped on her elbow, her face beside his. Her forehead was wrinkled in the middle like she might cry, but instead she stroked his face. It was the longest he could ever remember talking, his words pulling together one after another. He was probably a touch loopy from the blood loss. He found himself missing Sally and Jean Ann, his palm trees that he could see from his house in Terminal Island.

He heard himself continue. "I kept a picture of you." He tapped his temple. "Didn't fade, no matter how much I wanted it to. Not in Iraq, not in Leavenworth, not through two and a half years at TI. Maybe I didn't want to ruin that, that image. After Iraq I knew I would if I gave myself a chance."

Her cheeks glimmered in the neon light that managed to filter through the blurry back window. Her upper lip was slightly drawn, in anger or hurt or maybe both. "Coward."

"That, too, I guess."

A weak voice from the other bed. "Guys?" Sam had awakened, and his face looked yellow and bloated. "I don't feel so good."

A dog growled out front, and Walker stiffened. He crossed the room and fingered down the front blinds to see the Troubleshooter leading seven men in raid gear up the stairs.

Tim crept to Apartment 22, the brass numbers matching those that Morgenstein had scrawled on a torn bit of pizza carton. One of Pierce's portfolio companies had diversified into slumlording, this fine property north of the airport one of numerous holdings. MP5 in the high-ready position, Tim shouldered to the knob side of the jamb as Miller's explosive-detection dog cleared the door for booby traps. Maybeck's battering ram hit home, the door smashing open, and Tim charged in, the other ART members fanning out behind him to cover the rooms.

No people, no furniture, no bed—nothing but stained carpet and a startled rat in the far corner. Bear returned from the bathroom and stood beside Tim, half illuminated by the slash of streetlight yellow leaking through the splintered front door. Zimmer dropped his MP5, letting it dangle across his chest from the sling. Maybeck cursed, and Denley, still humming, poked at the rat with his boot.

Thomas said, "I'm getting tired of raiding empty rooms."

Bear's Remington shotgun swung at his side, its sawed-off tip brushing his knee. He dug the torn patch of pizza carton from his pocket and double-checked the address. "Lying piece of shit."

"Maybe." Tim used the tip of his gun to lift a torn strip of carpet by the door. A bullet lay just beneath the ripped seam, the cause of the tiny bump. Using his barrel, he flipped it out. Homemade. Awfully familiar tint to the bullet head. The missing bullet from Walker's recovered gun?

Thomas said, "Really?"

"Doubt it," Tim said. "Walker's not this careless."

"Even if he cleared out in a hurry?"

"He's trained for worse than a hurry." Tim stepped out into the floating hallway. He was standing on the short end of the L that formed the second floor, the staircase intersecting the nexus of the wings. A Latino guy in a towel, still glistening from a shower, peered out one of the doors across the way, then closed it quickly.

Why would Walker bother leaving evidence behind? To make them think he'd camped there, sure. But what benefit would that be?

Bear stood beside Tim, studying the pizza-carton corner. He spoke in a rumble of a whisper. "He'd want to know if we showed up. Because then he'd know Morgenstein leaked. The bullet's so we'd figure we missed him, that he already cleared out. So we'd know there's no sense in us sticking around."

"And he wouldn't want us to stick around because . . ."

Bear nodded. "He's watching us. Right now."

Tim said, "Let's ring some doorbells."

Sam held his stomach and moaned. From the window Walker watched the deputies fan out along the second floor, knocking on doors. He glanced at the back window. He'd tested it already—it screeched, and the rusty fire escape made a racket. Waiting it out was the best option. He still felt too weak to outrun eight men with MP5s.

Walker said, "Put him in the bathroom. Close the door. *Now.*" He caught Sam's eye. "If they hear you, someone's gonna have to die. I'm trusting you. That makes us family."

Kaitlin coughed out a note of disgust at Walker. With her help, Sam staggered to his feet. She sat him in the bathroom and said, "Honey, just hang on for a couple of seconds, okay?"

"No," Walker said, "keep the light off. And put the fan on for white noise in case he keeps moaning."

"I'll close the door, but I am *not* leaving him in the dark."

"I'm not scared of the dark," Sam said.

Through a sliver in the closed blinds, Walker watched the huge deputy flash a crime flyer at Humpy Gonzalez next door. No worries there, since Walker had been careful to come and go without being sighted. The flicker in Morgenstein's eye—greed? envy?—when he'd handed over the apartment keys to Walker had raised a red flag. As promised, the building was in an ideal nowhere location, peopled by nowhere tenants. Walker had taken advantage of his father's hospitality but moved down the hall into another empty apartment to find out if Morgenstein was as untrustworthy as Walker suspected. Unlike the proffered pad in the short wing, this apartment—the door of which an angry-looking deputy with a thick mustache was about to bang on—had a fire escape leading to an alley that fed into a network of back streets.

Kaitlin drew near and whispered fiercely, "His stomach's hurting. I'm *not* keeping him out of my sight for more than a minute."

"You won't have to."

A hammering on the door. They froze in the darkness, standing back from the front window. "Police. Open up, please." A pause and then another series of knocks. "Open *up.*"

Through the bathroom's closed door, above the hum of the fan, Sam's cough was barely audible. Walker eased the Redhawk free of his waistband. Kaitlin caught it on the rise, folding it in both hands and holding it firm so it pointed at her stomach. She shook her head—no way. Walker couldn't risk prying the gun free, not without risk to Kaitlin and not with a deputy three feet away, separated only by a two-inch hollow-core door.

If the deputy was coming in, he'd have a free shot at Walker.

Kaitlin matched Walker's glare until the deputy's footsteps ticked down the hall. She shoved the gun away and ran to the bathroom, throwing open the door. Sam lay sprawled by the toilet. Kaitlin let out a cry and flipped the light switch.

Splashes of bright red vomit stained the tiles.

The standby paramedics flicked their cigarettes through open windows and drove off. Tim cabled and padlocked his MP5 in the rear of his Explorer.

Bear stood on the runner of his truck, peering at Tim over the open door. He looked about nine feet tall.

Tim said quietly, "I think he's here. Make a show of clearing out."

"There's a few buildings there with a view," Bear called out, pointing to some office buildings a few blocks away. "Let's go take a look."

The deputies strung up along the block nodded and climbed into their various SUVs. Bear lowered himself into his truck and rattled off. Tim backtracked to the building, eyes on the ground, the walls, searching out any indication of Walker's presence. He jogged upstairs, his hand skimming the railing. Thanks to Maybeck's ram, the front door of 22 sat crooked and loose in the frame. Miller had secured crime-scene tape across the jamb to dissuade squatters until he could send a handyman out. Tim tapped the door open, ducked beneath the yellow tape, and crouched over the slit in the carpet. He was reaching to feel the edge when he noticed a stroke of red painting the insides of the fingers of his left hand. He smoothed a thumb across, and it came away sticky.

No sign of blood anywhere in the apartment. He checked the front-door knob. None there either.

He called Bear. "Any of the guys cut themselves on the entry? Anyone bleeding?"

"Not that I saw."

"You'd better come back here."

"Why?"

"Found some blood."

"Where'd you find it?"

"On my hand."

"Okay. We're up in the office buildings checking out sniper roosts—be there ASAP."

Tim went back onto the landing and looked at the doorknobs of the apartments he'd checked. No blood. He jogged down the stairs, halting halfway. He ran his hand along the dark wooden rail. Toward the bottom, he hit a run of wetness.

He stared at it a moment, then started back up.

Sam's head lolled weakly on his slender neck. "I tried. I tried to be so quiet."

Kaitlin sat on bent knees, wiping the blood from his chin. "Why didn't you call for me?"

Sam's voice came strained through a seized-up voice box. "They would've got him."

Walker stood speechlessly, idiotically, his feet stubbornly planted since Kaitlin had shoved open the bathroom door.

Kaitlin scrambled over to her purse, dumped its contents on the bed, and grabbed the cell phone. Rushing back to Sam, she keyed in three digits. She sat in the blood, cradling Sam's head in her lap, and stared at Walker, her eyes blazing reproach. Sam swayed, a stream of blood spilling over the side of his mouth. His lips goldfished as he dry-heaved.

Sam's eyes rolled north, giving a prize view of his yellowed sclera, and then his body went limp in Kaitlin's arms.

Tim heard the complaint of a window forced open. He sourced the noise to the last apartment Thomas had checked. No one had answered Thomas's knock.

Pressing his ear to the door, he heard murmuring and what sounded like soft sobbing within. Directly in his line of sight on the worn-down sill, a single drop of blood stood out, flecked at the perimeter with tiny splash petals.

Tim stepped back, drew his Smith & Wesson, jerked in a breath, and kicked. He landed the sole of his boot beside the knob, picking up the resistance of the lock assembly so he wouldn't wind up putting his leg through the cheap door, leaving the rest of him trapped outside. The dead bolt ripped through the inner frame.

His eyes took in the dim interior in a sweep that matched the movement of his .357. Blood, shockingly red against white bathroom tile. A little boy's legs and waist in view by the toilet, his torso blocked by the half-closed door. Kaitlin's sob-stained face looking up, panicked and helpless. A disposable cell phone pressed to her ear.

Directly across from the door, framed perfectly from the waist up by the open back window, Walker mirrored Tim, aiming straight back at him.

Chapter 71

Tim remained two strides into the dark apartment, gunfacing his shadowed double through the open window. The faint light thrown from the hall encompassed only Walker's figure, suspended, an orb surrounded by darkness. A Weaver shooting stance, both hands firmed around the revolver's grip, head slightly canted for sight alignment.

Tim shouted to Kaitlin, "What's wrong?"

Kaitlin was rocking Sam's body, yelling, "He's dying! He's unconscious!"

Walker shifted his weight, and the fire escape creaked. Neither he nor Tim lowered his gun; neither barrel wobbled even slightly. Given their proximity and aim, one shot would mean two and the likely end of them both.

"Sammy's not breathing," Kaitlin sobbed.

Without the slightest movement of his body or turn of his head, Tim said calmly, "Have you called 911?"

"They're on the way. I don't know how long. The operator didn't get it. Sam's condition is too complicated. Don't die, baby. Please, breathe."

Tim felt his adrenalized pulse in his neck, the back of his throat. He took his left hand off the grip, showing his fingers, then rode the hammer home with his right thumb and turned the gun sideways. He tilted his left hand toward the bathroom, asking permission.

Walker nodded, pulled his gun back, and vanished, hammering down the creaky metal stairs of the fire escape.

The ambulance screamed toward the hospital, making Tim, Kaitlin, and the two paramedics dig their feet into the floor and brace against the walls. The cramped space reeked of stomach acid. Tim's pants and sleeves, like Kaitlin's, were stained red. Sam drifted in and out of consciousness. Bear followed, his Kojak light blinking atop his rig.

After Walker had fled, Tim had turned Sam on his side and finger-swiped his mouth, clearing any blockage. It had taken a few rounds of messy CPR to get Sam's heart back on line; finally he'd coughed and started to cry hoarsely. Tim had radioed the paramedics who'd backed up the raid; they were only a few miles away. Bear had hustled the other ARTists, setting them on Walker's trail. LAPD had been alerted as well, a good sweep of the neighborhood already under way.

Sam had lost enough blood to drop his hematocrit, the paramedics said, plus his advanced liver disease was impeding his ability to clear ammonia. The combination left him woozy and mildly disassociated. They gave him a few boluses of saline and called ahead to the pediatric intensive care unit at the UCLA Medical Center. Sam seemed to regain clarity, wearing a grim expression and offering the paramedics one-word responses. The ambulance screamed into the bay, and Tim and Kaitlin jogged beside the gurney as it banged through three sets of double doors and landed in a procedure suite. The ER doc declared Sam stable almost immediately, and Tim and Kaitlin rode up on the elevator with Sam, a nurse, and a resident, Sam looking up at their drawn faces as if he found the gravitas mildly amusing.

Kaitlin kept her hand balled and pressed to her mouth. Finally her worry got the better of her. "Why are you so calm, Sammy?"

Sam said, "Because there's nothing I can do."

They got him set up with a private bed in the PICU, Tim waiting outside in the hall while Kaitlin settled him in. An extensive Mexican family had gathered at the far end of the hall. The kids were playing jacks, and the adults spooned posole out of thermoses and ate it with crisped corn tortillas. Tim wondered how long they'd been there. He grabbed a doctor leaving Sam's room and got the rundown. Sam had significant coagulopathy and elevated ammonia, which meant he was now in full-blown liver failure. The liver team could put in a request to upgrade Sam's status on the transplant list, but there were already two Status Ones ahead of him. His prognosis looked ominous.

Bear brought Tim up a fresh shirt from the gift shop. They checked in with Guerrera at the command post, and then Bear went back to his rig to retrieve some information from the field files. Thomas and Freed showed up, having had no luck with the pursuit. They kept near the elevators, walking tight circles with their cell phones pressed to their ears. Tim sat some more, a set of matte black handcuffs resting against his thigh.

Kaitlin finally came out. She'd pulled her hair back taut into a ponytail and changed into scrubs. She took note of the handcuffs. "He wants to see you," she said.

Tim slid the handcuffs back into their belt pouch, stood, and nodded at Thomas and Freed. Thomas squared himself so he was facing Kaitlin.

"Don't go anywhere," Tim said.

Sam was sweating, sheet thrown back from his bloated legs. His skin, so dry in places that it had cracked, had darkened to an olive-yellow shade.

Tim sat bedside and said, "Hey, Sam."

Sam coughed a bit. He sounded dry and raspy. "Kaitlin's not being all dramatic still, is she?"

"She's doing okay."

Sam's upper lids were puffy, more jaundiced even than the rest of his face. "I was thinking. . . ." he said. Tim waited him out. He coughed some more, then said, "If any of my other organs are any good, maybe some other kid could get 'em so his eyes don't have to turn yellow."

Tim lowered his head. Took a deep breath. Said, "Sure, I can have the doctor come talk to you about that."

"I wanted to tell you before Kaitlin. She's too emotional."

"I'll make sure she knows what you want."

Sam scratched his shoulder, leaving red tracks through the flaky skin, and drowsed off. The sleeve of his gown stayed shoved up. High on his flimsy biceps, Tim made out a Magic Marker tattoo, days faded. It was an imitation of Walker's—all yin, no yang. The tattoo was not featured on any of the photos of Walker they'd released to the press, nor in any of Walker's files.

Kaitlin was on the bench where Tim had left her, leaning forward with her elbows on her knees. She'd loosed her ponytail, her hair falling in sheets, hiding her face. Between her shoes, a few clear drops blurred the tile. She gripped the pager in both hands, just below the fringe of hair. Another tear tapped the floor.

Tim sat down beside her. "How long have you been in touch with Walker?"

"Just this night."

Not according to Sam's faded Magic Marker tattoo. Tim clenched his jaw, weighing the variables that had collided. He said, "Do *not* lie to me. I'm your friend here for about five more seconds. Then I'm not."

The anger in his voice snapped Freed's head around up the hall, but Kaitlin kept hers down. Tim counted to five, then pulled the handcuffs out. "Sam needs you right now. But if you won't cooperate, I'll take you out of here." He grabbed her right wrist and cinched metal around it.

"We never wanted any part of it," Kaitlin said quietly. She still hadn't raised her head. Tim keyed the cuff, releasing her wrist. She rubbed it like a weathered con, an instinctive reaction she'd likely picked up from TV. "He never told me anything specific about what he was up to. He broke into the house a few times to root through Tess's stuff, find clues, I guess, like you. He left when he was ready. Finally I told him he couldn't involve me and Sammy. That we never wanted to see him again."

"And tonight?"

"I went there to say good-bye. And to let Sammy do the same. I thought everyone deserves a good-bye."

"He bonded with Sam?"

"Yeah. Despite himself."

"When's the first time you saw him?"

"The morning after he got out."

Tim made a noise and sank back in his chair. "What else do you know? About where he was staying, what he was doing? Anything?"

"I don't know any more than what I saw on the news. He didn't tell me, and I knew better than to ask." Kaitlin spoke in a monotone. "He poked around in Tess's room and wanted revenge on the people he thought had killed her. That's it."

"If you're not being straight—"

"It's the truth." At last she sat up, swept the hair out of her face. She placed the pager on the bench beside her delicately, as if it were made of glass. "So what are you gonna do? Let Sam die alone? Put me in jail?"

"People are dead because you aided and abetted a fugitive."

She clutched her beat-up purse in both hands, as if holding on to it to stay afloat. A label on the worn leather read PURSE. She managed only a whisper. "What are you gonna do to me?"

"The cell phone Walker gave you . . . ?" Tim nodded at her purse, but Kaitlin didn't respond. "We're putting a trace on it."

Kaitlin removed the disposable phone from her purse, snapped off the cheap flip top, and threw it down the hall. It skittered across the tile, past the Mexican family, past Thomas. Freed, stepping out of the elevator, stopped it with a Ferragamo loafer.

Tim looked at her incredulously. "Why?"

"What do you know? How can I explain a thing like that? *Why.* Because I'm stupid. Because he picked me in a smoky bar with Merle on the jukebox and me with my two beautiful friends and he picked *me.* And he picked me every day, every day till he didn't. You have to do that. You make a choice every day, and you pick your spouse every day." Her dishwater hair, tired brown streaked with gray at the temples, hung lank. She glanced at Tim's ring. "I'm not sure if you know that or you don't. But that's how it works. Every day. He fought something out there in the desert he shouldn't have fought, and it's not fair, but that's how it is. But he's still my husband, and I still picked him. Every day. Even when he didn't pick me."

"Kaitlin—"

"I knew you'd never understand. You probably have a sweet wife and a quiet life with a bunch of healthy kids and they're great and they jump on you when you get home from work. And it makes sense, your world. There are *laws.* There are *answers.* There are *solutions.* Maybe we're too dumb to figure it out, or maybe we're too busy feeling sorry for ourselves. Me and Tess and Walk. We just can't get the fucking answers right. I had six miscarriages before the doctor told us to stop trying. *Six.* Every one like a piece of me bleeding away. I tried so hard, but I couldn't. The last one—I knew it would be the last—I went to the bathroom and there was blood everywhere, blood on the toilet and the tile, like today, today with Sam, and I sat on the toilet because I didn't know what else to do. I must've sat four, five hours before Walker came home. He put his hands here"—she gripped Tim's forearms so he faced her, their foreheads almost touching—"and he looked at me. Didn't say anything. And then he got some towels. And he wiped the floor. And he ran the water, ran it warm. And he cleaned me, the blood, from my feet, and my ankles, and here"—she touched the inside of her thigh—"and I sat there and I thought I might be dead, but here was this man on his knees cleaning me, cleaning every part of me. And I knew I wasn't dead. I knew I wasn't dead because of him. And that part of him, that part of him he lost somewhere along the way. And I don't want you to kill him for that."

A nurse went into Sam's room, trailing a fresh saline bag on an IV pole.

Tim shoved down his emotions. He hardened his face. He said, "I'm gonna get you another phone programmed with that number, and I'm gonna get you a warrant, and you're gonna answer it if it rings. If you don't, you'll be leaving Sam on his own and putting yourself in prison. It's my best offer, and it's good for about thirty seconds."

"I never had a good choice. Not in any of this."

He felt a pull in his chest—she was wrong, but only partly. "You put yourself here, Kaitlin."

The door swung open as the nurse left, and they could see Sam. An oxygen tube snaked under his nose. He waved, and the door closed.

"Fine." Tears ran down her cheeks. She looked at her hands. "I'll do it."

Tim put his back against the wall, and they sat side by side. He said, "He showed up at your house. He was controlling, dangerous. He threatened you and Sam if you ratted him out. You were scared. He demanded you show up at the apartment where we found you. You obeyed because you were worried he might hurt you if you didn't."

She kept her gaze on her lap as he rose. In a quiet voice, she said, "That's just how he told it." She fussed with her hands. "Thank you."

He paused over her, staring down at the floor, then kept walking.

Thomas got off the phone as he approached. "What are we doing with the broad?"

"Get her a new cell phone. Get her number transferred. Use Frisk if you have to."

"You think Walker'll call her?"

"Probably not, but we can't afford not to be set up if he does."

"You sure you're not just hunting out something for her to cooperate with to buy her lenience when the prosecutors bring the heat?"

"I'm not that bright. More important, I want you to go up live on the hospital line to Sam's room. Walker cares about that kid more than he's let on. He's gonna be in touch with him."

"Why?"

"Because Sam's gonna die soon. And he saw that in the apartment."

Thomas's mouth dropped, a rare show of emotion. "Days?"

"Maybe less." Tim moistened his lips and tried not to think about the resigned yellow eyes. "I want you at the switchboard, and I want to be patched in, live, before you put *any* calls through to Sam's room. And secure the floor in case Walker makes a personal appearance."

Tim rode down to the basement. He wound through endless white corridors before stepping out into the ambulance bay. Bear's truck was in the far corner; Tim could see the scattering of files across his dash. He headed over, passing parked ambulances, one after another.

An EMT with a shaved head sat on the tailgate, face buried in a newspaper. The headline read FUGITIVE MAKES APPEARANCE AT DEPUTY'S MOORPARK RESIDENCE. Tim cast his mind back through the chronology. Yes, that had been yesterday. This morning had begun, decades ago, with the sniper attempt on Dolan and Dean at the Vector investor meeting.

Without lowering the paper, the EMT called out, "Want me to take a look at that neck, pal?"

Tim raised his hand to the cut. A dribble of blood. The paramedic at Game had gotten in only three of five stitches before Tim had bolted for his father's. "No, thanks."

He got about halfway to Bear's rig when he stopped. Bear looked up through the windshield, puzzled. Tim raised a finger to Bear, turned around, and walked back to the EMT, standing before the wall of news-print.

Pete Krindon, freelance techie and man of infinite disguises, lowered the paper. His eyes went to Tim's neck, and he frowned. "Sit down." He threw a file in Tim's lap and snipped at the old stitches with a tiny pair of scissors. "Who sutured this? Dr. Frankenstein?"

As Pete pulled the old sutures out, Tim stared down at the top page. A blank e-mail, sent at 12:43 P.M. on June 3, carrying an attachment. For-warded from tuffnuff@pizzazzu.net to tess_jameson@westindentistry. com. The subject line read, simply, *Highly Confidential*. Tess must've found it by running a key-word search on Chase's BlackBerry that pulled up something in the attachment's contents.

Pete, who'd started resuturing the wound, said, "Sit still."

Tim flipped the page and was hit with a dense spreadsheet filled with abbreviations and numerals. It looked like a lot and not much at the same time. "Pete—"

"Shaddup for a second. I'm almost done."

"Wait a minute. What am I doing?" Tim started to pull away, but Pete was midstitch. "You're not an EMT."

"No, but I play one on TV." Pete produced a square mirror and held it up, barbershop style. "All done."

The sutures actually looked pretty good, but since Tim didn't want to concede the point, he returned his focus to the report that Pete had recovered from Tess's work computer, where she'd forwarded the e-mail. Charts, graphs, more numbers, nothing clearly labeled. The bot-tom sheet showed Tess's pizzazzu account access log. Tess had logged on the evening of Thursday, May 31, and then just past midnight on Sat-urday, June 2. Tim closed his eyes, recalling dates and constructing the likely story.

Monday, May 28, Tess discovers she's pregnant. She buys folic acid tablets and hires an attorney. Wednesday, May 30, she or her attorney alerts Chase that she'll be prosecuting him for rape. Dean calls and asks her to lunch on May 31, where he threatens to pull Sam from the study if she doesn't drop the case. In return for her cooperation, he offers to shepherd her—and Sam—back into Vector's fold. She accepts, planning to use the opportunity to dig for information she'd been pursuing. She discharges her lawyer the next morning, Friday, June 1. That night at The Ivy, Tess manages to switch her valet ticket with Chase's, get into his vehicle, and forward herself the e-mail with its attachment containing damaging information about Vector, perhaps involving covered-up risks of Xedral. She's careful to erase her tracks, deleting the record of her action on the BlackBerry, unaware that Chase's primary computer at work still holds a record of the forwarded attachment. At home she logs on, a little past midnight, reads the attachment, and forwards it to her work e-mail since she doesn't have a printer at home. Monday she goes in to work and prints it.

What she doesn't know is that Chase, back at the office to start the workweek, sees on his computer that the sensitive e-mail was forwarded Friday night. He has Percy do some digging, finds out that the recipient e-mail address belongs to Tess Jameson. Chase talks with Daddy Kagan, and they decide to wait it out and watch her, maybe tap her phone to see how she's going to respond. They know that Tess will likely tip her hand—*if* she deciphers the report—by dropping Sam from the trial herself.

That day Tess faxes a letter to Vector, withdrawing Sam from the study. Tuesday she contacts Melissa Yueh at KCOM and tells her she wants to see her, that she has something to show her. She's decided to blow the whistle. Kagan & Co., alerted that Tess understands the report and is willing to act on the conclusions she's drawn from it, deems her an unacceptable risk and puts out a contract on her life. Percy Keating sets up the deal online with a hit man he believes is the Piper. He has Ted Sands, a former Beacon-Kagan security worker, do the cash drop at Game the next day, Wednesday, June 6. Wes Dieter intercepts the cash and the job. He murders Tess two days later, safely before Yueh's return from Baghdad.

Only one question remained.

Tim tapped the sheaf and said, "What's hidden in these numbers that's so goddamned dangerous?"

Pete's thin shoulders rose and fell. "Beats me. Shit like this, it takes some decoding."

"You think Tess could've figured it out herself?"

"After what she staked to get it? You bet your ass. Remember, this was a research-savvy woman with an accounting degree. And she followed a trail that led her here. To the smoking gun."

Together they stared at the report.

"Given that she's dead," Pete asked, "who are you gonna talk to?"

Tim eyed the Vector logo on the document header. "Why not go to the source?"

Chapter 72

Seemingly relieved to be back in submissive charge, Edwin made Tim and Bear wait a solid five minutes in the parlor before Bear's escalating threats, conveyed in hushed tones through a house phone, bought them an escort back. They'd requested to see Dolan but wound up in Dean's study, alone with the progenitor. They'd left the confidential report that Krindon had recovered in Bear's rig outside, not wanting to show their cards until they were ready. And before leaving the hospital, they'd run off a few copies, leaving one with Freed so he could start making headway with the numbers in case they struck out here.

Dean rose as they entered. A sturdy security guard sat in one of the two club seats, flipping through the newspaper. He did not look up. A garbage-can-size paper shredder stood out in the corner, anomalous among the elegant study furnishings.

"We came to see Dolan," Bear said. "Why were we brought here?"

"Dolan's very shaken up from this morning. I don't think it's wise—"

"We didn't ask for your wisdom," Bear said. "We asked to see Dolan."

"He's too upset to see anyone."

"He's a grown-up. He can make his own decisions."

Dean cocked an eyebrow as if perhaps that wasn't true. "I understand you helped us at the presentation this morning, and for that I'm apprecia-tive, but that doesn't give you the right to storm into my house and make demands."

Tim said, "We know you had Tess Jameson killed."

The guard lowered the paper, his forehead wrinkling. Dean sat down, folding his hands across a knee, his dark gaze trained on Tim. "Would you go check on the rear-perimeter motion sensors?" He waited until the door clicked behind the guard, then said, "Can I be assured I'm not being illegally recorded this time out?"

"Of course."

"I'm not a stupid man, Deputy Rackley. I'm aware that you have your suspicions. Let me give you some advice. Don't waste your time here. If that fantasy of yours *were* true? You'd never, *ever* link me to it. I'd never be so foolish."

Tim's disgust settled into a calm anger. That's how they are, the privileged, when they decide that laws no longer suit them. They al-ways have men beneath them to make deals and move money, and when the lower floors start caving, the penthouse stays afloat.

"Well," Tim said, "then I'll have to find something else."

Dean smiled, white teeth against tan skin. "Happy hunting."

Tim walked over and rested a hand on the paper shredder. Still warm. "I can have a warrant for Dolan faxed here in minutes. If I get it, we're searching the entire house."

It was a bluff, but one Dean wouldn't want to call with his paper shredder still throwing off BTUs.

Dean studied Tim a few minutes, then said, "I'll call him in."

"No," Tim said. "We'll talk to him alone."

Dean said, "He's in his room. I don't think you'll find him infor-mative."

Tim and Bear made their way through the mansion to the second floor of the south wing. A guard stood at the door to the Kagan broth-ers' rooms like a bouncer, arms woven across a massive chest. A vein squiggled through the ball of his biceps, a firework's dying flare. He wore a benign expression, but there was no question he was blocking the door. He didn't move as they approached.

Bear said, "Out of the way."

Prudently, he stepped aside. Tim threw open the door. Dolan was sitting on the pool table, feet drifting in circles as if stirring water.

Bear said, "You're coming with us," and grabbed him by the arm, steering him out. Dolan whined and fired questions all the way to Bear's rig but didn't figure out simply to tell Bear to let go of him. Bear threw him in the front seat, and he and Tim climbed in on either side of him. The dashboard clock, at 1:32 A.M., had fallen back to an hour slow.

Bear drove a few blocks and pulled over on the quiet, dark street. He bent down, reaching beneath the floor mat. Dolan's concern changed to fear. He recoiled, practically scaling the bench seat, but there was nowhere to go.

Bear tossed the confidential report into Dolan's lap. Dolan took a moment to thaw. He looked at the top sheet, then turned a few more pages, rapidly, his interest growing. "Where did you get this?"

Tim told him.

Dolan held his stomach and leaned over as if contemplating throwing up. He said, "How do I know you didn't generate this yourself?"

"Because we don't know what the hell it is. We can't analyze this kind of scientific data."

"This isn't science."

"Then what is it?"

"It's accounting." Dolan flipped through the pages, zeroing in on a few abbreviations with his finger—*L12-AAT* mapped for comparison beside *X5-AAT.*

Tim noted his change in focus. "What?"

"These are the trial names for the latest generation of viral vectors I created. Lentidra and Xedral. Lentidra was back-burnered."

Bear said, "The permanent-cure vector? That was far along in the pipeline, right? Tess was all over it, had a bunch of info gathered on her hard drive. Early trials, the press release about the animal study going south, all that."

Tim recalled Tess's notation in the margin of the Xedral report stuffed into her bookshelf—*Why Lentidra fall off map?* Tim found himself, now at last, caught up to her inquiry. "Why was it back-burnered?"

"They ran into problems during animal trials. I looked at the data, but . . ."

"What?"

"The trial data are all outside my lab."

Tim imagined that such a vague answer from Vector's senior scientist would only have further fired Tess's imagination.

"And they withhold it from you?" Bear asked. "It's your company."

Dolan cupped sweat off his forehead. "They gave me the data. In a variety of formats, actually. I'm just not certain how . . . complete it was. It's something I've been looking into."

Tim said, "Are they similar? Lentidra and Xedral?"

Dolan adjusted his glasses with a little lift. "You're thinking if there was some problem with Lentidra, a design irregularity, something, it could reflect on Xedral, too? It's possible." He flipped to the next page. "But this looks more like—"

His cell phone rang, Bach's familiar Gothic trills. He caught himself, his shoulders rising in a half cringe.

"What were you saying, Dolan?" Tim said. "What do you think this report is?"

"I . . . I don't know."

"Bullshit," Bear said. "These are your inventions, Dolan. You can read this."

Dolan tilted his head down so his chin wrinkled. He looked scared, and much younger than his thirty-two years. The phone finally stopped ringing. "Take me back, please."

"Listen—"

"Take me back." Dolan shoved the document out of his lap. "Arrest me or take me back." Bear started to say something, but Dolan cut him off: *"Then let me out!"*

Bear tugged the gearshift down into drive, and they coasted smoothly back across the wide Bel Air streets. They pulled up to the estate, and Tim got out.

Dolan scooted across the seat, knocking the report onto the curb, and climbed out. He stood frail and bent; whatever he'd glimpsed had eaten away at his posture. At the end of the long walk, the giant house loomed, a few illuminated rooms granting it an uncanny vitality. He stared up at the house's impressive mass as if awed by it. Tim waited for him to move, but he didn't.

Dolan turned back to them. "I'm not like them. I'm weak."

Tim stooped and picked up the report from the gutter. He rolled it and pressed one end to Dolan's chest. "Don't be."

After a few moments, Dolan took the pages and stuffed them into his waistband. He pulled his shirt down, hiding them, and shuffled toward the porch that just four nights before had been the stage for Ted Sands's murder.

Chapter 73

Morgenstein stepped out of the shower with a shaggy bath mat wrapped around his waist, a stopgap towel that ended midthigh. He weaved a bit in front of the cracked mirror and took another pull from his fresh bottle of Bombay Sapphire. A used condom, infused with streetwalker-preferred strawberry flavor, stuck to the futon mattress behind him. He'd had a hell of a night, and still had seven hundred bucks of the snitch money hiding under the cap of his Speed Stick.

He shook his head, throwing flecks of water onto the stained mirror, then traded the square blue bottle for a Q-tip. He'd just inserted the cotton tip into his ear when a shadow flashed from the open closet to his left and struck his elbow.

He sagged back against the wall, a grasping arm knocking over toiletries and dirty glasses, the bath mat falling. He felt no pain, just a loud, constant rush, a seashell pressed to his left ear.

A revolver came into focus first, then Walker behind it.

Morgenstein's fingers scrabbled up his left cheek, growing sticky, and then he unscrewed the bent Q-tip from his ear canal. Blood ran through the fingers of his cupped hand.

He picked up the bath mat from the floor and secured it around himself, an incongruous act of modesty given what was at stake. The marks of his fingers were rendered on the cloth in crimson.

They'd told him Walker was going to come. He wasn't sure if he hadn't believed them or simply hadn't cared.

Grim comprehension hit him, a cold, chest-high wave. He cleared his throat, but it still felt coated with gin and phlegm. He couldn't hear himself well over the white noise permeating his skull. "Your father would never harm me."

Walker cocked the hammer with a thumb, the gun doing a tiny tilt and bob. "I'm not my father," he said, and squeezed.

Chapter 74

I heard you got shot."

Bear took a turn too hard, and Tim braced against the door, almost dropping his cell phone. "Shit, Dray, I'm sorry. I just got grazed. Coupla stitches."

"For a few stitches I wouldn't have bothered staying awake worrying." Despite her tone, her voice was uneven. She blew out a shaky breath. "I figured if you were dead, Guerrera wouldn't have mentioned it so nonchalantly."

In the background Tim heard Tyler fussing. "He's not asleep?"

"Same story." She sounded exhausted. "This case goes on much longer, I'm filing for hazardous-duty pay."

"Our space between sightings is shrinking. I'd say we're closing him down."

"Yeah? How many stitches has *he* got?"

"He's losing some blood."

"Do tell."

As Bear flew through stoplights, not bothering to distinguish red from green, Tim described the events since the last time he'd checked in with her, shortly after Walker's sniper attempt at Beacon-Kagan had hit the news channels. Caden Burke's emergence, the shoot-out at Game, Tim's visit to his father—this alone was met with stunned silence—the visit to Morgenstein, the raid on the apartment, Tim's standoff with

Walker, the trip to the hospital, and, finally, the failed interface with Dolan.

Not surprisingly, Dray zeroed in on a detail he'd long dismissed as insignificant. "Walker dumped the Camry in the airport parking lot, right?"

"We already checked, Dray. There were no other vehicles stolen out of there around that time."

"He drove away in *something*."

"He might've taken the bus. A cab."

"Covered in ash and reeking of trash? Maybe he wrote 'fugitive' across his forehead with a Sharpie, too?" Different tone: "No, you *can't* have a Scooby-Doo Band-Aid. Go back to sleep or I'm gonna put my head in the microwave. Yes, I'll send your daddy in when he gets home." Back to Tim: "Plus, why bother when you're gifted at boosting cars, which he clearly is?"

"So?"

"So check what cars were stolen in the surrounding area that night. He's not gonna swipe a car from the lot claiming he lost the ticket. They ding you for two hundred bucks. He'd have to grab something a block or two away."

The Ram screeched up to Freed's downtown high-rise. The doorman looked startled beneath his wannabe-Manhattan red cap.

Tim said, "The task force is on overload. Will you get on it?"

"Sure. Guerrera has the parking-lot ticket with the time stamped on it?"

"Yes. Thank you. Gotta run."

"Oh, and Timothy? Let's keep tonight's count to those five stitches. In you, I mean."

An elevator operator rode with them up to the penthouse floor. Freed's building was one of the crown jewels of downtown's gentrification, twenty-five floors of luxury living for Japanese businessmen, Europeans who missed real city living, and the occasional East Coast star whose career required a seasonal transplant to within limo range of the studios.

Freed answered the door in a silk kimono-looking robe that managed to be masculine but earned a behind-the-back eyebrow raise from

Bear nonetheless. They crossed a marble floor to a granite table suspended from the ceiling by two centered steel cables. His copy of the confidential report had been laid out, page by page, across the surface. Post-its with notes and questions, rendered in blue ink from Freed's Montblanc, lifted from the sheets like feathers. A floating fireplace magically burned logs. Someone rustled beyond the cracked bedroom door, but despite Bear's nosy detour in that direction, the identity—and gender—of Freed's visitor remained concealed. The wall-length window looked down on the rooftop bar and lounge of The Standard hotel. The pool cast a diffuse aqua glow over the scene-monkeys slurping bright name-brand drinks and rolling around on the waterbed cabanas. A projector Supersized *Casablanca* onto the side of the neighboring building.

Tim nodded at the pages on the table. "Make headway?"

"You could say that. I've got X5-AAT pegged as Xedral's latest model, but I've been trying to figure out what L12-AAT is."

"It was the final model of Lentidra," Tim said, "a viral vector they pulled back after they hit problems during animal trials."

"They pulled it back, all right, but not because of that." Freed looked troubled. He sat at the end of the table and scooted his chair in. "This report is, among other things, a risk assessment. It provides a comparative cost-benefit analysis of both viral vectors." He tapped a graph. "This part shows projected profit margins for Xedral, mapped against those for Lentidra."

Bear said, "Xedral's projected profits are higher."

"Significantly higher. Initially."

"And this chart?" Tim asked.

"The tipping point. For when the risks associated with Xedral outweigh the financial benefits."

"I'm not sure I follow," Tim said. "What are *these* figures?"

"The effectiveness quotient. It shows Xedral to be eighty-six percent effective."

"Sounds pretty good," Bear said. "So what 'risks' are we talking about here?"

Troubled, Freed jogged his Montblanc so it tapped the table's edge. "Lentidra's effectiveness is at ninety-five."

The guard came out of his chair when Dolan stormed into his father's study. Breathing hard, Dolan threw the report on his father's desk and crossed his arms. The guard, accustomed now to the pretense of discretion, dismissed himself quickly, leaving them alone. Dean held the report in a firm hand, perusing it at arm's length. The cold still hadn't left Dolan's face; he'd sat on the porch for the past forty-five minutes, reading by the faint light cast through the parlor window. Dean set down the report without lifting the top page.

"Well?" Dean said.

"You want to tell me what that is, sir?"

"An accounting scenario."

"That's why you gave me false data for Lentidra," Dolan said. "Not because it was flawed. But because it *wasn't*."

"Neither vector is one hundred percent."

"I don't see the same fail rate for Lentidra."

Dean's aggravation reached critical mass. "You don't see the same healthy profit margin either."

"Xedral is less effective. But you want it anyway."

"*Why* do you think that is?"

Dolan's eyes pulled to the framed poster behind Dean. XEDRAL. THE FUTURE HAS ARRIVED. THIRTY DAYS AT A TIME. "The boosters. You buried Lentidra because it was *too* effective. It achieves permanent transgene integration. There's no need for a maintenance shot every month, like Xedral requires. You don't want to *cure* AAT deficiency. You'd rather maintain a pipeline of sick monthly consumers."

"I don't expect you to comprehend the intricacies." And then, resigned to his disappointment: "You're not your brother."

"No. And I don't share his ethics either. We could have had Lentidra to market *months* ago. Saved who knows how many lives?"

"There's nothing illegal about what we've decided to do here. We own our research."

"Our research started with a grant from NIH. Taxpayer money."

Dean chuckled. "Do you know what your lab has spent since it opened?"

"A hundred and twelve million."

"Right. Of which your NIH grant was what?"

"Five hundred thousand."

"Correct. Your grant was a drop in the bucket. And you don't care where the rest comes from, do you? You don't bother to keep tabs. It could be from other people's gold teeth, melted down at Auschwitz and stockpiled in Paraguay, right? Ethics! Where do you think your operating capital comes from?"

"Investors."

"Right. Are the money managers bad people? No. Are their investors? No. They're just spoiled rotten. They've come of age in a time when a three percent dividend and four percent appreciation doesn't cut it. When stockholders see any equity that doesn't grow fifteen percent every year as a turd not even worth flushing. For better or worse, you are married to them. Those beady-eyed fund managers. Those rapacious investors. Their money, not mine, is what will turn Vector into a success. So don't you question my ethics until you can truthfully say you give a fuck how I've gotten my hands on that money for you."

"This isn't about money, or funding, or business. It's about putting people at unnecessary risk."

"Don't be such a pessimist, Dolan. These people—terminal patients facing certain death—are being offered an eighty-six percent chance at having their lives saved. If I was sitting in their chair at the roulette table, I'd take that bet. Say our worst-case estimate *is* right. Fourteen percent of patients have a problem. So what? They were going to die anyway. Of liver failure—a slow, horrible way to go. Until you developed Xedral. It's a godsend."

"Not when there's an alternative that provides a *cure*. With significantly less risk."

"An alternative that offers little incentive to this company to continue marketing and developing this and other lifesaving products. Grow up, son. This is part of doing business. We provide a service, and there are costs to providing that service. You want to . . . what? Bring one drug to market and not be able to fund the infrastructure to maintain it? Not to mention future R&D? How do you think that'll get funded?

You want to cure cystic fibrosis, Dolan? How are we going to do that without resources?"

"How are you going to explain why you knowingly withheld a superior vector?"

"Come on, Dolan. For every product we run *dozens* of models and sims like this. And thousands more showing potential problems and risks with all of our products."

"This report from your beloved accounting department is a bigger threat than you're letting on."

"Would it be a threat if it leaked? Yes. Would that threat be inconvenient? Yes. Would it be unmanageable? No. We've provided for that."

Dolan leaned over the desk, jabbing a finger into the report. "We're launching Xedral on Monday and going wide three months after that. To three hundred *thousand* humans. A nine percent effectiveness difference is what? Twenty-seven thousand dead? A *year.* Have you *really* got that accounted for?"

Dean, a portrait of calm in the face of Dolan's emotionality, studied him with something like enmity.

Dolan examined his stone façade and said, "We have a responsibility to release Lentidra."

"And we will when the time is right."

"No way. I can't let you sit on it."

"You *can't*? What do you have? A contingency scenario? A few pieces of paper obtained through questionable legal means? You don't have any hard data, do you? *Do* you? You don't have a scrap of leverage, so don't you *dare* threaten me."

"What about Tess Jameson?"

"What about her?"

"She found this."

"Yes. And she came to me, of course, to blackmail me with it."

"To give her Lentidra."

"As if we could just circumvent trials and FDA approval and stick the thing in her son's arm. Even if we *were* willing to trust her, to float our product out into the world where any general practitioner in Antelope Valley could raise an eyebrow at the miracle cure of this one kid."

"So you . . . ?" Dolan wanted to know and was afraid to know at the same time.

"So I told her I have a number of relationships in the medical community. Including the executive director of the United Network for Organ Sharing. If Tess were willing to walk away after signing a full non-disclosure regarding any and all knowledge she might have acquired as related to her involvement with Beacon-Kagan and Vector, perhaps expedited treatment could be arranged for her son."

Dolan could hear the rush of blood in his ears. "That's why she dropped Sam from the Xedral trial. To make him available for transplant. You offered her a liver."

"I tried to bring her into the fold—again. I tried to help her—again. And again she proved untrustworthy. She had a fit of conscience, backed out of our agreement, and was preparing to go public."

A fit of conscience. Tess had been placed in an impossible moral position. An illegal liver, attained for her son, at a cost of contributing to a corporate cover-up that would cost twenty-seven thousand children their lives every year. From what he knew of Tess, even her love for her son wouldn't make her participate in a scheme that would mean hundreds of thousands of children dying unnessarily. She'd thought she could go through with it, yet in the eleventh hour she couldn't. But in preparation for the liver, she'd had to sign away Sam's place in the Xedral study. She was stuck. So she'd tried to take another route—a legal route. Whistle-blow. And hope Sam could hang on until Vector was forced to release Lentidra.

Dolan's voice came weak, throaty. "So you ordered her killed."

"And what if I did?" Dean rose, speaking with pent-up force. "*And what if I did?* With what's at stake—the future of Vector, of Beacon-Kagan, the lives we save every day and will continue to save. You'd let one woman bring down the whole enterprise?"

"If she was right. Yes."

"Then why didn't you? You were in a position to know, Dolan. But you didn't want to. Instead you slurped at the teat all these years."

"Not anymore."

"Please. You may be naïve, but you're not a fool. You're not going to walk away from Vector, from your work. You're emotional right now, sure. But you'll calm down, see the road ahead. We'll work this out."

Dolan summoned a reserve of strength he never knew he had. "No, *sir*, we won't. I'm leaving. Now."

"You'll be killed." Dean's eyes pulled to the guard who had reappeared at the door, and Dolan felt a coldness run through his veins. His father might have been talking about Walker Jameson, but then again he might not have. Keeping his eyes on Dean, Dolan backed up into the hall. Immediately another guard appeared, flanking him. He tried to turn toward the foyer but was blocked, the men filling the breadth of the hall.

"Get the hell out of my way!"

But they remained, maddeningly mute, eyes downturned in a meretricious display of deference. Dolan moved back toward his room, and they permitted him, matching him when he jogged, safeguarding wrong turns, guiding him, a rat through a rigged labyrinth. He burst into the game room and slammed the door behind him, locking it.

He doubled over, hands on his knees, breathing deeply to stave off a panic attack. Finally he straightened. He picked up the telephone, pressed the receiver to his ear until the dial tone started bleating. What would he say? He had no proof, no hard data.

Setting the phone down, he pushed open the door to Chase's room. On the desk the termini of numerous computer cables shaped the blank space where the laptop had been. Dean must have had it removed in the past hour while Dolan was with the deputies. Under the circumstances the computer's absence struck Dolan as vaguely grotesque, an organ ripped free of its connective tissue. Dean had been at this game too long; he could think five moves ahead. Dolan didn't stand a chance.

He stared at the faint indentation in Chase's pillow, a remnant of his brother's final night of sleep. He tried to personalize his sense of loss, but it had little to do with Chaisson. It was more a diffuse sadness that his life and their brotherhood had amounted to nothing more than this.

A series of chirps came from the closet, disrupting Dolan's thoughts. He crossed and opened the door but was greeted with silence. After about thirty seconds, the sound repeated. He sourced it to a cell phone weighing down the pocket of Chase's favored leather jacket along with a set of keys. Dolan listened to the waiting message, but it was from a woman (screechy, loquacious, inebriated) berating Chase for not call-ing her.

He sat on the bed, clicking through the saved numbers. A lot of ini-tials, in case Chase's fiancée got ahold of it. He came upon an unnamed entry—*22498352*. A string of random digits, clearly not a phone number.

Vector's computer log-in security codes were eight digits long.

Dolan stared at the numbers, feeling his heartbeat grow louder until he sensed it pulsing at his eardrums. With renewed purpose he rose, sliding on Chase's jacket and stuffing the phone in his pocket. On his way out, he tapped the pillow, disintegrating the hollow where Chase's head last rested.

He jogged around the pool table, undid the various locks on the bulletproof window overlooking the backyard, and climbed out into the night. A guard stirred at his station near the rear gate and scanned the dark house. Dolan flattened against the second-story lattice until the guard turned back to the street. He'd require a more elaborate exit than the down-and-out he'd planned on. Honeysuckle scraping his face, he struggled his way to the next room.

The bathroom window was cracked. He clung to the lattice beside it, his body starting to shake from exertion. Supporting himself by two tenu-ous toeholds and one aching arm, he slid the pane open. He pulled him-self through and slipped out into the hall. Timing his dodges through the halls so as to miss the patrolling security guards, he eased out one of the service entrances. Chase's G-Wagen was parked outside the garages where he'd last left it.

Dolan flew through the remote-operated rear gate, offering a middle finger to the surprised security guard.

Chapter 75

Freed fussed at a contraption that looked like something out of a science-fiction movie; finally it clanked and spit out a dribble of espresso.

"Okay," Tim said, "walk us through the rationale."

Freed worked the knobs of the machine. "To my thinking, Lentidra's a contingency plan. No, a Plan B. They didn't back-burner it—it's ready to go. It's a holdback, a hostage drug for when the whistle blows or the pressure comes or whatever. If no nosy parent or probing journalist sniffs out its true effectiveness, it languishes in the vault. But if the heat of inquiry rises or a competitor puts a model in the pipeline that competes with Xedral, Vector has Lentidra poised to roll out. They claim they fixed it and unveil it as the new and improved lifesaver. The report indicates as much—they'll release it when it's in their financial interest to do so. That way they maximize profits on both products."

"So this isn't about undisclosed risks," Bear said. "It's not Xedral that's the problem."

"Right. It's not like Xedral kills anyone. It just doesn't *save* them as well. They would've died anyway. It's about Xedral's numbers versus Lentidra's. Get a jury of American dipshits to understand that bookkeeping wrinkle."

"So why would Tess drop Sam from the Xedral trial?" Bear asked. "I mean, unless she had Lentidra in hand?"

"If it was your kid, would you want him to have an eighty-six percent chance of living—or ninety-five?"

"But it's not like she knew she could get him Lentidra in any kind of time frame," Tim said. "For all she knew, Xedral was her only bet. Her decision doesn't make sense."

Freed shrugged. "I don't have an answer for you." He filled four petite mugs, double shots all the way around. One he carried back to the bedroom, Bear almost falling over to see through the opened door.

When Freed returned, Tim gestured at the report pages, still spread across the table like a feast. "This was enough to get Tess killed?"

"This in combination with her testimony, Sam's face on the news, former company mascot, all that stuff. It would've been enough to put a major crimp in the Kagan boys' plans on the eve of an IPO."

Tim finally popped the million-dollar question: "Is there anything here we can take to the U.S. Attorney's?"

"If you want to get laughed at. To prosecute Big Pharma, you need not just a smoking gun but footage of the gun being fired."

"If we got that footage, would the prosecution go federal or state?"

Freed wrinkled his mouth thoughtfully. "A big multinational corporation like this, I'd say the AUSA would probably team up with the SEC and hook it federal, like with Enron. Could be a career maker for someone. Plus, Vector was started with seed money Dolan acquired from NIH—not much, but if a nickel comes out of that pot, it carries with it a whole legal rubric of terms and conditions available for violation. If they buried a more effective drug that could've saved tens of thousands of lives, they're tangled up in all sorts of illegalities." He sipped his espresso. "But without hard data backing your case, all you have are contingency scenarios"—he gestured with his cup to the table—"and companies run those all the time. Dean Kagan's army of attorneys—and lobbyists—will have this respun before the AUSA returns our call."

"So where would the hard data be?"

"Well, you said Dean Kagan had a paper shredder working overtime at the house. Let's assume he followed similar protocol at the office and threw all key printed evidence in the circular file. What remains—for future corporate number crunching—are probably digital files hidden behind ten firewalls. But you know what a bitch it is getting warrants for corporate computers and getting to those computers before they've been processed in-house. Plus, our probable cause is wobbly. All we have are Tess's murder and a disquieting document, strung together by a lot of talk."

Tim's Nextel rang, clattering across the table. He caught it before it fell off the edge. "Rackley."

Thomas said, "I'm at the hospital switchboard, waiting to put through a call to Sam's room from a Dr. Norrath. None of the docs called for a referral from this guy."

Tim half smiled at the name, lifted from one of Sam's video games. "Put it through and patch us in."

Tim clicked the speakerphone button, set the Nextel on the table, and pressed a finger to his lips. Bear and Freed waited excitedly through two rings. A nurse picked up.

Walker's voice said, "Dr. Norrath for Sam Jameson."

A rustle as the phone was handed off.

Sam sounded hoarse and tired. "Yeah?"

"This is Dr. Norrath calling. Do you understand?"

A hesitation. "Yeah, I understand."

"How are you doing?"

Sam coughed a few times, then said, "If I'm a saint, doesn't that mean I get to go somewhere after this?"

"A saint?"

"Mom said I was a saint. She woke me up this one night. A few days before she died. She asked me, just for pretend like, if I could get a new liver but that meant that tons of other kids who are sick like me *couldn't* get better?" Sam took a few seconds to catch his breath. "Would I want it anyways? I told her I wouldn't feel so hot about that. So no. She said I was a saint. She cried and everything. *Mom* did. So I knew she meant it. She said she wouldn't be able to do it either and she hoped I'd know it wasn't because she didn't love me more than anything in the world." More labored breathing. "So what's that get me? Being a saint?"

"I wouldn't know about that," Walker said, "but don't worry. I'll make it right. I'll make it right for you."

In a quiet, hopeful voice, Sam said, "Promise?"

The pause stretched out to maybe ten seconds. Walker said, "Promise," and hung up.

Tim, Bear, and Freed remained silent, poleaxed by what they'd just heard, processing the implications.

Tess and Sam had walked away from a life guarantee, close at hand but questionably obtained, and they'd done it to bust Lentidra out of Big Pharma captivity. Dean's words returned as an echo in Tim's head: *bear in mind, once a patient begins gene therapy, he is removed from the organ-donor list.* Tess had to drop Sam from the trial to position him for the liver when she'd thought she could go through with it. But clearly, even with the Xedral trial no longer an option, the implications of saving her son's life had sat too heavy with her. Tim wondered if he'd be able to live with himself, choosing Ty's well-being, even if that meant tens of thousands of other children would die. Maybe more. He wondered if he could live with that knowledge. He wondered if he could live with Tyler's growing up under the weight of a secret that would crush him were it ever revealed.

Thomas came back on the line and told them to hold while he and Frisk sourced the call's origin. His voice jarred them back into the present.

"The kid's circling the drain," Freed said. "How's Walker think he's gonna make it right?"

"Just comforting him, maybe," Bear said.

"Not his style." Tim worked the inside of his cheek between molars.

Call-waiting beeped. Tim clicked over, catching Dray on the tail end of a vicious yawn.

When she recovered, she said, "I went out to a three-mile radius from the airport parking lot. There was only one car stolen that night. A red 2004 Honda Accord, registered to Brehanda De LaSalle, license number three-Nora-Charles-Sam-six-eight-four."

Tim thanked her and switched lines just as Thomas picked back up.

Thomas said, "He's still fucking with us. He routed the call through the Vector switchboard, like before."

Tim felt a stab of excitement. "No, he's *at* Vector this time. He's getting Sam the Xedral shots."

Freed was already dialing. He racked the cordless on its base so he could use speakerphone and keep his hands free. He maneuvered through Vector's automated phone system, reaching the ranking security guard on duty. The guard reported no breaches. Freed gave him the Honda's identifiers and asked him to radio his men and ask if anyone had spotted it.

"There's a red Accord parked right across the street here. Got a big-ass Cal State Northridge sticker on the back window?"

Freed grabbed his laptop from the kitchen counter. "Can you check the plate numbers?"

The guard huffed outside.

Bear said, "Walker would've switched the plates out."

With Tim peering over his shoulder, Freed Googled *Brehanda Delasalle*. The search engine delicately inquired, *Did you mean: Brehanda De LaSalle?* Indeed he did.

The guard said, "Nope, it's got dealer tags. Keyes Toyota Van Nuys."

Bear said, "What's an Accord doing with new-car plates from a Toyota dealer?"

Brehanda's search page loaded. The top entry read *classof04.alumni. csun.edu.*

As Freed scrambled back to throw on clothes and Bear ran to the door, keys jingling in his hand, Tim alternated between Thomas and the Vector guard. "Lock down the building. Call all local units. Assemble ART. Have LAPD set up a perimeter. I want the whole block flooded."

Freed jogged from his bedroom, ducking into the sling of his MP5. He called back over his shoulder, "Be back in a few, babe."

The elevator operator shrank against the back wall, so Freed knuckled the button himself. Tim flicked open the wheel of his .357 and gave it a spin, his ritual ammo check. As the elevator doors opened, Bear skidded to the front of the building, one tire popping up on the curb.

They hopped in, and he took off. They were a half block up the street before Tim managed to get the door closed.

Chapter 76

Timing his approach to dodge overlapping security patrols, Dolan arrived short of breath at the proximity reader guarding the back entrance above the parking-lot ramp. His own access-control card had been disabled as he'd predicted, and so had Chase's, but not Chase's generic guest pass, which he'd pulled from the G-Wagen's glove box. Just as the guard's footsteps rounded the corner, Dolan eased the door shut behind him and stood quietly inside the Beacon-Kagan Building, breathing in the darkness.

The rear of the floor was unfamiliar to him. He waited for his eyes to adjust to the dark, then eased slowly down the corridor. His sneakers padding quietly on the tile, he moved through the sliding glass doors into the test suite, passing beneath the oil portrait of his father. Agitated at the movement, the monkeys rattled their cages, flailing and screaming, the sound reaching a madhouse pitch. Dolan jogged through the heated production room, roller bottles filled with Xedral grinding all around him, and to his own bench. One of the junior researchers had left a champagne bottle, bow around the neck, on Dolan's chair. The attached card hung open, the note reading *Congrats on the IPO! Your hard work finally paid off!*

Working rapidly, he logged in to the system as his brother, using the code he'd pulled from Chase's cell phone. The monkeys' continued shrieking did little to settle his heartbeat. He waited, a held breath burning in his chest.

The log-in screen blipped away, leaving him with unrestricted access.

He searched the drives for key words, clicking past the reports teed up for public consumption and locating the data he was looking for—a set of files buried three folders deep on the C drive. Trial data, study databases, and finally, Lentidra's raw data. The *true* data. Most damning were interoffice memoranda circulated by Dean himself. Dolan gathered up an assemblage of key documents, compressed them into a neat packet, and attached them to an e-mail. He found Deputy Rackley's business card in his wallet and typed in the e-mail address.

His finger hovered above the mouse for maybe a full minute.

Lentidra had been ready for Phase I human trials months ago, but Dolan had slept through the backstage machinations that had removed it from the production line and sealed it behind a wall of secrecy. The cost of its delay was paid in human lives, as would be the cost of its continued captivity. All because Dolan had acted feebly, even in the face of his own suspicions.

He thought about Tess Jameson, with so much less to her name and more on the line. Up against vastly more powerful corporate muscle, she'd done everything to orchestrate her son's survival. And just when she'd gotten it within reach, her conscience wouldn't let her seize it. She'd fought to bring a cure to others, even knowing that Sam could die as a result. And now here Dolan was, Vector's principal investigator following the case laid out by a mother with limited resources, education, and opportunity.

The monkeys still hadn't calmed in the test suite, jungle cries echoing around the hard lab surfaces. The din ringing in his ears, Dolan clicked the mouse, sending the e-mail.

The icon spun as the data uploaded. Biting his thumbnail and waiting for the chime, he heard instead the sound of glass shattering in one of the accompanying suites.

A jumble of fears coalesced. Likely Dean had installed cameras inside the lab. So either Dolan had been spotted or soon would be. Maybe

Chase's guest access card had called up an alert on some remote security computer.

Slowly, he eased away from his bench, passing back through the production room, the heat of the incubator making his neck sweat. He groped around on the wall, finding the light-switch panel and disabling the motion-sensor feature before stepping fully into the test suite. The monkeys hopped around, their cages banging on the lab counters, but there was no sign of any guards. And no shattered beakers to explain the noise he'd heard.

The access card failed to open the exit in the back of the test suite. Numb with disbelief, Dolan tried again. The proximity reader gave him another flashing red light. Security had locked down the building.

The fire-escape door toward the end of the corridor was by law manually operated. Guards might be waiting for him outside, but he'd rather risk a public confrontation than wait in the dark for whoever broke the glass and was likely stalking him. He now had concrete evidence of what he'd sensed all along—his father was capable of anything.

Dean's painted face stared down as Dolan slipped through the sliding glass doors. Before proceeding up the corridor toward the exit, he turned off the motion sensor on the overheads. The window at the end of the corridor, normally lit by passing headlights, was a black square. Plotting each footstep, he crept along the tile. The monkeys had finally silenced, but the quiet was proving equally sinister.

A faint rustling in the vector-storage room stopped him dead. Through the vast internal window, he caught a partial view of the room. A refrigerator door hung open, casting a faint light across the floor. The freeze-dried Xedral vials, normally neatly lined on the shelves, had been pulled down. A few lay shattered on the concrete. A number of Styrofoam shipping containers had been knocked over, dry ice misting up from the floor.

Why would a guard ransack the vector-storage room?

Before he could flatten to the wall, the door kicked open and Walker solidified from the dark, shrouded in wisps of vapor.

The gunmetal, when pressed to Dolan's neck, felt like ice.

Chapter 77

Using his left arm to cradle twenty or so vials of Xedral against his stomach, Walker pressed the Redhawk to Dolan's throat. Calmly, he stuffed the vials and needle kit into his pockets.

Dolan said, "Listen—"

"Turn around."

Dolan pivoted haltingly. His spread fingers trembled.

"What did Tess get on you?" Walker said.

"She found out about a second viral vector I designed for AAT. More effective but less profitable, so my father and brother buried it. They lied to me about it, told me it was less viable than Xedral, and covered the trail with false data."

"Get on your knees."

"I *just* figured out—"

From behind, Walker kicked out Dolan's leg, and he hit the floor hard, his kneecaps knocking tile. Walker pressed the gun to the back of his head. He expected Dolan to cry, to plead, but he didn't. He just sat there, sagged over his folded legs, shoulders slumped.

Walker thought about Kaitlin in the apartment, steering his gun to her own belly so he couldn't aim at the deputy pounding on the door. He summoned his anger. "You were there. When Tess was raped."

"Yes." Dolan didn't move. His voice was quiet, resigned, almost peaceful. "And I did nothing to help her. I'm sorry."

Walker's finger tightened on the trigger, but then a spotlight struck the window at the corridor's end. Squinting through the glare, he made out a row of incoming flashing blue lights.

He hit the floor.

The Dodge actually caught air flying off the 405 at Wilshire. Tim's Nextel vibrated, and he snapped it off his belt. "Almost there."

Miller said, "Jameson's inside with an unidentified hostage. The perimeter's airtight, and a traffic-control team's locked down the surrounding blocks. We've got men at all the exits and windows and up on the second floor at the stairwells. The command team and negotiating team are en route, but we got the LAPD crisis negotiator in place already. We blocked the phone lines from the building, so if Walker calls out, he's talking to us. The negotiator's on with him now, obtaining proof that the hostage is okay. Guerrera's rounding up Jameson's mother and father and getting no cooperation. His platoon-mate—guy in the VA?—is too sick to be moved."

As Bear swept around the exit loop, a blanket of parked cop cars drew into view, the strobing reds and blues projecting false movement all around. The desolate run of street beyond the vehicle barricade looked bizarre; Tim had never seen Wilshire devoid of traffic. Freed whistled through his teeth. A spotlight blazed off the closed venetian blinds blotting out a window on the ground floor of the Beacon-Kagan Building.

Tim said, "Contact Kaitlin Jameson—she's three blocks over at the UCLA Med Center. And find Dolan Kagan."

Bear slowed at the sawhorses, flashing his badge to the cop. Up the block, in the eye of the spotlight, the venetian blinds flashed open, revealing a silhouette bound to an office chair, an arm reaching into view to press a gun to his temple. The blinds snapped shut again.

Miller said, "Unfortunately, I think we just did."

Bear steered slowly, threading through the parked cars.

"Walker said he won't talk to the negotiator anymore," Miller said. "Only to you."

Tim said, "We're here. Look west. Bear's rig? Have someone meet me with a cordless."

403

Bear slant-parked beside a fire engine, and Tim hopped out. A guy in a SWAT windbreaker trotted over and tossed Tim a cordless. Tim headed to the front of the barricade, pressing the phone to his ear. "Rackley."

Acrylic packing tape secured Dolan at the forearms, ankles, chest, and thighs, adhering him to the office chair. Gripping the back of his neck, Walker rolled him down the corridor on well-greased casters. He spoke into the cordless phone he'd swiped from one of the lab benches. "Bring Sam here now, or this fuck dies."

Through the phone Tim sounded slightly winded; he was jogging. "We can't move Sam. He's in full liver failure."

"Full liver failure? Then you'd better get him here quick."

"We can't do that," Tim said. "He's in bad shape."

"I have the Xedral shot. It'll make him better. Send Sam in to me. I give him the shot, then I let Dolan go free."

"There's a better vector. That's what Tess found out. That's why they had her killed."

Walker halted, Dolan grunting as his grip tightened. "That's what my hostage told me. You think we should believe him?"

"Tess got ahold of evidence. I've seen it."

"So there's another shot. A better shot." Walker pressed the Redhawk to the hollow of Dolan's eye. "Do you have it here?"

Dolan tried to recoil but had little room to move. The chair slid a little, and Walker moved with it, applying pressure to Dolan's face. The glass sliding doors hissed open, and they drifted into the test suite, the monkeys sending up a racket.

"Lentidra," Dolan said. "Yes, it's here. But it's too late."

"What do you mean it's too late?" Walker said.

"He's in liver failure? Sam?"

"So we give him the good shot. We fix it."

"Viral vectors can't work if the target organ is in failure. The administration of the transgene'll just damage the liver further. Gene therapy has to start earlier—it's not a late-stage cure."

A long pause. At the end of the line, Tim was silent; he'd been listening, too.

Walker tensed his mouth, scratched his head with the barrel of his gun. He said, into the phone and to Dolan, "I don't believe you. Put me through to Sam's room."

Tim said, "I can't do that."

Walker fired a shot across the suite—a computer monitor jumped, the bullet embedding in its side. The monkeys, bizarrely, silenced.

Tim said, reasonably, "Everyone okay in there?"

"Put me through to Kaitlin at the hospital, or so help me God I'll kill this motherfucker."

"I'll see what I can do."

A few seconds later, Walker got a ring, and then Kaitlin's voice. He said, "Kaitlin, it's very important you answer me straight right now. Did Sam's liver give out?"

"He's in a coma, Walk." She sounded deadened, on the far side of a sobbing jag. "I want to hear his voice. Just one more time. But they said I'm not gonna get to."

Walker felt his forehead crinkle. "How long's he have?"

"Morning. Maybe."

He waited until whatever was fucking with his throat subsided. "I'm sorry."

An indelicate nose blow. "You didn't do it."

"No," he said. "For being a coward. Like you said."

Her voice took on a note of suspicion. "Where are you? What's going on?"

"Are you high up? In the building?"

"Third floor."

"Get to a south window."

Sounds of Kaitlin running. She jerked in a breath. "Oh, honey."

"When the kid comes to, tell him I said he did good."

"Walker, they don't think he's gonna come to."

He hung up, crouched, and lowered his head, palming the back of his skull. Dolan started to say something, and Walker raised the Redhawk so it aimed at his face. His voice came low, gruff. "Do *not* say anything right now."

Between his feet the cordless rang. He picked it up.

Tim said, "You're a straight shooter, Walker. Here's how it is: We don't have anything to give you. You don't have anything to get. Dolan can't do anything for you anymore."

Walker started pulling Xedral vials from his pocket and throwing them against the far wall, one after another. A few of the monkeys reacted with anxious little calls. "How do you know I won't just kill this motherfucker anyway?"

"I don't. But you'd be killing the wrong guy. He wasn't in on Tess's murder."

"He was in on the rape."

"He was there."

"Being a coward don't buy you a pass."

"Sounds like Kaitlin just gave you one."

Walker threw another vial, finding the tinkle of breaking glass oddly pleasing.

"You're boxed," Tim said. "There's no way out that doesn't wind up at a dead end."

Walker said, "Dead ends don't scare me."

"You've got one move left. You let Dolan live, you walk out of there, we sit down with the AUSA and have a long talk about extenuating circumstances."

"Like they did for you."

"Like they did for me."

Walker laughed. "Somehow I don't think I'll get the same treatment." He set down the phone and turned to Dolan. "All you fucking people. When the chips are down, you hide behind them."

Dolan said, "You're right. But I had nothing to do with killing your sister. And I *never* would have. Stop and think what your sister put her life on the line for. I didn't see it until I came in here tonight. Sam was going downhill fast. She risked everything that mattered to her to give him something to die for. This drug my father and brother were trying to bury, she was gonna ransom with her own blood. For three hundred thousand people. This could be what Sam did with his life. Which is a lot more than my brother did with his. Or my father's doing with his fucking companies. With *my* company. Tess *died* trying to get the right AAT vector to the market. Now I'm the one who knows what it is and how to do it." His jacket had fallen open, and a few wet splotches appeared on his

T-shirt at the stomach. He bucked his head to wipe his nose against his shoulder. "Just give me a chance to set things right. Give me a second chance."

Walker killed the cordless phone. "No one ever gave me one." He leaned forward. Dolan recoiled, but Walker just reached into Chase's leather jacket and removed the cell phone from the inner pocket and set it on the counter. "People like me end up answering for your mistakes. We work your jobs, we take your falls, we fight your wars." He released the wheel of the Redhawk and spun it, watching the primers blur into a ring. "Assholes like you make big fucking messes. But it's guys like me gotta clean 'em up for you."

He jerked his wrist. The cylinder slammed home, and the gun stilled, its sights centered on Dolan's forehead. A dark voice spoke to Walker, a distant song.

A temptation, not a curse.

A return to what had always been natural.

A cold wind riffled the vinyl SWAT jackets and blew a swirl of trash into a minicyclone at the bus stop. Behind the three-vehicle-deep barricade, the crisis negotiator paced back and forth, tapping a black cordless against his thigh, the members of his team giving him space. At the makeshift command post behind two giant armored personnel vehicles, Tim and Bear huddled with Miller, Tannino, and the LAPD SWAT lieutenant. The other ARTists were arrayed around the building and in the stairwells, their olive drab flight suits standing out among the SWAT members with their black balaclavas, goggles, and Colt CAR-15s. Snipers from SWAT's D Platoon had rolled, regarding the various entrances through the three-by-nine scopes of their bolt-action Remington 700 .308 cals. The firepower assembled on site reminded Tim of a military operation; they were equipped to take down a small army.

Still pacing, the negotiator raised the phone to his face. Tim watched him walking and waiting as the phone rang and rang.

"What the hell's he doing in there?" Tannino said.

A movement on the blocked-off stretch of Wilshire caught Tim's eye. A blue-and-white ambulance motored up the center of the empty street.

He watched it as the SWAT lieutenant and Miller crunched endgame scenarios. The ambulance approached the LAPD officer working the sawhorses a half block up. Tim pivoted, regarding the two fire department rescue vehicles parked on the far side of the fire engine.

"Who called for a civilian ambulance?" His question went unanswered amid the banter, so he repeated it, louder.

The lieutenant said, "No one. Ours are right there."

The cop waved the ambulance through. Tim said, "Then you'd better have someone stop that vehicle and ID the driver."

The lieutenant spoke into his radio, and two black-and-whites lurched forward, halting the ambulance's progress. It screeched, banking off the skid, the familiar shield drawing into view on its side: UCLA MED CENTER, EMERGENCY MEDICAL SERVICES.

Tim's breath caught. "Damn it, Walker."

He shouldered past Tannino and the lieutenant, sprinting toward the Beacon-Kagan Building. An instant later, on cue, Walker kicked through the exit beside the revolving doors. Three spotlights zoomed over, casting the building front in daylight. Walker wore a ballistic vest over his T-shirt, and he held his Redhawk at his side. He was without Dolan. A piece of paper, pinned to his vest, fluttered in the breeze.

Tim hurdled two cop cars, parked hood to hood so the headlights kissed. He banged past an open car door, yelling, "Hold fire, hold fire!"

Walker halted. Tim stood alone in front of the blockade, mist rolling through the spotlights' glare. Walker faced him from about twenty yards, revolver dangling. Tim's gun was still at his hip, though the holster strap was thrown. His right hand was fastened around the stock, his elbow pointing back. His feet slid, found a shooting stance, but still he didn't draw. Around him Tim could hear puzzled murmurs and shouts.

Tim said, "Don't. We can figure something else out."

The SWAT sergeant yelled that he was blocking their angle, but Tim didn't move. He stayed frozen, his eyes on Walker's, the heat of the spotlights baking his back, the snipers ready with their armor-piercing rounds. Walker's lips moved, resignation taking shape as the faintest of grins. He gave Tim a little nod and raised his arm.

Tim drew and shot him through the forehead.

A chilled moment of silence, and then ART and SWAT lumbered out from their various posts, making tactical advances on the body, though there was no way there was still life in it. Thomas cleared the weapon, and the two fire department paramedics crowded the body.

Tim could make out the first few lines of scrawled writing on the paper safety-pinned to Walker's vest.

Last Will and Testament
I leave to Sam Jameson my

The sergeant said, "Why the hell would he show us he had a vest?"

Tim didn't slow his pace past the body. "So I'd know where not to shoot."

A paramedic unsnapped the vest, and a pack of ice fell out the right side. "This for his bullet wound?"

"No," Tim said. "Put it back in. Get the UCLA ambulance up here. They're set up for him already."

The paramedic looked puzzled. "How?"

"Because he called ahead." Tim shoved through the door, Bear following him offset to the right so he'd have more room for his Remington. A hidden button beneath the reception booth popped the door into Vector. Propping it open, Bear signaled the second team of paramedics to hold back, and he and Tim pressed forward down the corridor. Freed, Thomas, and Miller shuffled behind them, covering the rear.

Up ahead their dark corridor intersected another, that one lit. Rounding the corner, Tim felt his teeth grind. An office chair lay overturned, dumped forward, Dolan still bound to it. All they could see were his legs and the uprooted base, the wheels still rocking on their mountings. Tim sprinted down the corridor. Dolan's face and chest were mashed to the floor. His eyes flickered, and he tried to turn his head.

Beside his bruised cheek, six titanium bullets lay on the floor where Walker had let them fall.

Chapter 78

Edwin answered the door, regarded the FBI team soberly, nodded, and withdrew. Behind the cluster of agents, Tim and Bear waited by the koi pond. It had become the Bureau's case, but Tim had some pull with Jeff Malane, the special agent in charge, who requested Tim and Bear's presence for the arrest. A few years back with Tim and the Escape Team, Malane had busted up an incipient terrorist group trying to gain a foothold in Los Angeles, and he'd ridden the acclaim up the promotional ladder. Now he wore nicer shoes and a more pronounced scowl.

The 5:00 A.M. sky was a sheet of blued steel. After a few minutes, Bear made an impatient noise, but Malane held up his hand. They'd let Dean get dressed.

The other agents milled around the porch. A lot of rumpled button-ups and bad ties. Melissa Yueh was there, too, with a sized-down team. Tim had tipped her as repayment for her help earlier. She was made up and vibrant, her face flushed with an excitement that bordered on sexual.

The immense door opened with a groan of wood. Dean tugged a cuff free of his jacket sleeve. "The hell is this?" His glare pulled to the team of agents, the rolling TV camera.

Malane said, "I'm placing you under arrest for mail and wire fraud, health-care fraud, securities fraud, failure of corporate officers to certify financial reports, destruction of audit records, and criminal conspiracy to commit involuntary manslaughter. Those are just the Title Fifteens and Eighteens. I have an SEC investigator waiting to pile on charges. The asset-freeze order went through an hour ago—you'll have a hearing on it in ten days. In the meantime you can relax in the Metropolitan Detention Center."

Melissa Yueh slid into the scene as if on wheels, now front and center with her crew, offering the play-by-play. Instinctively, Dean raised a hand to hide his face, but Malane grasped his wrist and bent it down to the handcuff.

Dean was too wise and experienced to comment.

Gripping the handcuff chain, Malane steered him down the walk past the cameras, past the agents, past the deputies. Dean slowed when he caught sight of Tim and Bear.

Dean hunched against his cuffs, and Malane rested a hand on his coiffed hair, dipping him into the dark sedan. Malane nodded at Tim, who walked over and leaned in. The interior smelled of new leather and old cigarette smoke.

Tim spoke quietly. "You're right. We couldn't link you to Tess's murder. But she's responsible for your takedown. Remember that. See her face when you close your eyes."

Dean cast a vaguely bored gaze forward. "Whatever document you may possess means nothing on its own. You've got no evidence. I'll shake you boys off like fleas."

Tim lifted his stare to the tinted opposite window. Dean's brows drew together, and then he turned. Across the wide Bel Air street, Dolan leaned against Tannino's Bronco, his arms crossed. On one side of him the marshal, Guerrera on the other.

Dean's shoulders curled in an inadvertent cringe. His chin quivered ever so slightly.

Tim slammed the door and banged the roof, and he and Bear watched the sedan drift up the street, beginning the long drive downtown. It turned the corner.

When Tim looked back, Tannino's Bronco was gone, Dolan along with it.

"Well," Bear said, "that's that. What's for breakfast?"

Chapter 79

The desert scent of sage drifting through his open window, Tim cruised up Pearblossom Highway. Unfiltered by smog or clouds, the sun was a perfect blood-orange disk, hanging low in the western sky. He was due home for dinner, but he'd found himself on a detour after leaving the office.

This morning's *L.A. Times* had held no mention of Walker Jameson or Dean Kagan. In the five weeks that had passed since Walker's shooting, they—and the arrested Vector employees—had slipped farther back in the paper, the headlines moving on to terrorist chatter and earthquakes in India, until they finally fell off the back page. Tim's colorful career had left him familiar with the wax and wane of public interest. There'd be an upsurge before the trial, scheduled for early next year.

The task force had found no direct evidence linking Pierce to Walker. Morgenstein could've acted on his own, though they all knew he hadn't. His body had been found the morning after he'd been shot, the end of Walker's blood trail. The city was pressing forward with a suit against Pierce for his creative plumbing, but that would be months, if not years.

Tim threaded through the run-down community and parked in a long shadow across the street.

In his front yard, Sam Jameson crouched over the rebuilt anthill, his younger friend watching apprehensively from a few feet away. Sam lit a match, dropped it into the hole, and stood back. His little friend turned, ready to run. Red ants spilled out, swarming the top of the hill, and Sam giggled.

Kaitlin's voice sailed through the screen door. "What are you doing out there?"

Sam shoved the matches into his pocket. "Nothing."

The boys waited to see if she'd emerge, but she didn't. Sam picked up his Coke and carefully poured a rivulet down the side of the anthill, rewarding his charges.

They watched the ants dine.

A thrumming of bicycle tires over asphalt, and then the bully on the Huffy pedaled into view, approaching. Sam's head snapped up, his body tensed for fight or flight, but rather than slowing, the burly kid hoisted himself up on the pedals, lowered his head, and pumped harder. He flew past in a blur, his dirt bike curving out of sight into the park at the street's end. After a moment Sam relaxed.

Tim wondered what the hell that was about.

Kaitlin stepped outside and settled into a wicker chair on the porch, looking sad and tired and fulfilled. After a few minutes, she glanced over. Tim raised a hand in greeting, but she remained expressionless. She called out to Sam, then rose, the screen door knocking behind her. Sam said good-bye to his friend and headed in for dinner. He paused on the porch, his back to Tim. Somehow Tim knew he'd just registered his presence.

Walker Jameson had moved through prison bars and clawed his way from the trash-filled earth to avenge his sister, but in the end what he'd found to offer was a piece of himself. Blood type O, in all its universal glory. He'd balanced a cosmic account, spending his life to grant another.

On the porch Sam turned and looked across the street. He held Tim's gaze for a moment. His eyes were bright and curious, the sclera white as ivory. His mouth curved in a partial smile.

Then he went inside.

Tim stared at the dusty screen door for a few minutes before starting the drive home.

Chapter 80

The alarm chimed at 2:00 A.M. Dray's complaint was unintelligible. Tim got dressed quietly. She made a more forgiving moan when he kissed her on her sleep-soft cheek on his way out. The Typhoon had managed to flip upside down so his head was pressed to the footboard. Tim rearranged him, gripping his sweaty torso tightly so he wouldn't slip free.

Tyler flopped back onto his pillow, chuckled to himself, remarked, "Elmo wearing *diapers*," and resumed sleeping.

Tim enjoyed his first traffic-free drive to Pasadena. When his headlights swept the house, he was oddly relieved to see that the lawn had been cropped, the bushes fastidiously tended. Cleanly shaven and smelling of aftershave, his father opened the door before Tim could ring. He wore a double-breasted charcoal pinstripe that looked new. Tim wondered if he'd bought it for the occasion. They nodded at each other like competing salesmen. Tim's father stepped out and locked the door, then regarded the keys in his palm for a moment before sliding them under the mat. He followed Tim down the path to the Explorer.

Tim said, "What are you doing with the house?"

"I know a guy."

Tim nodded and pulled out. Corcoran State Prison was up the 5, between Bakersfield and Fresno. The trip would take the better part of three hours. They coasted wordlessly along the freeway, his father sitting still as a mannequin, watching the scenery roll by. As they headed over the Grapevine Pass, Tim realized he hadn't had time to check to make sure his father's prison sentence was real, that Tim wasn't being deployed on leg one of a scam. All through the flat wasteland of Kern County, Tim kept alert, waiting for his father to redirect him, for a carjacking, some new twist, but they just drove straight and silent. A glow came over the big squares of farmland flying past on either side, the first half hour looking more dusk than dawn. It wasn't until the sally-port gate came into view that Tim fully believed it was going to happen.

Corcoran caged six thousand inmates, Ginny's murderer among them.

And soon Tim's father.

Navigating through the two perimeter fences, in the shadow of the gray modules, Tim flashed his creds. Eyes lingered each time, the second correctional officer offering him a respectful nod. Tim's identity, duly noted, would be whispered into the right ears. Tim parked by the pedestrian entrance that led back to Inmate Processing. A prison bus dropping off cargo from Men's Central rattled in, and he and his father sat and watched the inmates unload. Many had to stoop to pass through the door.

Tim glanced at the man in his passenger seat. Fifteen years inside, even cut down by various sentence reductions, was too long for someone his age to be among men like this. It seemed improbable that he'd pass back out through these gates under his own power.

Tim checked the clock: 6:52. His father was due to report by 7:00.

"Well," Tim said.

"Well." His father did not move.

Though the sun was barely free of the horizon, heat was already radiating off the black dash. A road-worn Oldsmobile eased up beside them, forcing them to be privy to a weepy parting scene between a young couple. The tattooed kid ambled inside, wiping his face. Tim's father watched, lip curled with disapproval.

"Why would you do this?" Tim asked. "Submit to this indignity? You despise me. Why have *me* take you in?"

The clock changed, another precious minute gone. Tim's father's skin was dry, white dust by the mouth. His Adam's apple jerked with a swallow. "Mugsy's doing a dime. Frank got waxed last year. Mickey and Goose were rolled up. There's no one else."

6:57. 6:58.

Tim's father climbed out. He'd sweated through his dress shirt, something Tim had never seen him do. He pulled on his jacket, fastening the inner button with an expert tweak of his fingers. Erect and dignified, his father took a few steps. He paused, turned his face to the sun, closed his eyes.

He cleared his throat. "Maybe sometime I could meet my grandson."

"We'll see."

"Maybe he should see the world's ugly parts. Give him a shot to turn out better than me or you."

"I'd say that's a statistical inevitability, wouldn't you?"

With perfect posture his father started for the door. A correctional officer emerged.

"Move it along, pal. Door locks on the hour." The CO's face shifted with recognition when he looked at Tim, and he lessened the aggressiveness of his stance.

Tim stayed by his father's side. They reached the CO, the door.

Tim's father turned to face him. "I could count on you, Timmy. Despite everything, I could always count on you."

He offered his hand, and Tim shook it, and then the CO took him into custody with a respectful nod at Tim and led him away. He did not look back.

Dazed, Tim walked back and sat in his Explorer. He stared at the barbed wire, the chain link, the sally-port gate. Ten minutes passed. Then another ten.

He turned over the engine, but rather than heading for the gates, he drove around to the other side of the facility to the visiting area. He got out of the Explorer and started toward the building. The inmates were in the yard, pumping iron, bullshitting, gathering in protective clusters. In the wedge of shadow against the wall, there he was. Tim wasn't certain at first, but then Kindell stepped out to pick a rock from the dirt, and in the sunlight there was no question.

A pedophile and a child murderer—he wasn't supposed to last a month in there, let alone four years. For those four years, Tim had wanted him dead. He wanted him dead as much as ever. But even if Kindell were dead, he wouldn't be gone. He'd still be there. Always there.

His skin looked gray and hung on loose flesh. He'd put on weight—a lot of weight—his face blown wide around the familiar inexpressive eyes.

Whatever Tim had hoped to feel, he did not. Standing in the beating sun of the parking lot, he sensed a hollowness, not inside him but all around, as if he lay on the brink of a void too vast to comprehend. He grasped his own unimportance and, by extension, the insignificance of the man opposite the fence. It left him feeling dwarfed, though by what, precisely, he was not certain. There was a great horror in it, to be sure, but also a faint ray of a greater freedom he'd yet to encounter.

Kindell claimed his rock in a fist and withdrew back into shadow.

Tim looked at the visitor entrance, but, suddenly and clearly, he knew that he wouldn't go in, wouldn't confront Kindell through a mesh screen.

Tim thought of the vulnerability of his living child. He pictured the familiar scenarios—the kidnapping, the act of God, the proverbial bus. In every moment a hundred things can go wrong. But moment after moment they don't.

Right now Dray would be packing a picnic for the park. Tyler on the kitchen floor, wearing Evel Knievel and applying a Scooby-Doo Band-Aid to a knee scrape that had healed three days ago. Bear and Michelle Westin, D.D.S., on their morning walk, Boston running laps around them, an endless loop of Rhodesian Ridgeback.

Tim turned and headed back to the Explorer.

Ninety Days After Walker's Death

Kaiyer walk *hisself*."

"Okay, bub." Tim still guided Tyler through the penitentiary's outermost door. On its backswing the glass caught a reflection of the stern razor wire capping the double chain links. Tim paused, taking in the grounds. The place was removed from time, somehow. It seemed not a speck of dirt had shifted in the months since Tim had delivered the boy's grandfather.

Ahead the sally-port gate, the guard tower, COs with rifles.

And Dray leaning against the grille of her Blazer, arms crossed, face tilted to the sun. She took note of their accelerating progress back across the empty visitor lot. Tyler's steps grew shorter and choppier.

Halfway there he said, "Daddy up."

Tim held out his thumbs until the tiny hands grasped them, then lifted his son, seating him against his side.

They reached the Blazer and stopped. Tim took a breath and exhaled hard.

Dray said, "I bet."

Tyler squirmed a bit, so Tim set him down. Ty picked at the Scooby-Doo Band-Aid across the toe of his sneaker. Dray studied them, her face proud and tender, the sun shining straight through her ice green eyes.

"C'mon," she said. "Let's get you boys home."

Acknowledgments

I would like to thank a number of experts who lent me their time in order to make me appear smarter than I am. I'm hopeful that their efforts paid off. If they did not, then I'm dim *and* accountable.

As a former marine and Terminal Island correctional officer, and current deputy U.S. marshal, Mike Pennington proved to be my utility infielder, his knowledge second only to his affability. Christopher Murphy, a brilliant biochemist, exhibited endless patience while introducing me to the ins and outs of viral vectors.

I should also like to thank Kristin Baird, M.D.; Terel Beppu, my guns 'n' bullets guy; Ali Binazir, M.D., of Elite Communications; Jason Elliott, former Navy SEAL; Jimell Griffin of the U.S. Marshals Service; Bob Levy; Thomas Sendlenski; Pegeen Rhyne and Michael Winlin of the U.S. Attorney's Office; Cheryl Van Buskirk of Caltech; and Mason Wnyocker for his business acumen.

As always, I owe much gratitude to the efforts of Stephen F. Breimer; Marc H. Glick; Rich Green of CAA; Melissa Hurwitz, M.D.; Inkwell Management; Jess Nelson Taylor; and, of course, my entire team at William Morrow. Thanks additionally to the booksellers and librarians, who continue to show me much support.

And Delinah, Rosie, and Natalie. My family.